Andy McDermott is the bestselling  Eddie Chase adventure thrillers, w 30 countries and 20 languages. Hi *Atlantis*, was his first of several *Ne Valhalla Prophecy* is the ninth book in the series, and he has also written the explosive spy thriller *The Persona Protocol*.

A former journalist and movie critic, Andy was the editor of respected UK magazines *DVD Review* and the iconoclastic film publication *Hotdog*. Born in Halifax, he now lives in Bournemouth.

Praise for Andy McDermott:

'Adventure stories don't get much more epic than this' *Daily Mirror*

'An all-action cracker from one of Britain's most talented adventure writers' *Lancashire Evening Post*

'If Wilbur Smith and Clive Cussler collaborated, they might have come up with a thundering big adventure blockbuster like this . . . a widescreen, thrill-a-minute ride' *Peterborough Evening Telegraph*

'True Indiana Jones stuff with terrific pace' *Bookseller*

'A true blockbuster rollercoaster ride from start to finish . . . Popcorn escapism at its very best' *Crime and Publishing*

'A rip-roaring read and one which looks set to cement McDermott's place in the bestsellers list for years to come' *Bolton Evening News*

'Fast-moving, this is a pulse-racing adventure with action right down the line' *Northern Echo*

'A writer of rare, almost cinematic talent. Where others's action scenes limp along unconvincingly, his explode off the page in Technicolor' *Daily Express, Scotland*

'McDermott writes like Clive Cussler on speed. The action is non-stop' *Huddersfield Daily Examiner*

By Andy McDermott and available from Headline

Featuring Nina Wilde and Eddie Chase

The Hunt for Atlantis
The Tomb of Hercules
The Secret of Excalibur
The Covenant of Genesis
The Cult of Osiris
The Sacred Vault
Empire of Gold
Temple of the Gods
The Valhalla Prophecy

The Persona Protocol

ANDY McDERMOTT

THE VALHALLA PROPHECY

headline

First published in 2014 by
HEADLINE PUBLISHING GROUP

First published in paperback in 2014 by
HEADLINE PUBLISHING GROUP

7

Cataloguing in Publication Data is available from the British Library

ISBN 978 0 7553 8066 4 (B format)
ISBN 978 0 7553 9151 6 (A format)

Typeset in Aldine 401 by Avon DataSet Ltd, Bidford-on-Avon, Warwickshire

Printed and bound in Great Britain by Clays Ltd, St Ives plc

Headline's policy is to use papers that are natural, renewable and recyclable
products and made from wood grown in sustainable forests. The logging and
manufacturing processes are expected to conform to the environmental
regulations of the country of origin.

HEADLINE PUBLISHING GROUP
An Hachette UK Company
338 Euston Road
London NW1 3BH

www.headline.co.uk
www.hachette.co.uk

For Kat

Prologue

Novaya Zemlya, Northern Russia

30 October 1961

The temperature was below freezing, but Dr Serafim Volkov was sweating.

Part of the reason was purely physical. The pit from which he had just emerged was deep, and even though he had not descended all the way to the bottom, leaving the most dangerous part of his mission to his younger conspirator, he had still felt compelled to observe. Any mistakes could have deadly consequences.

But Surnin had secured the sample without incident, and was now making his way back up the series of ladders to the surface. Volkov waited for him, unpleasantly clammy inside his thick clothing even in the chill wind.

Not so much from the climb, but from fear.

Merely by being here, he was violating the orders of the most powerful man in the Soviet Union: Nikita Khrushchev himself. That alone would have led to life in the gulag, but if anyone discovered the reason for his unauthorised visit, it would mean a guaranteed death sentence.

Echoing clanks reached him from below as Surnin ascended the last ladder. Volkov tugged at the top fastener of his coat to let in a little cold air around his neck, then surveyed his surroundings. The sky was a solid dreary grey over the barren, snow-covered plain. A few hundred metres to the west stood the charred remains of several buildings: Volkov's workplace for the past several years, now nothing but fire-blackened hulks. The thought made him scowl. The facility had been destroyed on Khrushchev's orders – along with everything inside. All of Volkov's research, his experiments, his discoveries . . . reduced to ash.

All that the government *knew* about, at least. His secret experiment could still bear fruit.

If he escaped the Soviet Union alive.

He was sure that he could. The fact that he had made it back to the pit undetected proved that the exclusion zone around the islands of Novaya Zemlya, high above the Arctic Circle in the Barents Sea, was not impregnable. Volkov's pilot was a Samoyad, a former native who had been forcibly resettled when the long archipelago was designated a nuclear test site. He was waiting with his small fishing boat in an inlet a few kilometres to the north-west; the wily old man was the scientist's best hope of returning safely to the mainland with his precious cargo.

After that, he was entirely in the hands of the CIA. But so far, they had done everything they promised. His wife, now seven months pregnant, was already in West Berlin; once he joined her, they were only a jet flight away from a new life in the United States.

And his work could continue. He would have a new paymaster; a far, far more generous one. But the money, while certainly welcome, was not why he was transferring his loyalties. It was the promise of what he would be able to achieve in America, freed of limits. The world would change for ever . . . and it would be to his design.

He glanced into the pit. Surnin was nearing the top of the ladder, the thick steel cylinder of the sample container slung from his shoulder. Volkov backed away to give him room to climb out. The sled-dogs waited patiently nearby, their leather reins looped around a rock standing out of the ground like a gravestone.

The rock was the reason he was here – the reason anyone had taken an interest in this desolate patch of land. The entire archipelago had been photographed from the air as part of the preparations for nuclear testing so the effects of the detonations on the landscape could be seen. Someone with sharp eyes had spotted both the unusual standing stone and the black hole in the ground nearby, and a survey team was sent to investigate.

What they found was almost beyond imagination.

Seven years of work had followed; seven years of Volkov's life poured into his research. At first he had been following orders. Stalin might have been dead, but his legacy lived on: the Soviet Union needed weapons, so powerful and terrible that no enemy dared attack for fear of utter obliteration in reprisal. Atomic and hydrogen bombs were the most destructive, but there were others, in their own way even more frightening. Volkov's task had been to turn what lay at the bottom of the pit into one of these nightmares.

He had succeeded. But in the process, he'd realised that his research had the potential to produce something more than death. Quite the opposite, in fact. Whoever controlled it would have a power previously only in the hands of God.

Or *gods*, he mused, walking to the stone. He couldn't read the ancient runes carved into its face, but he didn't need to; they had been translated from Old Norse years before, and he now knew them by heart.

You great warriors, who have travelled far from Valhalla
Across the rainbow bridge and through the lake of lightning . . .

A crooked smile. The Vikings who'd visited this land over a thousand years earlier were barbarians, unable to comprehend what they found in the pit. So they had fitted it into their primitive mythology – or, more accurately, had shaped their mythology around *it*. It was almost a shame that no archaeologists would ever be allowed to visit the site; gods and monsters awaited them below.

Monsters. Another scowl. That one word had ended everything.

A curse under his breath at the thought of Eisenhov. He knew the younger scientist had no proof of his secret experiments – if that were the case, Eisenhov would surely have reported it, and arrest and execution would have followed – but had probably suspected after he'd subtly, but still foolishly, tried to sound him out as a potential ally. Eisenhov's reaction had made it very clear that he was opposed to – appalled by – the mere idea of his covert work. So Volkov had continued alone, making discoveries he dared tell no one about while getting ever closer to his goal . . .

Then came the accident. The deaths. The *monsters*. Everything was contained, an entire town wiped from the map as if it had never existed, but it was too late. Eisenhov, with his emotionally loaded weasel words, had poisoned Khrushchev against the whole project. Everyone at the Novaya Zemlya facility was taken back to the mainland. And the buildings and their contents were burned.

All that remained of Volkov's work was his final, greatest experiment, and the knowledge in his head. The Soviet Union had turned its back on his research – but America was more than keen to continue it. And the contents of the steel cylinder would allow him to do that.

Breathing heavily, Surnin reached the top of the ladder. Volkov strode to him. 'Turn around,' the scientist ordered. 'I need to check the sample container.'

'I didn't hit it on anything, Comrade Doctor,' Surnin objected, but he still meekly turned to present the cylinder. Obedience was one reason why Volkov had chosen to trust the big man to help him, along with his staggering lack of initiative. He would do what he was told by a superior and not even think to question.

The scientist examined the container, paying particular attention to the seal around its lid. There was no sign of any leakage. 'All right. Load it on to the sled. Carefully.'

'Yes, Comrade Doctor.' Surnin tramped through the snow to the runestone, petting one of the dogs before hesitantly lowering the cylinder into a padded metal case.

Volkov watched closely, finally satisfied that it was secure. 'Let's get back to the boat.' He was about to board the sled when he noticed that Surnin was staring at the dogs. 'What is it?'

'They hear something.' The animals had pricked up their ears, looking to the south-west.

Volkov strained to listen. All he could hear at first was the wind, but then he picked up a faint, distant rumble. 'It's a plane,' he said dismissively. 'One of our bombers.' The buzzing drone

5

of eight mighty propellers was a familiar sound on the military-controlled islands. 'Don't worry, it's a long way off. It won't see us through these clouds. Now let's go.' He took his seat and gestured impatiently for Surnin to do the same.

The other man unlooped the reins from the runestone and climbed aboard. At a tug on the leather straps, the dogs set off across the snowy ground, towing Volkov and his prize behind them.

The scientist's assessment of the sound had been correct. Its source was indeed a bomber, a Tupolev Tu-95 flying high above the clouds as it approached Novaya Zemlya from its base on the Kola peninsula six hundred miles to the south-west.

But it was no ordinary aircraft.

Designated Tu-95V, it was a one-of-a-kind variant, modified for a very special purpose. Its unique cargo was so huge that the bomb bay doors had been removed to accommodate it. Even stripped of all unnecessary weight and with its four massive twin-prop engines working at full power, the Tupolev was strained to its limit to carry the terrifying payload.

Its official designation was uninformative: Article AN602. But it had acquired a nickname during its rapid development and construction.

The Tsar Bomba. The Emperor of Bombs.

Twenty-six feet long and more than six feet in diameter, the Tsar Bomba weighed almost twenty-seven tons. This in itself made it the largest bomb ever constructed, almost three times as heavy as the British Grand Slam of the Second World War, but its size alone was no indication of its true destructive power.

It was a hydrogen bomb, the most powerful ever built.

The atomic device that destroyed Hiroshima had an explosive power of sixteen kilotons – the equivalent of 16,000 tons of

TNT. The bomb dropped on Nagasaki twelve days later had a twenty-one-kiloton yield. The first ever hydrogen bomb, detonated by the United States in 1952, had an explosive force of over ten *megatons* – ten *million* tons of TNT.

The Tsar Bomba was ten times more powerful still.

It was so powerful, in fact, that it had been adjusted at the last minute to deliver only around half its maximum predicted yield to minimise fallout. But a detonation of a 'mere' fifty megatons would still be over ten times as much as the combined power of *all* the explosives used in WWII – including the Hiroshima and Nagasaki bombs.

It was a bomb designed to destroy entire cities. But its current target was much more specific.

The spot marked by an ancient Norse runestone.

Volkov tugged back his sleeve to check his watch. Just after 11.25. If the weather didn't turn, he would reach the waiting boat around midday. It would be night by the time he got to the mainland, but that didn't matter. His CIA contact would be waiting for him, and then his own journey to the West to join his wife would begin.

The possibility that he might never make it had of course occurred to him. To that end, he had written a letter to Galina, with the express instructions that it only be opened if the CIA confirmed his death. There were secrets he had kept even from her. He hoped she would understand why he had done what he had . . . but even if she did not, the die was already cast. Whether he reached her or not, she would learn what he had done. The letter was his explanation, his justification.

His excuse, some part of his conscience sneered, but he forced the thought away. He had done what was necessary for his work.

He noticed that Surnin was again staring to the south-west – no, more to the west now. That meant the bomber was coming in from the ocean.

A bombing run? He dismissed the idea. The nuclear tests had been a recurring interruption of his work at the facility, all personnel evacuated the day before one took place and not permitted to return until at least a week after, once the local radiation levels had been declared safe. The senior staff were informed of upcoming tests in advance; if one were planned, he would have known.

Volkov leaned to look over Surnin's shoulder. The clouds ahead continued far out to sea, an impenetrable grey shield that would hide the fishing boat from watchers above. The aircraft was nothing to worry about.

A voice crackled in the pilot's earphones. 'One minute to drop. Confirm readiness.'

'I confirm readiness,' Major Andrei Durnovtsev replied, the calm professionalism of his voice masking his nervousness. All of the Tu-95's crew, and that of the Tu-16 jet acting as an observation aircraft off to starboard, were volunteers – and it had been made very clear that there was a chance they might not make it home. In theory, at the Tupolev's maximum speed it would reach the minimum safe distance with a small margin to spare . . . but theory and practice were two different things.

'Message received,' came the reply. 'Fifty seconds to drop. Wind speed and direction on your escape vector remain constant.' A pause, then: 'Good luck.'

Durnovtsev did not reply, instead checking his instruments, preparing himself. The actual release of the bomb was controlled from the ground; his job was to fly the bomber on an exact heading, taking the prevailing winds into account so the Tsar Bomba would parachute down as close to its target as possible. Even though it could destroy an entire city the size of New York, for whatever reason his masters at the Kremlin wanted their superweapon to hit the right spot. A demonstration to the West of precision as well as power, he supposed.

All musings vanished at another radio message. 'Thirty seconds to drop. Prepare for device release.'

'Confirm thirty seconds to release,' Durnovtsev replied, before switching to the aircraft's internal intercom. 'Thirty seconds! All crew, secure stations and confirm readiness!'

One by one his men reported ready, all systems green. 'Fifteen seconds,' said the ground controller. Durnovtsev's stomach knotted, but he held his hands firmly on the controls, ready to act. One last check of the instruments. Everything was as it should be.

'Ten seconds!' A glance at the compass. The Tu-95 was now heading almost due east, curving in towards its target; to survive, he had to turn the lumbering bomber to the south-west as quickly and sharply as possible. 'Drop in five seconds! Four! Three! Two! One – *drop!*'

The release mechanisms opened – and the Tupolev shot upwards as twenty-seven tons of death fell from its gaping bomb bay.

A massive parachute snapped open in the slipstream the moment the bomb was clear of the fuselage. Barometric sensors would trigger the detonators at an altitude of 13,000 feet above sea level. But even with the huge 'chute slowing it, the Tsar Bomba was still plunging earthwards at a frightening speed, giving the bomber and its chase plane less than three minutes to reach safety.

If they could.

Durnovtsev had already slammed the flight controls hard

over, throwing the Tu-95 into a sharp banking turn. The smaller Tu-16 held its course for a few more seconds, its cameras and observers tracking the bomb to make sure the parachute had deployed, before it too swung south-west. Its pilot immediately went to full power, the jet rapidly outpacing the wallowing turboprop.

'The payload has been dropped and the parachute successfully deployed,' said the voice in Durnovtsev's headphones, relaying the news from the second aircraft. 'Estimated detonation in two minutes and forty seconds. Go to maximum speed and initiate blast procedure.' Then, barely audible: 'God be with you.'

As a loyal communist Durnovtsev was not a believer, but he certainly appreciated the sentiment. The Tupolev came about on to its escape heading; he levelled out, one hand pushing on the throttle levers to the detent. The Tu-16 was already shrinking into the distance.

The airspeed indicator showed that the Tu-95 was now travelling at just over 510 knots, its four mighty engines straining. 'Begin blast procedure!' he ordered. Across the cockpit, his co-pilot pulled a pair of thick, almost opaque dark goggles down over his eyes. Durnovtsev waited until the insectile lenses were secure before donning his own. Day turned to night, the instruments barely visible through the tinted glass.

But he knew that the sky would become much brighter very soon.

Volkov stared up at the clouds again. Even over the sound of the dogs, he could now hear the bomber. The rumbling drone was subtly different, though. A Doppler shift; the aircraft was moving away from him.

He shook off a vague sense of unease. Whatever the plane was doing, it could have nothing to do with him – or the reason he was here. He touched the steel cylinder's case, making sure it was secured in place. It was. Reassured, he looked back as the sled crested a rise. The blackened remains of the facility stood out against the snow, the entrance to the pit an ominous yawning mouth. The runestone was a single broken tooth at its edge.

There was no sentiment as Volkov regarded his former workplace for the last time. What mattered above all else was the work itself; what he had discovered, and where it could lead.

He turned his back on the scene, a small smile rising. With the sample in his possession and a new life awaiting in the United States, that work would continue.

'Thirty seconds to detonation!' Durnovtsev barked into the intercom. 'All crew, brace for blast!'

He pulled his seat-belt straps as tight as they would go before clenching his hands back around the controls. The compass was an indiscernible shadow through the goggles, but holding the Tupolev on course was about to be the least of his concerns.

The ground controller continued the countdown. Twenty seconds. Ten. A last look around at the other crew in the cockpit. Dark shapes regarded him with impenetrable black eyes. One of the men in the seats behind him was holding a small cine camera, its lens pointed over Durnovtsev's shoulder at the front windows. The pilot gave him a brief nod, trying to dismiss the thought that it might be the last time anyone ever saw his face, then looked ahead once more.

Five seconds. Four. Three—

Even through the heavily tinted goggles, the sky suddenly became as bright as the sun.

★

11

Volkov checked his watch again: 11.32. The dogs were making better time on the return trip to the boat, perhaps as eager as he was to get off the bleak island—

The leaden grey clouds turned pure white.

A flash lit the landscape from high above, its reflection from the snow blinding. Steam rose around the sled, the bitter cold dispelled by a searing heat . . .

Volkov's last thought was one of horrified realisation – the bomber *had* been on a mission – before he and everything for miles around vanished in an unimaginable fire.

The Tsar Bomba detonated two and a half miles above the ground. Durnovtsev had done his job with great skill; even with the inherent inaccuracy of a parachute-dropped weapon, it was within half a mile of its target.

But a fifty-megaton hydrogen bomb did not need to be precise.

The nuclear fireball, over two miles across, was as hot as the sun's core. It never reached the ground, its own rapidly expanding shockwave bouncing back up off the surface to deflect it. But its flash alone, racing outwards at the speed of light, was enough to melt rock and vaporise anything lesser in a fraction of a second. Behind it came the blast, a wall of superheated air compressed so hard that it was practically solid. What little survived the flash was obliterated moments later.

The Tu-95 was almost thirty miles from Ground Zero when the bomb exploded. Even inside the plane, its crew felt a sudden heat as high-energy radiation, X-rays and gamma rays, passed through the aircraft – and their bodies. Sparks flashed around the cabin, the nuclear burst's electromagnetic pulse surging through the bomber's wiring. Durnovtsev heard an unearthly squeal in his headphones as their little loudspeaker converted the electrical overload into sound.

The brightness outside faded, but Durnovtsev knew the danger was far from over. The shockwave was on its way. Even with the Tupolev going flat out, it would catch up in seconds. He braced himself, hands on the controls ready to react . . .

It was as if the bomber had been rammed from behind by a speeding train.

For a moment Durnovtsev was stunned by the force of the impact, his restraints cutting tightly into his chest and crushing the breath from him. He struggled back to full awareness, gasping inside his oxygen mask as he pulled up the goggles. The sky was an angry orange-red, the fireball illuminating it like a miniature star. A colossal booming roar filled his ears: the sound of the atmosphere itself burning.

The artificial horizon was tumbling, the altimeter needle spinning rapidly down. A sickening feeling in his stomach told him he was in free fall. The Tupolev was dropping out of the sky, swatted like a wasp. It had already fallen a kilometre, and was still plunging . . .

The cloud layer below had been evaporated by the shockwave. The cold sea glinted through the windows – the Tu-95 was nose down. Durnovtsev pulled back hard on the controls to level out. The engines were still at full power; he eased them off to reduce the stress on the wings. The horizon slowly dropped back down through his view.

Nausea faded, the pressure on his chest easing. 'Is everyone all right?' he shouted over the crackling rumble. To his relief, all his crew replied in the positive. Next came a systems check. There had been some damage, but the aircraft was still in the sky with all four engines running. As far as Durnovtsev was concerned, that was a successful outcome.

He tried the radio. As he'd expected, nothing came through but a strange static screech. The explosion had ionised the atmosphere, making transmissions all but impossible. He had no idea how long it would take the effect to fade – all he could do was follow his orders and return to base.

The navigator provided him with the correct heading, but as he made the course change, Durnovtsev was stuck by a compulsion to see what he had wrought. He turned the bomber further so he could look back towards Novaya Zemlya through the cockpit's side windows.

What he saw chilled his blood. The Tu-95 had climbed back to its original altitude, over six miles above sea level . . . but the mushroom cloud had already risen far higher, demonic fire still burning within as it roiled skywards. A ring of smoke and ash was expanding around its base.

Nothing on the ground could possibly have survived.

Durnovtsev stared at the fearsome sight for one last moment, then turned his plane for home.

The landscape around Ground Zero was now unrecognisable from what it had been just minutes before. Snow had flashed to steam, the frozen soil beneath turned instantly to cinders before being blown away by the immense force of the blast. Even the very rocks had melted into a glaze covering the bowl of the newly formed crater.

Nothing remained of the facility. It had been atomised, along with the two men. Even the runestone, which had withstood the harsh climate for over a thousand years, was gone.

As was the pit.

The blast had sealed it for ever, countless tons of molten and shattered rock filling it in. The dark secrets it contained would now remain hidden for eternity.

Except . . .

The runestone, and the words inscribed upon it, were no

more. But they had been recorded, translated, and analysed. The men who had ordered Durnovtsev's mission knew what it said.

And knew the danger it still represented. A danger they could not allow to be released.

> *The guide-stone has brought you here*
> *To fight the final battle of Ragnarök*
> *One pit of the serpent lies before you*
> *The other awaits across the Western sea . . .*

1

New York City

Fifty-Three Years Later

'N ina, Eddie!' cried Lola Adams – née Gianetti – across the coffee shop. 'Long time no see!'

Nina Wilde hopped to her feet to greet her friend. Lola had, until five months earlier, been Nina's personal assistant at the International Heritage Agency. The reason for her departure was peering curiously at the world around him from a papoose on the chest of Lola's husband. 'Lola, Don, hi! Wow, it's so great to see you both again! And to meet this little guy in person for the first time. Oh, he's beautiful!'

Nina's own husband also stood. 'Yeah, that's not a bad-looking sprog you've got,' said Eddie Chase with a grin. 'Shame about the name, though.'

Lola pouted. 'What's wrong with Gino? It was my grandpa's name.'

'There's nothing wrong with it, it's just not as good as my suggestion. Now Eddie, *that's* a name for a baby.' He frowned.

'Wait, that didn't come out like I meant it to.'

Nina laughed. 'Accurate, though.' The balding Englishman pulled a face, to which Gino responded with a gurgling laugh of his own. 'Aw, look at that! He's so sweet.'

'He is,' said Lola, embracing the pair, 'when he's not occupying every moment of my time. And I thought you were demanding, Nina!'

Now it was Nina's turn to look affronted, while Eddie chuckled. 'Come on, sit down,' he said, pulling a chair out for the young mother. 'So being a parent's a bit stressful, is it?'

'You have no idea, man,' said Don as he unfastened the papoose. 'I thought being a firefighter was tough, but pulling people out of burning buildings is a cakewalk compared to watching out for a baby.'

'Don's worse than I am,' Lola said as she sat. 'There's danger everywhere, isn't there, hon? To him, every room looks like a deathtrap out of a *Final Destination* movie. It drives me nuts, 'cause now I can't even plug in my hairdryer without unlocking the gadgets he's put on all the outlets.'

'Safety's a serious business, babe,' Don replied, in a way that suggested it was far from the first time he had been teased.

The big-haired blonde took Gino from the papoose, settling the baby on her lap. 'Anyway, we're just about getting a handle on things, so we can finally catch up with everybody. What have I missed? What have you guys been up to? Have you found any more ancient wonders or saved the world again?'

'What, since the last time?' asked Eddie with a mocking snort. 'Come on, it's only been a few months. Give us a chance.'

'I'm enjoying the fact that we *haven't* been running around the world being chased and shot at and having everything blow up around us,' Nina said, with considerable relief. 'It means I get to do the things I joined the IHA for in the first place. Like

18

being an actual archaeologist, you know? Overseeing digs, research, writing papers . . .'

Eddie yawned theatrically. 'Yeah, it's thrilling.'

'Oh, shut up,' said the redhead. 'But it's amazing how much more productive you can be when you aren't being attacked by helicopter gunships and hunted by assassins.'

'And ninjas. Don't forget the ninjas.'

Don's eyebrows rose. 'Babe? You are *so* not going back to the IHA.'

Lola kissed Gino's head. 'This little guy's going to be my boss for the next few years, don't worry.' She looked back at Nina. 'If things are nice and easy at work, is that giving you more time to plan things at home?'

'What things?' Nina asked.

'You know.' Lola held up Gino, who let out a little squeak of delight, and kissed him again. 'Family matters.'

'Yeah,' added Don. 'You've been married for, what, two or three years now? I'm surprised you haven't got kids already.'

Nina found herself feeling surprisingly defensive. 'My work hasn't been exactly conducive to it, what with all the . . . ninjas and world-saving.'

The burly firefighter nodded. 'But now everything's quieted down, you're thinking about it, yeah? I mean, you don't want to leave it too late.'

Eddie huffed. 'We're not *that* old.' He put on a crotchety old man's voice. 'I'm hip to all the popular tunes of today's young people, you know.' Lola laughed.

'You're past forty, though, right? Me, I've just gone thirty and Lola's coming up on it, and we were worried that might be pushing it—'

'Donnyyyyy,' said Lola, singsong, through her teeth. Her

husband got the message and clammed up. 'So, what's new at the IHA? How's my replacement working out?'

'Melinda?' Nina said. 'She's fine, she's doing a good job.' Seeing Lola's face fall ever so slightly, she continued, 'Nearly as good as you.' The younger woman brightened. 'Okay, what else? Al Little got a job with Apple in California, Lucy DeMille got engaged, Bill Schofield got promoted – oh, and we got a new UN liaison after Sebastian Penrose, uh, retired.' The United Nations official's departure had been under a cloud, to say the least, but to avoid a media scandal the details were covered up. Nina had been dismayed at that, but the decision was made at far higher political levels than she had influence. 'A guy called Oswald Seretse.'

Lola searched her memory, then nodded. 'Oh – his dad's a diplomat too, isn't he? I met them at the UN once, before I transferred to the IHA.'

'Yeah, I think so. Anyway, that's all the big stuff.'

'You should come round to the office sometime,' Eddie suggested. 'There's a lot of people who'd love to see you and your nipper.'

'Maybe I will,' said Lola. She looked down at her son. 'Would you like to see where Mommy worked before she had you? Would you, little snooky-wooky?' Gino did not appear enthused by the prospect.

'Just make sure there aren't any frickin' ninjas there that day,' Don said.

'There won't be,' Eddie assured him. 'I shot 'em all.' The firefighter's expression wavered between amusement and a suspicion that the Englishman was not joking.

'Everyone would love to see you. And Gino,' said Nina.

Lola smiled. 'Then we'll come.'

'Good! In the meantime, I think it's time for some caffeine. What do you want?'

Lola and Don named their choices, then Nina turned to Eddie, only to find him looking at Gino, lost in thought. 'Eddie?'

He snapped back. 'Hmm?'

'You okay?'

'Yeah, yeah. Just thinking about something, that's all. What?'

'Coffee?'

'I'll get 'em. What's everyone having?'

Nina stood. 'It's okay, I'll go. You want your usual?'

'Yeah, thanks.'

She headed for the counter, looking back to find him again seeming preoccupied before returning to the conversation.

The same look was on his face that evening.

Nina was curled up in an armchair reading a book, ignoring the television. She raised her eyes to see her husband, stretched out on the sofa, paying just as little attention to the events on screen. 'Earth to Eddie.'

He blinked and lifted his head. 'What?'

'You were miles away. Penny for your thoughts?'

'Sounds like a good deal,' he said. 'If I'd had a penny every time I'd had a thought, I'd probably have about . . . oh, three pounds seventeen by now.'

'That much?' They both smiled. 'So what's on your mind? You had that same look this afternoon when we were with Lola and Don.'

Eddie hesitated before replying. 'I was thinking about . . . well, what Don said. About having kids.' He sat up. 'I'm wondering if he had a point. Do we want to have kids, and if we do, are we leaving it too late?'

'We've still got plenty of time to decide,' she assured him. 'Like you told him, we're not *that* old.'

He didn't seem convinced. 'I dunno. I'm past forty now,

you're coming up on thirty-five . . . I mean, Christ, my mum and dad were only twenty-one when they had me.'

'Times change, though. People had kids when they were younger back then. My parents were in their mid twenties when I was born.'

'I suppose.'

Realising that the matter was still bothering him, she put down her book and joined him on the sofa. 'Hey,' she said, putting her arms around him, '*do* you want to have kids?'

Another pause. 'I don't know. I really don't,' he said, closing a hand around hers. 'I mean, it's not like we haven't talked about it before, and it's one of those things you just sort of assume'll happen after you get married. But . . . there've been things that got in the way. Like mad cults and lost cities and psychos trying to start World War Three.'

She grinned. 'Minor distractions, then.'

'Yeah. Most people just worry about how it's going to affect their careers. We keep having the weight of the bloody world dumped on us.'

'It's not really something you want to make a child deal with, is it? Probably a good thing we haven't had one after all.'

Nina had meant the comment light-heartedly, but a sudden downcast twinge to his expression – which he hurriedly tried to hide – warned her that Eddie had taken it more seriously. 'Hey, hey,' she said apologetically, 'I was joking. I'm not ruling it out, not at all. But our lives have been, well . . . complicated.'

'Yeah, I know.' He intertwined his fingers with hers and squeezed her hand, then kissed her cheek. 'Although . . .'

'What?'

'Well, things are a bit less complicated at the moment, aren't they? All the IHA's operations are ticking along without any trouble—'

'Don't jinx it!'

He laughed. 'I'm right, though, aren't I? The Atlantis dig's back up to speed after what happened last year; the Egyptians asked us to help with the tomb of Alexander the Great—'

'If that's what it really is,' Nina cut in. Even the top experts in the field were not entirely certain whether the new excavations in Alexandria would bear fruit.

'Whatever, we've still got our hand in. And the Indian government's working with us on the Vault of Shiva, and even the Peruvians are letting the IHA get involved with what's happening at El Dorado.'

'Grudgingly,' she said, with a flash of professional annoyance.

'The point is, they've still asked for our help. So we've got all these digs going on at once, and you know what? They're all going smoothly.'

'You are *so* jinxing it!'

Eddie grinned. 'They're going smoothly,' he insisted, 'and you know why? Because you put people in charge of each of 'em who know what they're doing. So that means you don't have to micromanage everything any more.'

She treated him to a particularly sulky scowl. 'What do you mean, any more?'

'No, you never once looked over anyone's shoulder and told them to dig six inches to the left, did you?' he said, kissing her again. 'But the IHA's in a quiet patch at the moment. We've been talking about taking a break for a while – maybe now's the time. And there's the book thing too.'

'Right, the book thing,' Nina echoed. It was her turn to become thoughtful. 'I still don't know what I want to do about that.'

'What's to think about? For fuck's sake, love, they're offering you six figures to write about all the stuff you've discovered!

23

I know it's not like we desperately need the money or anything,' he waved a hand to encompass their Upper East Side apartment, 'but you've got to admit it'd be a hell of a bonus. Christ, if you want I'll write everything up for you. Although I can't type, so I'll have to scribble it all down in biro.'

'Just make sure you leave out all the things that are top secret,' she reminded him, amused. 'Oh, and the part where you were wanted for murder by Interpol.'

'And the part where you got a faceful of crap while you were crawling through a sewer pipe.'

She grimaced at the memory. 'It's all glamour being a famous archaeologist, isn't it?'

Eddie sniffed her cheek. 'You got most of it off. This book, though – it might be the perfect time to take a bit of a break and write it, while things are quiet at work. And we could also do some,' a lascivious smirk crept across his square face, 'other stuff.'

Nina feigned innocence. 'What kind of *stuff*, Mr Chase?'

'Oh, you know. Shagging like rabbits.'

She laughed, swatting his hand off hers. 'There's that subtle charm I fell in love with.'

'Yeah, it's irresistible, innit? I'm serious, though, and not just about a non-stop fuck-fest.' Nina giggled. 'I mean about the book, and having a break from work. We could take a really long holiday, somewhere we haven't been before – and with absolutely nothing to do with archaeology.'

Now she feigned horror. 'Oh, let's not do anything crazy . . .'

'Grant invited us out to Hollywood, remember? We could do that as part of a West Coast tour, maybe – start off in Seattle, then go down through San Francisco to LA to watch him filming his next movie. Even though it'll probably be as big a piece of crap as his last one.'

'I thought you liked action movies.'

'I like *good* action movies. *Nitrous 2* was absolute bollocks, though.'

'I think you mean *Ni-two-rous*,' Nina corrected with a smile. Their movie star friend Grant Thorn's most recent film had gone by the rather awkward moniker of *Ni2rous* on its posters, providing a source of endless amusement to the couple – as well as late-night talk-show hosts.

'Yeah, when nobody even knows how to pronounce the title, that's probably a bad start. It really was complete arse, though. That bit where he dived out of the car that went over the cliff and fired a grappling hook to grab hold of his mate's car that was jumping the other way? That was so fucking unrealistic they might as well have had him grow wings.'

'It wasn't any more unbelievable than his other movies, and you liked those.'

'I *used* to like 'em. Maybe I'm growing old.'

Her smile returned, wider. 'Maybe you're growing up.'

Eddie snorted. 'No danger of that, love. But I've got to admit, these days I'm happy just to watch Matt Damon moving purposefully for two hours. Still, actually getting to see Grant filming should be fun. Something to tell the grandkids.'

'That kinda presupposes kids,' said Nina. 'I guess this conversation's come round full circle.'

He shifted position to face her. 'So . . . what's your view on that? You're . . .' He paused, choosing his words. 'You're not dead set against it, are you?'

She also gave careful consideration to her reply. 'No,' she said at last. 'No, I'm not against it. It's just that, like I said, our lives have been complicated. But if things did get more straightforward, then . . .' Another moment of thought. 'I wouldn't say no.'

From the look of delight Eddie was trying hard to contain, it was clear he was happy with her answer. 'Nor would I.'

They kissed, then held each other tight. 'It's a big decision, though,' Nina said at last.

'Yeah, taking a sabbatical to get paid half a million dollars and have loads of sex. Big decision.'

Nina prodded him in the stomach, making him flinch and laugh. 'I don't mean like that. It's more about . . . well, what Don blurted out.' She became more serious. 'We *are* getting on, in a purely biological sense. The risks start to increase almost geometrically every year once a woman passes thirty, and the older the man is the more the likelihood of complications too.'

'What kind of complications?'

'Just getting pregnant in the first place becomes harder, for a start. Then there are things like an increased risk of pre-eclampsia, high blood pressure, gestational diabetes—'

'I thought you were a doctor of archaeology, not pregnancy!'

'Ah, well,' she admitted sheepishly, 'when Lola was still at work, I got worried about her and the baby's health, so I did some reading about any potential problems she might have. What?' she went on, seeing his mocking expression. 'She's the first close friend I've had who's been pregnant. I wanted to be prepared if anything happened to her!'

He chuckled. 'See? This is that whole micromanagement thing again. Pretty sure the UN has a couple of actual medical doctors on staff somewhere.'

'Oh, shut up,' she said, jabbing him again. 'The point is, it made me realise that the odds of anything going wrong with Lola's pregnancy were pretty low – but the risks start rising once a woman gets to my age.'

'But they should *still* be pretty low,' Eddie said. 'I mean, you're in good nick – you exercise, you're not a lard-arse, you don't eat junk, you don't even drink all that much any more. And I'm still in exactly the same shape I was in when I left the SAS.'

Nina eyed his midsection sceptically. 'Uh-huh.'

He made a rude sound. 'Okay, so maybe I've put on a *little* weight in nine years. But I'm not spending every day running twenty miles with a full pack of gear any more, so what do you expect? Anyway, we're both in decent nick, so that should put us in a better position than most people our age right from the start.'

'It's not just about health, though. There are some things that are still a danger even if both people are in perfect condition. I don't want to be morbid and depressing, but the chances of a miscarriage go up enormously after thirty. And then there are higher risks of delivery complications, birth defects—'

'Birth defects?' Eddie said sharply, straightening.

'Yeah, I'm afraid so. Autism's more common in kids with older parents, as well as Down's syndrome and other genetic disorders.' She took in his oddly stricken expression. 'What's wrong? Sorry, I didn't mean to bring you down so much.'

He shook his head. 'No, it's okay.'

'Is that something you're worried about?' But there was something deeper to his reaction, she realised. 'Something you've seen?'

His reply took a moment in coming. 'Yeah.'

'Where?'

'On a job,' he said, tone becoming brusquer. 'Can't talk about it.'

After six years together, she was attuned enough to her husband to pick up the nuances of those rare occasions when he discussed his professional past – first as a British special forces soldier, then a hired troubleshooter. 'A job, not a mission?' The difference was small, but crucial. The latter were covered by the laws of state security; any secrets from the second stage of his career, however, would be kept for more personal reasons.

'Doesn't matter. Let's just say I've seen that kind of stuff. And that I don't really want to talk about it.'

Nina decided not to push him. 'Okay, no problem. You and your secrets, though,' she continued, deliberately teasing in the hope of changing the subject. 'I think I know you fairly well by now. And after everything we've been through together, I can't believe there's anything in your past that could shock me.'

Eddie smiled. 'Nah, probably not.'

But she couldn't help noticing that he hesitated before replying.

2
London

Eight Years Earlier

Eddie Chase stared disconsolately up at the flaking ceiling, debating whether it was worth getting out of bed.

There was little to look forward to if he did. It was unseasonably hot and unpleasantly humid, the temperature in the cramped studio flat already uncomfortable even at this time of the morning, but things would be no better outside. He had no job, was almost out of money . . . and in the middle of a bitter separation from his wife.

What the hell had gone wrong? He and Sophia had married less than a year and a half earlier, in a mad whirlwind of passion that he thought would last for ever. But everything collapsed with shocking suddenness, leaving him stunned and blinking in the wreckage.

The wedding – practically an elopement – was only a month after they met, so the first time Chase was introduced to Sophia's father was after the honeymoon. And Lord Blackwood had made it clear with every aristocratic curl of the lip that his daughter's marriage to a soldier – not even an officer, but a common squaddie! – was something of which he utterly disapproved. Sophia soon afterwards found herself cut off from her father's money for the first time in her life – and not long after *that*, Chase began to find himself on the outside looking in as she renewed old friendships. Friendships exclusively of the male, young, upper-class and wealthy variety.

So now he was here, alone in a crappy rented flat overlooking a congestion-clogged main road through one of the grottier parts of London. He couldn't even open the window to let in cooler air without it being joined by noise and diesel fumes.

Staying in bed was not an option, he finally decided. If nothing else, years of military routine made inactivity seem almost criminally wasteful. He shoved away the covers and rolled upright.

The sight of his surroundings lowered his mood still further. One room; that was what his life had been reduced to. He even had to share a bathroom with one of the other tenants.

But the damp-stained studio was not nearly so depressing as what was on the little folding table by the door. Chase stared at the documents poking out of the torn envelope like spilled guts from a small animal. They were from Sophia – or rather, her solicitor – and one of them, once he signed it, would probably be the last thing she ever wanted from him.

If he signed it.

He let out a sound that was somewhere between a sigh and a growl. Sophia was seeking a divorce, to get rid of him as soon as possible so she could hook up with whichever rich, braying arsehole from the City she'd set her sights on. Under British law, before a divorce could be granted husband and wife needed to be separated for at least two years, or there had to be reasonable grounds.

Adultery was one of these, and it had certainly been a factor; Sophia had practically rubbed his face in it before he finally moved out, unable to tolerate her taunting any longer. But there were two problems. The first, in which he saw the hand of her father, was that Sophia wanted *Chase* to be the one who admitted to an affair. Daddy dearest was protecting the reputation of his daughter – or, just as likely, the Blackwood name. An heiress sleeping around behind the back of her war hero husband was irresistible gossip fodder, whereas some yob from Yorkshire betraying a beautiful aristocrat would arouse nothing but sympathy for her.

The second was more simple. He didn't *want* to end the marriage.

For all Sophia had done to him, for all the arguments and screaming and unfaithfulness . . . he still loved her. He had made a commitment to her, a promise, and the thought of breaking that promise was almost physically painful. Though he was no longer a member of the armed forces, he still placed a high value on duty, honour and loyalty – even if Sophia did not.

It also implied surrender, failure. As a former member of the Special Air Service, he was unwilling to accept either.

Another sound, this time definitely a sigh. Chase forced himself to his feet and stretched, working the stiffness out of his muscles. The mattress was as unforgiving as his wife. He crossed the room to the counter that acted as his kitchen and filled the kettle, preparing – however reluctantly – to start the day.

Half an hour later, he had eaten, showered and dressed. To his disappointment, the letter had not magically vanished in the meantime.

'Buggeration and fuckery,' Chase muttered, glaring at it. Sophia's solicitors, he already knew from experience, would not hesitate to follow up on their enquiries by phone or even in person if a response didn't come immediately. Their letterhead said they were based in the City of London, so they were probably charging her father a thousand pounds per hour for their time, while his own financial situation forced him to traipse across two boroughs to get what free help he could at the nearest Citizens Advice Bureau.

He tried to suppress a churning feeling of disgust. Money. That was what everything came down to. Sophia was used to it, couldn't live without it, wanted more of it – and now that she had access to it again, was using it against him.

And she knew his sense of dignity wouldn't allow him to beg others for it. He had friends all around the world, but while he could always rely on them for a favour, since he in turn would always help them if they needed it, the one thing he couldn't bring himself to ask for was money.

So now he was trapped by his own pride. Whether he caved in to Sophia's demands or asked for monetary help from others to fight her, it would feel like failure either way. At least in combat there was always the *possibility* of beating the odds to reach victory, but right now he couldn't see any good way out short of a miracle . . .

His phone trilled. Chase knew it wasn't Sophia; he had set her ringtone as Cliff Richard's 'Devil Woman', but this was the cheap pre-paid Nokia's default. He picked the phone up and flipped it open, seeing on the screen that it was a London number. 'Is that you, Jesus?'

'I've heard some strange things from your mouth, Eddie, but that's got to be near the top of the list.' Not a miracle, but the familiar voice was nearly as welcome.

'Mac!' Chase cried, smiling for the first time in several days. 'Fuck me, I wasn't expecting to hear from you. I thought you were out of the country?'

'I'm back, for the moment,' said the Scotsman. 'I'll tell you about it – well, as much as I can within the bounds of the Official Secrets Act – if you'd like to meet up. Are you busy?'

'Let me check my Filofax,' Chase said sarcastically. 'No, I'm free. Where do you want to meet?'

'Come round to my place – you remember where it is?'

'Yeah.'

'Good. Half eleven or thereabouts? Oh, and there'll be someone else here I'm sure you'll be pleased to see again.' Even over the phone, Chase could detect the amusement in the other man's voice. 'An old friend.'

'Well, fucking hell,' said Chase, unable to hold back a grin. 'Look who it is. Hugo Castille, the Belgian waffler.'

The lanky Castille sniffed through his beaky nose. 'And Edward Chase, as polite and charming as always.' He peered at the shorter man's head. 'Your hair . . . it is getting a little thin, no? Especially on top.'

'Oh fuck off, Hugo.' Still grinning, Chase shook the mustachioed Belgian's hand, before the pair embraced and clapped each other on the back. 'Christ, how long's it been? A year?'

'More than that,' Castille replied. 'I have not seen you since the wedding.' His expression became mournful. 'Mac told me what has happened with you and Sophia. I am very sorry.'

'It's okay,' said Chase, rather brusquely, before moving the conversation along. 'Everything's good with you, then? Coping with civilian life?'

'I have a new line of work. Not too different from my old one,' he added with a sly smile. 'I will tell you about it. You might find it interesting.'

'Can't wait.' Chase turned to his former commanding officer. 'What about you, Mac? How's the leg?'

Jim 'Mac' McCrimmon shifted his stance to put his left foot forward, supporting himself on a metal cane. A faint creak came from the ankle joint – not of bone, but aluminium and plastic. 'Bearable. They think that given another two or three years, I should regain more or less full mobility. I intend to do it in one.'

'Anything I can do to help, you just say the word.'

The tall, bearded Scot smiled. 'You already did, Eddie. If it hadn't been for you, I would have lost more than just a leg to those Taliban bastards.' He gestured for Chase to take a seat in one of the deep red leather armchairs in his living room. 'In fact, we might be able to help you.'

The Yorkshireman didn't move, his expression darkening. 'I'm not here to take charity.'

'And I didn't ask you here to offer it. I know you better than that, Eddie. Come on, sit down. I'm going to, whether you do or not.' He rapped his left shin with the cane. 'Standing on this bloody thing isn't exactly comfortable.'

Chase reluctantly sat as Mac and Castille did the same. 'So,' he said, 'you've become a spook, eh? You bloody sell-out.'

Mac chuckled. 'Yes, I remember what you think of the men and women of our intelligence services. But they're not all that bad. Well, a few of them. Actually, I've been working with somebody you've already met.'

Chase pulled a disgusted face. 'Aw, not that fucking Capri-driving bell-end Alderley, surely?'

'The very same.'

'How's his nose?'

'Still crooked where you broke it.' A wry grin. 'He remembers you too, funnily enough.'

'Good. Can't believe you're working with that twat! At least I'll never have to deal with him again. Tosser.'

'So, you have been in Africa, Mac,' Castille said. 'What have you been doing there?'

The older man's grin widened. 'Nothing I'm going to tell you about, Hugo. I know you don't mean any harm, but if I even gave you a hint, you'd be chatting to some random stranger in a bar about it before the end of the day.'

'That is not true!' Castille protested. 'I do not give away secrets.'

'Only because the rest of us tackle you to the fucking floor every time you open your mouth,' Chase told him, laughing.

'Let's just say I've been doing some consulting work on behalf of Her Majesty's Government, and leave it at that,' said Mac. 'The main thing was, it got me back on my feet – foot – and actually doing something useful again. Which after three months in hospital and most of a year withering away convalescing was a huge relief. It felt better than any amount of talking to the shrinks, put it that way. Made me realise just how much I need to *do* things, to contribute. To have a purpose.'

'I think we are all like that, no?' added Castille.

Chase eyed him. 'This is the bit with the hard sell, right? The reason you asked me here?'

'Partly,' Mac admitted. 'But Hugo was right – I think you'll be interested in what he's got to say.' A hint of concern entered his level gaze. 'It might be exactly what you need right now, considering what Sophia's been putting you through.'

'You seem to know a lot about it, for someone who's been out of the country.' Chase gave him a suspicious look. 'For that matter, how'd you get my number? I only got that phone after I moved out.'

'I've been working with MI6, not 118. They can do quite a bit more with their directory enquiries. But that's not important.' He nodded towards the other man. 'Hugo, why don't you tell him about the job?'

Castille straightened in his seat. 'I am working for a private contractor,' he told Chase. 'There is a job that has just come up – I would like you to join me on it.'

Chase shook his head. 'I only got out of the military last year; I don't want to be going right back into it under another name. And I know it's big business right now, but I *really* don't want to traipse around some godforsaken desert shithole acting as a human shield for a bunch of arseholes from an oil company.'

'No, no,' said Castille, gesticulating enthusiastically, 'this is nothing like that. Do you remember Hal Sullivan?'

Chase glanced at Mac. 'Your old mate from the Kiwi SAS?'

'More than just a mate, Eddie,' Mac told him, nodding. 'He taught me practically everything I know about being a soldier. He's a good man.'

'I have been working for him,' Castille continued. 'And it is not bodyguard work. It is, how to describe it? Aid and rescue work – in places where there are men who do not want people to get aid or rescue.'

'Troubleshooting,' added Mac. 'Humanitarian work, but with a fist in the glove if it's needed. Hal actually approached me about being a partner, and I might have considered it if not for this.' He thumped his artificial heel on the carpet. 'It's right up your street, though. You'd be using your skills to help people. And I know how important that is to you.'

Chase considered his words, before cautiously asking Castille: 'What's the job?'

'A rescue mission,' said the Belgian. 'A team of aid workers in Vietnam has been kidnapped by bandits. The father of one of them called on Hal to rescue them; he is putting a team together now.' A beseeching look. 'You would be a great help, Edward. You have experience of just this kind of mission.'

'Yeah, and look how it turned out,' Chase replied, voice drenched with sarcasm. 'I married the hostage. And why isn't the Vietnamese government sorting it out, instead of someone having to hire mercs?'

'They're dragging their feet, apparently,' said Mac. 'From what I gather, these bandits have the local authorities in their pockets. And going through normal channels in Hanoi could take days – which the hostages might not have.'

'I am flying out from Heathrow tonight,' Castille said. 'Do you have a visa?'

Chase nodded. 'All the stuff I got in the SAS is still valid, far as I know.' As part of the preparation for a mission in Cambodia – the very one on which he had met Sophia – he had been issued with visas for all the neighbouring countries, in case the team needed to exit the region by an alternate route.

'The plane takes off at nine o'clock.' Castille regarded him hopefully. 'It would be very good if you were on it with me. I would like your help.'

Chase said nothing, conflicting thoughts running through his mind. His practical side knew he should be demanding more details: the exact location of the operation, who else would be involved, pay and conditions, extraction options. But all those were irrelevant without another question being answered first. 'Why'd you come to me?' he finally asked. 'I've been out of the Regiment for a year, and I haven't exactly been keeping in shape. Married life does that to you – the most exercise I've had has been dodging the plates Sophia's thrown at me.' That was an exaggeration, as she had only done it once, but it had been a deciding factor in prompting him to move out. 'And don't say it's to help me out of a bind. I told you, I'm not here to accept charity.'

Castille held up his hands. 'And I am not here to offer it. Edward, I came to you because you are my friend, and I know how good you are at what you do.'

'Only I don't do it any more.'

'There's nothing worse than a man who wastes his potential,' Mac said quietly.

'Oh, for fuck's sake,' Chase snapped, with genuine irritation. 'I'm in the middle of a fucking divorce! I've got her solicitors breathing up my arse trying to make me sign something I don't want to – if I jet off to bloody Vietnam, they'll probably use it against me as a case of unreasonable behaviour.'

'Eddie, you may not want to hear this, but that could be the best thing for you as things stand,' said the Scot.

'Maybe it would,' Chase countered, bitterness now entering his voice, 'but maybe I don't want what's *best* for me. Maybe I want what I want – which is not to get fucking divorced!'

Mac shook his head. 'I know exactly how you feel. I've been there. But sometimes these things happen – they *have* to happen. It hurts at the time, but it's less painful in the long run.'

Chase fixed his former commander with a penetrating stare. 'And that's how you felt about splitting up with Angela?'

Mac's own gaze did not waver. 'I did what had to be done. The fact that I wasn't at all happy about it didn't stop it from being right.'

Another silence, this one longer, before Chase turned back

to Castille. 'Hugo, I'm sorry, but . . . no. I can't do it. Thanks for the offer, but . . . things are just too fucked-up and complicated right now.' Castille's expressive face clearly revealed his disappointment. 'You'll have to find someone else.'

'But you are the best person by far,' the Belgian objected.

'What about Jason Starkman?' Mac suggested.

'Starkman? *Fuck* him,' Chase spat with a vehemence that startled both the other men. On their questioning looks, he continued: 'He's one of the people Sophia was banging behind my back!'

Mac was genuinely shocked. 'Jason did that to you? I would never have . . .' He shook his head in dismay. 'Bastard.'

'Yeah,' said Chase, still seething. 'So I wouldn't exactly recommend him.'

'He was not on my list,' Castille said apologetically, 'but I shall put him on it so I can cross him off again!'

'Why weren't you considering him?' asked Mac.

'I do not know where he is. I heard he had been approached by some organisation, but since then . . .' A shrug. 'He has vanished. Nobody knows what he is doing.'

'If he's got any sense, he'll stay a long fucking way from me,' Chase growled. 'But I can't do this, Hugo. Sorry.'

The Belgian sighed. 'I am sorry too, but . . . I understand.'

There was an awkward pause, which Chase broke by leaning back in his armchair with exaggerated casualness. 'So. What else have you two arseholes been up to since I saw you last?'

Castille's offer was not mentioned again during the couple of hours Chase spent with his former comrades, although its shadow was ever-present. Finally, and somewhat reluctantly, the Yorkshireman said goodbye, making mutual promises to keep in touch. 'If you change your mind...' said Castille hopefully.

Chase shook his hand firmly. 'Good luck in Vietnam, Hugo. Keep your head down, eh?'

'I will.' Again, Castille's disappointment was obvious, but this time he let the matter drop. 'And you do the same, no? I would rather be dodging bullets than dodging lawyers!'

'Yeah. At least when you're dodging bullets you get to shoot back.' Another handshake, both men grinning, then Chase turned to Mac. 'See you around.'

'Fight to the end, Eddie,' Mac replied.

'Always do.' They shook hands once more, then Chase departed, heading back out into the cloying urban heat.

He had barely turned the corner from Mac's house before despondency settled over him like a heavy cloud. Castille's offer might have come out of the blue, and – Chase kept telling himself – it just wasn't practical to accept right now, but at least it would have been *something*. Would tramping through a jungle on a rescue mission really be any worse than sitting around in his miserable little flat?

That thought kept returning during the two bus journeys it took him to return to said residence. There was mail waiting for him, but any hope that there might be a job interview amongst it was soon dashed; it was all junk. He slumped into the lone armchair. The flat was hotter than ever, but the clatter of traffic outside reminded him that opening the window would bring its own unpleasantness.

'Fuck,' he muttered.

He stared blankly across the room for several minutes. This wasn't how he'd expected his life to turn out after leaving the SAS. Then he'd been newly married and in love; now, he had a table strewn with divorce papers, and whatever his own feelings for Sophia, they were not mutual . . .

Cliff Richard squalled tinnily from his phone. Speak of the devil.

He flipped it open. 'Hi, Soph.' At the back of his mind he still had hope as he waited to hear her voice. Maybe her tone would have changed, maybe she would want a reconciliation . . .

That hope was impaled by a stiletto heel. 'Eddie,' Sophia said, her crystal accent filled with impatience and disdain. 'Where the hell have you been? I've been trying to get hold of you all morning.'

'Turned my phone off,' he replied. 'Had a . . . job offer.'

She expressed no interest. 'Well, I need to talk to you. Can you come round to my house?'

'Not sure I know where that is, Soph,' said Chase. 'Is it anywhere near *our* house?'

He expected a sarcastic retort, but got only a huff of irritation. 'You know exactly what I mean. Come over as soon as you can.'

'That could take a while, seeing as I don't have a car any more.'

'Then take a cab.'

He could no longer hold in his own exasperation. 'Fucking hell *fire*, Sophia! I guess you forgot what it was like when your dad cut you off. Remember, when you *had no money*? When your credit cards might as well have been cream fucking crackers for all the good they were? I can't just hop in a taxi and cruise over to Chelsea, because I can't. Fucking. *Afford*. It. You get that?'

Another huff, this time overflowing with undisguised disgust. 'Oh, very well. If it'll get this sorted out, I'll come to you. Where are you?'

He gave her the address, then closed the phone with an angry snap. 'Fuuuuuck . . .' he said, kneading his forehead.

Sophia arrived a mere twenty minutes later; considering London's traffic, Chase imagined she had driven at Formula 1 speeds through the city's rat-runs. Not wanting to give her any further ammunition, he went down to meet her on the street rather than letting her inside the dismal apartment. 'Nice car,' he snorted on seeing what was parked on the double-yellow lines, hazard lights flashing. 'Which Hooray Henry did you get to pay for that?'

'No one you know,' Sophia told him, giving the brand-new Maserati Coupé a casual glance through her sunglasses before curling her glossed lips at the surroundings. 'So, this is where you're living now? I'm not impressed.'

'Can't say I am either, but needs must. What do you want?'

She took off the glasses and shook out her long black hair. 'My solicitors told me you haven't replied to their last letter yet. I thought I'd see if a personal visit would prompt a response.'

'I didn't reply to it 'cause I don't agree with it. You're asking me to say something that isn't true. I wasn't the one who was sleeping around.'

Sophia bared her teeth. 'We've been through this, Eddie. It'll make things much simpler if you just bite the bullet and go through with it.'

'You mean it keeps your name clean while I get shat on.'

'A crude way of putting it, which I suppose I should expect by now, but yes. You have to admit, the financial settlement we've offered is more than adequate.'

'The financial . . .' Chase shook his head. 'You make it sound like a fucking business deal. It was a *marriage*, Sophia! Maybe that doesn't mean anything to you, but it does to me. I made a promise.'

'Sometimes promises have to be broken.'

'Not by me. If I give someone my word, I move heaven and fucking earth to keep it.'

'Ah, the knight in shining armour rears his head again.' Sophia looked away, taking a breath before rounding on him once more. 'Eddie, I'm sorry to be so blunt, but clearly I have to in order to penetrate that armour – I don't want you any more.' Chase felt as if he had been kicked in the chest, but she kept talking. 'We were in love once, but that was the past. Things change. I changed.'

'I didn't.'

'Maybe that's the problem. You have all these noble, romantic ideas about true love and how marriage should last for ever . . . but this is the real world. It didn't work; it's over. The best way for you to avoid any more pain is simply to sign the papers and finish it, quickly and cleanly. I'll expect my solicitors to hear from you soon.' She returned to the Maserati, hesitating as she opened the door to give him a slightly softer look. 'I'm sorry, Eddie, but we just weren't right for each other. Maybe someday you'll meet the right person for you. I hope you do.'

Chase wanted to reply, but found his throat clenched tight by a torrent of emotions. By the time he managed to force them down, Sophia had climbed into the sports car and started the engine. The Maserati carved out into the traffic with a V8 bellow, leaving him standing uselessly on the pavement. He stared after it, hoping it would turn around and bring her back to recant, but it was quickly lost to sight.

Numbed, he headed indoors, collapsing once more into the armchair. The solicitor's letter was still on the table, taunting him. *Just sign, and it will all be over . . .*

His clenched fist thumped down on the chair's arm. 'Fuck that!' he snarled. Mac's words echoed in his head: *fight to the end*. His SAS unit's unofficial motto, but one that he lived by. He knew now in his heart that he would never get Sophia back, but he wasn't just going to surrender meekly to whatever she wanted.

And he wasn't going to roll over and die in his own life, either. He was going to *do* something.

Chase took out his phone and thumbed back through the recent calls to return one. 'Mac,' he said on getting an answer. 'What's Hugo's number?'

3

New York City

'Eddie, get up,' said Nina, coming back into the bedroom to find her husband still in bed, the covers crumpled back to expose his muscular, if scarred, body from the waist up. 'It's nearly time for work.'

Eddie didn't move. 'You're the boss – tell everyone we're having the day off. It's not like the planet will explode if we don't turn up.'

'You're jinxing it again!' She went to prod his side. 'Come on, move your—'

Fast as a snake, he grabbed her wrist and pulled her on to the mattress beside him. She yipped in surprise. 'Move my what?' he said, smirking.

'Your ass.'

'Arse.'

'Ass.'

'*Arse.*'

'Po-tay-to, po-tah-to, you still have to move it.'

The smirk widened. 'I was planning to. Only in a sort of

45

repeated up-and-down motion. 'Cause if we *are* going to have kids, after what you said yesterday we need to get cracking on it.'

She laughed. 'I know, but I wasn't thinking in every available moment.'

'I bloody was!'

'Edward J. Chase, you've got a one-track mind.' Nina kissed him, then sat up. 'Seriously, though, time to move. I've got a meeting at nine thirty. And I'm sure you must have something to do as well.' She cocked her head and gave him a mocking smile. 'What exactly *is* it that you do at the IHA?'

'Save the world and shag the boss, mostly.'

'I can't dispute that. Come on, get up.' She pulled the covers off him, then eyed what was revealed. 'Ah, I see you already *are* up.'

Eddie cackled. 'I don't hang about. So you just drop your kecks, then hop aboard . . .'

She gave the upstanding member a playful swat. 'It'll have to wait until tonight, sorry. But you hold that thought.'

'If I do that, I won't be able to walk all day!'

Nina laughed again, then tugged away from him and stood, checking her watch. 'I'm out the door in fifteen minutes. And you *will* be with me. Preferably fully dressed.'

'Oh, so I've got a choice?'

'Ha! You're a married man, you have no choice in anything.'

'Yeah, I learned that in my first marriage.' He huffed, then rolled out of bed. 'Well, if the world needs saving again, suppose I'd better bloody do it.'

'Hopefully it won't need our services today,' Nina told him. Now it was her turn to smirk. 'Because I've got plans for tonight.'

Eddie grinned, then headed for the bathroom.

★

'Can't believe you're still cold,' said Eddie as they entered Nina's office.

'What?' she complained, unzipping her coat. 'It feels like the middle of winter!' She pointed at the cityscape beyond the windows. The view across her native Manhattan from the United Nations' towering Secretariat Building was still dappled with snow from an unexpected flurry a few days earlier, and a chill wind had whipped around them as they crossed First Avenue and the plaza outside the UN complex.

'You were the one who wanted to take the subway rather than getting a cab.' Eddie took off his battered leather jacket, looking entirely unfazed by the weather.

'And you should have tried harder to convince me that was a bad idea!'

'When have I ever managed to do that?' He hung up his jacket, then watched with amusement as his wife shrugged off layers of clothing. 'So what's in today's diary, then?'

'Jeez, at least let me get to my desk.' Finally shorn of wool, Nina sat and opened her laptop. 'Okay, there's the international relations meeting at nine thirty, the general accounting briefing at eleven—'

'Count me in! Fucking thrilling.'

'The IT upgrade group at two, and the interagency communications meeting at four.' She leaned back, shaking her head. 'You know what's missing from all of those? Anything to do with actual archaeology.'

'See? This'd be a good time to take a long break. There's nothing new actually going on.'

'It's tempting. Very tempting.' She started to check her emails, but was interrupted by the intercom. 'Yes?'

'Dr Wilde?' said Melinda, Lola's French replacement. 'There

is a Mr Trulli asking to see you. He does not have an appointment, but—'

'Matt?' said Nina. 'That's okay, let him in.'

Eddie raised his eyebrows. 'Matt's here?'

'Must have come back early from down under.' Before long, there was a knock at the door. 'Come in!'

Matt Trulli entered. 'Morning, guys!' said the Australian cheerfully. The couple had not seen him for a few months, and in that time the Oceanic Survey Organisation's chief engineer had topped up his tan and also acquired a sun-bleached beard and several extra pounds around his already ample midsection. 'Great to see you both.'

'You too,' replied Nina, getting up to greet him.

Eddie shook his hand. 'Welcome back! How was your trip home?'

'Bloody brilliant, mate. Just what I needed to relax after everything that happened down at Atlantis.' The previous year, Matt had almost died in a crippled submarine amongst the ruins of the lost city. 'Spent the time designing a new sub – with a two-way release on the docking clamps this time! – and building a couple of ROVs.'

'Your idea of relaxation ain't the same as mine,' said the Englishman. 'That's not what I call a holiday.'

'It wasn't really a holiday, mate – it was technically a sabbatical. *Working* holiday, the best sort.'

'My thinking exactly,' said Nina, embracing Matt. 'Maybe I married the wrong man . . .'

'Oi!' protested Eddie.

Matt laughed. 'Wouldn't dream of splitting you two up, mate. For starters, I know you'd beat the crap out of me!'

'So you're back at the OSO?' Nina asked.

He nodded. 'Don't start again until next week, officially, but

I fancied coming in to clear the decks beforehand. I've been out of the office for months, so I hate to think what my inbox is going to look like! But I wanted to pop in and say hello to you guys first.'

'Aw, thanks, Matt,' she said with a smile. 'Glad you're back.'

'Nice to be back. Although the weather's a bit crook! So what have you two been up to? Got anything exciting going on?'

'Not at the moment,' said Nina. 'Lots of meetings, bureaucracy, budgets . . .'

'There's no bloody pleasing her,' Eddie scoffed. 'When things are going smoothly, she complains. When she's being shot at or thrown out of blimps, she complains!'

Matt looked surprised. 'You were thrown out of a blimp?'

'No,' Nina assured him. 'Although it's about the only thing we *haven't* been thrown out of.'

'Yet,' added her husband.

She jabbed a finger at him. 'What did I tell you about jinxing things?'

'Glad to see you two are the same as ever,' said Matt, smiling. 'Anyway, we'll have to have a proper catch-up soon. If you're free one evening this week, maybe we could grab a bite somewhere.'

'Sounds good to me,' Eddie said. 'Lola yesterday, now you, and we were just talking about going to see Grant Thorn in LA – it's like we're getting the gang back together.'

'If we see Grant, we'll probably see Macy too – they're an item now,' added Nina. 'Huh, wonder if we'll catch up with anyone else?'

'Probably Peter bloody Alderley, knowing my luck.'

She smiled, and was about to reply when the intercom sounded again. 'Yes?'

'Dr Wilde, Mr Seretse is here,' Melinda announced. Nina and Eddie exchanged glances; the UN liaison was not one of their scheduled meetings for the day. 'He says it's a very important matter.'

'Thanks, Melinda. Send him in,' said Nina. 'Wonder what he wants?'

'Whatever it is, I doubt it's any of my business,' Matt said. 'I'd better get going.'

'See you later,' said Eddie, clapping him on the shoulder.

'No worries, mate. Catch you again soon, Nina.'

She kissed his cheek. 'Bye, Matt.' He smiled and departed, the door barely having time to swing shut before it was opened again by the morning's second unexpected arrival.

Oswald Seretse was a tall and handsome black man in his late forties, straight-backed and aristocratic in bearing. He carried a slim, expensive briefcase. 'Ah, good morning, Dr Wilde, Mr Chase,' he said, his Gambian accent largely masked beneath the patrician tones he had acquired while studying at Cambridge.

'Please,' said Nina as she shook his proffered hand, 'call me Nina.' Seretse's attitude was considerably more formal than his predecessor's. 'We don't really stand on ceremony at the IHA.'

'Very well. Nina.' He did not sound entirely comfortable with doing so. 'Eddie.'

'Oswald,' said Eddie as he shook the official's hand and grinned cheekily. 'Or can I call you Ozzy?'

Seretse gave him a heavy-eyed stare. 'I would really prefer that you didn't.'

'What can we do for you?' Nina asked, gesturing for him to take a seat on the couches in one corner. 'I wasn't expecting to see you until the end of the week.'

'Something has come up.' Seretse sat, carefully straightening the trouser creases of his immaculate blue suit before setting his briefcase on the low coffee table and unlocking it. 'A matter that I think you will agree concerns the IHA.'

Eddie took the place on the adjoining couch beside Nina. 'Security business?'

'That is the IHA's purview, so yes.' He took out a manila folder. 'Now, Doct— Nina. How much do you know about Norse mythology?'

'The basics,' she answered, curious. 'I read *Beowulf* at high school, and Viking history was part of my coursework for a semester as an undergraduate. And there was a degree of crossover when I was doing my research into the various legends of Atlantis, because the Vikings were linked to some of them – although just about every ancient civilisation was linked to Atlantis at one time or another, so the connections were tenuous at best, and as we've since found out, they had no basis in fact. But I wouldn't call myself an expert by any means.'

Seretse nodded. 'I see. But you have heard of Viking runestones?'

'Of course. In fact, I know a specialist in them, David Colway. He's not a full-time member of the IHA, but he's worked with us before. If you want, I can call him.'

The diplomat firmly shook his head. 'As I said, this is a security matter. It must remain classified for now.' He opened the folder and handed her a photograph. 'This is what has become known as the Valhalla Runestone.'

Nina recognised it immediately. 'Found last year in Sweden. David actually went over to Stockholm to study it for a few days. Are you sure you don't want me to bring him in on this?'

'Absolutely.'

Eddie took a closer look at the photograph. The runestone

was a long, rugged slab of moss-covered granite, lying on a cloth-draped bench to allow for detailed examination. A ruler beside it provided scale: it was around seven feet in length, some two feet wide at the base and tapering to half that at the top. The rock was about a foot thick. Line upon line of thin, angular characters had been chiselled into its face, along with patterns and symbols surrounding a circular piece of much darker stone set into a recess some two thirds of the way up it. 'So what's so important about it? It doesn't actually tell you how to find Valhalla, does it?'

He had said it jokingly, but Nina's reply was serious. 'Actually . . . kind of, yes.'

'What? You're kidding.'

'No. If I remember, it supposedly described the route the Vikings would have taken to find it. There was a lot of excitement about it at the time; people were wondering if Valhalla was more than just a legend, like Atlantis. That's why I asked David to check it out for us.'

'What did he find?'

'Nothing concrete – what was written in the runes was too vague. The Swedes are still working on it, but everyone else has pretty much lost interest.'

'Not everyone,' said Seretse. 'Someone is very interested in the runestone. Interested enough to steal it – and to kill for it.'

Nina gasped. 'What?'

Seretse took out another photograph. This was a wider angle, showing the bench from the previous image in its surroundings, a laboratory.

It was empty.

'Last night, thieves broke into the Museum of National Antiquities in Stockholm and took the runestone,' the official

52

told them sonorously. 'They also shot and killed a security guard.'

'They stole it?' Eddie said, looking back at the first photo. 'Christ, if that thing's seven feet of solid granite, it must weigh a ton!'

'Very nearly. Nought-point-nine metric tons, in fact.'

'They'd need a lot of people to move it.'

'They had them. They hacked into the security cameras and shut them off before breaking in, but a camera on another building nearby caught them. There were at least eight people involved, probably more.'

'Why would they steal it?' Nina wondered. 'Every inch of it's been photographed, and all the runes have been translated. Why go to the risk of taking the actual stone when you could just look it up on Google?'

'That is what the UN would like you to find out,' said Seretse, straightening. 'A flight to Stockholm has been arranged for this evening, so you will arrive there tomorrow morning.'

'What?' she said, taken aback.

'Guess we'll have to tell Matt to take a rain check,' Eddie muttered.

'Wait, I don't understand,' Nina went on. 'This is a job for the Stockholm police, not the IHA. What's it got to do with us?'

Seretse took out a final photo and placed it in front of them. The scene was dark and grainy, a CCTV still taken at night. Several figures wearing black clothing were clustered around a van, features obscured by hoods and caps.

Except one. This particular frame had been singled out because one of the robbers had inadvertently revealed his face, even if only for a fraction of a second. His hood had slipped back as he climbed into the van, exposing his features to the wash of a nearby street light.

Both Nina and Eddie knew him at once.

'*That* is what it has to do with the IHA,' said Seretse, seeing their recognition. 'The thieves were led by one of your people.'

4

Vietnam

Eight Years Earlier

Chase stared up at the slowly turning ceiling fan. 'Saigon. *Shit.*'

'What?' Castille gave him a bewildered look from his nearby chair. 'We are not in Saigon. This is Da Nang.'

'I know, but I always wanted to say that.' On his friend's uncomprehending blink, he went on: 'Come on, Hugo! *Apocalypse Now*?'

'Is it?'

Chase snorted and shook his head. 'You need to watch more movies.'

'Or you need to watch less.'

They both looked around as the hotel room's telephone rang. Castille, closest, picked it up. 'Hello? Yes, we are here . . . Okay.' He replaced the receiver. 'That was Hal. He is with the client in room 503. They are ready to meet us.'

'About time.' Chase grunted as he stood, flexing and

stretching. The flight from London to Ho Chi Minh City had taken over twelve hours, and then the pair had taken a shuttle flight to the coastal city of Da Nang, more than 500 miles to the north. Even having taken every possible opportunity to sleep during the journey, he was still tired.

The fan did not exactly provide an ice-cold blast, but made enough of a breeze to take the edge off the tropical heat – which returned in full force as Chase and Castille left the room. It was not the first time that Chase had experienced such conditions, but the cloying, humid atmosphere was still far from pleasant. The Belgian also made a disapproving face, dabbing at his neck with a handkerchief. 'I do not mind a little heat,' he complained, 'but this? Ugh!'

'And I thought London was sweaty,' Chase agreed as they reached the elevator. A wait for the elderly device to grumble up to their level, then they entered and ascended to the fifth floor. They headed down another sweltering hallway. From the distance between doors, Chase guessed that guests on this floor had suites rather than mere rooms. They stopped at the third door, Castille knocking. A voice from inside told them to enter.

The cool air that greeted Chase as he stepped through was a huge relief. He had been right about it being a suite, and with the extra space also came the luxury of air-conditioning. He automatically surveyed the room as he entered: two other exits, plus French windows to a balcony overlooking the port. Five men waiting for them. No visible weapons, but he could tell immediately from the equally calculating looks he was getting in return that four of them had been in the military.

One of them he recognised, having met him very briefly several years earlier: Hal Sullivan, a former colonel in the New Zealand Special Air Service. In his early sixties, Sullivan nevertheless remained an imposing, dangerous figure. He was six feet tall with the solid build of someone who trained every day, and completely bald – which made his greying handlebar moustache all the more distinctive. His tanned skin had the colour and texture of a walnut. 'Hugo, mate,' he drawled. 'Good to see you. Come on in.' He shook Castille's hand, then turned to his companion. 'And you must be Eddie Chase.'

'I must,' Chase replied, extending his own hand. Sullivan's grip was strong, and he could tell that it could easily have been crushing if he so chose.

'Mac spoke very highly of you, which as far as I'm concerned is as good as a royal seal of approval. Glad to have you aboard.' He released Chase's hand, then indicated the other men. 'These are the rest of the team. John Lomax,' a close-cropped, bearded Caucasian man, 'Fernando Rios,' thick black eyebrows and swigging from a can of Coca-Cola, 'and Carl Hoyt.'

Hoyt was the tallest man in the room, wiry rather than muscular and with bony, deeply sunken cheeks. A hand-rolled cigarette hung from his clenched lips. 'Join the gang,' he said, his accent American.

Chase and Castille greeted the group, then Sullivan waved for them to sit as he stood beside the last man. 'This is our client: Ivor Lock. Mr Lock, if you'd like to explain the situation?'

Lock had a neat goatee beard and was wearing a tailored suit and shirt, his sole concession to the climate being an open top button. Chase guessed him to be around forty, and from his smooth skin and slicked-back brown hair took him to be a lawyer or business executive. Like Lomax and Hoyt, his accent revealed him as American. 'Gentlemen, good afternoon,' he began. 'Some background first: there is a charitable organisation, Aide Sans Limites, that travels around Third World countries providing free medical care for the poor. One of their groups has been working in Vietnam. Two days ago,' he leaned forward, expression becoming more intense, 'the team was taken hostage by a group of bandits operating in the jungle near the Laotian border, fifty or so miles west of here. The local authorities have been . . . unhelpful. Which is why I approached Mr Sullivan to expedite their rescue.'

'I know suggestin' this is kind of against my own economic interests, since it'd mean we weren't needed,' said Lomax, 'but couldn't you go to the US embassy and get them to put pressure on the Vietnamese government?'

'None of the group are Americans,' Lock replied. 'They're mostly European, but different nationalities, so it would mean going through multiple embassies, multiple bureaucracies. And the Vietnamese will try to hush the whole affair up. Tourism's becoming big business for them; the last thing they want is to scare people away with news stories about bandits and kidnappings.'

Rios, a Spaniard, spoke. 'But the story will get out eventually.'

'Not soon enough to help the people who've been kidnapped.'

'What's your connection to them?' asked Chase.

Lock took a breath. 'My daughter is one of the volunteers.'

'Thought you said there weren't any Americans?'

'She's a German national.' Lock's flinty eyes narrowed; he did not appreciate being questioned. 'Natalia Pöltl, my daughter from my first marriage.' He took out his wallet, opening it to reveal a small photograph of a young blonde woman. 'Now you see why I'm involved, Mr Chase – and why I want this situation dealt with as quickly as possible. I want my daughter rescued from these . . . animals. Before anything happens to her.'

'We've got information about the bandits' area of operations,' said Sullivan, 'and narrowed their location down to a few square kilometres.' He crossed to a large map taped to one wall, and pointed out a particular section. 'It's about eighty klicks west of

Da Nang, so we'll take Highway 49 to a point north of the target area, then head south. We'll have to search, but it seems these jokers have been operating with free rein for some time. If they're not worried about being tracked down, they shouldn't be too hard to find.'

'So what do we do when we find them?' asked Castille.

Hoyt grinned coldly. 'I've got a few things in mind.'

Sullivan raised a warning finger. 'We use lethal force only as a last resort, understood? Our number one priority is to recover the prisoners safely. Considering Vietnam's past, they really don't like having groups of Westerners marching through the jungle shooting people, even if they are bandits. If they decide to crack down, they could make it hell for us to get out of the country. Trust me, I did it the hard way back in '73, and it was not fun.'

Chase took a closer look at the map. The area Sullivan had indicated was hilly, judging from the contour lines, and there were few signs of civilisation nearby. 'Is it just jungle out there?'

Sullivan nodded. 'There are some small villages along the main river valleys, but past them it's pretty much solid all the way to the border, and beyond. We're not far south of the old DMZ, so this whole part of the country got ripped apart during the war. It's been left to recover ever since.'

'A good place to hide,' said Castille dolefully.

'We'll find them,' Sullivan assured him. 'So, here's the drill. A local friend of mine, Thuc, will take us in and out. From the drop point, we start a search. Once we find the hostages, we rescue them – minimum force unless absolutely necessary, remember – and take them to an extraction point on this river,' he pointed at a thin blue line on the map, 'where Thuc will be waiting with a boat. That should be the quickest way to get them back to the highway. From there, we return to Da Nang. Job done.'

'What about gear?' asked Lomax.

'I've got a good man with access to weapons and equipment. He's on his way over right now. In the meantime,' he handed out larger-scale maps of the target area, already marked with the drop and extraction points, 'familiarise yourself with the terrain. Mr Lock, you don't need to stay around if you don't want to.'

'Thanks,' said Lock, 'but I'd like to see. My daughter's out there, remember.'

Sullivan nodded, then began a more detailed briefing. Chase paid close attention; having served in Vietnam during the war as a young NZSAS officer, the Antipodean's first-hand knowledge of the jungle would be invaluable. Hoyt, meanwhile, was more occupied with rolling a new cigarette.

After twenty minutes, they were interrupted by a knock on the door. Sullivan opened it. To Chase's surprise, the man who entered was another familiar face. 'Jesus, if it isn't Eddie Chase!' he said after greeting Sullivan. 'And Hugo Castille too. Christ, we're only a couple short of a full Afghanistan reunion.'

'Bluey!' cried Chase. 'Fucking hell, you were the last person I expected to see. What're you doing here, you farty old bastard?'

'Supplying this sheep-shagger and the rest of you drongos with guns and gear,' said Bob 'Bluey' Jackson, giving Sullivan a cheery nod. 'So, Sully, you roped Eddie and Hugo into this? Well, they'll get the job done, even if they are a right pair of wankers.'

'As Edward would say, "Fuck off, you wombat-shagging twat,"' Castille grinningly told him in a very poor imitation of Chase's Yorkshire accent. The Australian waggled his bushy eyebrows in amusement. 'Are you coming with us?'

Bluey shook his head. 'Fuck no, mate. I've been living here

for a bit now; last thing I want to do is get into trouble with the local wallopers. And the girlfriend'd kill me!'

'Amazed anyone'd have you,' said Chase.

'Me too, sometimes! She's a lovely girl – well, a bit loud, but she keeps me in check. We're planning to move back to Oz together. Immigration paperwork might be a pain, but she's got some tricks.' A knowing smile, then he saw Sullivan's growing impatience. 'Anyway, Sully, I brought your gear. The guns're all forty-sevens; a bit scruffy, but I checked 'em and they're in decent nick.'

Sullivan nodded. 'What about radios?'

'Got you a set of Motorola walkie-talkies and headsets. On the old side, but they work fine. New batteries in all of 'em.'

'Good. Thanks for this, Bluey. Where is everything?'

'In my van,' said the Australian. 'It's all boxed up, so you won't get any stickybeaks freaking out when you unload it. When're you setting off?'

'As soon as Thuc arrives with his minibus.' Sullivan turned to the others. 'Is everyone ready to move?'

'Just let me take a piss first and I'm good to go,' Chase replied.

Sullivan gave him a weary look. 'Mac warned me that you were like this . . . Everyone else set?'

The remaining mercenaries confirmed their readiness. 'Let's get started,' said Hoyt.

'Good luck,' Lock said to Sullivan. 'I'll be waiting to hear from you. Bring my daughter back safely.'

'We'll find her,' the New Zealander replied. He glanced past Lock at the French windows, peering out at the sky over the ocean. 'Oh, a heads-up,' he said, turning back to his team. 'The weather forecast says there's a tropical storm due to make landfall this evening, with a chance it might become a typhoon by then. Even though we'll be farther inland, we're still going to get wet. Hopefully Bluey remembered to pack some rain gear.'

'Sod this, then,' Chase said. 'I'm off back to England!'

That produced muted chuckles in the group, which were cut short when the phone rang. Sullivan answered it. 'That's our ride,' he told them as he hung up.

The men filed out of the room, back into the stifling heat of the Vietnamese day. 'Here we go, then,' Chase said to the Belgian. 'Back into action.'

'Are you ready for it?' Castille asked quietly.

'Yeah,' Chase replied.

He hoped he was telling the truth.

5

Sweden

Nina stared at her laptop, even after multiple viewings not quite able to believe what she was witnessing.

Seretse had shown her a still image in New York; this was the full version, footage from a security camera. Because it had been watching a neighbouring building rather than the museum itself, the robbers were almost incidental, tucked away in one corner. Had their van been parked ten feet to the right, it was unlikely that any of their faces would even have been captured in frame.

But one had. And she knew it well.

'Logan Berkeley,' she said to herself, shaking her head. 'What the hell are you doing?'

Eddie, reclining beside her in the airliner's business-class cabin, raised his head to glare at the screen. 'Never did like that tosser, even before what he did in Egypt. You should have punched him harder. And whatever Seretse said, he's not part of the IHA any more. He got fired when he was arrested.'

'When he was convicted,' Nina corrected, even as she spoke wondering why she was giving her former colleague – and rival

– any benefit of the doubt. Dr Logan Berkeley had been in charge of an excavation in Cairo, opening up the long-lost Hall of Records hidden beneath the Great Sphinx of Giza. After Nina beat him to it, on live television to boot, the enraged and humiliated Berkeley had ended up taking a payoff from a cult to locate an even greater prize, the legendary Pyramid of Osiris. It wasn't until the pyramid was plundered and the cult leader murdered by his own psychotic brother that Berkeley realised he had thrown in his lot with the wrong people, but by then it was too late to repent; according to Seretse, he had only been released from an Egyptian prison a few months earlier.

'Whatever. He's still a complete cockwipe. And now he's involved in robbery and murder.'

'So it seems,' said Nina, with a small sigh. 'I just don't understand why.'

Eddie smiled sardonically. 'A year in an Egyptian nick's probably enough to turn anyone into a nutter.'

'No, I don't mean that. I mean, why steal the runestone at all?' She tabbed to another application, the photograph of the monolith filling her screen. 'All the text on it's already been translated by experts, so there's nothing new that anyone could get from it in person. And except for the inset,' she indicated the circle of darker stone set into the face of the monolith, 'there's nothing unusual about the runestone physically. It's just a block of granite.'

'So there could be something special about that thing.' Eddie also pointed at the inset. 'There are some markings on it – maybe it's a map.'

'Well, hopefully we'll find out more from Dr Skilfinger.'

'Ha! We're meeting a Bond villain?'

'I'm sure she's one of the good guys. At least, I hope so!' They both grinned. 'She's the person who found the runestone in the first place, and has been researching it ever since. If anyone knows what it is, she will.'

Eddie leaned over to peer out of the porthole. A snowy, tree-covered landscape slid past below. 'So, this is Sweden, eh? Never actually been here before.'

'I'm kind of surprised,' said Nina. 'I thought you'd been everywhere.'

'Norway, Finland and Denmark, yeah, but I somehow missed this one. Still, I think I know everything I need to about it. IKEA, Volvo, high-quality porn, Abba, girls with dragon tattoos.' Another, more lecherous grin. 'All I have to do is drink loads of coffee, eat lots of open-faced sandwiches and be blandly heroic, and I'll get to have no-strings-attached sex with every woman I meet.'

'You will *not*,' Nina told him firmly, then they both laughed. 'I'm pretty sure there's more to the country than that, though.'

'Well, obviously. There's also meatballs, the Swedish Chef . . .'

'Okay,' she said with a smile as the pilot announced that the plane was making its final approach to Stockholm Arlanda airport, 'if any Swede asks what you think of their country, it'd probably be a good idea if you just said, "It's very nice." Otherwise they might rethink their neutrality policy.'

Ninety minutes later, their United Nations diplomatic visas having seen them whisked through customs, Nina and Eddie arrived at the Swedish National Museum of Antiquities in Stockholm, after a brief detour to a hotel to drop off their luggage. Despite the snow blanketing the countryside, the capital's streets were impressively clear, traffic moving at a brisk pace. 'We should hire these guys to plough the streets in Manhattan,' said Nina.

'We should get 'em to do the whole of bloody England,' Eddie countered as he climbed out of the taxi. 'One flake of snow and the entire country falls apart.'

Nina paid the driver and joined him. The museum was a large, pale beige block abutting a triangular plaza on a broad tree-lined boulevard, banners advertising its current exhibits adorning its facade. Vikings featured prominently upon them. She regarded the bearded warriors. 'I guess they know what sells . . .'

They trotted across the chilly plaza to the main entrance, finding a member of staff and asking for Dr Skilfinger. They were expected; the rapid clacking of high heels barely a minute later heralded the arrival of their hostess. 'Dr Wilde, hello!' said the tall, slender blonde, her flustered air suggesting that she had hurried from the far side of the museum to meet them. 'I'm Tova, Tova Skilfinger. It's a great honour and pleasure to meet you.' Though she had a strong accent, her English was perfect.

'It's good to meet you too, Dr Skilfinger,' Nina replied as they shook hands.

'Please, Dr Wilde, call me Tova.'

'Then call me Nina.'

'Agreed.' Tova beamed at her. Nina guessed she was in her late forties or early fifties, but age had not diminished the Swedish historian's striking looks. Her hair was held up in a loose bun, all her snugly fitting clothing black. 'I have been following your work for several years – you could say I am something of a fan.' She blushed faintly.

Nina did the same. 'Thank you. This is my husband, Eddie Chase.'

'Good to meet you,' said Eddie.

Tova shook his hand. 'And you. Have you come straight from the airport?'

'More or less,' Nina told her. 'I wanted to talk to you about the runestone as soon as we arrived.'

'We can do that in my office – I have all my notes ready for you. Please, this way.' They started down the hall. 'The reason I said I am a fan of yours is that your work allowed me to rethink my own, and look at it from a new perspective.'

'How so?' asked Nina.

'Well, although I am primarily a historian, I also have a great interest in Old Norse mythology – though there are few people in Sweden who have not!' She smiled. 'Your discovery of Atlantis in particular, but also other finds such as King Arthur's tomb and El Dorado, caused a resurgence of euhemeristic theory.'

'Yoo-hoo who?' said Eddie.

'Euhemerus was an ancient Greek scholar,' Nina told him. 'He had the idea that myths and legends were derived from actual historical events, which were exaggerated and distorted over time. Early Christians used it as a way to explain away and discredit what they saw as pagan gods.'

'It is an important part of the *Prose Edda*,' added Tova. Seeing the Englishman's questioning look, she continued: 'One of the most important texts about Norse mythology. It was written in the thirteenth century by an Icelandic poet and historian called Snorri Sturluson. He was a Christian, so used the *Edda* to promote his belief that the ancient Norse deities – like Odin and Thor – were once kings, who aroused such devotion in life that cults formed to honour them after death. Over time, their stories turned them into gods.'

'Clever,' said Nina. 'It meant that he got to preserve the pre-Christian mythology of his people, while debunking it at the same time.'

'But people like that were actually right, weren't they?' Eddie said. 'After all, we discovered Atlantis, and a lot of what the myths said turned out to be true. And we know Hercules was a real bloke and not a god, 'cause we found his tomb.'

'Which led me to change my approach to my work,' said Tova as they entered a new section of the museum: the Viking exhibition. Cabinets of Norse artefacts and recreations of scenes of Viking life lined the long, softly lit hall. 'By applying euhemeristic principles to my earlier research, on the theory that they might contain some amount of truth rather than being purely myth, I was able to work out the location of the Valhalla Runestone.' She paused by one of the exhibits. 'It was a runestone much like this that gave me the clues, actually.'

Nina examined the display. This stone was considerably smaller than the one she had seen in the photograph, only about two feet tall. An elaborate carving of what appeared to be a snake encircled the outer edge of the roughly triangular stone, runes etched along its length like patterns of scales. The serpent's elongated head snapped at an axe-wielding man at the centre of the image. 'That's a representation of Thor at Ragnarök, I'm guessing.'

Tova nodded, then set off again. 'The stone I was working from described a location where the Norse gods met to settle conflicts between tribes. It had of course long been considered a myth, but I thought: what if it was true? The runes named people and places, some of which were historical rather than mythological, so I researched all of them too. When I put everything together, they pointed to a place near Gamla Uppsala, called Iarlsta – a site that had been excavated in the past, but which was not considered very important. I was able to arrange a new dig, and deeper down we found the remains of a much more ancient settlement. And in *that* . . . we discovered the Valhalla Runestone.'

'A big find,' said Nina.

Tova nodded appreciatively. 'Thank you – though not as big as Atlantis! But it did prove that applying euhemeristic principles to Old Norse finds had the potential for even greater discoveries. And when I translated the runes on the stone, I realised where this could lead.'

'From the name of the runestone, I'm guessing Valhalla?' suggested Eddie.

'Yes,' Tova replied. 'The great hall where the warriors chosen by Odin awaited the call to the final battle.'

She led them through a side exit and down a corridor, unlocking a door at its end. Her expression became more solemn. 'This is the lab from where the runestone was stolen,' she said. 'The security guard, Arvid . . . he was shot in there.' She pointed out a doorway marked with yellow and black police tape.

A much larger set of double doors occupied the rear wall, daylight visible through small windows set into them. 'That's where they took the stone out of the building?' said Eddie.

'Yes. The runestone was so large and heavy, it could only come in through a service entrance.'

Nina surveyed the scene. The bench on which the stone had been laid was at the room's centre, the white cloth crumpled on the floor beside it. 'The police have examined everything?'

'Yes, but they did not find anything useful.' Tova's face fell further. 'There were no fingerprints or DNA evidence. The robbers were very professional.'

'We might have a lead, though,' Nina told her. The Swede was surprised; clearly she had not been told about Berkeley's appearance on camera. 'But we still don't know *why* they wanted to steal the runestone, so hopefully you can tell us something that'll explain it.'

'I will help however I can, of course. My office is over here.' She gestured towards a cubicle in one corner.

The space was cramped, but also oddly barren. It took Nina a moment to realise what was missing: Tova's work. The desk was devoid of papers, and there was a faint discoloration on its surface that suggested a laptop had been in long-term residence. 'Did they take your research as well?'

The older woman nodded miserably. 'I had backups of everything at home, fortunately, but yes – it was a horrible shock. First the runestone and Arvid's murder, and then I found all my work had gone . . . I thought I had lost everything.'

'That means they don't know exactly what they're looking for, though,' Eddie said thoughtfully. 'If they need your work as well, then whatever they're after, they're not as close to it as they'd like.'

'But what *could* they be after?' Nina wondered. 'What's so special about this runestone?'

Tova opened a large satchel, taking a thick folder from it. 'I printed out my research from the backups. I have photographs, translations of all the runes, any connections I found to mythology or historical fact, everything I could think of. Hopefully the answer is in here.' She gestured for her guests to sit.

Nina did so, Eddie pulling up a second chair beside her. 'I suppose the best starting point would be the runes themselves. What do they say?'

Tova opened the folder and leafed through the pages within, handing several to Nina. 'I have an English translation here. It may not be as accurate as the Swedish, but it will give you a good idea.'

The American quickly scanned through the text. 'An account of the preparations for Ragnarök?' she said before long, looking up at Tova.

'That is why it would be better if you could read the Swedish version,' Tova replied. 'There is more nuance. It is not exactly an account, more . . .' She frowned; despite her excellent command of English, the correct words eluded her. 'It is not the right tense, you could say. Calling it an account implies that it is in the past tense, a description of something that has already happened. The text on the Valhalla stone is more like . . .' Another frown, before it came to her. 'Like a *prophecy*.'

'A prophecy?' said Eddie. 'About what?'

'Ragnarök,' Nina told him. 'The end of the world.'

He moaned. 'Not again!'

Tova gave him a confused look, then turned back to Nina. 'That is right. In my belief, it tells the warriors what to do at Ragnarök.'

Nina was still reading, but wanted to hear Tova's own interpretation. 'Which is what?'

'To travel to Valhalla and gather the weapons they will need to kill Jörmungandr and Fenrir – the serpent and the wolf,' she elaborated. 'Jörmungandr is the Midgard Serpent, a giant snake that encircles the earth beneath its surface, and Fenrir is a huge and monstrous wolf. When they return, it heralds Ragnarök. Although it is not quite right to say it is the end of the world,' she corrected Nina. 'The translation is closer to "the twilight of the gods". It is more like the end of a cycle, as the world will renew in time, but there will be much destruction and death before that happens.'

Nina nodded, and kept reading. The large runestone had been crammed with text; the translation took up several pages. Eddie, meanwhile, had questions of his own. 'So the stone actually tells you how to find Valhalla? I guess that's another place we can add to the "thought they were legends, turns out they're real" list.'

'It's not quite like getting directions from Google Maps,' said Nina, still perusing the text. 'It seems more like riddles.'

'In a way,' Tova replied. 'This runestone tells you to reach Valhalla by travelling up a river until you reach Bifröst – the rainbow bridge that in myth joined the earth with Asgard, the realm of the gods. Once you cross it, you are not far from Valhalla. The runes tell you the path to take. But they do not say which river to follow.'

By now, Nina had reached a relevant part of the translation. 'There's a second runestone?'

'Yes. The first gives a clue on how to find it, saying that a true warrior will understand it.' She leaned across the desk, pointing out a particular passage. '"At the fellowship hall, the other part waits." I believe it refers to a site in Norway. I would imagine that the other runestone is much like the first, but tells you which river to follow – without telling you how to reach Valhalla.'

'It's a security code,' Eddie realised. 'You need both rune-stones to find the place – but even if you've got one stone, unless you're a proper Viking warrior you won't know where the other one is.'

'So what happens once you get there?' Nina asked. 'The text mentions a guide-stone . . .'

'A sun compass,' Tova told her. She took a photograph from the folder; it was a close-up of the circle of black stone set into the face of the granite monolith.

Nina regarded the picture. Faint lines were inscribed on the dark surface, lines arcing across it from one side to the other. The outer edge was also marked, angular chevrons evenly spaced around the circumference. Further runic symbols appeared in the spaces between the lines. 'I've seen these before. The Vikings used them for navigation.'

Eddie peered at the image. 'Looks a bit like a ship's chart.'

'It's similar – they used them to determine latitude. The Vikings didn't have magnetic compasses, so they needed another way to navigate at sea.'

'Actually, that is still uncertain,' Tova remarked. 'The compass set into the runestone is magnetic. It is a carved piece of magnetite; a lodestone. But we don't know if it was used to magnetise needles to point north, or was simply considered special *because* it was magnetic. Nobody has found proof that the Vikings used magnetic compasses, though.'

Eddie nodded. 'That hole in the middle looks like it's for a stick or something, so you can use it like a sundial.'

'That's basically right,' Nina told him. 'The lines,' she indicated the various arcs, 'represent different times of year to match the sun's path in the sky, and you'd use the shadow to work out how far north you were. I think they were quite accurate.'

'A skilled user could work out their position to within one degree of latitude,' said Tova, with a hint of pride in her heritage.

Eddie was impressed. 'Smart. There was more to the Vikings than pillaging and helmets with cow horns, then.'

'There is no evidence that they ever wore horned helmets in battle,' insisted the Swede, slightly testy. 'That is as much of a myth as Odin and Thor.'

'Maybe more of a myth, if you're right about the runestone giving directions to Valhalla,' said Nina. She looked back at the translation. 'So the sun compass . . . "the two parts together brought, shall alone open the death-gate of Valhalla"? Do you know what that means?'

'I'm afraid not. But there is a reference to a gate to Valhalla in the *Poetic Edda* – another of Snorri Sturluson's works,' she added for Eddie's benefit. 'Depending on the translation, it is referred to as a "holy gate", a "sacred gate" – or a "death-barrier".'

Eddie sighed. 'Based on our luck in the past, I know which one it'll turn out to be. If you find the place, watch out for booby-traps.'

Tova seemed alarmed at the prospect. 'I had not thought of that!'

'We've got prior experience,' Nina told her mournfully. 'Lots and lots of prior experience.' She stared at the pages, thinking over what she had learned. 'Okay, then. I think it's safe to say that the Valhalla Runestone was stolen because someone,' she avoided mentioning Berkeley's name, mindful of Seretse's advice, 'wants to find Valhalla itself. Presumably they're looking for the second runestone as well.'

'Unless they've already got it,' Eddie said.

'Let's hope not. But the question is: why do they want to find Valhalla so badly that they're willing to kill for it?'

'I do not know,' said Tova, shaking her head. 'The poem *Grímnismál*, in the *Poetic Edda*, describes Valhalla as "golden" and roofed with shields. In some interpretations of the poem they are made of gold, so perhaps the robbers think they will find treasure there.'

'They'd have to be pretty bloody sure it was more than just a myth to murder somebody for it,' said the Englishman.

'Yeah,' Nina agreed. 'Is there anything more in the runes that might be useful?' She looked back through the translated text, searching for clues.

Tova took the Swedish version of the ancient writing from the folder. 'The runes tell you how to find Valhalla – or half of the route, at least – and then say you need the sun compass to get through the gate. There is little description of what is inside, though. All it says is that the warriors shall find every-thing they need to reach the battlefield where they will face the serpent and the wolf at Ragnarök. "The serpent's venom lies thick deep below, black eitr that can kill even a god . . .'"

She continued, but Nina's attention shifted to her husband as he reacted to Tova's words, straightening in his seat. 'Eddie? What is it?'

'Nothing,' he said, suddenly curt.

'But you just sat up like you'd realised there's a bomb under the table.' She looked back at Tova. 'What was that about poison?'

'The Midgard Serpent's venom is called eitr,' Tova told her, surprised by the couple's shift of focus. 'It—'

'It's what killed Thor,' Eddie cut in. 'It's supposedly the source of all life in Viking legend, but it's also lethal if it touches you. Thor killed the snake, but he got poisoned by it and died straight after.'

'That is right,' said Tova. 'According to myth, the first giant, Ymir, was birthed from eitr, and all other life came from him. But Eddie is right; it is also a deadly poison. Thor only took nine steps after killing the serpent before he fell.'

Nina looked askance at her husband. 'How did you know about that?'

'Learned about Viking legends at school,' he replied. But his tone was still taciturn, and she recognised a subtle shift in his attitude that warned her he would not elaborate further without her risking escalating the discussion into an argument.

Right now, she had larger concerns. 'You said the second runestone is in Norway?' she asked Tova.

'I believe so,' the historian replied. 'But I am afraid it will be impossible to reach. The site is at the bottom of a lake – it was flooded when a dam was built in the 1930s.'

'Well, that's the end of that, then,' said Eddie, sounding oddly relieved.

'Slow down, Mr Defeatist,' Nina teased. 'The IHA's got the resources to take a look if we need to.'

Tova was a little taken aback. 'You would explore the lake to find the other runestone? What is the IHA's interest in this?'

'It's what we do. If Valhalla is more than just a legend, then it's our job to protect it from looters.'

'Hmm. That is the IHA's *official* purpose, but . . .' She gave Nina a calculating look. 'I have heard stories that the IHA has something to do with global security.' The American tried to keep her expression neutral. 'Is that why you are here? Will finding Valhalla be dangerous somehow?'

'It didn't even occur to me that somebody might be trying to find Valhalla until you just told me,' Nina answered, truthfully. 'All I can tell you right now is that we possibly have a lead on who that somebody is. Would you be willing to help us?'

'Yes, of course. I want to find out who did this, and why – but I have to admit that . . . I also want to find Valhalla.' A slightly sheepish grin. 'With a name like Skilfinger – there is a "Skilfingr", without an "e", mentioned in the *Prose Edda* – I suppose I have a connection to the mythology.'

'Looks like it's more than just a myth,' Eddie said quietly.

Nina still wanted to quiz him further on his reaction to the mention of eitr, but decided it could wait. Instead, she told Tova: 'That's great. We'll go back to the hotel and I'll contact New York to make the arrangements, then we can start work. Hopefully we'll find the truth.'

'I hope so too,' the Swede replied. 'Are you taking a taxi?'

Nina stood and put on her coat. 'Absolutely. I don't want to walk in this weather!'

'Wuss,' said Eddie, shaking off his distracted air as he rose.

Tova picked up her own coat. 'I will call one, then walk you to it. Since you do not like the cold, I do not want to leave you standing out in it for too long!'

She made a short phone call, then the trio made their way back through the museum. 'So, if you were able to organise a dig, I guess you're an archaeologist as well as a historian,' Nina said.

'I go both ways,' Tova replied, prompting a snort of barely contained laughter from Eddie followed by an irked glare from his wife. 'In an ideal world I would do both, but there was never enough time. Especially once I had children.'

'You've got kids?' Eddie asked.

'Two boys. Well, men now – they are both grown up. It was hard to keep working once they arrived, but I managed thanks to my wonderful husband, God rest him. The past has been my passion since I was a child, so even though I love my sons, giving it up would have been like giving up a part of myself. Do you know what I mean?'

'Yeah, I do,' said Nina, suddenly wistful.

'But you managed to keep your career and still have kids at the same time,' Eddie said, with a pointed look at Nina. 'So it *is* possible.'

'Oh, yes. If something is very important to you, you will always find a way to do it – even if there are other things that are important too! If there is one thing I have learned about life, it is that.'

'Hear that, love?' He prodded Nina's side. 'Sounds like good advice to me.'

'It's something to think about, certainly,' she replied, giving him a warm smile.

They reached the main entrance. Tova peered through the glass doors. 'I think that is your taxi,' she announced, seeing a dark blue Mercedes pulling up at the edge of the plaza.

'Thanks,' Nina replied. They stepped outside. 'Oh, damn! Jeez, it's freezing.' She hunched more deeply into her coat.

'You should visit when it is *really* cold,' said Tova, amused. 'You are not bothered by it, Eddie?'

'Got a magic jacket,' he replied with a grin. Ahead, a black Audi made an abrupt stop behind the taxi. Two men in dark coats and baseball caps got out of the back, a third emerging from the front passenger door. 'Helps when I—'

For the second time that afternoon, Nina saw a sudden shift in his attitude. 'Eddie? What . . .'

He had already taken up a defensive posture, right hand instinctively reaching into his jacket for a gun that wasn't there before he arrested the movement. 'Nina, Tova – *run!*'

But it was too late.

The approaching men also reached into their coats – but unlike Eddie, they had weapons concealed inside. Three pistols came up. One man shouted in Swedish. Nina didn't understand the words, but the meaning was clear: *don't move!* Two of the men kept their guns aimed at Eddie and Nina while the third grabbed the startled Tova, burying the muzzle of his weapon in her side.

A bystander saw the commotion – and the guns. She shrieked, alerting other people nearby. The taxi driver's eyes bugged wide in shock as he saw what was happening, then he stomped his foot to the floor and set his vehicle fishtailing away as quickly as it could go.

'Oi!' Eddie yelled as the third man hauled Tova towards the waiting Audi S4. 'Let her go!'

'Shut fuck up, and get back!' one of the others snarled, jabbing his gun at the Yorkshireman. His companion did the same to Nina, making her flinch away.

Tova screamed, her heels scraping through the snow as her captor dragged her across the plaza. The Audi's engine revved, its driver signalling for his comrades to hurry up. The man holding Nina at gunpoint said something – *Russian*, she thought – to his companion and ran to help the third kidnapper manhandle their prisoner into the back of the car.

'No fucking move!' the remaining man ordered, swinging his gun back and forth between Nina and Eddie. He backed up, risking a glance at the car once he was sure the gap was wide enough to prevent Eddie from charging him. 'You move, I kill you!'

'Just let her go, and nobody has to get hurt,' said Nina, more afraid for Tova than herself. If the Russians wanted her and Eddie dead they would have killed them already, but there was no way to know what they had in store for their victim.

'Shut up, get fucking back,' was his only reply. Behind him, the other two men had forced the struggling historian into the car. Gun still raised, the last of the three jogged backwards and clambered into the remaining seat. Before he had even fully closed the door, the Audi peeled away, snow spraying up from its tyres.

Eddie ran after it, but knew he would never catch up. The S4 had four-wheel drive, easily finding grip on the ploughed road. He searched for another car he could flag down to give chase . . .

The only approaching vehicle was not what he had in mind. 'You're fucking joking,' he said under his breath, checking the other side of the boulevard for something, *anything* better. But he was out of luck.

No choice. He ran into the street, waving furiously for the driver to stop.

Nina had taken out her iPhone to alert the police, but saw that others on the plaza were already making emergency calls. Instead, she ran after her husband. To her dismay, she realised that he intended to pursue the kidnappers – and her alarm only worsened when she saw what he was about to commandeer. 'Eddie, what're you doing?'

'I'm going after them!' he shouted back as he pulled the startled driver, a young man in thick-framed glasses and multiple layers of trendy clothing, from his vehicle. 'Hope you speak English,' Eddie told him, '''cause I need your car.'

'That's not a car,' Nina protested as she reached him. 'That's a golf cart!'

It was actually a Renault Twizy, a minuscule electric buggy with a futuristically styled – and open-sided – pod-like body. It had only two seats, a small passenger space directly behind the driver's position. 'It's all we've got,' insisted Eddie. The driver made a flustered objection; the Englishman pushed him away. 'Sorry, Bjorn. Just call the police. *Polis, polizei?* Whatever they are in Swedish, call 'em!'

Nina was already squeezing into the cramped second seat. 'You seriously think I'm going to let you leave me behind?' she said, anticipating her husband's response.

'Yeah, I should've bloody known by now.' He dropped into the front seat, ignoring the continuing squawks from the Twizy's owner, and stepped on the accelerator.

The little electric car's response was not exactly Ferrari-quick, but it was better than running. Eddie saw the kidnappers' car rapidly disappearing down the boulevard. Pushing the accelerator pedal as far as it would go, he set off in pursuit.

6

Vietnam

'Welcome to the jungle!' sang Chase tunelessly as the mercenary team began their trek.

They were some fifty miles west of Da Nang, Sullivan's local contact having driven them from the city to their drop-off point in an elderly Volkswagen minibus. The road they took was marked on the map as a major highway, though Chase considered it no more than a country lane by British standards. But it was paved, so the journey was relatively straightforward – even if Vietnamese traffic discipline was far looser than anything in Europe.

The minibus had turned south off the highway on to a dirt track, heading through a small village and continuing on as rough farmland gave way first to scrub, then actual jungle. Once they entered the dense woodland, it did not take long before the track petered out entirely. After checking their surroundings to make sure they were not being observed, the team armed up with the gear Bluey had provided. The weapons were AK-47s, almost certainly dating back to the Vietnam War, but Chase found that the Australian had been as good as his word. The rifles were still in working order.

The rest of the gear was also as promised. Once everyone was kitted out, the VW departed, heading back north. Hoyt watched it go as he lit another cigarette. Sullivan checked a map, then directed his men deeper into the jungle.

'If our info's right,' said the New Zealander as he took the lead, 'we should go five or six klicks before we get into our bandits' area of operations. But watch out before then, eh? We don't want to run into any sentries.'

'If that storm reaches us, it could make them hard to spot,' Castille said.

'Could work for us, though,' Chase countered. 'It'll give us some cover too, and if it's pissing it down, the bad guys'll want to stay in the dry.' He peered up through the overhanging canopy. The weather had definitely started to turn, the sweltering tropical heat falling as the sky clouded over and the wind picked up. The storm was due to make landfall in a couple of hours; if it continued along its predicted course, the worst of it would strike them about an hour later. 'But yeah, I'll keep my eyes open.'

They continued south, Sullivan checking the map every so often. The terrain was rough and crumpled with hardly a flat piece of ground to be found. The jungle itself also slowed their progress; there were no paths, so thick undergrowth frequently needed to be hacked through. All the team members had been on missions in similar conditions, accepting the strenuous nature of their progress with weary shrugs.

There was something about this particular jungle that set it apart from the others Chase had traversed, however. It was impossible to escape a constant sense of foreboding – a feeling that death was all around them. Part of the infamous Ho Chi Minh Trail had run through the region during the war, feeding North Vietnamese troops and supplies into the South, and as a result the whole area had been subjected to massive herbicidal assaults by American forces to kill the vegetation and strip away their enemies' cover. Even though the environment had recovered to an extent after over three decades, dead trees still lurked all around, rotting monuments to chemical warfare. The Englishman was the first to admit that he was not burdened with an overactive imagination, but there was still something unsettling about the poisoned land.

After two hours, the light had dropped considerably, and not just because evening was approaching. 'Wind's really pickin' up,' said Lomax. Heavy clouds roiled ominously above. 'Storm'll be on us soon, I reckon.'

'Looks that way,' Sullivan replied. 'I'd say we've got no more than ten minutes before the rain hits us. You might want to put on your gear now.'

'Sounds good to me,' said Chase, shrugging off his pack and taking out a hooded nylon poncho with a mottled green camouflage pattern. 'Although if the storm's turned into a typhoon, we'll get wet no matter what.'

'I will take a little dryness over none at all,' said Castille, donning his own poncho before taking a plastic bag from his pack.

Chase sighed. 'What weird fucking fruit've you got now, Hugo?'

Sullivan retreated, making a face. 'It'd better not be a durian. They smell like a chimp's arse.'

'Ah, you people,' said Castille with cheery disdain. 'You never want to discover new tastes. No, it is not a durian. It is a longan.' The Belgian took one of the brown spheres from the bag and squeezed it to split the shell, revealing the pale, almost eyeball-like fruit within. He popped it in his mouth and chewed. 'Delicious.'

'I'll stick with *Golden* Delicious,' Chase told him, producing a mocking snort from his friend.

Rios checked his map. 'If the bandits are in this area, where will they be?'

The others joined him. 'If they're stupid,' said Hoyt, 'they'll be in this valley here.' He pointed it out. 'It's flat ground, so it'd be easy for them to make camp – but they'll have boxed themselves in.'

'I doubt we'll be that lucky,' Sullivan told him. 'If they know the jungle, which I imagine they do, they'd know somewhere like that would flood in typhoon season. But . . .' He ran his finger across the map from the valley to an area above its steep western side. 'That would be a better choice. The ground's fairly level, it's defensible – but there are avenues of escape if they need them.'

Chase examined his own map. 'If we come in from this big hill to the north-west, that gives us higher ground and a better vantage point.'

'If that is where they are at all,' Castille pointed out.

Sullivan surveyed the location. 'If they've got prisoners, they'll have to secure them somewhere, so they can't just bivvy down and be ready to move at a moment's notice. They'll need space for an actual camp.' His eyes flicked over other possibilities. 'That's as good a place as any. If they're not there, then we just continue the search – but it's our most likely target.'

Hoyt hefted his AK-47. 'Good. Then let's go in there and get 'em.'

'Minimum force,' Sullivan reminded him sternly. 'I want this to be easy in, easy out if we can manage it.'

'You're the boss,' said the American mildly, though he kept his gun raised.

Chase took a compass bearing. 'That way,' he said, pointing

south-east. 'About a mile. It'll be dark by the time we get there, though.'

Castille peered unhappily up at the swaying trees. 'The storm will have reached us, too.'

'All the more reason to stop talking and start walking,' said Sullivan. 'Okay, let's move.'

The rain began soon after.

Even beneath the tree cover, it was a deluge. The rising winds tore through the canopy, exposing the ground beneath to the torrential fall. Soil turned to mud, the thick, cloying sludge clinging to the team's boots with every step. The last daylight had faded too, turning the jungle almost pitch black. Even though their eyes quickly adjusted to the darkness, the mercenaries were forced to slow even further, each footfall perilous on the uneven ground.

Crossing a slope, Chase almost stumbled where a rivulet of running water had loosened the topsoil. He held in an obscenity, mindful of the need for stealth. 'Are you okay?' Castille whispered from behind him, holding up one hand to warn the others to stop.

'Yeah,' Chase replied. 'Watch your step, there's a lot of water coming down the hill.'

'If it gets much worse, there could be a mudslide,' Sullivan warned. 'Everyone stay close to those large rocks down there.' He pointed at a line of rain-slicked shapes below their current path.

Chase was about to move again when he caught a flicker of movement in the distance. He raised his hand, this gesture signalling potential danger. The other men immediately crouched, drawing their weapons. 'What is it?' hissed Castille.

'Saw something.' The Englishman shielded his eyes from the

rain, watching the site of the movement intently. He spotted nothing but the vague shapes of trees swaying in the darkness for several seconds . . . then it reappeared.

A light. Faint, but in the black of the jungle it stood out like a beacon. It bobbed between the trees, then vanished again, obscured by the trunks.

Chase didn't need to see any more. The only person who would be strolling through the jungle at night with a typhoon bearing down on them was a sentry. 'It's a torch,' he whispered as Sullivan moved up to join him. 'We've found them.'

The news sent a crackle of electricity through the group. They had been alert before; now they were fully focused, ready for action. Hoyt spat out his damp cigarette and crushed it under his boot. 'Okay,' said Sullivan at another glimpse of torchlight, 'he's about two hundred metres away. We'll stay on this level and move in to one hundred for a better look. We don't get any closer until we've got an idea of how many there are – and *where* they are. Spread out to five-metre spacing. Eddie, lead on.'

Chase slung his rifle over his shoulder and crouched, almost on all fours as he began his cautious advance. Castille waited until a gap had opened up between them, then followed. The other men picked up the trail one by one after him, Hoyt at the rear.

By the time Chase had covered roughly half the hundred metres, he had already spotted further signs of life. The torch definitely belonged to a sentry, trudging back and forth along a curving path. There was at least one other sentry farther away, forming a perimeter. Within the circle, more lights were revealed as he got closer. Diffuse glows gradually took on the form of several tents with lamps inside, and a lantern hung at the entrance to another shelter.

He stopped a hundred metres from the camp. Beyond the

tents was some sort of building, a boxy cabin. Reflected light picked out the rain running in sheets down its slab-like sides. A faint glowing rectangle marked a window in one wall. It didn't seem to be a bunker left over from the war; it looked more like a caravan or shipping container.

He had more immediate concerns than the mystery structure, however. The two sentries were still slogging around the perimeter, and as he watched, a man emerged from one of the smaller tents and scurried across the camp to enter the largest of the shelters. The guards were not the only bandits still awake.

The other mercenaries reached him. Chase gave them a brief summary of his observations. 'No idea what that cabin is, mind,' he concluded.

Sullivan took out a pair of binoculars and scanned the camp. 'Can't see a damn thing in all this rain,' he muttered. 'The small tents, I'd say you could get three, maybe four men in each of them at a squeeze. The big one . . . ten, or more.'

'So we're looking at, what, up to thirty guys?' said Lomax unhappily.

The New Zealander shook his head. 'I doubt it. The hostages are probably being held in the big tent – it'd be a lot easier to keep them all together in one place. So that's eight people accounted for already.'

'Still twenty-two against six. I don't like those odds.'

'We've got surprise on our side,' Hoyt pointed out. 'We could take most of 'em out before they even knew we were here. If we had to,' he added, as Sullivan frowned at him.

'If the aid workers *are* in the big tent, I think we can get to 'em without being seen.' Chase pointed at a patch of darkness between the shelters and the path the first sentry was following. 'If we timed it right, we could hide in the bushes and get across the perimeter when that guy's heading away from us, then sneak right up behind the tents.'

'Has he followed the same route every time?' Castille asked.

'Since I've been watching him, yeah. He's probably made a path and doesn't want to move off it in the dark.'

Rios bit his lip. 'We need to be sure where the hostages are. If we go in, and they are not where we think . . .'

'I know,' said Sullivan. 'We need a better idea of how many other guys we're dealing with, too. Somebody'll have to take a closer look.'

'I'll do it,' said Hoyt at once.

Sullivan regarded him with an unreadable expression, then shook his head. 'Eddie, Mac told me you've got recent experience in jungle infiltration *and* hostage extraction work. Correct?'

'If two years ago counts as recent, then yeah,' Chase replied.

'Think you can get in closer without being seen?'

He gave the encampment another look, judging distances, paths of approach and exit, the movements of the sentries . . . 'Yeah. I can do it.'

'Good man,' said Sullivan. 'Hugo, you're with me – we'll move down to those rocks there and cover him. The rest of you, stay here and keep watch.'

Lomax, Rios and Hoyt all nodded, then spread out to positions where they could observe what was happening below – and maintain a clear line of fire. The other three men moved carefully down the slope to the rocks. Castille and Sullivan stopped, watching the tents, as Chase prepared to advance. 'Good luck,' Sullivan whispered.

'Fight to the end, Edward,' added Castille.

'Always do,' Chase replied, nodding to his friend before dropping low and moving into the undergrowth. A brief look back; the two men were little more than shadows from a distance of just fifteen feet, the three higher up the slope practically invisible in the darkness and rain. Hiding from the bandits would not be a problem.

Nor would locating them. The man on patrol was making no attempt to conceal himself, the light of his torch standing out clearly, nor was he being all that attentive to his surroundings. The beam spent far more time aimed at the ground ahead of him than sweeping the jungle. Nevertheless, Chase froze once he got close to the approaching sentry's route.

From his hiding place, lying beneath the drooping branches of a large plant, he watched the man as he passed twenty feet away. The bandit was wearing a long rain cape and a wide-brimmed khaki hat, water streaming off both. From the glimpse of his expression in the torchlight, he was not at all happy to have been assigned sentry duty.

The light also glinted off his shouldered weapon. A Kalashnikov, no surprise there . . .

But a surprise to Chase was the particular *type* of Kalashnikov. His SAS training had taught him to identify weapons at a glance, and this one's short barrel revealed it as an AKS-74U, a cut-down version of the AKS-74 assault rifle. It was designed for mobility and easy concealment rather than range and stopping power, and was generally only issued to special forces units. Not the kind of thing normally found in the hands of a jungle bandit. He would have expected something like his own far older AK-47.

He put the thought to the back of his mind as he watched the sentry trudge away, waiting until he was out of sight behind the trees before moving. The man's patrol route was clear to see, squishy footprints in the mud leading in both directions. Chase raised his head to confirm that the bandit was still retreating, then stood and hopped over the path, keeping his own telltale prints as far from the track as he could. Then he dropped low again and resumed his advance.

Moving slowly and silently, it took him almost five cautious minutes to reach the camp. He peered over a mouldering log. Six tents; five small, one large, two of the small ones unlit. Even over the drumming of raindrops on the canvas he could hear the low murmur of conversation. Shadows shifted in some of the shelters, their occupants rendered on the fabric as magic lantern displays.

Chase remained still, gathering intelligence. At least six men in the smaller tents, plus however many were inside the two without lights. The big tent was harder to judge, but he estimated no fewer than another six people within. Assuming that the aid workers were being held together under guard, that made a minimum of nine bandits: six in the small tents, one man watching the hostages, plus the two sentries.

There was still the mysterious cabin to consider, though. It was definitely not a wartime leftover. The structure was a block some fifteen feet to a side, standing clear of the ground on supports resembling a helicopter's skids. The window he had seen earlier turned out to be set into a door, a slatted blind on the other side of the glass. On the roof was what looked like a satellite dish, and even over the rain and wind he could hear the flat rattle of a generator. The encampment was more than a mere hideout.

Movement caught his attention. The front flap of one of the small tents opened, a man emerging and jogging to the nearer of the two unlit shelters. He said something in Vietnamese. After a few seconds, a light came on inside, someone replying.

That now made at least ten enemies, but Chase had registered that this man was also armed with an AKS-74U. One uncommon weapon might have been happenstance, but two? He didn't buy it. Either someone had issued them to the bandits . . .

Or they weren't bandits at all.

The man finished his discussion, then hurried back to his tent. Chase remained still for a long moment before setting off again. Whatever was going on, he still had an objective: locate the prisoners. He crawled over the log towards the largest tent.

There were two small polythene windows in the side nearest to him. He crept up and peered through the transparent plastic.

Hooded figures, hands tied behind them, sat or lay upon blankets, unmoving. The aid workers. A Vietnamese man was on a small stool by the entrance, with a second guard at the other end of the tent. Both were armed with 74Us.

He took a headcount. Seven prisoners. So where was number eight?

The noise of the generator suggested a possibility.

Chase slunk back into the undergrowth, then started on a circuitous route around the camp towards the structure. He had covered about two thirds of the distance when movement prompted him to freeze. Three people came out of a tent, and headed for the cabin. All wore nylon ponchos and hats, though these were baseball caps rather than the round-brimmed cloth kind of the bandits. With their heads down and their backs to the lights, he couldn't see their faces.

He could hear their voices, though. And they were not speaking in Vietnamese.

Russians? He only knew a few phrases of the language, but the accents and intonations sounded familiar. What the hell were they doing here?

The figures crossed to the hut and went inside. Chase caught a brief glimpse of the interior, but the flash of stark white paint and stainless steel told him nothing. He edged closer. After a few minutes, the door reopened and the three men emerged. This time, he saw their faces. Definitely not Vietnamese.

One was in his fifties with a reddish beard, another a stocky man in his late twenties with a thin and untidy attempt at a moustache. He was engaged in discussion with the third Russian. Chase didn't know what they were saying, but one thing was clear from their attitudes alone: the last man was very much in charge. The tallest of the three, he looked to be around Chase's age, in his early thirties, with angular features and a hard, pale-eyed gaze, which he turned dismissively on his younger companion at some unappreciated suggestion. Cowed, the man with the moustache fell into sullen silence.

The Englishman waited for them to return to the tents before moving again. Before long, he reached the cabin. He sidled along its wall and climbed the metal steps to the door.

He gently tried the handle. It turned. Readying his gun, Chase opened the door and quickly slipped inside.

He'd had no idea what to expect, but what he found still came as a shock.

A glass partition wall divided the cabin. The narrow section in which he stood had the feel of a viewing gallery, where people could observe what was happening on the other side.

Medical experiments.

He had found the last prisoner. He recognised the young blonde from the picture Lock had shown him as Natalia Pöltl, the American's daughter. She was asleep – drugged, he saw, a number of intravenous drips running into her bare arms. There were bruises on her skin where more needles had been inserted. She was wearing only a white surgical gown, which appeared to have been made specifically for her; a flap over her abdomen was secured by a Velcro strip, the bulge of dressings beneath it. Stark blue-white light from a circular lamp cluster illuminated her from above, pinning her like an animal on a taxidermist's table.

Filled with a growing sense of revulsion, Chase surveyed the rest of the chamber. A large stainless-steel cabinet in one corner resembled a fridge; for storing samples? Another corner was home to a small steel washbasin, glass-fronted cases alongside it containing glinting surgical equipment and flasks of chemicals. A laptop computer sat atop a small chest of drawers near the head of the operating table.

Whatever was going on, it was obvious that this was no random kidnapping by bandits. Someone had gone to a great deal of effort to get their hands on Natalia.

But finding out why would have to wait. Natalia was not the only prisoner. His first priority was to make his way back to Sullivan so that the team could plan the rescue.

Fighting every instinct to free the young woman and take her to safety, Chase turned and opened the door a crack. The torrential rain was still keeping her captors in their tents. 'I'll be back for you soon,' he promised the sleeping figure as he slipped outside.

7

Sweden

Eddie accelerated, sending the Twizy southwards down the boulevard after the kidnappers. A long way ahead, the Audi made a skidding turn to the right. He glanced at the speedometer, trying to judge how long it would take him to reach the intersection. For a moment it seemed the little electric car was surprisingly fast – then he remembered that the number was in *kilometres* per hour, not miles.

'Eddie!' Nina shouted from behind him. 'Go right, down there!' She pointed at a street angling away to the south-west, her iPhone gripped tightly in her hand. The screen displayed a 3D aerial view of Stockholm. 'It's a short cut, we'll catch up with them!'

Eddie made the turn, sweeping the Twizy to the wrong side of the road to pass a slow-moving car. The road was a cul-de-sac, trees across its end, but a cycle path ran between them. The Renault was narrow enough to fit – he hoped. 'What's down here?'

Nina rotated the map. 'A river. The only way they can go is along it. The road's called, uh . . . Strandvägen.'

Eddie sounded the Twizy's horn, startled pedestrians leaping away as he swerved on to the cycle path. Snow and slush spattered him and Nina through the buggy's open sides. 'Where does it go?'

'How the hell would I know? I've never been here before!'

Her call on the short cut had been good, however. The Audi powered past just ahead of them, heading west along the riverside. Still shrilling the horn, Eddie swung on to another broad boulevard in pursuit. Tramlines occupied the lanes on each side of the tree-lined central reservation, three-coach trains trundling past the dawdling traffic. The S4 was forced to weave aggressively between the cars to avoid being blocked.

The much skinnier Twizy slipped through the gaps with ease. 'Okay, I'm starting to see the point of this thing,' Eddie admitted. 'We're catching up.'

Nina tilted the map to get a better view of what lay ahead. 'If they don't take one of these side streets, they'll have to keep going along the river for about a half-mile. They must be heading for one of the main roads out of the cit*eeee!*' She squeaked as Eddie guided their vehicle between two cars with only inches to spare on each side. 'Don't miss them like that!'

'You'd rather I *hit* 'em?'

'You'd rather I hit *you*?'

'Not really – wait, look!' Two lanes ahead were full of stationary vehicles, a tram in the third closing off the only open avenue before the kidnappers could reach it. The Audi's brake lights flared. 'They're stuck!'

'Or not,' said Nina as the S4 made a slithering power slide, barging a smaller car out of the way and crossing the lines just behind the tram to traverse the central reservation. A man walking along the path down its centre had to dive out of the way, the car jinking to avoid him at the last second. The Audi vaulted the kerb on the other side and skidded again, still heading west – but now facing into oncoming traffic.

Eddie used the lowered kerb at a pedestrian crossing to follow, angling across the grassy central divider. He weaved between the trees before dropping down heavily into the empty bus and tram lane on the other side. The Audi's driver tried to cut back across the road to get into the clear space ahead of the Twizy, but couldn't find a large enough gap between the approaching cars. Frustrated, he swung the other way and rode up on to the pavement along the waterfront, sounding the horn and flashing his headlights. Terrified pedestrians cleared the S4's path.

'Jesus!' Nina gasped as the Russians pulled away. 'Someone's going to get killed!'

'Yeah, probably us!' Eddie replied in alarm. The Twizy's lane was no longer empty, the headlights of a tram directly ahead – and getting closer with worrying speed. The kerb to the right was high enough to flip the small-wheeled Renault if he tried to ride up over it, but going into the oncoming cars would be even more dangerous . . .

Out of time. The tram rushed at them.

He went left—

Nina screamed as the tram flashed past to her right, traffic blurring by on the other side as Eddie threaded the needle and straddled the dividing line between the two lanes. An approaching driver instinctively swerved away in fright and sideswiped the car alongside him with a *whump* of crumpling sheet metal. Traffic stopped sharply behind them with blaring horns and the cracks of fender-benders.

The tram passed. Eddie immediately darted back into the empty lane. His wife thumped his shoulder with a balled fist. 'I *told* you not to do that!'

He ignored her, searching for the kidnappers. The black

Audi was still racing along the pavement. But it had slowed, slaloming to avoid pedestrians. That told him something: the kidnappers were not totally ruthless, trying to avoid collateral damage to innocent bystanders.

But it didn't mean Tova was safe. He brought the Twizy back to its maximum speed, such as it was – though right now it was enough to gain ground on the kidnappers. 'What's coming up ahead?' he shouted.

Nina zoomed in closer on the map. 'Looks like a big intersection. If they're trying to get out of the city, they'll have to go straight on . . .' She paused, listening. 'I can hear the cops!'

Eddie picked up the wail of a siren a moment later. He looked ahead. The two sides of the boulevard rejoined past the end of the tree-lined reservation. Beyond it the route forked, pulsing blue strobe lights approaching down each leg.

But not all the kidnappers' escape routes were closed off. To the left was a small inlet lined with moored pleasure craft, another road curving in a semicircle around its end. The Russians had seen it too, one of the silhouettes in the Audi gesturing furiously. The S4 followed the pavement around the little harbour before finally finding a clear section of road and dropping back on to it with a suspension-straining crash.

Eddie swung the Twizy between the stalled traffic and followed. 'Where does this road go?' he demanded.

Nina hurriedly scrolled across the map. 'It's called Nybrohamnen, and it goes . . . nowhere!' The screen revealed that the road in question ran around the edge of a spit of densely built-up land jutting into the river before looping back to rejoin the main shore. 'If we cut across, we can get ahead of them!'

The Audi was pulling away fast, but stayed on the waterfront. The driver wasn't familiar with Stockholm's complicated geography either. Eddie glanced back as he brought the Twizy around the curve. The police cars were struggling to squeeze between the backed-up vehicles, rapidly falling behind. 'Where can we cut through?'

'Down there!' Nina pointed to the right. There was a narrow road between a pale stone hall with banners proclaiming it as the 'Musikaliska' and a large hotel.

He saw warning signs at the junction. 'It says no entry – it's one-way.'

'It's the *only* way – we'll never catch up with them otherwise.' The Audi's lead kept growing. A few more seconds and it would be lost to sight as the riverfront curved.

Eddie started to make the turn – only to see that both lanes were blocked by traffic waiting at the lights. These were not cars he could slip the Twizy between, either. One was a garbage truck, the other a snowplough, the two metal hulks filling the side street. Railings made it impossible for him to ride the Renault up on to the pavement. 'Whoa! No go,' he said, hurriedly swinging back on to Nybrohamnen.

The Russians were now out of sight. 'We've lost them!' Nina cried in dismay.

'No we bloody haven't,' he insisted. He powered their little vehicle down the length of the ivy-covered Radisson hotel – then made an abrupt stop. The Twizy skidded sideways, ending up pointing straight at the hotel's main entrance.

'Oh, you're not . . .' she moaned.

'Oh, I am!' Eddie stamped on the accelerator. The Twizy bounded over the low kerb and raced through the doors into the hotel's lobby.

Guests screamed and dived aside as the little Renault zipped through the building. Eddie sounded the horn in a shrill tattoo. 'Get out of the way!' An elderly couple were too slow and befuddled to react, forcing him to swerve. The wet tyres slithered on the tiled floor, and the buggy wiped out a table and sent a tall lamp flying before he regained control. 'Come on, shift your arses!'

'Sorry,' Nina added.

More yells and shrieks followed them as the Twizy continued through the lobby. The reception desk loomed at its end, staff gawping as the buggy charged towards them. Eddie made another hard right turn, fishtailing around a corner and scattering someone's luggage. 'Hope there's a way out down here,' he said.

'Oh, *now* you're thinking about that?' Nina shot back.

'You've known me for six years – how often have I ever planned anything in advance?'

'If we have kids, you're going to have to start!' She spotted a sign on the wall with an arrow pointing right. 'There's an exit down that corridor.'

'It'll just take us back the way we came,' Eddie objected. He saw a set of doors ahead and aimed for them, sounding the horn again. 'This looks better.'

'No it doesn't!' But it was too late to stop. She braced herself—

The Twizy rammed the doors open, almost ripping one from its hinges. Waiters leapt away on the other side, plates scattering. The couple had burst into a restaurant, what had once been a courtyard now protected from the elements by a glazed ceiling high above. Diners reacted in shock to the unexpected intrusion.

Eddie weaved between the tables. 'Where's the bloody way out?' Large parts of the walls were covered by black curtains. He finally spotted the glow of an exit sign through a gap in the drapes and angled towards it.

'Ah, don't mind us,' said Nina, cringing at the stunned gazes of the patrons. Some displayed recognition: she was, after all, a public figure. 'Oh boy. Another day in the papers.'

'Thought you'd be used to it by now. 'Scuse me,' Eddie added, sounding the horn again to prompt a waiter to clear his path. The man had been carving a roast on a trolley beside a table; an idea came to the Englishman, and as the Twizy passed he snatched up the big knife.

'What're you doing?' Nina asked.

'Planning ahead!' He wedged it blade-down beside his seat and steered between the curtains towards the exit. To his relief it was a swing door, the buggy barging it open and humming through. A long corridor stretched out ahead. He accelerated. 'Where are we going to come out?'

'I don't think the app covers the insides of buildings,' she complained as she checked her iPhone's screen again. 'Hold on . . . okay, this corridor looks long enough to go to the back of the building, so . . .' She rotated the image, getting a better angle on the 3D representation of the hotel. 'There's a parking lot at the back – if we can get into that, then if we go right we'll be back on that one-way street.'

Eddie bleated the horn again, more hotel staff jumping out of their way as the Twizy entered another lobby at the hotel's rear. A large arched doorway led outside. A man with a staff name tag rushed to the exit as if to block their escape, but when the Renault showed no sign of slowing thought better of it and threw the doors open to save them from damage. 'Cheers, mate,' the Englishman said as he whipped past.

Nina gave the man an apologetic look. 'I feel like we should have tipped him . . .'

Cold air hit them as they emerged into the open. The paved area between two wings of the hotel was indeed a small parking lot, a gate open to a road. Eddie drove through it, turning right, then immediately left to rejoin the one-way street. He zipped between the oncoming cars. 'Okay, which way?'

'Straight on,' Nina told him. 'If they followed the waterfront around, they'll be coming from the left.'

He nodded in acknowledgement. 'Hope we're still ahead of 'em.' The right lane was now clear of traffic; he swung into it. They were approaching a busy intersection at one end of a bridge over the river, cars and buses milling.

No sirens – or angry horns. The kidnappers hadn't got here yet. But with their massive speed advantage over the little electric buggy, they couldn't be far away. Steeling himself, Eddie pushed the Twizy to its full speed and shot out of the side street on to the waterfront.

Now he heard horns, furious blasts sounding to his left. 'Here they come!' Nina yelled, seeing a sleek black shape carving through the traffic towards them.

'Hold tight!' Eddie warned, sweeping across the lanes to inter-cept the Audi. It was already almost upon them, engine snarling. He grabbed the knife as the S4 skidded through the intersection.

The Twizy was distinctive enough to have stuck in the kidnappers' minds. The driver reacted with surprise on seeing the Renault again, then veered sharply at it. Eddie jerked the wheel, swinging away. The Audi's front wing scraped the pod-like body. 'Shit!' Nina yelped as the Russian straightened, then made another attempt to sideswipe them.

Her husband was less worried about the driver than the man beside him. The front passenger window whirred down – and a gun emerged, pointing at him—

Eddie braked hard – and stabbed the knife into the Audi's rear tyre as it shot past.

Pain exploded through his fingers as the blade slashed the rubber before being snatched away. The larger car shimmied, knocking the Twizy into a skid – then the damaged tyre ruptured with a flat gunshot *bang.*

The Russian driver sawed at his steering wheel, but not even four-wheel drive could help him keep control as the speeding Audi slewed around on the wet surface. The man in the front passenger seat was thrown against the door, dropping his gun. He tried to pull back inside the cabin – then screamed as he saw what was rushing at him—

The Audi slammed side-on into an articulated bus. Windows shattered and showered passengers with glass. The S4 bounced off and spun to a standstill in the middle of the road. The gunman slumped dead out of the battered side of the car, his face and most of his arm embedded in the shredded concertina connecting the bus's two halves. The car's other occupants were left stunned by the impact.

Their pursuers had not escaped a crash either. Despite Eddie's best efforts to counter its skid, the Twizy wobbled, then overturned—

He gripped the wheel, Nina clinging to his seat to hold herself up as the buggy rasped across the road on its side. It hit a kerb, the Renault's curved roof absorbing the blow with a vicious crack.

Passers-by ran to help, worried faces peering down into the vehicle. Eddie winced as he moved; the pain in his left hand had been joined by a throb in his right shoulder where he had scraped the ground. But nothing was broken. His concern was more for his wife. 'Nina!' he gasped, struggling upright. 'Are you okay?'

'No, I'm frickin' *not*!' she cried as the onlookers helped her up. She had struck her head on the icy road, blood running from a gash above her temple. She put a hand to her forehead, and immediately wished she hadn't as more pain stabbed through her skull. 'Son of a *bitch*, that hurts!'

Someone in the growing crowd spoke English. 'I'll call an ambulance.'

'Never mind that, call the cops,' Eddie ordered, turning to locate the Audi. The driver clambered woozily out. 'Shit! They're still moving.'

'What about Tova?' Nina asked in alarm, concern overcoming discomfort.

Eddie scrambled out of the capsized Twizy. The Russians were pulling Tova from the Audi—

No, they were *trying* to pull her out. But she was limp, apparently unconscious. Her captors seemed little better off. One man hobbled around the car, his hard gaze darting between the historian and the onlookers before he barked a command to his companions. The trio abandoned Tova and ran towards a park to the north-west.

'Nina, make sure she's okay,' said Eddie as he set off – not to intercept the Russians, but back towards the bus, where he had spotted something on the road.

'What are you going to do?' she demanded.

'Find out who they are,' he called back. He reached what he had seen – the dead man's fallen gun. He picked it up. It took him a moment to identify it: an SR-1 Vector, a high-powered sidearm used primarily by the FSB – the Russian intelligence service that had succeeded the KGB. That pretty much confirmed *who* had tried to kidnap Tova Skilfinger – but the question now was *why*?

Only one way to find out. As Nina climbed from the wrecked Twizy and started for the Audi, he raced after the fleeing men.

The leader was hurt, running with a limp, but he clearly had the training and fortitude to overcome the pain. As he and his comrades reached the park entrance, he glanced back and saw Eddie following. Another barked order, and one of his men skidded to a halt on the sidewalk, then drew his gun—

Eddie dived and rolled behind a stationary Volvo as the Russian opened fire. The woman in the car screamed and hunched down in her seat as bullets struck her vehicle.

'Jesus!' Nina gasped, dropping low beside the Audi at the crack of gunfire. Panic spread amongst the people nearby, sending them scattering like terrified birds. The Russian kept shooting, blowing out some of the Volvo's windows, then looked back over his shoulder for a moment to see how far his companions had gone—

A moment was all Eddie needed.

He popped up and fired through the car's cabin in front of the hysterical driver. Two bloody bullet wounds burst open in the Russian's chest. He crumpled to the ground. The Englishman offered a quick apology to the woman, then ran across the road to kick away the Russian's gun in case he was still a threat.

He was not, eyes frozen wide. Eddie gave the dead man an angry look, then ran into the park after his companions.

Nina watched him go, then rose and leaned into the Audi. Tova was sprawled on the back seat, unmoving. 'Tova?' the American asked fearfully, reaching out to check her neck. 'Are you okay?'

For a moment she felt nothing . . . then she found a faint but steady pulse. Tova reacted to the touch, flinching before crying out in Swedish. 'It's okay, it's okay!' Nina told her. 'They've gone.'

The historian stared at her, still frightened. 'Who were they? What did they want with me?'

'I don't know, but you're safe now. The police are on their way. Are you all right?'

Tova sat up, putting one hand to her head. 'I – I think so. I hit my head when we crashed . . .' She took in Nina's own injury. '*Oj herre Gud!* You are hurt!'

'I'll live,' Nina replied through gritted teeth.

'And what about Eddie? Is he okay?'

'God, I hope so.' She turned to see her husband running into the park.

Eddie hurdled a low fence, pounding across a snow-covered flower bed to cut a corner before reaching a wide path. The two Russians were about fifty metres ahead, having passed a large statue on a high stone plinth. The limping leader looked back again, seeing that Eddie was still in pursuit. Another barked order, and the other man stopped and raised his gun.

'Shit!' Eddie yelped, hurriedly changing direction to put the plinth between them. The supersonic whipcrack of a bullet passed just behind him. More screams echoed across the park as people realised the firefight was coming their way.

He reached the statue. Castings of old-fashioned cannons or mortars acted as fence posts at each corner, chains hanging between them. He jumped over the obstacle and pressed his back against the plinth. Raising his gun, he edged sideways to peer around the corner. Was the Russian just trying to slow him down, or actively attempting to kill him?

A gunshot and a shower of stone chips from the plinth's corner as he hurriedly ducked back into cover gave him an answer. Until the car crash the Russians had minimised collateral damage, but now that the kidnappers had lost their target and were in danger of being cornered, all bets were clearly off.

He leaned back out as far as he dared, trying to see what his opponents were doing without exposing himself to fire. The leader was cutting across a lawn in the direction of a red church beyond some trees. Even with his limp, it wouldn't be long before he was lost to view – and Eddie had no doubts that he had been well trained in melting away into a city's population.

If he got away, then Tova was still at risk of another kidnap attempt – or worse. He couldn't let that happen.

But he had to deal with the gunman first . . .

Eddie shrugged off his leather jacket. He threw the garment out from one side of the plinth – as he darted out into the open on the other.

The Russian fired – at the first target, the jacket twitching in mid air as a bullet punched through it. The man was quick to realise that it was a decoy, already swinging round to take aim at the second—

Eddie was quicker. His shot hit the shooter squarely in the forehead, a wet spray erupting from an exit wound in the back of his skull. The man almost somersaulted backwards to land in the snow, red flowering across the white expanse.

No need to check if his target was dead this time. Eddie hopped over the chains, snatching up his punctured jacket and running after the last Russian.

He quickly gained, the kidnapper's painful ankle slowing him. The Russian left the park and ran up a road past the church. Eddie closed the gap. Twenty feet, ten. The man heard him coming and looked back, raising his gun—

Eddie tackled him to the ground.

Both men skidded through the snow before tumbling to a stop. The Russian's cap came off. Eddie drove a punch at his groin. He made contact, but his opponent had twisted so the blow struck his hip. His foot lashed out in retaliation. Eddie jerked away. The man's heel hit his shoulder. The Englishman rolled back, whipping up his gun.

As did the kidnapper—

They each got their first clear view of the other's face – and froze.

Eddie's gun remained locked on the other man – just as the

Russian's own weapon stayed fixed on him. The kidnapper was taller than his pursuer, intense pale eyes set in a hard, lean face. They regarded each other for a long moment.

The other man broke the silence. 'You know why I am here, Chase.' A statement, not a question.

'Yeah,' was Eddie's only reply. The kidnapper nodded, then lowered his gun. Eddie did the same.

The Russian's level gaze remained fixed on him, thoughtful, calculating – then without a word he stood and hurried away. Eddie rose, silently watching him round the red-painted church and disappear from sight.

Only when the limping figure was gone did he move, putting his battered leather jacket back on and slipping the gun inside. He heard someone approaching from behind and turned. 'Eddie!' Nina called, running to him. 'Are you okay?'

'Yeah, I'm fine,' he replied.

She looked round, worried, but saw no sign of the kidnapper. 'What happened? Where did he go?'

'He got away.'

'But you were right behind him.'

'He got away,' Eddie repeated flatly. He started back towards the park, leaving the bewildered Nina staring after him.

8

Vietnam

'This whole thing's not right,' said Chase. 'I don't like it.'

'Beggars can't be choosers,' Sullivan told him, though with considerable disquiet. 'We've still got to get those hostages out of there, no matter what. But . . .'

'But they are obviously not just bandits,' Castille said, finishing his thought.

'Then who are they?' asked Rios.

'You said they were all carrying 74Us?' Sullivan asked Chase, who nodded. 'The only Vietnamese who are issued those as standard are members of their special forces – or TC2.'

'What's TC2?' said Lomax.

'*Tông cuc Tình báo* – Vietnamese military intelligence, officially, but it also acts as secret police and a spy agency. But I can't think of any reason why they would be taking aid workers hostage.'

'And what about these Russians?' Chase asked. 'It looked like they were in charge of whatever they were doing to Natalia. But what *were* they doing, and why her?'

'First things first,' the New Zealander said. 'We've got to rescue her and the others – and if these people really are TC2, then that makes doing so with a zero body count even more important. If we kill members of their secret police, then believe me, we *will* be hunted down.'

'I don't see how we're going to manage that,' said Hoyt. 'If there's as many of 'em as Chase said—'

'We find a way,' Sullivan snapped. 'Understand? I got a taste of communist Vietnamese hospitality in the seventies. I wouldn't wish it on my worst enemy – and I sure as hell don't want to experience it again!'

'If we're going to go in stealthy, this is the best time,' Chase pointed out. 'The storm'll give us cover. No bugger'll go out into this if they don't have to.' Even in what shelter they could find, the mercenaries were still drenched.

Sullivan peered over the rock behind which they were crouching. 'There's still only one sentry on this side of the camp,' he reported, spotting the speck of torchlight. 'Looks like he's sticking to the same route. If we time it right, we should be able to take him down without any trouble. Non-lethally,' he added, giving Hoyt a warning look.

The American made a sarcastic sound. 'Yeah, yeah. I got the message.'

A plan was rapidly worked out, then the six men advanced on the camp. Having already covered the ground, Chase took the lead. Pausing occasionally to confirm the sentry's position, he moved in until he reached the line of footprints, then signalled to the others.

No words were needed; everyone knew what to do. Chase hunched down behind a bush a few feet from the path, while Castille took up position nearby. The other men spread out behind them, ready to react if needed.

The wind gusted, raindrops bursting against the Englishman like little bombs. For all the dryness his poncho provided, he might as well not have bothered wearing it. But it served another purpose, the blotchy camo pattern breaking up his outline. With his head low and the bush's branches further hiding his shape, the sentry wouldn't see him until he was just a few feet away.

He hoped . . .

A glance to the side revealed a crouching shadow: Castille. In the other direction, the light gradually got closer, its bearer taking on form as he plodded along the track. A faint gleam of wet metal showed that the gun was still slung over his shoulder. As before, the torch's beam was mostly following the path, only occasionally checking the undergrowth on each side.

Fifteen feet, ten. Chase tensed, ready to strike. Five feet, and the torch briefly swept over the bush – then abruptly snapped back towards him—

He sprang, slamming his shoulder into the Vietnamese man's stomach and knocking him to the ground. The sentry tried to cry out, but only managed a choked gurgle as he took a savage elbow to the groin. He convulsed in pain. Chase rolled and wrapped one arm tightly around his throat as Castille rushed over to toss the AKS into the bushes.

Chase tightened his chokehold. The man writhed, clawing at his face with one hand, but then Castille pinned him and the result was inevitable. Eyes bulging, the sentry made a last strangled moan, then went limp. Chase maintained the hold for a few more seconds to make sure he wasn't faking, then eased the pressure. The man's head lolled. He quickly checked his pulse. He was still alive.

Shapes rose from the undergrowth. 'Is he okay?' Sullivan asked.

'He's out,' Chase reported, pushing the unconscious man away and standing.

'Good.' Sullivan looked round. 'Hoyt, Rios, tie him to that tree there. Gag him, too – he probably won't be able to shout loud enough for anyone in the camp to hear him over this wind, but let's not take chances. The rest of us'll move on. Eddie?'

Chase took point again, retracing his earlier path to the edge of the encampment. Before long, the team were in the bushes behind the largest tent, Rios and Hoyt soon catching up. 'No one in the open,' said Castille, surveying the scene.

'Two men guarding the hostages, yes?' Rios asked.

Chase nodded. 'Better check nobody else has gone in there, though.'

Hoyt glanced towards the dark block of the cabin. 'What are we going to do about the girl?'

Sullivan considered the question. 'We deal with the guards inside this tent first,' he decided. 'Once they're out of the way, you and Eddie go and get her while we secure the rest of the hostages.'

'The two guards were at opposite ends,' warned Chase, 'and there's only one entrance. If one of them raises the alarm we're fucked, so how're we going to get 'em both at the same time?'

Sullivan grinned, reaching under his poncho to take out a glinting knife. 'Make another entrance. Okay, let's move.'

The group split into two teams of three, Chase accompanied by Castille and Sullivan. They went to the closed end of the large tent, while the other mercenaries crept towards its entrance. The Englishman peered through the plastic window again. 'Still two guards,' he whispered as he rejoined his companions. 'One's sitting by the door – back to it, watching the prisoners. The other's got his back to the other end of the tent.'

Sullivan quietly used his radio headset to relay the information to the others. Rios gave him a thumbs-up. 'All right,' said the New Zealander, 'let's open up another door . . .'

He examined the tent's corner, then with intense concentration and precision pressed the tip of his knife against it, about four feet above the ground and right beside the supporting pole. The wet canvas strained, then split as he applied more pressure. The constant beat of the rain covered the thin crackle of fibres being severed. Slowly he forced the blade downwards. It was extremely sharp; the fabric peeled apart as if he were slicing a boiled egg. Castille held the material in place as the cut lengthened.

Finally the blade reached the groundsheet. Sullivan withdrew it, taking hold of the bottom corner of the slashed canvas to prevent it from flapping in the wind. A nod to Chase, who in turn leaned around the side of the tent and signalled to the men at the other end. He got another thumbs-up in reply. 'They're set,' he whispered.

'Weapons ready,' Sullivan ordered. Making sure Rios and the others could see what he was doing, Chase carefully unshouldered his Kalashnikov. They did the same. He nodded to the mercenary leader to confirm this. 'Okay. Tell them to go in five.'

Sullivan moved back a little, using his boot to hold the canvas in position as he readied his AK. Castille took up a firing stance as Chase held his hand out, all five fingers extended. He waited until he was sure the other three men had seen it, then brought in his thumb. Four. Forefinger, three . . .

With the countdown established, there was no need to keep displaying it. All six men knew exactly how long they had to wait. Chase gripped his gun in both hands, feeling a rush of adrenalin. Ambushing the lone sentry was one thing, but any mistakes here and people would die.

Two, one—

Sullivan yanked back the flap, hissing a warning in Vietnamese for both guards to freeze as Chase ducked through and jammed the muzzle of his AK-47 against the closest man's neck. Castille was right behind him. Simultaneously, the tent's entrance was thrown open and Rios and Hoyt rushed in. The Spaniard pointed his gun at the startled second guard beside it – but Hoyt had already flipped his rifle around and smashed its butt against the man's skull. He tumbled to the floor. 'Don't you fuckin' move, Charlie,' Hoyt growled, planting a foot down hard on his back and bringing his AK back round to push it against his head.

'Enough of that,' snapped Sullivan as he entered the tent. He issued an order in the guards' language. Chase's prisoner scowled, but raised his hands behind his head before kneeling. 'Are we still clear outside?'

Lomax peered in through the entrance. 'Yeah, we're good.'

'All right. Keep watch.' The American nodded and returned to his position outside. 'Secure these two.'

The weapons pointed at them deterred the guards from offering any resistance as they were bound and gagged. Once they were secure, Chase checked the hooded figures. The nearest was a woman; her clothes were dirty, but with no sign of blood. The other captives were in much the same state. A couple of the men had visible bruises, but they were days old, received when they were taken hostage rather than from subsequent beatings.

'Okay, we're here to rescue you,' Sullivan announced quietly. 'We're going to untie you. Don't make any noise, okay? If you understand me, nod your head.' All but two of the prisoners responded. 'Free the ones who nodded so they can tell their friends that we're getting them out of here,' he told his team, before signalling to Chase and Hoyt. 'Okay, you two get Natalia. Be careful – we still don't want to risk a firefight.'

'Don't marry her,' added Castille with a smile. Chase flicked him a cheery two fingers before ducking out of the back of the tent.

The rain hit him again like a fire hose. Behind him, Hoyt muttered an obscenity. 'Which way?'

'Round here.' Chase dropped low and made his way through the undergrowth around the edge of the camp. As he approached the cabin he spotted the second sentry's light amongst the trees, but it was some way distant. There was no movement in any of the smaller tents. 'All right, here we go.'

He emerged from the bushes by the cabin, Hoyt following. The slatted blind behind the single window was still closed; no way to tell if the Russians had gone back inside. He readied his rifle and climbed the steps. 'Okay, on three . . .'

Another silent countdown – then he turned the handle and darted inside.

Natalia was still unconscious on the table. But she was not alone.

The red-bearded man, wearing a white lab coat, was taking a blood sample from her arm. He looked round, annoyed at being interrupted – then his expression flashed to fear as he saw the two armed intruders. He whirled, rushing for a walkie-talkie beside the computer—

Chase shoved open the sliding door and thrust the Kalashnikov at him. 'Freeze!'

Hoyt took aim at the Russian's head. 'You heard him. Don't move.' The man hesitantly retreated.

'Watch him,' said Chase, entering the inner chamber to check on Natalia. The syringe that had been inserted into her arm was slowly filling with dark blood. Even asleep, the young woman's expression was one of discomfort. He rounded on the Russian again, frowning. 'What've you done to her?'

Hoyt stepped closer, hefting his weapon threateningly. 'Answer him, Ivan. Or don't you speak English?'

The man blinked. '*Vy Amerikanskya?*' he said, before following it with a rapid-fire protest in Russian. Chase had no idea what he was saying, but the man's fear was mixed with anger – or outrage.

Hoyt's response was to shove him hard against the wall. 'Just stay there and shut the fuck up,' he said, holding his AK with one hand while he started to open the drawers and cabinets with the other. 'She okay, Chase?'

'No fucking clue, I don't know what they've been doing.' The bruises on her arms stood out clearly under the harsh overhead lights. He turned angrily to the – doctor? Scientist? 'What's in those drips? Will it hurt her if I take them out?' The man regarded him uncomprehendingly, so he took hold of one of the plastic intravenous lines as if to pull it out. The Russian's expression changed, but not to the worry Chase would have expected of a doctor faced with a threat to his patient; more a dismay that he was about to lose something important. 'I'll take that as a no.'

He peeled away the tape holding the needle in place, then pulled out the IV feed. A small bead of blood swelled at the centre of the exposed bruise. The scientist objected; Hoyt thumped him in the stomach with his rifle butt, the Russian collapsing to the floor. Chase removed the other lines, then carefully extracted the little syringe from Natalia's arm and tossed it away. 'Natalia?' he said, leaning closer. 'Can you hear me?' Her eyelids twitched slightly, but she was a long way from being conscious. 'Bollocks. We'll have to carry— What're you doing?'

Hoyt had shrugged off his backpack, sliding the laptop inside before resuming his search of the drawers and stuffing handfuls of what Chase guessed were research notes in with the computer. 'Finding out what they're working on.'

'That's not why we're here. Help me get her up.'

'In a minute. She ain't going anywhere.'

'She won't be if you don't give me a fucking hand,' Chase

complained, but the American was still rifling through the cabin's contents. 'For fuck's sake,' he muttered, before turning back to the young woman. He gently patted her cheek, but there was no response.

She was still connected to the medical monitors. Chase glanced at them, hoping they would show some change in her condition.

Hoyt was reflected in one of the screens. His gun swung towards the Russian, who was trying to push himself back upright—

The Kalashnikov's thudding bark was almost deafening in the small space as it unleashed a three-round burst. The scientist's white coat erupted with splashes of deep red as the bullets tore through his chest.

'Jesus *Christ*!' Chase yelled, his ears ringing. 'What the *fuck* are you doing?'

'He was coming at me,' Hoyt replied.

'No he wasn't – he was just sitting there, you fucking psycho! Now the whole fucking camp knows we're here—'

The smoking AK swung round on a new target: Chase. 'Drop your gun,' the American ordered coldly. 'Do it, or I'll put you down too.' Chase reluctantly let his rifle clatter to the metal floor. 'Okay, you're gonna be my pack mule. Pick her up. Now!'

The Englishman lifted Natalia off the table. She moaned faintly, but was still limp. 'You bastard,' he growled as Hoyt closed his backpack and reshouldered it. 'You knew they were doing this to her, didn't you?'

Hoyt ignored his question, instead gesturing towards the exit. 'Okay. Get her outside, and we'll—'

The door opened. The man with the feeble moustache rushed in, rain-soaked hair draped over his forehead. He started to say something in Russian, only to halt abruptly as he took in the scene. Hoyt's gun locked on to him. The new arrival stared at the American, watery blue eyes wide – then with a startled gasp he stumbled backwards down the stairs into the storm.

Hoyt watched him run, then snapped his gun back to Chase. 'Go.'

Chase carried Natalia to the door and looked outside. The gunfire had roused the camp, people scrambling from the tents. The running man reached one just as another Russian emerged. Chase recognised him as the lean-faced man who had been with the scientist earlier. He was not just the leader of the Russians; from the responses of the Vietnamese as he shouted orders, he was in overall charge of whatever was going on.

'Move it!' Hoyt shouted. Chase descended the stairs to the waterlogged ground. Natalia was instantly soaked by the lashing rain, her thin medical gown sticking to her skin. 'Get to the trees!'

Two of the 'bandits' ran towards the cabin, their AKS-74Us raised – but an urgent command from the head Russian stayed their fire. Hoyt, however, had no such restraints. He unleashed a swathe of bullets that took down both men, then leapt from the doorway to follow Chase into the undergrowth.

Shouts came from the big tent. Chase saw a Vietnamese man rush from its entrance, waving frantically. He wasn't one of the guards: that meant Sullivan, Castille and the others had already got the prisoners out without being seen.

But they couldn't have gone far in so short a time. He expected some of the kidnappers to start after them – but instead their entire focus was on the two men and one woman who had just left the cabin.

They want Natalia back – but why?

Chase had no time to dwell on the thought. Squinting as the wind sent stinging rain into his face, he ran deeper into the jungle. Behind him, Hoyt stopped and took something from a pocket. He lobbed it through the cabin's open doorway. A couple of seconds later there was an explosion, followed by a swelling, crackling roar. An orange light washed over the encampment. The grenade was an incendiary, setting the laboratory – and everything still inside – aflame.

The American set off after Chase. But the gap between them now gave the camp's inhabitants a chance to fire without risking Natalia's life. More yelled orders, the Russian commander's voice joined by angry calls in Vietnamese. Shots ripped through the trees. Chase looked back. The spreading blaze provided enough light to show Hoyt ducking into cover before returning fire. A scream came from the camp as another man was hit.

The Englishman also saw others spreading out, trying to cut off his escape. He changed direction, weaving between the swaying trunks. Getting away from Natalia's captors was now his primary objective – but escaping from Hoyt was a close second. He didn't doubt for a moment that the American would kill him to protect his secret.

Hoyt and the Vietnamese exchanged more shots. Chase kept running. He had lost his bearings in the confusion, pounding across a steepening slope, but couldn't do anything more than head away from the camp. No way to tell where Castille and the others were . . .

The radio. He could warn Sullivan about Hoyt!

Chase raised his arms, clumsily shifting Natalia's weight as he tried to switch on the walkie-talkie. He finally found the dial and turned it, hearing a click from the headset. 'Hal! Can you hear me? This is Eddie, do you read me? I've—'

The ground disappeared in front of him.

With a yelp, Chase threw himself on to his back just in time to avoid careering over a near-vertical drop. Natalia was not heavy, but she still weighed enough to wind him as she landed on top of him. He dug his heels into the mud and pushed himself away from the precipice. He was at the edge of the valley he had seen on the map, the dark chasm below ready to swallow the unwary.

He struggled back to his feet. The radio crackled, Sullivan's voice barely discernible. 'Chase? Where are you? Are you okay?'

He set off again, angling up the slope. 'Hal, I've got Natalia, but Hoyt—'

The crack of a gunshot and the thud of a bullet hitting a tree right beside him were simultaneous.

Chase spun, adrenalin and fear surging. He expected to see Hoyt, but the shape approaching through the rain-filled murk was smaller. A woman – one of the Russians – took on form, a white coat partly visible under her rain gear and a pistol in her outstretched hand. She shouted at him, but he didn't understand the words.

Sullivan spoke through the headset again, but Chase didn't answer. The woman advanced, aiming at his head. She almost stumbled as a gushing rivulet caused mud under her foot to slip away, but with Natalia in his arms Chase couldn't do anything to take advantage.

The Russian repeated her demand, flicking the gun towards the ground for emphasis. *Put her down. Now.* She was easily close enough to shoot him without risking injury to Natalia; the only reason she hadn't done so already was that if he dropped her, she might roll down the slope and go over the edge.

They were determined to keep her alive, then. But that wouldn't help him without a major distraction . . .

One arrived – from an unexpected source.

A hissing rumble came from uphill, growing louder every second. The streams of water running down the slope suddenly became torrents, spray bursting up from rocks and roots. Chase and the Russian woman both looked around—

For a moment he thought the whole hill was melting . . . before realising he was staring into a mudslide.

Part of the waterlogged hillside had given way under the relentless force of the tropical storm, and now it was thundering straight at him. The sludgy wave front was only about eight inches high, but that was more than enough to sweep the muddy ground out from under his feet.

Still clutching Natalia, he toppled and slithered helplessly down the slope – and fell with the screaming Russian over the edge into the blackness below.

9

Sweden

Nina read through Tova's translation of the Valhalla Runestone for what felt like the millionth time. The words may have been in English, but by now they seemed to have lost all meaning.

Following the thwarted kidnap attempt on the historian, she and Eddie had been taken to the headquarters of Stockholm County Police. Despite Tova's statement on their behalf, the couple had been threatened with arrest for crimes ranging from grand theft auto through possession of illegal firearms to murder. To avoid being charged, Nina had reluctantly been forced to draw a big gun of her own: legal immunity. As the director of a United Nations agency she had the de facto status of a senior diplomat, and the same privilege was automatically conferred on her spouse. She had as a result endured an uncomfortable telephone discussion with Oswald Seretse the previous evening, the normally calm and urbane official sounding as close to apoplexy as he ever got before she explained the circumstances, and had no doubt that more questions would come when she returned to New York.

But for now, she and Eddie were both free and able to work. She was working, at least, her laptop linked to the IHA's database and trawling for any information that could suggest why Russians might want to steal a runestone or kidnap a historian. That kind of research was not Eddie's forte, so he had left her to it.

For that matter, where *was* he? She had been so engrossed that she only belatedly realised he was no longer in the hotel suite. Trying his phone got no reply, the call going straight to voicemail.

He might just have forgotten to turn it on, but the fact that he had left without telling her where he was going – or even saying goodbye – perturbed her. She turned back to the laptop, the thought still nagging.

Several minutes later, her phone rang. But a glance at the screen told her it wasn't Eddie. 'Hello?'

'Hello, Nina?' It was Tova. 'Are you okay?'

"I should be asking you that.'

'I am fine, thank you. But I am still worried about you and Eddie. I told the Ministry of Justice that you were trying to rescue me, but—'

'That's okay,' Nina told her, not wanting to relive the diplomatic debates. 'Are you at home?'

'Yes – and there is a police car outside, to watch for the kidnappers if they try again.'

'Good.' While Tova seemed calm, Nina could sense the stress in her voice. It was a feeling she knew herself, from unwelcome personal experience. 'What can I do for you?'

'I have, ah, been trying to take my mind off what happened by concentrating on work.'

'I know that feeling,' Nina told her with black humour.

'Yes – I said I had been inspired by your work, but I did not expect to have the same kind of experiences as well! I am happy to stay in the lab or my study. But after you told me you were going to look again at all the information about the Valhalla Runestone, I decided to do some more research of my own – about the clue in the runes to the location of the second stone.'

'You said you thought it was at the bottom of a lake?'

'Yes, but before, I did not look any farther. There did not seem to be any point. Now, I have gone back to my research and I think I have got closer to its exact position. It is remarkable how bad things can focus the mind.' An attempt at a laugh. 'But I do not have access to information that would help me confirm if I am right – not easy access, I mean. I would have to search for it in archives, it will take time.'

'What kind of information do you need?'

'Maps, mostly. Old maps of Norway – not only from Viking times, but from one or two centuries ago as well.'

'The IHA database should have that kind of thing. I can access them from my laptop. You can have whatever you need.'

Tova sounded surprised, but pleased, by the offer. 'Oh, good! I can bring my notes to your hotel.'

'No, no, we'll come to you,' Nina insisted. 'The cops can still keep an eye on you – and to be honest, I'm suffering from cabin fever after spending most of the day in here. What's your address?' She wrote it down. 'Okay, we'll be there soon.'

The two women said their goodbyes, and Nina hung up before trying Eddie's phone again. No answer. 'Dammit, Eddie,' she muttered as she tied her long red hair into a ponytail, then collected her notes and packed her laptop into a bag. She was about to get her coat when the door opened. 'Eddie?'

'No, Russian kidnappers,' came the reply. 'Who'd you think it was?' Eddie entered the suite, a colourful scarf hanging down over his battered leather jacket and wetness on his boots where he had been in the snow. He was carrying something about eight inches long in a brown paper bag.

'Where were you? I tried calling, but it went straight to voicemail.'

'Police station. I turned my phone off while I was there.'

'Why did you go back there? Until we hear otherwise, our immunity's still in effect.'

'They wanted to ask me some more questions about the kidnappers,' he said, his tone curt. 'Thought if I told them, they might let me know if they'd found out anything more themselves.'

'And had they?'

'Nope.' He headed for the suite's bedroom.

'What did you buy?' Nina asked, regarding the bag.

'Hmm? Oh, just some thicker socks.' He didn't look back at her as he went into the other room. 'My feet got a bit damp during all that business, wanted to make sure I didn't get frostbite.' Nina heard the clunk of his suitcase being opened and closed, then he returned. He glanced at her laptop bag. 'You off somewhere?'

'Tova did some more research about the location of the second runestone. I was about to go over to her place rather than have her come here; the cops are watching it in case the kidnappers come back.'

'They won't.'

Nina cocked her head. 'You seem very sure of that.'

He looked irritated at being doubted. 'There were four guys, and now three of 'em are dead. The one who's left'd be pretty fucking stupid to try anything, especially now that every cop in Stockholm's after him. Why, what did you think I meant?'

'Nothing, Jeez,' she said defensively. 'I was just saying, that's all. Why are you in such a mood?'

''Cause I just spent a couple of hours in a police station. So I'm going straight out again, am I?'

'You don't have to come if you don't want to.'

'Nah, I'll come.' He smiled, exposing the gap between his front teeth. 'Got my scarf just how I like it, so it'd be a shame to take it off.'

Nina grinned back, relieved that his moment of ill temper had passed. 'Okay then, Doctor Who. Let's go.'

Tova lived in a small but comfortable apartment in southern Stockholm. As she had said, there was a police car on station in the street outside, the two officers within watching the visitors suspiciously as they entered the building.

The Swede's greeting was warmer. 'Nina, Eddie! Hello again, I am so happy to see you both.'

'Thanks,' Nina replied. 'How are you? Are you okay?'

'Still shaken, I am afraid,' Tova said as she took the couple's coats. 'Being kidnapped, it is . . .' She tried to suppress a shiver. 'I am just a historian. This is crazy. I never imagined that my work would cause this.'

'I don't think they'll be coming back,' Eddie told her. 'You shouldn't have to worry about 'em.'

'I hope so! But thank you again for saving me, both of you.'

'All part of the job,' said the Englishman with a small smile.

Nina opened her bag. 'I brought my laptop, so if the IHA database has anything that can help you, we'll be able to access it.'

Tova nodded. 'I will show you what I have found out so far.'

She led them through the apartment to a small room lined with bookshelves heavily laden with volumes on Scandinavian history and mythology. On a desk was a map of Norway, along with numerous printed notes. Tova sat and gathered together several pages. 'This is the English translation of the section of the runes from the Valhalla Runestone that describes the journey to Ragnarök,' she said, placing one of the pages on the desktop. It was the same text that she had shown them at the museum. Nina read it again, Eddie this time taking considerably more of an interest.

> O great Norse warriors!
> When Ragnarök is upon you
> You must travel to Valhalla
> To prepare for the final battle
>
> The serpent and the wolf have risen before
> From their lairs in the lands of ice
> The serpent's venom lies thick deep below
> Black eitr that can kill even a god
>
> This dark stone is but one of two
> That reveal the true way to Valhalla
> On this, the path that leads to its doors
> The other, the river to follow
>
> Up this river you must travel
> Until great Bifröst is reached
> Across, follow the stream to the falls
> At their summit is Odin's hall, now of the slain
>
> Before you is the guide-stone
> One half of the whole that leads to battle
> At the fellowship hall the other part awaits
> A place known to all true warriors

The two parts together brought
Shall alone open the death-gate of Valhalla
Within its halls are found the paths
That lead to Ragnarök

At the final battle, wolf and serpent shall fall
Slain at last by our mightiest heroes
Though the price to be paid shall be great
Those who fight shall be honoured for all time

Nina was first to finish. 'There's nothing more on the other runes that were on the stone?' she asked.

Tova shook her head. 'Not that seemed relevant. Most of the other text is a list of those present when the stone was made.'

Eddie straightened. 'Okay, so if I'm reading this right: you use the clues on the two runestones to find out how to reach Valhalla, then when you get there, you use the two halves of the dark stone to open the gate, and inside Valhalla there are two maps telling you where to find the eitr pits. That it?' The blonde historian nodded.

'Two maps?' Nina asked, looking back at the text.

'It says "are found the *paths*", plural.' He pointed out the relevant line.

'That might just mean the route to Ragnarök involves going across the sea as well as overland.'

'No, Eddie is right,' said Tova. 'As I told you yesterday, this English translation does not have the nuance of the original. The Old Norse text definitely refers to two different locations for the final conflict. Ragnarök is an event, not a place.'

Nina was slightly irked at herself for not having considered that, and at her husband for his smug smirk. 'So does that mean they didn't know exactly where the battle of Ragnarök would take place?'

'Looks like it,' said Eddie. 'They've got a choice of two locations – these lairs of the serpent and the wolf. They must both be way up north somewhere if they're in the "lands of ice". So presumably once they're at Valhalla and have the maps, one lot of Vikings toddle off to find the first eitr pit while their mates head for the other. Whichever one's got monsters coming out of it, that's your battle of Ragnarök.'

'That is . . . a new way of putting it,' said Tova, amused, 'but yes.'

'But before you can find them, you've got to find Valhalla,' Nina noted. 'And to do that, you need the other runestone.'

Tova moved the translation aside to show them the map. 'I shall show you where I think it is.' Her fingertip moved to a long lake in western Norway. 'This is Tinnvatnet – it is a valley that was flooded in the 1930s when a dam was built. But an archaeological site was also found there. Unfortunately, it was not fully catalogued before the water rose over it.'

'They didn't delay the dam work until it was done?' Nina asked, faintly outraged.

'It was a different time; archaeology was placed second to progress, sadly. But the man in charge of the dig, Tollak Enberg, made as many notes as he could.' She picked up another sheaf of papers. 'The site was called Félagthing – which literally means "the fellowship assembly" – by the Vikings, and like Iarlsta, it was a meeting place where differences between various tribes were discussed and settled. A kind of high court, somewhere of great importance.'

'Important enough to be known about by tribes a couple of hundred miles away in Sweden?' suggested Nina. She indicated one section of the translation. '"A place known to all true warriors", in other words?'

'I believe so, yes,' said Tova. 'A meeting of the tribes there would only be called on rare occasions, and it would be for something very important.'

'Like Ragnarök,' Eddie said thoughtfully.

'Yes. Which is why I first thought it might be the place mentioned on the Valhalla Runestone – the fellowship hall. When I read Enberg's notes, that made me more certain that I was right. They said there was a runestone at the site with a black circle set into it.'

Amongst Tova's papers was a photograph of the stolen runestone. 'Like the sun compass,' said Nina, indicating it. 'But I'm assuming that Enberg didn't translate the runes or take any photos of it, otherwise we wouldn't be having this discussion.'

'I am afraid not. He dismissed the text on the runestone as mere myth, and instead concentrated on the historical finds. And he did not have long to work there – even though the site had been discovered a few years before, it was only when the dam was almost completed that Enberg was able to arrange a dig. He and his people were working right up until the waters reached them.'

'Nothing like a deadline to spur you on.' Nina looked back at the map. 'But that means the runestone's still there under the lake, somewhere. Do you know where the site is?'

'Only the general area,' admitted Tova. 'The lake is very long, almost thirty kilometres. Many of the landmarks Enberg described are now underwater also, and do not appear on modern maps. That is why I wanted to check in the archives, to see if older maps show them. With those, I can find the location more accurately.'

Nina took out her laptop. 'I think I can help with that. Just give me your Wi-Fi password, and I'll see what the IHA database can turn up.'

'Not that it's going to make any difference,' said Eddie, almost forcefully dismissive. 'It's still at the bottom of a lake. The chances of digging the thing up have got to be pretty much zero.'

'Almost zero isn't the same as zero,' said Nina. 'And the people who stole the Valhalla Runestone and tried to kidnap Tova are obviously determined to get hold of the other stone so they can find Valhalla. If they're willing to go that far, a bit of water isn't going to stop them. I think it's the IHA's job to make sure that doesn't happen. Don't you?' She deliberately added a faint tone of challenge to her words, curious to see his reaction.

He merely shrugged. 'Like I said, it's at the bottom of a bloody lake. Even if you figure out where it is, we'll still have a hell of a job finding it.'

Nina smiled. 'Not necessarily. I know just the man to call . . .'

10

Vietnam

Pain and discomfort forced Chase back to groggy consciousness. He tried to move. The rippling burn of bruised muscles made him groan, but while his ribs and hip had taken a heavy impact, nothing was broken as far as he could tell.

He opened his eyes – and immediately squeezed them shut as raindrops smacked down on them. 'Ow, fuck!' he muttered, annoyance followed by an odd amusement. If water in the eyes was his biggest complaint, he couldn't be that badly hurt.

Turning his head, he opened his eyes again to see . . . nothing. A flash of panic: was he blind? No, there was a very low light, the moon's glow diffusing faintly through the heavy clouds above. Bushes and trees slowly took on ghostly form through the rain. Where was he? A forest? No, a jungle . . .

He snapped back to full wakefulness. Vietnam – he had been carrying Natalia, but one of the Russians had caught up. Then the mudslide sent them all over the cliff—

'Natalia!' Chase sat up, more pain coursing through his ribs. No answer. He looked round. A pale shape lay nearby: the young blonde in her white medical gown. He called her name again.

No response. He was about to check if she was still alive when he remembered they were not alone.

The Russian—

Another figure was sprawled on the muddy ground about ten feet from him. Even in the darkness, though, he could tell she was no longer a threat. A rock glinted wetly beneath the Russian woman's neck, her head twisted at an unnatural angle.

Chase crawled through the sludgy dirt to Natalia. He found a pulse, slow but steady. She was still out cold, either from the drugs or as a result of the fall. Her landing had been softer than his; a dull throb across his chest told him he had unwittingly acted as her cushion when they hit the ground.

He looked up, trying to judge how far they had fallen. The slope was not quite vertical; he had bounced off several earthy steps as the rushing mud swept him down. The jungle at the top was hard to make out – thirty feet above? Forty? Not an easy climb, up or down, in the dark, slippery conditions.

But that did not mean he and Natalia were safe. Over the storm, he heard shouts from on high. Russian or Vietnamese, he couldn't tell, but one thing was clear – they were getting closer. A shaft of torchlight stabbed out over the edge like a lighthouse's beam.

Chase went to the dead woman. Where was her gun? He scoured the ground for telltale glints of metal, but saw only mud and stones.

No time to widen the search. He hurried back to Natalia and raised her to a sitting position, patting her cheek. 'Natalia! Are you awake, can you hear me?'

Fore the first time, she responded, whispering something. Chase leaned closer, trying to catch it, but his knowledge of her language was too basic to understand what she said. 'My name's Eddie – your father sent me to rescue you,' he told her, hoping her English was better than his German. 'We've got to get out of here.'

She spoke again, her voice barely audible. '*Mein Vater* . . . my father?' Her eyelids flickered as she tried to look at the man holding her.

'Yeah. Can you walk?'

Natalia wriggled, but there was no strength behind it. '*Nein*, no, I . . .' There was more, but it tailed away below the threshold of audibility.

'Guess not.' Straining as more aches and bruises made themselves known, he picked her up. Her head lolled against the radio headset, which had been partially dislodged by the fall. He nudged it back into place. 'Hal, Hugo – can anyone read me?'

There was no response – not even static. He looked down at his belt to find the walkie-talkie missing, its headset wire dangling loose. 'Shit!' He turned, searching for any faint glow of LEDs on the ground, but saw none. The Motorola was either broken by the fall or buried in the mud.

They were on their own.

He still had his backpack, which meant he also had a map, but getting away from their pursuers was his highest priority.

The vegetation along the foot of the cliff was sparse. There were thicker trees off to his right – to the east, he worked out, remembering what the map had shown him earlier. Going that way would take him away from the extraction point, but they needed cover. Natalia's white robe, even rain-soaked and dirty, would stand out clearly from above. Raising her higher, he started for the denser jungle.

More lights shimmered through the trees above the top of the cliff. The shouts were clearer, closer. There had been no more gunfire, which he took to mean that Sullivan's team had got the other hostages clear.

What about Hoyt? The thought of the American set an ember of anger burning in his stomach. If he saw him again . . .

He put ideas of revenge aside. They were unprofessional, and he had more important concerns – like survival.

The boundary of the overhanging jungle canopy was about forty feet away. He lumbered towards it, feet sticking in the thick mud as if walking through a nightmare. Someone shouted urgently. Fear surged – had he been spotted? A glance back revealed the lights converging where the mudslide had rushed downhill. It would only be seconds before they realised what had happened and made their way to the edge of the ridge to look down . . .

Mud tugged at his boot. He pulled it free, almost losing his balance. Natalia gasped as she jerked back to wakefulness. He recovered and pressed on. Almost at the trees, wet bushes swatting at them as he pushed through. Another look back. The lights were picking their way down the slope towards the drop.

The rain's pounding eased as Chase reached the shelter of the foliage overhead. But he still needed to keep moving until he and Natalia were blocked from view—

The beams lanced down into the valley as the searchers reached the edge. They swept across the undergrowth – then one flashed over him as a hunter's sharp eyes caught movement. A shout. More lights locked on to the fugitives.

Gunfire—

Chase dived behind a tree, Natalia crying out as he landed on top of her. Bullets thunked against the bark. One of the Russians yelled furiously and the shooting stopped.

But now they knew where their prey had gone. And they would soon climb down to track it.

He risked a peek around the tree. The overhanging branches meant that the men from the camp no longer had a clear line of sight on him. That gave him a short window in which to move out and force them to search for his trail.

He picked Natalia up again. The thought of abandoning her did not even cross his mind. His job was to get her to safety, and he would do just that – or go down fighting.

The ground was muddy, but not as bad as it had been nearer the ridge. If he stayed close to the trees, he could use roots and stones to keep his footprints to a minimum. Which way? He tried to recall the map. The cliff ran roughly north–south, parallel to a nearby river . . .

'Okay, hold on to me,' Chase told Natalia as he headed in what he hoped was the right direction. She managed to raise one arm and cling weakly to his shoulder.

He made his way as quickly as he could through the jungle. His feet sought out the unyielding firmness of rocks and roots, but sometimes he had no choice but to cross soft, wet ground. With Natalia's weight added to his own, his boot prints would not be hard to spot. All he could do was keep changing direction in the hope of forcing their pursuers to waste time reacquiring his tracks.

Minutes passed. His progress was as good as it could be given the conditions, but Chase was all too aware that Natalia was slowing him considerably. And a look back revealed torchlight in the distance – on the ground, not above. They had descended the cliff and were on his trail.

A new sound rose above the storm's din. Running water. They had reached the river.

Chase emerged from the jungle on to its edge. The river was swollen by the downpour, white froth gushing around the bases of the trees where it had burst its banks. More pale splashes on the far side told him it was about fifty feet wide, but it was impossible to know how deep it was.

No choice. The sure knowledge that the Vietnamese and Russians were getting closer every moment forced him to commit to his plan. If he didn't cross the river, not only would he be hemmed in, but there would be no break in his trail. They would quickly catch up.

'Natalia?' he said. She turned her head towards him. 'The men who kidnapped you are coming after us. We've got to cross this river to get away from them. We're both going to get wet. You understand?'

'I already *am* wet,' she sighed.

Chase gave her what he hoped was a reassuring smile. 'Okay. Just keep hold of me. Here we go.'

He stepped into the torrent.

Even with only a few inches of water covering his boots, he could still feel the relentless pressure behind it. He continued onwards. The river deepened with each step. No time to play games of bluff and double bluff with his pursuers to make them unsure if he was heading up or down the river; he needed to get across as quickly as possible, following a direct line to the far bank.

The rushing water was now up to his waist, every step a strain against the current. Cold spray splashed Natalia's back. She gasped and tensed in his arms, the thin material of her robe providing no warmth. 'Hang on,' he said. 'This is where it gets *really* bad . . .'

Another couple of steps – and the riverbed dropped away underfoot, plunging them both into open water.

It was much deeper than Chase had feared. Natalia screamed, then the sound was cut off as her head went under the surface. The coldness of the water squeezed his chest like a giant's hand. He raised his arms and pushed her back up, kicking furiously to hold position.

It wasn't enough. The river was sweeping them along, deep enough that he couldn't find bottom. Natalia gasped before being submerged again. A wave smacked against his face. He coughed, blowing water from his nostrils, then pulled his arm out from beneath Natalia's legs while gripping her torso more tightly. Her head came up as her feet went down. She took in a choked breath.

With one arm free, Chase now had some control over their direction, however limited. 'Keep your head up!' he spluttered, trying to raise the young woman higher in the water as he headed for the other bank.

'I'm trying!' she wailed. 'I can't see!'

She was close to panic. Chase steeled himself and thrashed his free arm to bring them around, then raised her as high as he could before leaning forward in the water. 'Use your legs, kick! We've got to swim for it!'

It took her a moment to take in what he was saying, but then he felt her move, thighs beating first against, then in time with his. The line of froth at the base of the trees slowly drew closer. 'Keep going!' Chase shouted as the toe of one boot made contact with the riverbed. He scrambled for purchase, foot slithering in the submerged mud before finding grip. 'We're almost there!'

Natalia managed to bring up one arm, making increasingly powerful strokes as they neared the bank. Both the Englishman's feet found solid ground. He took her weight again, the water dropping lower with each stride. 'Yeah, yeah!' he grunted. 'We did it, we're there!'

He hoisted the young German up in both arms once more and half ran, half staggered the final metres to the bank. They entered the trees. The ground was far from dry, but to Chase it felt like a rocky desert. Panting, he lowered Natalia so she could lean against a tree. 'Are you okay?'

'No,' she gasped. 'I thought I was going to drown!'

'Close bloody call,' he agreed, coughing. 'But we can't stay here. They're still coming after us.'

The shock of being submerged in chilly water had shaken her out of her drugged befuddlement. 'Who is coming? What . . . what happened to me?'

'You don't remember?'

'I . . . do not know.' A pause as she searched her memories. 'We were travelling, then . . . they stopped us! Some bandits—'

'Yeah,' he cut in, 'but they aren't really bandits.'

'Who are they?'

'I don't know, but some of them were Russian. I think they took your whole group hostage just to get you.'

'Russian?' she exclaimed, shocked. 'But why would Russians . . .'

Her words trailed off. To Chase, it seemed as if some horrible realisation had just struck her – but whatever it was, explanations would have to wait. 'We've got to go. Can you walk?'

She pushed herself upright, wobbling before steadying herself. 'I – I think so.'

'Good. Come on.'

He took her hand to lead her deeper into the jungle. She hesitated. 'What . . . what did you say your name was?'

He looked back at her. 'Chase. Eddie Chase.'

Even in the gloom, he saw that she had managed a small smile. 'Oh – like Bond, James Bond?'

'*Better* than James Bond. Except for Roger Moore.'

That confused her, but: 'All the same, I am very pleased to meet you . . . Eddie.'

'Don't thank me until I've got you somewhere safe. You ready?'

'Yes.'

'Great. Let's go.'

*

Despite Natalia's insistence that she could walk, it was not long before she began to falter, the effects of her captivity and the exhaustion of the swim catching up with her.

And that was not all that was catching up. Their pursuers had followed their trail to the edge of the river – and crossed it. Shouts and flashes of torchlight warned Chase that they were moving through the jungle behind him.

They were spreading out, though. That meant they had not found his and Natalia's tracks – yet. So far all his efforts had been put towards simply running, but now a new option presented itself. If the Russians and Vietnamese dispersed too widely, he might be able to slip through the gaps in their net . . .

Natalia suddenly cried out in pain, almost tripping. 'What's wrong?' Chase asked.

'I stepped on something sharp,' she replied, close to tears.

He crouched; she was holding one foot off the ground like a cat with an injured paw. Gingerly touching her bare sole, he found a large splinter of wood or bark jutting from it. He pulled it out and wiped away dirt, but there was not enough light to see if the puncture wound was superficial or something more serious. 'Can you walk?'

She lowered her foot, flinching and stifling a gasp as she put weight on it. 'I think there is still a piece in my skin.'

Chase swore under his breath as he turned to locate the hunters. He got a long enough view of one of the torches to judge its distance before it disappeared behind the trees. Less than two hundred metres away. And getting closer.

'I'll carry you,' he said, picking her up. Another gasp, but this was of surprise. He set off again, glancing back every few steps to find their followers.

They were definitely fanning out. The current had swept

Chase and Natalia further downstream than the Englishman had intended, and so far it didn't seem that anyone had found where they'd made landfall. The odds of escaping were increasing. Very slightly, but Chase would take whatever he could . . .

Natalia mumbled something in German. Her voice was slurred, and she was having trouble holding her head up. An after-effect of the drugs? 'What's wrong?' he asked, concerned.

'I feel . . . very tired,' she answered. 'And . . . sick.'

Chase suddenly realised that if she had no memory of being held in the cabin, then she had been kept unconscious the whole time – and had not eaten, maybe for days. Even if one of the IV lines had been feeding her nutrients, her body would be close to exhaustion, and she was now also cold, wet and hurt. She needed warmth and rest.

She would get that when they reached the rendezvous and were taken out of the jungle, but – he reluctantly had to accept – the Vietnamese and Russians would probably catch up long before then. Simply running would not be enough. He needed another course of action.

Natalia began to say something more, but the words faded away to silence. She went limp. Chase stopped, trying to assess her condition. Her breathing was worryingly shallow. 'Shit,' he whispered, moving behind a tree and looking back. One of the men was heading in his direction. A chill of dismay ran through him as he realised the man would cross his tracks. If he spotted any footprints, he would alert the others and bring them running like hounds.

Although . . .

He kept watching. Other lights winked in and out of view between the trees – but further away. Chase felt a surge of hope: the hunters had spread out *too* far. They would be able to pick out their companions' lights in the distance, but their voices would be lost under the ceaseless hiss of the rain. Even if the approaching man found a footprint, he wouldn't be able to call to anyone else. The mere fact that they had been communicating by shouts gave away that they didn't have radios.

A new option presented itself. *Attack*.

Chase's gaze went back to the torch, judging distance, direction . . . then he turned and surveyed his surroundings. He needed somewhere safe to leave Natalia. A large rock rose from the ground at an angle, bushes overhanging one side. He pushed the branches aside with his body before carefully laying the young woman down alongside the stone. When he retreated, the bush bent back into shape, covering her.

Not well enough. Her white gown was still discernible through the leaves. He should smear it with mud to break up her shape—

A shout, close by. Out of time. His trail had been found.

He ducked behind a tree and peered into the jungle. Another urgent cry in Vietnamese. The man was less than eighty metres away. He shouted again, waving his flashlight. Chase rapidly checked to each side. Those other hunters that he could pick out by their torches were advancing in a widely spaced ragged line, some of them now level with his position. Unless they looked back and happened to have a clear line of sight on their companion, they would not see or hear his warning.

What would the man do? Leave the trail to run after the others – or follow it?

The latter. The torch beam moved back down to the ground, then began to advance on Chase's position. Fast. The man was moving at a near-run, certain he had his prey's scent.

The trail would lead him past Chase's hiding place. He dropped low, keeping the tree between himself and the approaching light.

The man shouted again, excited triumph clear. Rain-dripping metal gleamed; his gun. The AKS came up, tracking back and forth as he searched for his quarry.

Chase hunched lower. He heard squelching footsteps over the wind and rain. The Vietnamese man was almost upon him.

The hunter jogged past the tree – then slowed, the torch warily sweeping the surrounding vegetation. The boot prints had become muddled, tracks crossing over each other. He hesitated, then started to follow one set.

Towards Chase.

The Englishman kept moving around the tree as the Vietnamese lifted his torch. Its beam followed the trail to the base of the trunk. Chase sensed his sudden wariness, afraid of an ambush.

Gun and torch came around in unison as he turned the light on the undergrowth. Chase tensed as it reached him—

A low moan. Natalia.

The man spun, torch beam locking on to the wet rock – then the figure in white beside it as she lifted her head. He raised the gun—

Chase burst out from behind the tree and dived at him.

The man whirled to shoot, but the Yorkshireman had already lashed out at his gun as they collided. His arm caught the magazine, knocking it out of the receiver and sending it spinning into the darkness. Both men hit the ground, mud splashing around them.

But there was a round already in the rifle's chamber. If it fired, it would draw all the other hunters to their position.

The Vietnamese knew this too. Chase was on top, but the other man still held the AK in his right hand. He tried to bring it around to fire into his attacker's side. Chase felt rather than saw the movement and snapped his left hand across as the man pulled the trigger—

It didn't move. Chase had thrust his thumb through the trigger guard – behind the trigger itself.

The hunter squeezed it again, harder. Metal dug into Chase's thumb like a guillotine blade, nerves and tendons crunching. He gasped in pain, but kept his grip on the gun.

The Vietnamese snarled as he struggled against Chase's weight – then jerked his left hand free and smacked his heavy flashlight against the side of the Englishman's head. Chase cried out. The light swung again—

Chase moved – not sideways to avoid the blow, but *down*, delivering a punishing headbutt. The man shrieked as his nose broke, cartilage cracking like damp wood.

The crushing pain on Chase's thumb suddenly eased. He yanked at the gun, wresting it from the Vietnamese's grip and tossing it out of reach. The other man was still paralysed by pain, bloodied face scrunched up in the spill of light from the torch, but Chase knew he only had moments before he recovered his senses.

He rolled off his attacker and grabbed him by the throat, hauling him over to clamp his arm around his neck. The Vietnamese realised what was happening and struggled, kicking furiously and slamming his elbows into the Englishman's body, but Chase grimaced, withstanding the pain of the blows, and tightened his hold. The hunter's fury turned to panic as he choked, but there was nothing he could do. His attacks grew weaker, then stopped. His body convulsed before going limp.

Chase eased his grip, taking several seconds to recover his breath and let the adrenalin rush subside, then brought up his aching hand to check the man's pulse. It was slow, but steady.

He pushed the unconscious form away and painfully rose to his knees.

Natalia had also risen. She stared at him in horror. 'You – you killed him!'

'No, he's still alive,' Chase rasped, 'but we've got to get away from here before his friends realise he's missing and come looking for him.' He picked up the Kalashnikov, the rifle feeling unbalanced without its magazine. A rapid check of the ground around him revealed no trace of the curved metal clip, and he had no idea where it had landed. 'Bollocks!'

He helped Natalia up. She gasped when she put weight on her foot, so he hoisted her over one shoulder in a fireman's lift and, the AK in his right hand, moved off into the jungle, angling away from the other probing lights.

It wasn't long before he heard shouts from behind. The Vietnamese man had regained consciousness and was yelling for help. By now, the gap in the search line had been noticed, some of the other hunters having turned to investigate. All Chase could do was keep going, trying to camouflage his tracks as much as possible.

He pushed on for five more minutes, ten. A look back. The pursuing lights had finally been lost in the storm. But could he risk trying to find a hiding place?

A feeble moan from over his shoulder forced an answer. Exhausted from the drugs and whatever experiments the Russians had been carrying out on her, drenched and cold in only her thin surgical gown, Natalia had reached the limit of her endurance. If he didn't find shelter for her soon, there was a definite danger that if she passed out again, she might never wake up. He clambered over more roots, eyes straining to pick out details in the darkness.

A shadowy shape on the ground resolved itself into that of

a fallen tree as he approached. One end was higher than the other, propped up by a hunk of half-buried stone. A black void told him that the log was hollow. He went to the open end, using the rifle to probe its interior – partly to check if it was large enough to fit Natalia, and also to make sure it was not home to any venomous snakes. It seemed big enough to accommodate her – just – and nothing hissed at him.

He bent forward, carefully letting the young German slide off his shoulder and taking her weight with his arms. 'Natalia, I don't know if you can hear me, but I'm going to put you into a hiding place. I'll be right here with you.' He lifted her again, this time trying to manoeuvre her bare legs into the open end of the log. It felt like trying to push wet spaghetti through a keyhole, but after a couple of attempts he finally got both limp limbs into the gap and eased her inside. When she was fully swallowed by the log, he shrugged off his backpack, then removed his rain cape and draped it over her as best he could.

There was a low hollow beneath the trunk's raised end. Another quick check for snakes, then Chase squeezed down into it, keeping the gun with its single bullet at the ready as he stared into the jungle back the way they had come. No lights, no movement but the sway of trees and bushes in the wind and the constant falling rain.

He kept watch for as long as he could, but tiredness inevitably caught up. Despite his best efforts, sleep eventually swallowed him as completely as the night.

11

Norway

Eddie gazed out across the long frozen lake. 'So, somewhere under that . . . there's a Viking village?'

'That's what we think,' Nina replied. 'That's what we *hope*, anyway.'

Tova, standing beside them on the shore, had a concerned, apologetic expression. 'Oh, I really hope I am right, Nina. You have organised this so fast! People, equipment, machines, all of this in just two days. It is a lot of money. And if I am wrong about the location . . .'

'If *we're* wrong,' the American corrected, giving her a reassuring smile. 'If we don't find it, I'll take the hit – you don't need to worry about anything. This is what the IHA does. When we need to move, we've got the resources.'

'Yes, so I see. I have to admit I am a little jealous!' Tova waved an arm at the vehicles lined up along the lake's edge. 'But you have brought all this, even though we do not know if the runestone is even here.'

'If it *is* here,' Nina pointed out, 'we'll need to secure it as quickly as possible. The people who stole the other stone and murdered the security guard – and tried to kidnap you – are obviously desperate to get hold of it.'

'If they're the same people,' Eddie said quietly.

'Hmm? What do you mean?'

He shook his head. 'Nothing. Just that if the first lot stole the runestone because they want to find Valhalla, maybe the Russians went after Tova because she was the next best thing to having the actual stone.' He shrugged. 'Just a thought. I'm probably wrong.'

It was not an idea that had occurred to Nina. 'God, I hope you are. If there are two sets of bad guys after the stones, we don't want to be caught in the middle if they start shooting it out!'

'Well, wouldn't be the first time.' He gave her a sardonic smile. 'So, we've got diving gear, we've got pumps, lights, drills, flotation bags, winches . . . everything we need to get a ton of stone up from the bottom. All we've got to do is find the bugger.'

Nina turned at the sound of more approaching vehicles. 'Well, hopefully this is the man to do it.'

A long-wheelbase pickup truck was carefully making its way to the shoreline. Mounted in its rear bed was a crane, the arm rotated to rest over the cab. When it was turned the other way, it would extend several feet beyond the tailgate. Another, smaller pickup followed, a blocky object secured in the cargo area beneath a tarpaulin. Both trucks lined up alongside the parked 4x4s.

Nina, Eddie and Tova went to greet the driver of the second vehicle as he emerged. 'Strewth and g'day, cobber!' said Eddie.

Matt Trulli shivered, wrapping his coat tightly around himself. Its down quilting made him look even chubbier than he already was. 'Was that meant to be Australian, mate? Sounded more like Welsh.'

'I keep telling him he's terrible at accents,' said Nina playfully. 'He won't listen.' Eddie sniffed.

'Yeah, well, one of these days I won't listen to you when you ring up and say, "Matt, there's something underwater that we need. Can you bring one of your subs to the arse-end of the world to get it?" Especially when the place you want me to come to could freeze the balls off a brass monkey!' Matt belatedly registered an unfamiliar face in the group. 'Oops, sorry for the language,' he told Tova.

'That is . . . okay,' she replied, her politely bewildered tone suggesting that she hadn't understood him enough to be offended.

'Tova, this is Matt Trulli,' said Nina. 'He works for the Oceanic Survey Organisation at the UN, but he helps the IHA out from time to time. Matt, this is Tova Skilfinger, a historian and expert in Viking culture.'

Matt's face lit up. 'Vikings, eh? Now there's an interesting bit of history! Amazing shipbuilders and navigators for their time.'

'Trust you to find that the most fascinating thing about them,' chided Nina. 'And *all* history's interesting.'

That prompted mocking snorts from both men, which in turn roused looks of professional disapproval from the two PhDs. 'Just taking the piss, love,' Eddie reassured his wife.

Matt shook Tova's hand, then regarded the lake. 'So, it took me two days, but I've rounded up the gear you asked me for. What are we actually trying to find?'

'A Viking runestone,' Nina told him. She led them to one of the parked off-roaders, taking a photograph from a case inside. 'It's probably going to look a lot like this.'

The Australian examined the picture of the Valhalla Runestone inside Tova's lab. 'Fairly hefty. That's why you brought all those IBUs, then?' He glanced at the bright orange cargo of another truck.

'IBUs?' Tova asked.

'Inflatable Buoyancy Units. Airbags, basically – they lift stuff underwater. Those look like two-fifty-kilo bags, and you've got eight of them, so it could be anything up to two metric tonnes?'

'The runestone that was stolen weighs about nine hundred and ninety kilos,' the Swede told him.

'Stolen?' Matt gave Nina a look of weary suspicion. 'And let me guess, the guys who took it probably want to get their hands on its twin as well?'

'Uh . . . yeah,' she admitted. 'They killed a guard at Tova's museum to steal it, then tried to kidnap her as well.'

'Right. Why am I not surprised?' He shook his head. 'One of these days I'll learn to ask you about this kind of stuff *before* I bring all my gear out into the field!'

'It, ah . . . sounds as if you have experienced this sort of thing before,' Tova said, with slight worry.

Matt made a sarcastic sound. 'Oh Christ, yeah. I've lost count of the number of times these galahs've almost got me killed! Let me tell you about it—'

'No, don't,' Eddie cut in with a grin. 'It'll give her night-mares.'

'It's not nearly as bad as it sounds,' Nina insisted, seeing that the older woman appeared about to re-evaluate her decision to join the expedition. 'And I made sure the IHA's security procedures were put in place. The number of people who know what we're doing is very small, and they're all aware of the need for secrecy given what happened in Stockholm – there shouldn't be any trouble.'

'Famous last words,' said Matt.

'Nobody knows we're here. Tova and I worked out the location of the second runestone, and outside of the people here, only a couple of senior Norwegian officials, and Seretse and a few people at the IHA, know exactly where that is.'

'Someone else might,' Eddie suggested darkly.

'Who?'

'The people who stole the first runestone.'

'Yeah, I was kinda hoping that wouldn't come up. But,' Nina went on, 'their expert doesn't have nearly the amount of local knowledge and experience that Tova does, or any more access to the IHA database.'

'Wait, wait,' said Tova. Now it was her turn to adopt an expression of dawning suspicion. She chose her words carefully. 'You *know* who stole the runestone and shot Arvid?' When Nina did not answer immediately, she continued: 'You *do* know! Why did you not tell me?'

'I . . . yes, I know,' said Nina, shamefaced. 'I didn't tell you because it's a security issue – an *IHA* security issue. One of the robbers – possibly even their leader – used to work for us, before we fired him.'

The Swede was outraged. 'I cannot believe you did not tell me! Have you told the police?'

'The UN told your government, and Interpol. I don't know if they passed the information to the Stockholm police, although I'd certainly hope they did. But there's no record of him entering or leaving Sweden, so he's presumably travelling on a fake passport. We don't even know if he's still in the country.'

Tova stared at the icy ground, processing what she had learned before fixing the American with a stern gaze. 'Who is this man?'

Nina hesitated, before deciding that after what she had been through, the older woman deserved to know the truth. 'His name's Logan Berkeley.'

Tova blinked, surprised. 'I have heard of him.'

'He was the IHA archaeologist overseeing the dig at the pyramids a couple of years ago. So yeah, his face was all over the papers and TV – he was big on self-publicity.'

'He's keeping a lot lower profile now,' said Eddie.

Tova nodded. 'He opened the chamber under the Sphinx – but you were already inside!'

'And he never forgave me for upstaging his big moment,' Nina said. 'He sold out to the people who tried to raid the site – and went to prison for it. He was released about six months ago. It looks like he's been selling his services again.'

'Wait,' said Matt, puzzled, 'if this guy's an Egyptian expert, why would he know anything about Vikings?'

Nina was a little affronted. 'I'm the Atlantis expert, so why would I know anything about Alexander the Great or Ancient Rome, right? Archaeologists aren't fixated on one era from the moment they're born.'

Eddie laughed. 'No, you're fixated on *all* of 'em.'

'Logan had just as broad a grounding in history and archaeology as I did. And you too, I imagine,' she added to Tova, who nodded. 'We may have specialised in certain areas, but that doesn't make us ignorant of everything else.'

'All right, Jesus!' said Matt, holding up his hands in mock surrender. 'Didn't mean to impugn the entire archaeological profession.'

'And actually, there was a connection between the Vikings and the Egyptians,' Tova said. 'The Vikings' voyages were very far-reaching – they traded with Byzantium and the Caliphate of Baghdad, and are also believed to have had trade links with Egypt.'

'How far did they go?' asked Eddie.

'A long way. They reached the Americas centuries before Columbus, and also colonised Greenland and Iceland, travelled into Russia all the way to the Caspian Sea, deep into France and Germany – and Britain, of course. By the eleventh century they had settled most of England. Your own ancestors may even be Vikings!'

Matt put a finger to his chin, studying the Englishman with affected interest. 'You know, I can see that. Eddie the Balding.'

Eddie held up a warning finger. 'Oi.' His friend grinned. 'That's a pretty impressive amount of conquering, though,' he told Tova. 'Didn't realise they'd gone so far.'

'I guess you were only listening to the gory bits when they taught you about the Vikings at school,' Nina joked. He seemed confused. 'You know, when you learned about eitr?' she prompted.

'Oh yeah, yeah,' he replied, before quickly changing the subject. 'Anyway, Berkeley – a security camera caught him coming out of the museum with the guys who stole the runestone, so we know it's him. I suppose the big question is: why does he want it?'

'Maybe he just needs the money,' Matt suggested. 'The IHA fired him, his professional reputation's up the Swanee – he might want a nest egg.'

'But even if he's only doing it for the money, that means someone else paid him – and all the other people involved – to take the runestone and presumably decipher it,' said Nina. 'So why do *they* want it so bad? What do they think they'll find at Valhalla?'

Tova's flare of anger had subsided. 'Perhaps we will find out if we locate the second runestone.'

'In that case, I guess we'd better get cracking,' said Matt. 'And I've got just the thing for the job. I hope so, anyway – it'd be a bloody great waste if I'd had it flown all the way here for nothing!'

He gave the photo back to Nina, then led them to his pickup truck, dropping the tailgate and hopping into the bed. 'Here's my new toy,' he announced with pride as he pulled back the tarp. 'Ain't he a beaut?'

'If submarines are your thing, then sure,' Nina replied. The machine was a pale blue rectangular block around five feet long and three high and wide, thruster pods protruding from its sides. Gleaming steel manipulator arms were folded like insect limbs on each side of a 'head' containing cameras and spotlights. Painted along its flank was the word *NELSON*. 'So what does that stand for? Nautical Exploration, uh, Logistics Submersible . . . something beginning with O . . . no, I got nothing.'

'It doesn't stand for anything,' said Matt, amused. 'It's in capitals because I liked the font, that's all. It's just a name. You know, from Admiral Nelson?'

'Oh. Yeah. That works too.'

'But he's designed for endurance work, including under ice, so he should be just what you need. The OSO commissioned me to build him to work in the Arctic – give it a few years, we're going to see some major disputes over territory and drilling rights, so the UN wants to be able to check that one lot isn't slant-drilling into someone else's oilfield, that kind of thing. Full sea trials aren't scheduled for another few months, so I was able to borrow him.'

Eddie took for a closer look. 'How's it controlled?'

'Fibre-optic remote link.' He pointed at the head and its baleful mechanical eyes. 'Got 3D cameras, plus a LIDAR for longer-distance scanning. My usual bag of tricks. Endurance should be about twenty hours on a full charge.'

Nina glanced out at the frozen waters. 'How much of the lake will you be able to cover in that time?'

'It's a bloody long lake,' Eddie added.

Matt patted the fibreglass outer casing. 'He moves at a decent clip, no worries. And when you told me that what you're after probably has a lodestone set into it, well . . .' He crouched, indicating a black box mounted on an equipment rack at the bow. A long metal rod extended backwards from it beneath the craft's belly. 'That's the MAD.'

Tova raised her eyebrows. 'Why is it mad?'

'It takes after the bloke who built it,' said Eddie.

The Australian's round face creased into a half-grin. 'Cheers, mate. No, it stands for Magnetic Anomaly Detector. This one was designed to track pipelines; anything metal causes a change in the earth's magnetic field, and the MAD picks it up. If the lodestone's as big as the one you just showed me, it'll easily find it. It's just a matter of following a search pattern until something pings.'

'How soon can you start looking?' Nina asked.

'How soon can you chop me a big enough hole in the ice?' came the cheeky reply. 'He's fully charged, so I'll just need time to put up a shelter for the remote console and the support gear, then we use the crane to lower him into the water.'

Nina nodded. 'Okay, I'll tell Mikkel' – their Norwegian liaison and guide – 'and his people to start making a hole for you. Eddie?'

'Oh, for fuck's sake,' he said with a sigh. 'Don't tell me: I'm on ice-breaking duty, am I?'

'I don't think you'll be going out there with a pickaxe,' she assured him. 'I saw a couple of chainsaws in one of the trucks.'

His face brightened. 'Chainsaws? Oh, well, if you insist . . .'

Nina laughed. 'Okay – let's break the ice.'

To Eddie's annoyance – 'I've been conned!' he protested – Mikkel limited use of the chainsaws to himself and one of his small team, the Yorkshireman joining the other Norwegians in the more strenuous job of hauling out the blocks of ice cut from the hole in the frozen lake. But the operation was accomplished with practised efficiency, an opening twelve feet by eight being sliced into the surface before Matt had even finished assembling his equipment inside a pop-up tent.

At this time of year the ice was well over two feet thick, more than enough to take the weight of the crane truck and the remotely operated vehicle now suspended from it. All the same, its journey from the shore – Matt had picked a point sixty feet out from the lake's edge to be sure that the water beneath was deep enough for *Nelson* to manoeuvre – was made with great patience, Mikkel and his companions constantly checking how much stress was being put on the surface. Nina was unnerved by the squeals and crackles coming from under the truck's chain-wrapped tyres, but it made it to the hole without incident.

Matt came out to oversee the lowering of his charge into the frigid depths. 'All right, start bringing him down,' he called, once he was sure the submersible was well clear of the hole's edges. 'Gently now.'

The crane operator said something in Norwegian with a long-suffering tone, prompting laughter from his countrymen. Tova, who had strolled on to the ice with the unconcerned air of someone well used to the potential dangers, giggled. 'He said, "No, I thought I would drop it straight in,"' she told the Australian, who was not amused.

The ROV began its leisurely descent. Eddie walked out on to the lake to watch; Nina, still nervous about being on the ice, hesitantly followed. A stiff wind blowing down the lake made her shiver. Even though the sky was fairly clear and the sun was shining, it was still bitterly cold. She looked along the opposite shore. Nothing but snow-draped trees for miles in either direction. For the first time, the isolation of the location really struck her. If anything unexpected happened, they were a long way from help.

She tried to shake off the unsettling feeling as Matt called out, 'Okay, ease off! Release the cable!' *Nelson* was in the water. Everyone gathered around the hole to watch as he unwound a cable from a relay box he had placed on the ice, then hopped on to the submersible's back and screwed it tightly into a connector. 'Control line,' he explained as he returned to the ice. The relay box was linked via another cable to the remote controls in the tent. 'The spool's on the sub rather than the surface, so if the water freezes over, the line won't snag.'

'How long's the line?' Nina asked.

'Long enough, don't you worry!' He crouched to check the connection on the box, then stood, satisfied. 'Okay! I just need to run the diagnostics, then we're good to go.' An apologetic smile. 'Afraid that's where the boring part starts. No telling how long it'll take before the search turns anything up.'

'We are not far from where the old records said the Viking site was found,' said Tova. 'That is the most likely place for the runestone to be.'

'Well, if we find it in the first five minutes that's all well and good. All the same, you might want to have a Sudoku app on your phones.' He started back to the shore.

The others followed, the crane truck crawling along behind them. 'If there's a chance he might find it pretty quick,' said

Eddie, 'we'd better get the diving gear ready just in case. No point wasting time standing around when it's this bloody nippy.'

'I was planning on sitting in the truck where it's warm rather than standing out in the cold,' Nina replied with a smile. 'But are you sure you want to go down there? Peder and Mathias can handle it – that's why I brought them.'

'I've dived in worse than this,' he said, shrugging. 'And the more hands we have down there, the quicker we'll get the thing to the surface. It gets dark pretty early this time of year – it'll be a pain in the arse if we have to leave and come back tomorrow to start all over again.'

'You have not been on many archaeological digs, have you, Eddie?' Tova asked, amused. 'They usually take days, or even weeks. I think working for the IHA has made you think things always happen very quickly!'

Nina grinned. 'I'd love to have a nice long, slow, good old-fashioned dig in the dirt sometime,' she said, prompting an earnest shake of the head from her husband, 'but yeah, things do often tend to race away when the IHA's involved. Hopefully not this time, though.'

They reached the shore. While Matt went to the tent, Nina joined Eddie and the two divers as they checked their gear. They would not be wearing standard wetsuits, but insulated double-layer drysuits better suited to the frigid conditions. 'Sure you don't want to come down and see the thing first-hand?' Eddie joked to the two women, waggling the neoprene arms of his suit at them.

'Oh no, no,' was Tova's emphatic reply. 'I am not a good swimmer. And I do not like the cold.'

'But you live in Sweden,' Nina pointed out.

'Yes, and it is beautiful – in the summer!'

'There needs to be more archaeology on tropical islands,' said Eddie. 'You're in charge of the IHA, Nina – sort it out.' He checked the pressure on his gas cylinder: nitrox, a mix with much higher oxygen content than normal air. 'Okay, this is all set.' Peder and Mathias confirmed that their own diving gear was ready for use. 'Now we just need to find the thing.'

'That's up to Matt,' Nina said. They went to the tent. 'Is everything ready?' she asked, entering the little shelter.

'Keep that closed, will ya?' the Australian complained. 'It's bloody freezing in here!' He had a halogen heat lamp hooked up to the same portable generator powering his equipment, but was still huddled up tightly in his cold-weather gear. 'But yeah, *Nelson*'s ready to go.'

'Great. Do your thing.'

Matt regarded a map on a laptop, then checked another window on the screen before working the controls. A monitor showed the view from one of the ROV's cameras; the glare of the sky quickly disappeared as the machine submerged. 'Okay, I've switched on the MAD. I'll take him to the middle of the lake and start a radial search to cover the area you said was the most likely place to find this old village. If nothing turns up, I'll switch to a grid and move out from there.'

'Sounds good.' Nina watched a symbol slowly move across the map, then regarded the view from the on-board camera. The diffuse light coming through the ice was already fading to darkness as the submersible descended. 'Let's see what's down there.'

'If there is anything,' Eddie added from behind her.

She couldn't help thinking from his tone that he was almost hoping there was not.

★

The first hour of the search passed slowly, and fruitlessly.

The readings from the MAD turned out to be a source of frustration for the uninitiated. Within minutes, there was excitement as something distorted the background magnetic field enough to trigger an alert – but Matt dismissed it almost immediately as nothing more than a piece of inert metal rather than an actual magnetic source, and was proven correct when he took *Nelson* in to investigate. The sub's floodlights fell upon nothing more than a rusting boat anchor. Further signals turned out to be equally disappointing: a corroded car door, a piece of unidentifiable scrap. 'Told you to bring an app,' Matt told Nina after the fourth false alarm.

She was half wishing she did have something to pass the time, but all the same there was something oddly fascinating about the slowly changing view from beneath the surface. The valley had been as full of trees as the surrounding hills before it was flooded, and their remains were still there, standing in their hundreds like decaying grave markers. It was an eerie sight.

Eddie was less impressed. 'Bollocks to this,' he said, retreating from the tent. 'I'm going for a walk. Give me a shout if anything interesting turns up.'

Nothing did for the next hour. The Yorkshireman eventually returned to find the view on the monitor little changed. 'Found any more buckets?' he asked.

'Enough to open a bait shop,' Nina replied, stifling a yawn. 'And some bits of boats, something that looked like an engine . . .'

'No runestone, though,' Tova said glumly. 'And I am sure we started searching near the old archaeological site. Perhaps I was wrong, and it is not here at all.'

'Give it time,' Nina insisted. 'It's not as if they could get an exact GPS fix in the 1930s. If they were down in the forest and couldn't see any landmarks, they could easily have gotten their position wrong.'

'Yes, but by how much? The submarine is almost half a kilometre from where the search started. They would not—'

A chime from the computer signalled another find for the MAD. 'Hold on, this looks interesting,' Matt announced after checking the results. A graph displayed the readings as a series of fluctuating lines – one of which had just spiked considerably. 'Definitely not a bucket. This is something actually magnetic, not just metal.'

Eddie peered over his shoulder. 'You've found it?'

'Let's take a look . . .' The Australian worked the controls, guiding the ROV between the drowned trunks. The lake bed came into view in the spotlights. Silt deposits had built up over the decades since the dam was constructed, but several large rocks were still visible.

One stood out. Where the others were craggy, this had a more regular shape.

Nina felt a surge of exhilaration. 'Tova, look at this,' she said, moving aside so the Swede could get closer to the monitor. 'Is that the second runestone?'

Tova let out an audible gasp. 'It – it could be,' she stammered. 'I think it could be!'

Matt brought the submersible closer. The lights picked out features on the rock's flat face: lines scribed into the stone.

Runes.

'What about the other part of the compass?' Eddie asked. 'Is that there?'

The camera panned down. More runes were revealed, and an image below them – a stylised carving of a wolf. The beast was curled around something set into the surface beneath it . . .

'That's it!' Nina cried as darker stone came into view. Curving lines ran across the disc, notches cut into its edge. 'It's the other sun compass! We've found the second runestone.' She turned to Tova, who was gazing at the image with astonishment. 'And once we get it out of the water, it'll tell us how to find Valhalla.'

12

Vietnam

Chase drifted through a nightmare. He was trapped in darkness by endless trees, slimy trunks blocking every line of escape as his pursuers drew nearer. He tried to run, but his feet sank deeper into the cloying mud with every step. The trees closed in, branches wrapping ever tighter around him, covering his face—

He jerked awake, confused – then realised something *was* on his face. Barely holding in a startled yelp, he swatted away a centipede that had been exploring his cheek.

The sounds of the jungle surrounded him, an incessant chatter of insects and birds. He straightened, muscles and bones aching from the night spent curled up beneath the hollow log. The storm had passed. Shafts of bright sunlight cut through the canopy above to send up ghostly wafts of steam from the sodden ground. He was far from warm, though. His clothes were as damp as the soil, sticking unpleasantly to his skin. 'Welcome to the fucking jungle,' he muttered as he started to stand . . .

Memory forced its way through his mental fug. Chase

instantly dropped back down and grabbed the Kalashnikov, the weapon awkward and unbalanced without its magazine. His gaze darted over his surroundings, hunting for movement, danger . . .

Nobody was there. He was safe.

For now.

More cautiously, he rose again and peered into the open end of the log. 'Natalia? Are you okay?'

Matted blond hair slowly emerged from the folds of the camouflaged rain cape. '*Wo bin* . . . Where am I?' Natalia croaked as she squinted at the light.

Chase saw fear rising over her bewilderment. 'It's okay,' he said, keeping the gun out of sight as he raised his free hand to show that he was not a threat. 'It's me – Eddie, remember? Eddie Chase? I brought you here last night.'

Natalia stared up at him – then suddenly started to writhe against the claustrophobic confines of her shelter. She whimpered, crying out in German as her fists beat ineffectually against the mouldering wood. 'Hey, hey!' said Chase, trying to calm her. 'It's okay – I'll get you out of there.'

He reached into the log. She resisted his touch for a moment, before her own addled memory returned. 'You . . . were carrying me, we were in the rain.'

'Yeah, that's right.' Taking care not to catch her skin on any protruding splinters, he eased her out of the hiding place.

She looked around in alarm. 'Someone was chasing us! You – you had a fight with him.'

'I know. But we escaped. We're safe for now, but we need to get moving. I've got friends waiting for us, but I'll need to figure out where we are before we can reach them.'

He set her on the ground. She winced as one bare foot touched down. 'It hurts.'

'Lift it up.' Chase shouldered the rifle, then crouched to examine her foot. A small fragment of wood was stuck in her sole, the skin around it red and swollen. 'Hold still.' He carefully teased it out, blood beading in the little puncture wound. Natalia's face tightened, but she endured the discomfort. He retrieved his backpack from under the log and took out a first aid kit. A minute's work, and a bandage was in place, antiseptic ointment applied under it. 'That should be okay for now, but you'll need to have it checked by a doctor when we get out of here. Drawing blood in the jungle's never a good idea.'

'I know, I have been working here for four months. We—' She stopped, dawning terror on her face. 'We were attacked! They took us prisoner, they—'

'It's okay, it's okay,' Chase said, holding her as she began to shake. 'We were sent to rescue you. My mates got all the rest of your people out of there. We got cut off, but we'll catch up with them. I promise.'

Her trembling slowly subsided. 'What happened to us? We were driving to another village when the bandits blocked the road. They had guns, there was nothing we could do. They put a blindfold on me, and then . . .' Her brow furrowed as she struggled to recall events. 'I don't remember anything. I woke up, and . . . and I was with you.'

'You don't remember anything at all?' She shook her head. 'You were in a camp in the jungle. Your friends were being kept in a tent, but you were in a cabin, on your own. Do you remember that?'

'I don't know. I . . .' Another, deeper frown. 'There was a very bright light, in my face. And my arms hurt . . .' Natalia looked down at them – and gasped as she saw the bruises. She tried to pull away from Chase. 'What did they *do* to me?'

He eased his grip, but didn't fully let go, concerned that she would panic and try to flee. 'I don't know what they did. It looked like they were doing some sort of tests.' That reminded him of Hoyt, shooting the Russian scientist in cold blood and stealing his work, but this wasn't the time to worry about the traitor's true motives.

She froze. 'Tests?' she said, voice childlike, barely a whisper. 'Like . . . experiments?'

'I suppose, yeah.' She was still afraid, but something about her fear had changed. 'Do you know why they were doing it?' Her only reply was another shake of the head. 'Some of the people at the camp were Russians,' he reminded her.

'Russians, yes.' The knowledge was clearly distressing, but the reason was something she either did not want to talk about . . .

Or did not want to face.

Whatever it was, there were bigger concerns. He released her and checked his watch. It was slightly after eight in the morning. He used the angle of the sunbeams cutting through the trees to work out which way was north. 'We need to get moving. Can you walk?'

Natalia hesitantly put weight on her bandaged foot. 'I think so.'

'Good. If it starts hurting, let me know and I'll carry you. Ready?'

'Yes.'

'Okay.' He was about to set off, then paused, spotting something hanging from a nearby small tree. 'Who'd have thought, Hugo actually said something useful . . .'

'What are you doing?' Natalia asked.

'Getting you something to eat. I think they're called longans.' He plucked a bunch of orange-brown fruit from one of the branches. 'No idea what they're like, but a mate of mine from Belgium likes them, so hopefully German tastes aren't too different.'

He gave them to her. She looked uncertain, but hunger won out and she split open one of the small round fruits to test the pale flesh inside. 'Oh! This is good.' She devoured it and spat out the black stone, before giving Chase a sheepish look. 'Sorry. I am usually more polite . . .'

He grinned. 'Don't worry about being polite around me, love. But those are okay?'

'Yes, I have had them before, in one of the villages. I just had not seen them growing on a tree.'

'If you like 'em, then tuck in. I might even try one myself. Once you're full, I mean – you need to eat more than I do.'

Natalia opened another longan, nibbling at it with more decorum. 'Thank you.'

'No problem. All right, let's find a way out of here.'

He set off, heading north. Natalia followed, still eating.

Although Chase knew they were going in the right direction to reach the rendezvous, he was not sure of their actual position. He took out the map, but it was little help; no landmarks were visible through the dense jungle. 'We need to get to higher ground,' he said. The ground to the north-east rose up a slope. 'If I can see the landscape, I can figure out where we are.'

Natalia peered with interest at the map. 'The camp where you rescued me – where was it?'

He pointed it out. 'About here.'

'Let me see.' She took the map and examined it more closely. 'I know this place!' she said excitedly, tapping on a small black square marked with Vietnamese text. 'This is Ly Quang – the village where we were working before we were . . . before we were taken.' Her tone became more sombre. 'We were driving from it when they stopped our bus.'

Chase saw that the village was about two kilometres north-east of the camp, another few kilometres south of the highway. 'You got friends there?'

'Yes, yes! We were there for four days. We helped them – we gave them medical treatment, vaccinations.'

'Anyone there have a phone?'

'There is one telephone, yes.'

He silently debated the options. Sullivan had given him an emergency number; it would, hopefully, allow him to contact their Vietnamese driver, who had a satellite phone. If he reached Thuc, he could find out the status of the rest of the team and the hostages, arrange to be picked up – and warn Sullivan about Hoyt.

The danger was that the kidnappers would also know about the village. It would be an obvious place to search for the fugitives . . . or lie in wait for them.

'We'll try to get there,' he decided. The benefits outweighed the risks; reaching a phone would save them a longer trek to the rendezvous point, and he was confident he could spot an ambush. 'We just need to work out how.'

'Do you know where we are now?'

He waved a finger over the area east of the camp. 'Here, somewhere.'

Natalia regarded the map again, then indicated a spot south of the village. 'There is a tower on the top of a hill,' she said thoughtfully. 'It is from the war, the Americans built it. The people in Ly Quang told me about it. You can see it from the village – it is quite high. If we can see it too . . .'

'We'll know where we are,' Chase finished. He put away the map, then turned to her. 'How's your foot?'

'I am good, thank you.' She lifted her bandaged foot to examine it, pale skin almost hidden by dirt. 'It is . . .' She searched for the English word. 'Sore. But I will be okay.'

'Good. If you have any trouble, tell me.'

'Thank you,' she said again. Chase smiled, and they started up the hill. 'Mr Chase . . .'

'Eddie. Call me Eddie.'

'Okay. Eddie.' A coy grin, which quickly faded. 'Last night, you said my father sent you?'

'Yeah. Me and some other guys were hired to rescue you and your friends.'

'You are soldiers?'

'Used to be. We're mercenaries, technically. But the good kind.' The thought of Hoyt darkened his expression. 'Mostly.'

Natalia was too concerned with her own thoughts to notice. 'He does not know any soldiers, or mercenaries – and he does not have a lot of money. How did he afford to do this?'

'I dunno. But he's waiting for you in Da Nang.'

Her face lit up. 'He is here?'

'Yeah. And I'll get you to him. That's a promise. Once we're out of this bloody jungle, that is.'

They continued up the slope. Chase checked for any signs that their pursuers were nearby, but there were none, just the constant drone and flutter of insects and the calls of birds. Even though it was still early in the day, the heat was already rising. 'You told me the people who took me were Russians,' said Natalia, also thinking about her former captors. 'Do you know what they were doing to me?'

'No,' he admitted. 'They had you drugged, and they were taking blood samples. But I don't know what they were looking for, or why they were doing it.' He glanced at her;

the fearful expression, though veiled, had returned. 'Do you know?'

She clearly did, or at least had an idea, but it was equally obvious that she was unwilling to discuss it. 'If you don't want to tell me, that's not a problem,' Chase went on, giving her a reassuring smile. 'My job's to get you to somewhere safe, that's all.'

Her only reply was a quiet 'Thank you.' Deciding to let her talk again when she was ready, Chase plodded on up the steepening hill.

Before long, brighter daylight flared through the jungle canopy to the north. He angled towards it. The slope flattened out. Ahead, the ground dropped steeply away to reveal the lush green carpet of the rainforest spread out below. The hill was not high, but it was enough to clear the tops of all but the tallest trees.

He took out the map again. Now that he could see the lie of the land, it would not take long to work out their position. However, Natalia had already found a way to speed up the process. 'Look, over there!' she said, pointing to the north-east. Chase advanced until he had a clearer view and followed her gaze. There was a higher hilltop around three quarters of a mile away. A spindly tower rose from its summit. He guessed that it had been a radio mast. Decades of neglect had taken its toll, the top crooked and missing parts of its gridwork. 'The village is about a kilometre from there,' she continued.

He quickly translated the view to the map's two-dimensional grid. 'Okay, that puts us here,' he said, tapping the paper. 'If we go, let's see . . . east across the top of this hill and then follow it down, we can go round the bottom of the hill with the tower and head north to the village.'

'Wouldn't it be quicker to get to this road?' Natalia asked, indicating a thin line running south-east from Ly Quang.

'Yeah, but I want to stay in the jungle until I'm sure it's safe. The bad guys'll still be looking for us.'

Her face fell. 'Oh. Yes, I see.'

'Hey, it's okay,' he said, trying to perk her up. 'Once we reach the phone, my friends'll be able to come and get us.'

'What about *my* friends? Will they be safe?'

'They're probably on their way to Da Nang already. Those people at the camp looked like they were only coming after us.'

That produced mixed emotions. 'I hope they got away, but . . . that is not good for us, if they want me so badly, is it?'

'I'll do everything I can to get you back to your dad,' he assured the young woman. 'And the quicker we start moving, the sooner that'll be.'

They set off across the hilltop. 'You do not like to keep still, do you, Eddie?' said Natalia with a half-smile.

'Sitting around on my arse has never been my thing,' he said, amused. 'I like to *do* stuff, you know? Feel like I'm actually accomplishing something.'

'I know exactly that feeling,' she replied. 'It is one of the reasons why I came to Vietnam – to make a difference, to help. The people in this part of the country are very poor; they cannot afford even simple medicines and vaccinations that can save lives – and there are also after-effects of the war, even now.' She gestured in the direction of the radio tower, now hidden again behind trees as they began to descend the other side of the hill. 'The stupid fight between the East and the West brought nothing but misery to the people caught in it. I wanted to do something to make up for it.'

Chase gave her a curious look. 'Sounds like you take it personally.' He couldn't imagine why; she only appeared to be in her early twenties, barely old enough to remember the end of the Cold War.

Natalia shook her head. 'Not me, but my family. Some of them were involved in things that . . . I do not like.' She fell silent again.

He decided to let her stay quiet for now. The hill became steeper. He used the rifle as a makeshift walking stick, helping the young blonde down the slippery slope with his other hand.

It took several minutes for them to reach flatter ground. 'That is better,' Natalia said with a sigh. She wiped caked mud off one foot, then set off through the trees.

'Hold on,' Chase told her as he took out the map. 'Let me see where we are.'

'If we go north now, we will get to the hill with the tower,' she countered as she kept walking. 'Then if we go around it, we will reach the road, no?'

'I know, but I want to take the quickest route.' He used his watch's hour hand in relation to the direction of the sun to locate north. 'Okay, so . . . that way.' He pointed.

Almost directly at Natalia. 'You see? I was right all along,' she said, smiling. Chase shot her a sardonic grin and started after her. 'I told you, I have been here for four months. I have learned some—'

Click!

The sound was metallic, not the crackle of breaking wood.

'*Freeze!*' Chase yelled, trained instinct sending him diving to the ground even before the cry fully left his lips. 'Don't move! Whatever you do, *do not move!*'

A muted sound of pain escaped through Natalia's clenched teeth. She had started to lift her foot – but froze on his shout, forcing herself to hold still. Chase raised his head. Something was poking through the mud and rotten leaves, grubby metal visible beneath the young woman's sole.

Three narrow prongs jutting up from a dull green cylinder. The trigger and fuse assembly of a landmine.

'Stay still, stay *very* still,' Chase warned. He put down the gun, then crawled towards her. He recognised the particular type of weapon as he drew closer: an American M16A2 'Bouncing Betty'. Hundreds of thousands, maybe even millions, of similar mines had been laid during the Vietnam War, strewn throughout the jungles to hinder and kill the Viet Cong.

Many were still there. And still deadly.

Suddenly sweating, and not from the rising heat, Chase reached Natalia and examined the weapon. His SAS training had included mine defusal; the Bouncing Betty had been one of the types covered. He knew that, in theory, he could render it harmless fairly simply.

In theory.

In tropical conditions, an M16A2 had a life expectancy of twelve years. The Vietnam War had ended in 1975, so even if this particular mine had been laid on the very last day of the conflict, it was nineteen years beyond that. Time might have rendered it inert, moving parts rusted and clogged with mud, its explosive charge of tetryl broken down by microbes in the soil.

Or . . . it could have become so unstable that a hard jolt would detonate it.

Natalia whimpered again, from pain rather than fear. One of the prongs was digging deeply into her foot. There was no blood, so it had not broken the skin, but she didn't dare pull away. 'What is it?' she whispered.

Chase looked up at her. 'Natalia, I need you to stay calm, and keep very still. Okay? Promise me you'll do that.'

'I will,' she managed to say.

'Good.' He kept his gaze locked on hers. 'You've stepped on a landmine. Keep calm, stay calm,' he added as she tensed. 'It's not working properly, otherwise it would have already gone off. It's called a Bouncing Betty – it's meant to spring up in the air and explode after someone steps on it, but even if they keep their foot on it, it'll still blow up. This one hasn't, so the fuse is probably jammed 'cause it's so old. But if you move your foot, it might still go off – unless I defuse it.'

'Can – can you do that?' Her voice was trembling.

'Yeah. I can. I know it hurts, but stay still.' He finally broke eye contact, bringing his head right up to the mine and gently blowing damp leaves away from the fuse.

A small metal ring protruded from its side. If the weapon had been rigged to explode when a tripwire was pulled, the line would run through the ring, but there was no sign of one. That meant it was pressure-detonated. Natalia's footstep had triggered it – and now her weight was all that was holding it in check.

But was it a dud . . . or would any movement finally set it off?

He didn't know. All he could do was try to recall his training. 'Okay,' he said, speaking as much to keep Natalia's mind occupied as to focus his own thoughts, 'I know how to defuse it. There's a little hole where the safety pin went.' With great care, he used the tip of his smallest finger to brush dirt away from the fuse assembly, revealing a small circular opening in the side of a metal protrusion between the three prongs. 'I'll need to put something in it.'

A twig? No, too thick. It would have to be a piece of wire or similar, but where would he find one in the middle of the jungle? There was nothing in his gear—

Wait – there was. The radio headset. Its connecting plug was too large to fit the hole, but the wire itself . . .

'Keep still, I'm going to get up for a minute,' he warned. Natalia nodded. Chase moved back, then carefully rose to his knees. He pulled off the headset and used his thumb and forefinger to give the plastic-sheathed wire an experimental crimp. It seemed to hold its new shape.

With a nod of reassurance to the German, he took out his Swiss Army knife and unfolded the scissors to snip a short length of wire. He then got back down on his belly to begin his work.

Right away he saw there was going to be a problem. 'Natalia, I need you to keep still,' he said. Her foot – no, her whole body – was quivering. The prongs flexed under her weight.

'I'm trying,' she said, voice strained. 'But my foot is hurting – and my leg is shaking. I cannot stop it.'

'All right, okay. Er . . . where are you from?'

She was surprised. 'What?'

'Tell me about yourself, it'll help you stay calm. Where are you from?'

'Uh . . . I am from Hamburg.'

Chase waited a few seconds, but she said nothing more, and her shakes were not subsiding. 'I've never been there. Nice place?' he prompted.

'Yes, it is a beautiful city.'

'Do you have any brothers or sisters?'

'No, there is only me.'

The trembling subsided, slightly. Chase took that as a good sign and started the delicate task of sliding the wire into the hole. 'I've met your dad – what about your mum? Does she live there too?'

'No, she . . .' Sadness replaced fear in her tone. 'She died, a few years ago. From cancer.'

'I'm sorry. My mum died of cancer too.'

'I am sorry,' Natalia echoed. Another silence followed, but this time she broke it without prompting. 'My grandmother died from cancer also. She was Russian, she came to Germany in 1961.'

'What, she got out of Russia?' The wire was almost in the hole, but Natalia's shuddering was making the mine wobble. Chase used his other hand to brace the device.

'Yes. She was actually supposed to be taken to America with my grandfather, but . . .'

'But what?'

There was an odd – hardness? Bitterness? – to her words. 'He did not make it out of Russia. So my grandmother did not go any further than West Germany. My mother was born there a few months later.'

'Well, at least she made it to the right side of the wall.' The wire finally slipped into the hole. It was a tight fit; he slowly applied pressure to push it in deeper. 'West Germany sounded a better place to grow up than East Germany.'

'Yes, I suppose so.'

'You don't sound too sure.'

'East and West – they are both bad, in different ways. Not the people,' she quickly added, 'but the politicians, those in charge.'

'Can't argue with that too much.' The wire gradually disappeared into the hole. Chase kept pushing – but another thought had come to him. 'So . . . your grandparents were Russians? You think there's any connection to those Russians at the camp?'

Natalia drew in a breath, as if about to make a confession—

Click.

A much softer sound than before, accompanied by a tiny but

discernible amount of resistance that Chase felt through the wire. According to his training, the fuse should have been deactivated.

Should have – but then the mine should have exploded a couple of seconds after Natalia stepped on it. Its safety features might be as faulty as its detonator. He withdrew his finger. The wire stayed in place.

'Okay, Natalia,' he said. 'When I count to three, I want you to very slowly lift up your foot. Are you ready?'

The reply was barely even a whisper. 'Yes.'

'Right. Now, one, two . . . *three*.'

She hesitated – then raised her leg.

The spring-loaded prongs rose back into position . . . and stopped. No sounds came from inside the mine's casing.

It was safe.

An explosion did come, though – from Chase. '*Fuck!* Buggering fuck-bollocks arse and *shit*!' he cried, pent-up tension finding release. 'Fuck. Ing. Hell! God, I hate mines.'

Natalia still had one foot raised, balancing like a flamingo. 'Is it safe?'

'Yeah, it's safe. You can put your foot down now.'

She did so – and began to cry. 'I'm sorry. I should have been more careful . . .'

Chase bent the end of the wire to hold it in place, then unscrewed the fuse from the mine's body and carefully lifted it out. The metal was scabbed with rust; the trigger had jammed. 'Hey, it's not your fault, okay? Blame whichever arsehole dumped millions of mines in the jungle and then forgot where they put 'em.'

She shook her head. 'No, I should have known. When I was at Ly Quang, they warned us not to go too far into the jungle. One of the boys in the village lost a leg last year to an old mine.'

'The Yanks probably planted them to protect the radio tower.' He put down the fuse and sat up. 'This one should be safe now, though.'

Natalia wiped her eyes. 'Should be? Is there still a danger?'

'Depends how unstable the explosive is. It might have totally broken down by now, or it might go off if it takes a hard knock.'

'We cannot leave it like this, then. Another child from the village may set it off. Can you make it blow up from a safe distance?'

'Yeah – but a bang like that'll be heard for miles. The people who're after us'll know where we are. We'll just have to tell your friends in the village to watch out for it.'

'But we do not know exactly where we are!' she protested. 'The Vietnamese government has people who destroy mines when they are found, but they need to know their precise location.' She thought for a moment. 'If we take it with us, we can leave it near the village so it can be found and destroyed safely.'

Chase stared at her. 'You want me to pick up a landmine.'

'Yes.'

'And carry it through the jungle.'

'Yes.'

'While bad guys are still after us.'

'That is not a good idea, is it?'

'Nope. But,' he went on, 'you've got a point. We're not that far from the village, so there's a chance someone else might find it.' Another reason for taking the mine had occurred to him: if their pursuers found them again, it would give him an extra weapon – however dangerous – with which to fight them. For obvious reasons, he kept this to himself. 'So long as we're careful, we should be okay. The explosive in these mines can get unstable, but it's not like nitroglycerine or something – it takes more than just a tap to set it off.'

He bent down again and gently scooped the earth away from the mine's casing. There was a chance it could have been booby-trapped – a Vietnam-era tactic was to bury a live grenade beneath a Bouncing Betty so that if the mine were moved the hidden bomb would go off – but it didn't take long to confirm that had not been done here. A deep breath . . . then he raised the weapon out of the ground.

'Well, we're still here,' Chase announced after a moment. Natalia let out a nervous giggle. 'Okay, I'll carry it. You take the gun.' Her expression changed to one of concern, or even disgust. 'What?'

'I am a pacifist,' she said, regarding the Kalashnikov on the ground as if it were a venomous snake. 'I do not want anything to do with guns.'

'You want to carry the mine instead?' Seeing that she did not appreciate his sarcasm, he softened slightly. 'Look, it's okay – it's got no magazine, and the safety's on. Even if you pull the trigger, it won't fire.'

'It is not about whether it can fire. It is about what it was built to do. To kill people. I do not want anything to do with weapons of war.' Her resolve belonged to a much older and more world-weary person.

Chase's own view on the subject boiled down to *some people just deserve to be shot*, but this was something else he opted to keep to himself. 'Okay, I'll take 'em both,' he told her. 'I won't be able to carry you if you have trouble with your foot, though.'

She nodded. 'Okay. I did not mean to insult you,' she added, suddenly apologetic. 'You are a soldier, you use weapons as part of what you do. But it . . . it is not for me. I only ever want to help people, not do anything to hurt them. I hope you understand that.'

'Yeah, I do.' He smiled at her; she seemed a little surprised by his ready acceptance. 'What? I want to help people too, and it's not like I go out of my way to hurt anyone. Only an idiot, or a psycho, actually *looks* for a fight. It's just that sometimes, people do bad stuff and, well . . . a stern letter isn't going to stop 'em.'

Natalia regarded him uncertainly. Questions crossed her face, but the one that finally emerged was: 'Have you ever killed anyone?'

His reply was simple. 'Yes.'

'Were they doing . . . bad stuff?'

'Yeah.' He stood, still holding the mine. 'If you really don't want to carry the gun, it's no problem – I'll take it. But can you put the fuse in my rucksack? It'll be safe as long as the wire stays in place, but be careful with it anyway.'

She gingerly picked up the fuse and slipped it into one of his pack's outer pockets. 'What happens if the wire comes out?' she asked.

'Maybe nothing; it's all buggered up with rust and muck. Or it might go off. There's a gunpowder charge in it, enough to take off some fingers if you're holding it.'

There was a startled gasp from behind him. When he looked round, he saw that she had retreated by several steps. 'You want to walk in front of me?'

'Please.'

He grinned. 'If it hasn't gone off by now, it's probably not going to unless someone tries to make it happen. And I'm not going to do that, not while I'm carrying the bloody thing!'

The young woman did not seem entirely convinced, but still managed a faint smile. She picked up the AKS as if it were covered in thorns and handed it to him. 'Here.'

'Thanks.' He slung it over one shoulder. 'Okay, now which way were we going?'

Natalia pointed into the trees. 'That way.'

'Great. Let's get to this village of yours. Oh,' he said with a grin as they set off, 'watch what you're treading on this time, eh?'

13

Norway

Eddie emerged from a tent, rubbing his hands rapidly up and down his neoprene-sleeved arms. 'Buggeration and fuckery! It's a bit nippy.'

'I told you that you don't need to do this,' said Nina. She gave the tight-fitting drysuit a cheekily approving look. 'But you know, you look rather good in that.' Even though her own fitness regimen had started to slide of late, her husband worked out enough to keep himself in solid shape, muscles visible even through the layers of cold-water gear.

A smirk spread across his face. 'I've been saying *you* look good in tight rubber for years. If you weren't such a bloody prude, you'd buy that dress with holes in all the right places.'

Nina blushed as she realised they had an audience; Matt and Tova had just rounded the tent. The Swede widened her eyes, while the Australian's response was little more than a heard-it-all-before shrug. 'Ignore him, he's just joking,' she hurriedly said.

'No, no, it is quite all right,' Tova replied. She smiled at the couple. 'It is healthy to discuss your sex life – and keep it interesting.'

'Mm-hmm,' said Nina, blushing even more. Eddie cackled.

'So, *aaaanyway*,' Matt said, keen to change the subject, 'we've got all the IBUs ready. *Nelson*'s waiting in the hole in the ice – once you and the other divers load up his topside rack with the gear, you can just grab on and he'll tow you to the dig site.'

'You noticed how everyone says "the hole in the ice" and not "the ice hole"?' Eddie remarked, still grinning as he tugged the drysuit's hood up over his head. He put on his best Arnold Schwarzenegger voice. 'Fuck you, ice hooole.'

It got a smile from Matt, at least, but Tova didn't seem to understand what he had said, and Nina just gave a weary sigh. He snorted. 'Well *I* thought it was funny. So we're ready?'

'No time like the present,' said Nina. Even though it was only early in the afternoon, at this latitude and time of year they only had a few more hours of daylight. She started for the shoreline, the others following.

'Keep that burning,' Eddie said as they passed a campfire that Mikkel had started. 'I know we've got heaters in the tents, but sometimes a big roaring pile of wood's the best thing you can have.'

'Oh, don't you worry,' Nina told him. 'I'm going to spend the rest of the day sitting by it while you work. I may even toast some marshmallows.'

Eddie collected his nitrox tanks and a small toolbox. 'Yeah, right,' he scoffed. 'I know you better than that. You'll be looking over Matt's shoulder and getting annoyed that you can't micromanage us the whole time.'

'The man knows his wife,' Matt said, laughing.

Nina pouted. 'Shut up. Although yeah, he's totally right,' she admitted to Tova. The older woman grinned.

The group set out across the ice, joining Mikkel and the two IHA divers waiting at the hole. Eddie donned his breathing gear, weights and flippers, then attached the toolbox to his belt. Nina noticed that neither of the other divers had anything similar. 'What's in that?'

'Just some bits and bobs in case I need 'em,' came the non-committal reply.

'Like what?'

'Like the kinds of things you normally find in a toolbox. You know, *tools*?'

'Okay, jeez,' she said, a little taken aback by his waspish sarcasm. 'I just wondered.'

He didn't respond, instead pulling down his goggles before giving his mouthpiece one final check. 'Okay, I'm set.'

'We are too,' Mathias told him.

Eddie gave him a thumbs-up. 'Stand back if you don't want to get splashed,' he warned, before putting the rebreather into his mouth and hopping into the water. His head popped back above the surface a couple of seconds later, his wide-eyed grimace giving those above a clear indication of the temperature.

'You okay?' Nina called to him as the two other divers also dropped into the lake.

He gave her another thumbs-up, which then drooped to a more uncertain angle, but his expression assured her that he was not serious. The three men checked each other's gear to make sure the watertight seals were secure, then, with the aid of those still on the ice, loaded the buoyancy units on to the submersible. Once everything was secured, Matt headed back to his little shelter on the shore, Tova following him.

Nina stayed to watch her husband go. 'See you back here soon,' she said. His hand broke the surface to wave at her. 'And don't get cold – oops, too late.' The hand rotated to give her a two-finger salute. She laughed. 'Go on, get going,' she said, waving back. Eddie dipped beneath the surface, the two other men following suit. She watched them disappear into the darkness below, then returned to the shore.

'Jesus, Eddie was right,' Matt complained. His tone was light, but there was still an edge of genuine irritation.

Nina was indeed watching over his shoulder, gazing intently at the images from the ROV's cameras. 'Sorry, sorry,' she said, moving back – a few inches. 'It's just frustrating not being able to communicate with them.'

'Not being able to boss 'em around, you mean.'

'Well, yeah.' They shared a chuckle.

The main screen showed the runestone poking up from the lake's bottom, pinned by the hovering submersible's spotlights. The three divers had cleared away some of the silt, exposing more of the monolith – but while Nina and Tova's interest was in what was inscribed upon the stone, the men at the site were concerned only with securing high-tensile ropes around it. Three sets of lines connected by nylon webbing now encircled the slab; each line would have two lifting bags attached, which based on the weight of its counterpart would be more than enough to raise it to the surface.

One of the divers attached a hook to the ropework, then gave two thumbs-ups to the camera. 'Either they're ready, or Eddie's just seen a really good movie,' said Nina.

'Probably not one of Grant Thorn's, then,' Matt said; he too was acquainted with the Hollywood star. He zoomed in the camera, taking a closer look at the rigging. 'Well, Mathias and Peder know their knots, and I'm guessing Eddie does too, so all that seems nice and tight.'

Tova was still nervous. 'Is there any danger that the stone might be damaged?'

'Riskiest parts are going to be the moment it's actually pulled clear of the hole it's been stuck in for however many hundred years, and when the crane brings it out of the water,' Matt told her. On the screen, the divers swam to the ROV, then passed above its camera to reach the equipment rack. 'If it's going to break, that's when it's most likely to happen. But,' he went on, seeing her now decidedly worried expression, 'it looks pretty solid – there aren't any obvious cracks or anything. I don't think we'll have much trouble.'

'I hope not!' she replied, still not entirely reassured.

'They've done this sort of thing before, don't worry,' said Nina. All the same, she was feeling a degree of tension herself. It would not even take major damage to end their mission; if a small but crucial piece of the carved text sheared away and was lost on the lake bed, the search for Valhalla would end before it had even begun.

She watched as the divers reappeared on the screen, each now carrying an Inflatable Buoyancy Unit. In their empty state, the IBUs resembled bright orange sports bags with compressed air tanks attached; once filled, they would balloon enormously into sausage-shaped cylinders. They hooked them to the webbing, then returned to *Nelson* for the second set. Before long, these too were attached.

'Okay, they're ready,' announced Matt on a signal from one of the men, but Nina had already seen it; she had returned to her former position, peering over his shoulder like a pirate's parrot. He shook his head, then flashed the ROV's lights to indicate that the message had been received. 'Let's bring this thing up.'

The divers opened the valves on the air tanks. The IBUs unfurled, the creases in the tough PVC quickly smoothing out as they expanded. They rose in the water, the lines to which they were connected taking the strain.

Nina switched her attention to the lake bed. 'Matt, can you zoom in on the bottom of the stone?'

He did so. As they watched, the glutinous silt shifted. 'It is coming up,' Tova said, excited – but also tense. Nina felt the same.

'Not yet,' Matt told her. 'They've only got three two-fifty-kilo bags inflated at the moment, so it won't be enough to lift the thing. It'll take the weight off it, though. When they inflate the next three, *that's* when it'll really shift.'

'It's not going to pop out of the ground and shoot up to hit the ice, is it?' Nina asked.

Matt laughed. 'That'd be a hell of a sight, but no. They'll get it to neutral buoyancy so *Nelson* can tow it to the hole.'

'Great.' Reassured, she turned her attention back to the screen. Matt zoomed out again to follow the divers' progress. With the first three bags now pulling hard on the lines, they began to inflate the second set.

Before they were even half full, the lake bed surrounding the stone bulged visibly. 'It's moving, all right,' Matt said. 'The thing's going to come right out like a bad tooth. And speaking of teeth, will you stop doing that?'

Nina realised she had been grinding hers. 'Sorry,' she said, moving away from the Australian's ear.

Two of the men adjusted the IBUs' valves to slow the inflation. The third – Eddie, Nina realised – did nothing, until one of his companions gestured firmly for him to turn his own tank down. He did so . . . with what she couldn't help thinking was a degree of reluctance. 'What's the rush, Eddie?' she said to herself.

She was still close enough for Matt to hear. 'Maybe because it's bloody freezing down there?' he said with a grin.

'Well, there is that.' But she still felt there was something . . . *odd* about Eddie's response.

The IBUs kept swelling. Fissures appeared in the bulges on the lake bed, spreading outwards. Tova put a hand to her mouth, whispering in Swedish before adding, 'Oh, please be careful . . .'

'It's coming – it's coming!' Nina gasped. Part of the ground around the runestone's foot finally split apart, a wash of swirling particulates blotting out her view. The entire monolith shifted sideways – and then upwards.

'They've got it,' Matt reported. The two IHA divers made further adjustments to the valves. The runestone's ascent slowed, then stopped. 'They'll check there aren't any obvious stress fractures, then if everything looks okay they'll bring it up.' He looked round at Tova, whose expression was caught somewhere between panic and elation. 'Don't worry, should all be plain sailing from now.'

'Let's hope,' said Nina. She turned to Tova. 'We did it, though – you found the second runestone, and it's intact. It's an amazing discovery.'

'No, no, *we* found it,' Tova insisted. 'I couldn't have done it without you and the IHA.'

'And the OSO,' Matt added pointedly. 'It's not all about the archaeologists!'

'And the OSO too, thank you. But it is a joint effort.'

'It all started with you, though,' said Nina. 'It was your research, your find. I just helped out.'

'Well . . . okay, if you insist,' Tova said, finally breaking into a smile.

Nina looked back at the screen. 'Matt, if you get the sub in closer, we can take some photos of the runes. Just in case.'

Matt took the controls, flashing the spotlights to warn the divers that the ROV was about to move. Two of them swam clear, but the third stayed in front of the floating runestone.

'Come on, mate, shift your backside,' he said, with another flash of the lights.

Nina saw the toolbox attached to the man's belt. 'It's Eddie. Why isn't he moving?' Her husband appeared engrossed in checking one of the IBUs. 'Come on, honey, you're blocking the cameras!'

'I could extend one of the arms and bat him out of the way,' Matt suggested, less than seriously.

'Don't tempt me.' Eddie remained still. Matt brought *Nelson* closer and flashed the spotlights once more. This time, it got a response – though not the one Nina was hoping for. Eddie turned and waved sharply for the submersible to pull away.

'He must be worried about something,' said Matt. 'I'll back off to be safe.'

'Worried about what?' Nina complained. As far as she could tell, all the lines were holding firm, and the runestone itself seemed unharmed despite its extraction.

The Australian gave her an apologetic shrug. 'He's there and we're not – he's got the best view. Better safe than sorry, eh?' The image of Eddie and the runestone slowly shrank as he guided *Nelson* into a retreat.

Nina knew it was sensible not to take any chances, but she was still irritated. 'He could at least have moved so we could take a couple of pictures, dammit.'

All she could do now was watch impatiently as the divers prepared to bring the runestone up to the surface. They gradually pumped more air into the IBUs, using their own drysuits' buoyancy compensators to rise with them, until the ancient stone was about six feet beneath the ice covering the lake. Matt turned the ROV around so tow lines could be attached, then started the laborious trek back to the hole.

Nina checked her watch, then briefly pulled back the tent's

flap to look at the sky. 'The sun'll be down by the time we get it out of the water,' she lamented.

'So long as it's on the crane by then, it'll be fine,' said Matt. 'We've got plenty of lights, so they shouldn't have any trouble loading it on to the flatbed.'

'Yeah, but it'll be even colder than it is already.' The brief exposure to the outside air had been enough to make her shiver.

'Don't know why you think it's so bad. You're from New York, you're used to cold winters. I'm an Aussie – anything below twenty Celsius is like freezing for us!' Nina grinned, then resigned herself to a long wait as the overhanging ice slowly crawled past the camera.

It took well over an hour before the submersible and its cargo finally reached the hole in the ice. The sun was edging down to the western horizon, the sky reddening. Nina reluctantly left the shelter's warmth to watch the recovery operation as Mikkel and his team moved back on to the lake. They first used the crane to lift the ROV from the water and return it to the pickup on the shore, Matt reconnecting it to the controls in his tent so he could perform systems checks. Then they took the truck back to the hole. The runestone was manoeuvred to a position beneath the opening, and the divers pumped more air into the IBUs, little by little, to bring it up.

At last, the bright orange airbags broke the surface. The runestone's upper end followed, a rime filling in the inscriptions. Tova joined the group and peered expectantly down at the ancient text, trying to read it. 'It is so close! This is very exciting.'

Mikkel waved to the crane truck's driver, who extended its arm out over the hole. 'It should not take long to bring it out of the water,' he told the two women.

'Good,' Nina said, though her attention was now on the

divers as they breached the surface. A familiar face swam to the edge.

'Fuck me, it's cold down there,' said Eddie, pulling off his goggles. He rubbed at his cheeks with a gloved hand. 'Can't feel a bloody thing!'

'We kept the fire going for you,' Nina told him, kneeling. 'What were you doing down there?'

'What do you mean?'

'I wanted Matt to get some photos of the runestone, but you waved back the sub.'

His eyes briefly flicked away from hers. 'Didn't want it to get too close in case its backwash knocked the bags around.' He paddled back to the nylon nest between the IBUs. 'Just got to hook it to the crane and lift it out, and you can take as many piccies as you want.'

The operator got out of the cab and worked the crane's controls to lower the steel line. The hook on its end used to lift the submersible had been replaced by several chains, which the divers attached to the lines around the runestone. 'Okay, everything's secure,' Eddie called. Peder and Mathias swam to the edge of the hole and climbed out.

Eddie stayed in the water. 'Aren't you coming?' Nina asked.

'Just going to give this a last look over. You should get back to the shore before they start winching it up, though.'

'He is right,' said Mikkel, to Nina's disappointment – and also Tova's. 'We don't know exactly how much the stone weighs, so it is dangerous to be too close to the crane. The ice should be strong enough to support it, but you never know for sure.'

'I'll see you back there,' said Eddie as he re-donned his goggles. 'Chuck a few extra logs on the fire for me, will you?'

'Will do,' Nina replied. Still struck by the nagging feeling that there was something not quite right, she followed the others back to the shoreline. The crane driver put on a lifejacket, then on a nod from Mikkel activated the winch. The chains pulled taut, and the runestone began its slow ascent into open air.

Eddie arrived at the camp soon after Nina, having jogged across the ice. Frost crystals glinted on his drysuit in the light of the setting sun. 'The heater'd better still be on in that tent,' he said as he unhooked his breathing apparatus and set down the nitrox cylinder.

'Nah, mate, we turned it off to save power,' said Matt with a smirk. 'Gave your underpants a soak in some nice cold water too. That was what you wanted, wasn't it?'

'Ice hole,' Eddie retorted. He pulled off his gloves and warmed his hands over the fire, then detached the toolbox from his belt and dropped it to the ground with a hollow clatter. 'I'll be back out once I've got all my kit on,' he said to Nina as he opened the tent – then added, almost in warning: 'Don't go on to the lake.'

'See you soon,' she said, before turning to Tova. 'Did you manage to read the runes?'

'A few lines,' the Swede replied. 'I cannot wait to see the whole thing, though!'

'Me neither.' She looked back across the lake, watching the runestone's recovery. The orange sausages of two IBUs had risen above the surface, but the truck blocked most of her view.

Leaving Tova near the fire, Nina tramped a short way along the shore in the hope of finding a better angle, but the result was little better. 'Mikkel!' she shouted. The Norwegian, who was keeping watch on the ice beneath the truck, looked around. 'Is it safe?'

'It is okay so far,' he answered, 'but don't get too close to the truck.'

Keeping a cautious eye on the frozen surface, Nina made her

way towards the hole, circling around well clear of the crane to get a view from the side. The runestone's top was a couple of feet above the water, encrusted with frost. She could pick out some of the ice-filled runes.

What did they say? What was the secret they had been hiding for over a thousand years? She moved closer for a better look, wishing the crane would go faster.

More of the runestone emerged. One of the now unsupported IBUs drifted in front of the monolith; Nina moved again to keep the runes in view, now almost directly opposite the crane. Something glinted – a metal cylinder the size of a shampoo bottle, held in place against the black circle of the sun compass by the nylon mesh. She almost dismissed it as part of the rigging . . .

A frown. It looked more like it had been pushed into place after the stone was secured, the webbing stretched around it. What was it?

'Nina!'

Eddie's voice from the shore, urgent. He had changed back into his clothes – and was running past the startled onlookers on to the lake, waving his arms. Mikkel also heard the commotion and turned, surprised. 'Get away from it, get back!'

The Norwegian gestured sharply to the crane operator, who immediately stopped the winch and scuttled away from the truck. Mikkel retreated, eyes scouring the ice for cracks.

But he saw none. Neither did Nina. With the winch halted, an eerie silence had descended – with no alarming noises from the ice. As far as she could tell, everything was solid and stable. So why was Eddie nearly in a panic?

'Nina, get back!' he screamed again as he sprinted across the ice. Now suddenly scared, but unsure what to be afraid of, she edged away from the hole. 'No! Not that way, the other—'

His conflicting instructions caused her to freeze. He broke

off in frustration, changing direction as he passed the two Norwegians to head for the crane truck. Nina watched in astonishment as he ran past it – and made a flying leap from the edge of the ice, arms windmilling, to land with a heavy thump on the runestone.

The chains clattered as he grabbed them, the truck lurching with the extra weight. Frigid water sluiced up around the stone – and the Englishman's boots. He hauled himself higher and clawed at the metal cylinder. 'Nina, get to the shore! *Run!*'

'Eddie, what are you doing?' she cried.

'It's a *bomb*! Go, *go*!'

He pulled the object free and hurled it out towards the centre of the lake. Nina was still confused – but the word *bomb* cut through her bewilderment and she broke into a run.

Eddie leapt after her – but the unstable surface and lack of a run-up made him fall short. He hit the edge of the hole hard, legs splashing into the water. Gasping in pain, he clawed at the ice . . .

His gloved fingertips couldn't get a firm grip. He slid back into the lake, up to his thighs, his waist—

Nina skidded to a stop, then turned and raced back to him.

'No!' he yelled. 'Get out of here, go!'

She ignored him, grabbing his wrists and pulling. Her boots scrabbled for grip on the slick surface. Eddie kicked as she hauled him higher, managing to get one knee over the edge. He scrambled out. Nina almost stumbled as she released him. 'Are you okay?'

He jumped to his feet. 'Yeah – now *fucking leg it*!' he shouted, pulling her after him as he ran for the shore—

The deep crump of an explosion echoed around the lake.

Nina and Eddie both dived flat as churning water and chunks of shattered ice were blasted high into the air. They looked at each other in a mixture of shock and relief as they found they were unhurt – then shielded their heads as frozen debris hailed down around them.

'What the hell was— *Ow!* Son of a *bitch*!' Nina yelped as an icy lump bounced off her arm. She rubbed it, then fixed her husband with a look as cold as their surroundings as realisation sank in. 'You *knew* that bomb was there.'

He didn't reply, instead pulling her up. 'We've got to get off the ice. It might not be safe.' Mikkel and the driver were already hurrying towards land.

'I'll tell you what's not safe,' she snapped as they started back to the shore, giving the hole a wide berth. The runestone was still swaying on its chains, sending ripples across the slushy water. '*Bombs!*'

'If you'd run when I told you, it wouldn't have been a problem.'

She gave an incredulous laugh, pointing back to the site of the explosion. The blast had ripped a ragged opening in the ice almost six feet across. 'You think *that's* not a problem? If that had gone off on the runestone, it would have blown it apart—' She broke off abruptly, fragments of memory suddenly clicking together to tell a story.

The toolbox on Eddie's diving belt, empty as he discarded it; his blocking of the camera; then staying in the water to do something to the stone while everyone else left . . .

Nina stopped. Eddie continued for a couple of paces before realising she was no longer beside him. 'What're you doing?'

'I could ask you the same thing,' she said with barely contained anger. 'You didn't just know the bomb was there. You *put* it there.'

Hiding his feelings was hardly one of her husband's strengths, and she could see the conflict in his eyes. But the side that won was not the one she had hoped for. 'Dunno what you mean,' he said.

'Eddie, I *know* you did; it's the only possible explanation! You had it in that toolbox – it's the only way it could have gotten there. You put the bomb right over the sun compass so you could be sure it would be destroyed. And you deliberately blocked us from taking photos of the runes.' Her voice rose as the truth hit home. 'You're trying to make sure we can't use it to find Valhalla! Why?'

A strained shake of his head. 'I can't tell you.'

'Why not?'

'I made a promise.'

'To whom?'

Still conflicted, he opened his mouth as if about to confess . . . then turned away and resumed his walk back to the shore, head bowed. Nina followed, barely able to hold back her fury. 'Eddie? Dammit, *Eddie*! Talk to me! What's going on?'

'I've said as much as I can.'

'What is it? Some military secret? I know you won't talk about that stuff, but how can a Viking runestone have any connection . . .'

Nina suddenly saw that the people on the shore were reacting to something, looking west along the lake. As she fell silent, she registered a sound breaking the quiet of the snow-muffled forest. A rumble, getting louder, closer . . .

Eddie heard it too. His head whipped around to hunt for the source. 'Choppers,' he said. 'You didn't call 'em in?'

'No.'

'And they wouldn't have, so . . .'

'Who's "they"?' she demanded.

Again he didn't answer. 'Come on, quick!' he said instead. He grabbed her hand and ran.

'Eddie, what's going on?' She looked down the length of the

lake. The sun was a red sliver on the western horizon – and silhouetted against it were two dark shapes, the bright stars of spotlights beneath them. The helicopters were heading straight for the camp. 'Who are they?'

'Probably Berkeley's lot! They got the first stone – and now they want the other one.' A glare. 'And you bloody found it for them!'

'What? Don't you try to—'

'They killed that security guard, and they'll kill us too to get what they're after!'

They crossed the shoreline and ran to the waiting vehicles. The other members of the team were milling about, the combination of the explosion and the arrival of the helicopters throwing everyone into confusion. 'What is going on?' asked Tova, worried.

'Trouble,' Eddie told her, before raising his voice. 'Everyone into the trucks, now! We need to get out of here—'

Too late.

One of the pickups jolted with a harsh metallic *thunk* as something hit it, scabs of paint scattering like sharp-edged snowflakes from a thumb-sized hole in its bonnet. The echoing boom of a large-calibre rifle caught up with the supersonic bullet a moment later. A second shot followed, another truck taking a hit that ripped through its engine block.

'Cover! Get to cover!' Eddie yelled. 'Into the trees!'

The helicopters split up, one swinging out over the lake while the other swept along the shore. More shots came from the latter – the chatter of automatic fire. A couple of team members who had started to run for the forest hurriedly reversed direction as a fountaining line of bullet impacts stitched across their path. A third vehicle jerked on its suspension as a sniper round punched into its engine compartment.

'Shit!' shouted Eddie, looking in desperation for anything he could use as a weapon. Nothing presented itself. 'Mikkel! Where's your gun?'

The Norwegian had brought a .22-calibre hunting rifle to ward off bears and wolves. 'In the truck!' he replied, pointing – at the vehicle farthest from them. Anyone trying to reach it would have to run the gauntlet of gunfire.

Nina cringed as one of the choppers, a Jet Ranger, made a low pass overhead, kicking up a whirlwind of ice crystals. It slowed to a hover, turning to let the gunman leaning from one of its doors keep the expedition in his sights as it descended. The other aircraft, a larger Eurocopter EC175, swept over the hole in the ice as if checking that the runestone was safe, then it too moved in to land. The sniper kept his rifle raised, his targets now human, not machines. 'What do we do?'

Eddie gave her a grim look, then turned as if about to run for the trees – but Mathias set off first, only to stumble as another burst of fire crackled out. Nina gasped, thinking he had been shot, but then he recovered and scrambled back the way he had come. The shots had been a warning. The attackers didn't want them dead.

At least . . . not yet.

The two choppers touched down at opposite ends of the camp. The doors opened, men scrambling out to surround the expedition. All were armed.

Almost all, Nina corrected herself. The last man to emerge from the EC175 carried a briefcase rather than a weapon. He winced at the cold and tugged up the hood of his thick coat, then followed his companions to the little encampment.

Nina recognised him at once. 'Hello, Logan,' she said with undisguised disdain as he reached her.

Logan Berkeley sneered contemptuously back at her. 'Nina. I can't exactly say it's a pleasure to see you again.'

Eddie, meanwhile, was focused on the sixteen gunmen closing in around the group. His gaze suddenly snapped on to one in particular. Tall and wiry, with deeply sunken cheeks and a weathered tan . . .

The new arrival grinned malevolently, locking his gun on to the Englishman. 'Well now, there's a face from the past,' said Carl Hoyt.

14

Vietnam

'There is the road,' Natalia said excitedly, pointing through the trees ahead.

'About bloody time,' Chase grumbled. Their trek had taken longer than expected, partly because of the need to watch out for more landmines, but mostly because of the one he was already carrying. Even though he was now fairly confident that the explosive inside the rusted casing had decomposed to harmlessness, there was still just enough doubt in his mind to encourage him to handle it very carefully.

They emerged into bright daylight. The road was nothing more than a muddy track, but tyre ruts told Chase that it was reasonably well used. Nobody had driven along it so far today, though; branches dislodged by the previous night's storm were scattered all over, and none had been crushed into the wet soil. The search for the fugitives might not have reached this far – yet.

He was still wary, though. 'Keep to the grass along the side,' he warned Natalia. 'So you don't leave a trail.'

The young woman took heed and stopped at the roadside.

She looked in each direction. 'The village is . . . that way,' she announced, pointing to the left.

'You're sure?'

'Yes. Both roads out of it go up hills.'

The pair set off down the slope. Before long, they encountered the first signs of a settlement: scattered garbage in the undergrowth. 'That's civilisation for you,' Chase said with a wry smile.

To his surprise, Natalia became defensive. 'They do the best they can,' she said. 'They have so little – no money, and the land here is not good for farming. They cannot afford to take their trash to be recycled.'

He remembered a comment his late grandfather had once made – 'You're never too poor to pick up after yourself' – but decided she wouldn't appreciate the piece of Yorkshire wisdom. Instead, he asked, 'How many people live here?'

'About eighty. It is only small.'

'And you stayed here for, what, four days? Wouldn't have thought it'd take that long to give everyone a jab.'

'A jab? Oh, a vaccination. No, we treated everyone who needed one on the first day. But we were doing other things also. Actually, that was the reason I came to Vietnam, not just to give out medicine.'

'Yeah?' Chase was about to ask more when he saw movement ahead. Someone was walking up the road. 'Get down,' he growled, sidestepping into the concealment of the undergrowth.

Natalia laughed. 'It is okay – I know him!' She waved, calling out in Vietnamese.

'No, the guys looking for us might— Oh, for fuck's sake.' Seeing the man waving back, Natalia ran to meet him. Chase carefully put down the mine and raised the rifle, senses on alert for any signs of danger.

There were none. Natalia spoke to the man, who appeared delighted to see her, then waved for the Englishman to join them. Still annoyed, he collected the Bouncing Betty once more and followed her. 'All right, who's this?'

The man's happy expression quickly became one of trepidation when he saw the mud-splattered, gun-toting Westerner advancing on him with a landmine in one hand. Natalia hurriedly gave him what Chase guessed was an assurance that he wasn't a threat. The villager – he seemed quite elderly, though given his hardscrabble lifestyle it was possible he was only in his late forties – didn't seem completely mollified, but his face at least now displayed more curiosity than fear.

She kept talking. The man reacted in surprise to something she said, an intense exchange following, then he gestured for them to follow. 'He says to come with him to the village,' Natalia told Chase. 'They will help us.'

'Ask him if anybody's been there today asking about us,' he said. She did so, getting a shake of the head in reply. 'That's something, then.'

It only took another five minutes before they entered Ly Quang itself. The settlement was not impressive, just a small cluster of shacks near a riverbank. Most of the structures were wood and thatch, though some were partially built of corrugated metal. The storm had inflicted damage, people patching up holes in the roofs of several houses.

Chase was more interested in something else: telephone poles, running along the road heading north out of the village. The line ended by one of the largest buildings, a single cable leading down to it. 'I need to use the phone,' he said.

Their arrival had already attracted attention. Everyone seemed genuinely pleased to see Natalia, even if their reactions to her travelling companion were more uncertain. Chase made a point of shouldering the AK across his back out of easy reach, though he kept hold of the mine – which encouraged the villagers to keep their distance. After sharing greetings with everyone, the German had a brief discussion with one of the men, then turned to Chase in disappointment. 'He says the telephone is not working. The storm took down the line – it could be days before it is repaired.'

'Arse chives,' he muttered, looking down at the Bouncing Betty. 'They won't be able to call anyone to deal with this either. What do they normally do with mines if they find 'em?'

Another rapid conversation. She smiled at the Englishman. 'They usually go to a safe distance and throw stones at them until they explode. They think you are crazy for carrying one all this way.'

'Christ, you try to do a good deed . . . So what do I do with this?'

'There is a place by the river where you can leave it,' she told him after getting an answer. 'They will make sure nobody goes near it.' A young man, beaming broadly despite missing several teeth, stepped forward. 'Thanh will take you. You can leave the gun there too.'

Chase was less happy about that, but nevertheless went with the smiling youth to deposit the weapons amongst some rocks, taking the detonator from his backpack and leaving it beside the mine. By the time he returned, the reunion had moved into one of the houses. A middle-aged woman signalled for him and his guide to come inside.

'You weren't kidding about having friends here,' he said on entering. Natalia sat on a rug, older villagers looking on with amusement as several laughing children clung to her. One boy had a crude prosthetic leg below the knee. The young German had replaced her filthy medical gown with a donated wraparound skirt and a faded T-shirt bearing the logo of some Vietnamese product he didn't recognise, as well as a pair of sandals.

'I wanted to work with children,' she replied, grinning. Then the smile faded. 'And when I heard what had happened here, that made me want to help them even more.'

'What *did* happen?'

Natalia spoke to two of the women, gesturing towards Chase. They regarded him with suspicion, but a plea eventually drew reluctant nods. 'I told them you are English, not American,' she said. 'The people here, they . . . they try to forgive for the war, but it is hard.'

'Is it something to do with the landmines?' he asked.

A deep sadness crossed her face. 'Worse than that.' She spoke to each of the children, managing to pluck them off her one by one before standing. 'I will show you.' One of the women rose as well. 'But I have to warn you, it is . . .' She paused, searching for the correct word. 'Upsetting.'

Unsure what to expect, Chase followed them out of the little house to the building where the telephone line terminated. The Vietnamese woman opened the screen door and called out, getting a reply from someone inside.

They entered. Insects flitted around an electric light hanging from the ceiling; he heard the flat puttering of a small generator somewhere outside. A woman in her thirties, pretty but tired far beyond her years, greeted them. A curtained doorway led to an adjoining room. The sound of a softly crying child came from beyond it.

The woman pulled aside the curtain. Natalia gave Chase a look of both warning and apology. 'Please, do not be afraid, or . . . disgusted. They are children, they have done nothing to deserve this. The people here do everything they can to help them.'

'What happened to them?' Chase asked.

Natalia stepped through the doorway and nodded for him to follow. 'Come and see.'

He hesitated, then entered the next room with her.

What he saw would haunt him for the rest of his life.

There were five beds, each occupied by a child. Their ages ranged from around three years to twelve.

All were terribly, cruelly deformed.

Chase now knew why Natalia had issued her warning. His first response to the sight was an instinctive revulsion – followed at once by shame at his own feelings, then sadness as he realised the extent of their suffering. One child had stunted arms and a hugely swollen, lopsided head, dark eyes peering pitiably out from an unnaturally wide expanse of skin. Another's jaw was only partially formed, a gaping hole in her cheek exposing gums and the twisted roots of teeth. The youngest of them had no limbs at all, just gnarled stumps. Her entire skull was stretched almost to a point, eyes bulging, her small chest rising and falling rapidly as she struggled to draw in each breath.

'Jesus,' he whispered, a shiver coursing through him despite the heat. He had witnessed plenty of death in his military career, bodies smashed and mangled in horrifying ways, but the knowledge that these figures were still very much alive made their injuries – he wasn't even sure that was the right word – all the more disturbing.

Natalia went to each bed in turn. The children recognised her, responding with sounds of delight. She smiled back, hugging and caressing, speaking softly in Vietnamese. The woman who had come with them spoke; Chase didn't understand her words, but could tell from her tone that she was expressing gratitude.

'We brought them things for the children,' Natalia explained. 'Medicines, mosquito nets, food, toys . . .' She gestured at a doll on a small table beside one of the beds. A photograph was pinned to the wall above; it showed the young German hugging the little girl in the bed, who was clutching the plastic figure. 'We gave them as much as we could, though it was still not enough. There is never enough,' she added sadly.

The Englishman suspected that he knew the cause, but felt compelled to ask all the same. 'What happened to them?'

'Chemical warfare. Agent Orange.' Chase nodded; he had been right. 'The Americans dumped millions of litres of poison on the jungle during the war, without caring for a moment what effect it would have on the people who lived there. Or even their own soldiers. The children of American troops have suffered deformities and cancers because of what their fathers were exposed to . . . but nothing like this. The poison is still in the ground, in the water and plants, everywhere. And the children are paying for it, even after all this time.'

'I'm sorry.' It was all he could say. He could barely begin to imagine the horror and heartbreak the parents must have been through when their children were born.

She looked up at him, tears in her eyes. 'This is why I came here, to help children like this. There are many more in other villages in this part of the country. I wanted to do as much as I could for them. I *had* to.'

Chase sensed an almost confessional tone to her words. 'Why?'

She looked away, gently touching the head of the smallest child. 'Because . . . because I am a part of what happened to them.' Before he could ask what she meant, she went on: 'And because I am *one* of them.'

She stood and turned, pulling up the T-shirt to expose the left side of her torso to him. In the jungle, the gown had covered what lay beneath; now he got a clear, chilling view. A twisted scar ran from below her armpit almost to her waist, smaller branches lancing off it around her chest and back. 'I had tumours removed,' Natalia said, seeing his shock. She pulled the shirt back down. 'The doctors did not know what caused them. But I did.'

She said goodbye to the children, then spoke briefly to the Vietnamese women before going back outside. Chase went with her, blinking in the bright sunlight. 'What was it?'

She did not answer the question at first, wiping her eyes as they wandered through the little village. 'My mother had the same tumours. So did my grandmother. They both died from them. I will too.'

'You don't know that,' said Chase, unsettled by her matter-of-fact acceptance.

'Yes,' she sighed. 'I do. It is my family's curse, and the reason why I must never have children of my own – because they will suffer it too.'

'What do you mean, your curse?'

There was a makeshift bench by one building, a plank supported by two old oil drums. Natalia took a seat, then beckoned him to join her. 'My grandfather was a man named Serafim Volkov,' she began as he sat and put his pack down under the bench. 'He was Russian, a scientist in the Cold War. He was going to defect to the West with my grandmother, but died before he got out of Russia.'

Chase nodded. 'Yeah, you said.'

'He gave my grandmother a letter, only to be opened if he did not escape. She told my mother that she did not open it for over a year, in the hope that he was still alive. When at last she did, she thought it would tell of his love for her and his hopes that their child would have a better life in a new country.' She paused, taking a mournful breath. 'It did not.'

'What *did* it talk about?'

'His work. What he had been doing for the Soviet Union – and what he planned to sell to the Americans. He was creating weapons. Awful, terrible weapons.'

'Chemical warfare?'

'Yes. And biological too – the difference is sometimes small. That was true of what he had created.' A pause as she shook her head. 'No, that is the wrong word. He did not create it. He . . . *exploited* it. It was something the Russians had found.'

'What kind of thing?'

Another pause. Natalia stared silently at the ground before finally looking back at him. 'Do you know anything about Norse mythology, Eddie?'

'You mean like Vikings?' he asked, surprised by the change of subject. 'Not really. I never paid much attention in history class.'

'I did. My mother encouraged it, especially to do with Norse legends. I did not know why until just before she died. But there is a substance in their myth called eitr. It is a black liquid, a deadly poison . . . and it is also the source of life.'

He frowned at the contradiction. 'How does that work?'

'In the myth, there was a sea of eitr, and from the drops of a splash rose the first giant, Ymir. From him came all other life. But the eitr remained, still a poison, hidden beneath the ground.' Her expression became grave. 'The Russians found it. There was a Viking runestone in the Arctic at the entrance to a pit full of eitr. My grandfather wrote the first lines of the runes in his letter; they told how the Vikings had travelled from Valhalla across a rainbow bridge and through a lake of lightning to fight a giant monster and prevent the end of the world.'

'You mean the legend's *real*?'

'No – not really. I do not believe there were giants and gods and serpents that circled the whole of the earth – the blood of the serpent was eitr, and in their legends it was what killed Thor. But it is based on something that *was* real. The eitr was deadly, but it also had . . . other effects. My grandfather discovered them. He was trying to turn the eitr into a weapon the Soviet Union could use against the West, but began his own experiments – which he was going to take to America.'

Each word seemed to weigh her down a little more. Chase realised that something awful was coming. 'What sort of experiments?' he prompted.

'Human experiments,' she whispered. 'On my grandmother. He used her to see what eitr would do to a living person – and her unborn child.'

'Shit,' he said, shocked. 'He actually poisoned his own wife? While she was pregnant?'

'He was an evil, evil man.' A new tear ran down her cheek. 'I am ashamed that I have anything to do with him.'

'It's not your fault. But why did he do it?'

She raised her head. 'The eitr is not just a poison, even though according to his letter just a few drops on the skin can kill a person – they tested it on prisoners.' Utter disgust and loathing twisted her features for a moment. 'In smaller amounts, it is a . . . a *mutagen* is I think the English word. It causes mutations in DNA, sometimes huge. My grandfather believed these mutations could be controlled to create a new breed of human. Supermen, a master race.' Another expression of revulsion, this time at the connections to her own country's past. 'The Soviets only cared about turning the eitr into a weapon, so he continued his work in secret. After testing on animals, he put a tiny amount into my grandmother's food to see the effect it would have on people.'

'And it gave her cancer?'

'And eventually killed her. But because it caused mutations at a genetic level, they were passed down to my mother while she was still in the womb – and then to me.' She looked down at her side, one hand tracing the line of the scar. 'The tumours appeared when I was sixteen. They almost killed me – I was in hospital for half a year. By the time I came out, my mother was suffering from them too. But with her, the doctors could not risk removing them; they were too advanced. All I could do was – was watch her die.' She sniffed, wiping her eyes again. 'I am sorry, it is still hard to talk about.'

'That's okay,' said Chase, with deep sympathy. He had been through the same terrible experience with his own mother.

'Thank you. Oh . . .' She released a long, sighing breath, then looked round as the child with the prosthetic leg hobbled up and hugged her tightly, chattering and laughing in Vietnamese. Natalia managed a smile, giving the excitable boy a kiss on the forehead before sending him back to his mother. Another sigh. 'I love children, I do. But I can never have any of my own – it is too dangerous. That is my family's curse, Eddie. My grandfather poisoned us for ever.'

'Christ. I'm sorry. I can't even imagine what it must have been like to find out.'

'My grandmother gave the letter to my mother on her deathbed, telling her the truth about how they had come to Germany,' Natalia continued. 'The CIA was supposed to take her out of Russia, first to West Germany and then on to America. But when my grandfather did not make it, they abandoned my grandmother. She had to make her own life in a new country. Which she did – until the eitr at last killed her. My mother kept the letter, but did not tell me about it. Until she too was on her deathbed.'

'If she'd told someone what was causing the tumours, couldn't they have done something about them?'

The young woman shook her head firmly. 'We did not want

to tell *anyone* about my grandfather's experiments, or the eitr. That was something my grandmother made my mother promise, and she made me promise. It is a promise I meant to keep. I did not even tell my father.'

'But you're telling me now.'

'Someone else already knows.'

Chase glanced towards the jungle. 'The Russians?'

'It is the only possible reason why they would have taken me. They want to start the experiments again.'

'So why would they want you? Couldn't they just go to wherever they found this eitr stuff and get more?'

'Because it was destroyed. My grandmother worked out what must have happened. The letter said the eitr was discovered on Novaya Zemlya, off northern Russia.'

'That was where the Russians tested their nukes,' he remembered.

'Yes, but a research facility was also built where they found the eitr. That was where my grandfather worked. I do not know the details, they were not in the letter, but there was an accident involving the eitr. Many people died. Khrushchev ordered the project to be closed down. That was when my grandfather decided to defect, and take his research with him. But he needed a sample of eitr to give to the Americans. There was only one place he could get it – the pit in the Arctic. So his plan was to go in secret to the facility to steal some, then the CIA would get him out of the country. He never came back. A nuclear test took place on the same day.'

'So . . . you're saying they *nuked* the place?'

'They must have wanted to be sure that no one would ever have the eitr. They dropped the biggest bomb ever made—'

'The Tsar Bomb.' Chase saw her questioning look. 'I paid attention to *military* history.'

'But you did not know the real reason why they dropped it, did you? It was to destroy the facility, and the eitr. I read about the results of the explosion. Nothing was left – even the ground was melted.'

'I still don't get why they'd need you, though. It's not like you've got eitr running through your veins.'

'No, I do not. But . . .' Natalia stared at the ground again, deep in thought, before continuing. 'I have been *exposed* to it. Through my mother, and my grandmother. My DNA has been mutated by the eitr. If these Russians had samples, they could compare them to normal DNA and find out *how* it had been mutated. That could tell them enough about what the eitr does to create more, or create something that has the same effect.' She turned back to him, fearful. 'They want to *use* me. They want to take what my grandfather did to me, and turn it into a weapon. Eddie, that cannot happen! I will not let it.'

'It won't,' he assured her. 'I'll get you out of here, I promise.'

'That is not a promise you can keep!' she cried. 'They are still hunting for us, they must be – if I am so important to them, they will not let me escape. If they find us—'

He put a hand on her arm. 'I won't let them take you.'

'How? With what? A broken landmine and a gun with one bullet?' She straightened, suddenly resolute. 'The bullet – you must keep it for me.'

'What?'

'I am serious. You saw those poor children in there.' She jabbed a hand towards their building. 'That is what chemical warfare did to them, and that was just a – a side effect. Agent Orange was created to kill plants; they did not even think about what it would do to people. But if the Russians create more eitr, it will be as a weapon of deliberate mass murder. Anyone who is exposed to it will die, either from the poison or the mutations

211

it will cause. I will *not* allow that. It is against everything I believe in. If I let it happen, I would be as evil as my grandfather! It cannot happen. It cannot.' She began to cry again. 'Promise me *that*, Eddie. Promise me that.'

'I am not going to promise to put a fucking bullet in your head, Natalia!' he said, dismayed. 'But I'll stick to the promise I already made. I'll get you out of here, trust me. It'll take a bit longer since the phone's out, but once I meet up with the others at the rendezvous, we'll take you somewhere safe. These Russians won't get hold of you.'

'But they are working with the Vietnamese, they must be,' she protested. 'The man you knocked out . . .'

'Yeah, I know. One of my mates reckoned they were secret police – something called TC2.' From her stricken expression, he guessed their infamy was widely known. 'But they won't catch us either. You know I said I was a soldier?'

'Yes?'

He gave her a small but meaningful grin. 'I wasn't just some squaddie. Trust me, I'll—'

He snapped his head around at a sound from the north. An engine. Someone was driving down the track into the village. 'Oh, fuckeration. Time to go!'

'Do you think it is them?' Natalia asked as he jumped up.

'I'm not taking any chances that it's not!' He looked up the hill. The vehicle was not yet visible, but he glimpsed flickers of colour between the trees as it approached. The land around the village had been cleared, making their chances of escaping before the new arrivals spotted them slim. 'Did you tell the people here what happened to you?'

'Yes, but—'

'Are they your friends?'

'Yes, absolutely, but—'

'Then tell 'em we need to hide!'

He ran with her to the nearby villagers. Natalia hurriedly spoke to them, then cried, 'Here, quickly!' She and Chase rushed for the building that was home to the Agent Orange victims, one of the Vietnamese women going with them. A call drew out the woman inside. Natalia exchanged rapid words, then the nurse bustled them into the children's room.

The only hiding places were under the beds. The woman led Natalia to one of them, then gestured for Chase to get under another. He dropped to his belly and slithered beneath it. There was barely enough room, his back touching the slats supporting the thin mattress; he realised at once that it was also too small to conceal him fully. Even if he positioned himself to be hidden from someone coming through the door, if they walked past the bed he would be visible.

Natalia, smaller and slimmer, was better covered, but the most cursory search would expose her too. She gave the Englishman a fearful look across the grubby floor. One of the children made a sound, excited at seeing the young blonde again, but the carer quickly hushed him.

The vehicle drew closer. For a moment Chase thought it was going to drive straight through the village, but then it downshifted rapidly before stopping. He heard voices, a man with an unmistakably commanding tone calling out.

Natalia tensed. 'It is the men from the camp,' she whispered. 'He is asking if they have seen any foreigners. They are telling him no, but . . .'

The sudden silence as the new arrivals switched off their vehicle's idling engine was a clear sign that they were not convinced. More words were exchanged. 'He says he is from the government,' she continued. 'And that . . . Eddie, he is telling them that you have kidnapped me!'

'Let's hope your friends don't believe him,' was his grim reply.

She kept listening to the unfolding discussion. The voices of the villagers became agitated. Were they going to give the fugitives away? Chase checked the room for other possible exits. A window with a half-open shutter, some uneven planks in one corner that might break if charged with enough force . . .

Natalia's breathless whisper brought his gaze back to her. 'They are still saying they have not seen us!'

Chase strained to listen, trying to read the emotional state of those outside from their voices. If the villagers were *too* insistent about not having visitors, it would arouse suspicion.

Had they convinced the secret police? Or would a house-to-house search be ordered? Chase looked back at the window, working out the quickest route to his weapons by the river . . .

'They're going,' Natalia gasped. The commander issued orders with grudging acceptance. His men climbed back into their vehicle. 'My friends did not give us away. I knew they would help us.'

Chase remained silent. The man was still talking; he guessed he was reminding the villagers of their duty to report any sightings of the kidnapper and his prisoner. Their replies sounded like assurances that they would. One of the women called out, 'T m bi t,' which even after only a short time in Vietnam he knew meant 'goodbye'. They had done it . . .

A child's chatter and laughter caught his attention. It was the one-legged boy who had hugged Natalia earlier, scurrying from one of the houses to see the new visitors. His mother shouted for him to come back, but he was already in the middle of the group, asking excited questions. Chase held in a sound of irritation. The kid was going to hold up the secret police's departure—

Natalia's sudden look of horror warned him that he was doing more than that. 'What?' he whispered.

She waved him to silence, listening intently. The commander was speaking again, but now in a much more amiable tone. The boy laughed and gave him a happy reply. The other villagers were conspicuously silent.

'He's asking if he's seen me,' she told Chase, frightened. 'He calls me "the girl with yellow hair", and – and he said yes!'

'Shit,' Chase hissed. Outside, the car's doors opened again. Still sounding friendly, the commander asked another question. The boy's response was enthusiastic.

Too enthusiastic. He hurried to the door of the building, calling out. Natalia swallowed. 'He told them I'm in here!'

Options flashed through Chase's mind. He didn't like any of them. Both potential escape routes would put them only a matter of yards from their pursuers, but if he tried to stand and fight he would be outnumbered and outgunned—

Out of time. The boy ignored his mother's pleas to come back to her and entered the building – then the room. Behind him, Chase saw tough leather boots beneath khaki trousers. The commander. A second man, then a third, followed him. One of the children in the beds made a sound of fearful surprise at the sight of the strangers.

Adrenalin surged through the Englishman's body as the boy limped towards him, then stopped – but not by his bed. Nor Natalia's. The boy eagerly beckoned the commander to look at something.

One of the other men chuckled quietly, drawing an irritated exhalation from his superior. He spoke to the boy again, now more patronising than friendly, then issued an order. The three men turned and clomped out of the building. The boy went after them, still asking questions.

Natalia started to crawl out from under her bed, but Chase waved for her to remain still. He waited until the car had restarted and driven away before finally signalling that it was safe for her to move. Hands shaking, she slowly emerged. 'What happened?'

Chase had already got to his feet and found the explanation. 'You *were* in here, and he brought them to see.'

The realisation made her laugh, though it was a pure release of tension rather than humour. 'So I am,' she said, gently touching the photograph of herself. 'Oh God, I thought they had found us . . .'

'So did I.' He took a slow breath, trying to calm down. 'It's too risky to stay here – they'll probably come back. They know that you knew about this place, and since it's the nearest village, they'll expect you to come here sooner or later.'

'I cannot let anything happen to my friends because of me,' she said, nodding. 'You are right, we have to go.'

A thought occurred to Chase. 'Bollocks!'

'What is it?'

'The mine. We can't leave it for a bomb-disposal guy to deal with – they'll know we were here.'

'How?'

''Cause they'll realise that someone with training did their job for them. And I'm guessing that even if we're long gone, it won't be good for your friends if anyone finds out they sheltered us.'

'It will not,' said Natalia gloomily. 'It is getting better, but . . . it is still not a free country. So what do we do?'

'We'll have to take the bloody thing with us. Once we get to the rendezvous, I'll blow it up just before we leave.' He went to the window and pushed open the shutter. The villagers were clustered outside, several still staring anxiously up the road after the departed vehicle. 'You say bye to your friends while I get the mine and my gun. Tell 'em thanks from me too.'

'I will,' Natalia replied. She began to say goodbye to the children.

Chase left her, giving hurried gestures of gratitude to the people outside before retrieving his rucksack and jogging back to the river. The Bouncing Betty and the AKS were still there, untouched. He shouldered the rifle, then carefully picked up the mine and detonator before starting back to the village. A flustered Natalia met him on the outskirts. 'I told them that if I get caught, I will not tell them I went to the village,' she said. 'But I—'

'We won't get caught,' Chase cut in firmly. 'I'll take you to the rendezvous, and then we'll be out of here. We just need to get across the river.'

She pointed downstream. 'There is a shallow place where we can cross. It goes to a track on the other side.'

'Great.' He had already memorised the relative positions of the village and the rendezvous on the map; the journey through the jungle would take only a few hours. Cradling the landmine in the crook of one arm, he led the way along the riverbank, Natalia right behind him.

15

Norway

Nina stared coldly at her former colleague. Though only in his late thirties, a spell in jail had aged Logan Berkeley considerably, a streak of grey in his brown hair and deep creases around his eyes that were definitely not the product of laughter. There was also a lump in his nose – though that had come from Nina's fist rather than incarceration. 'So, Logan, you mind telling me what all this is about?' she demanded, struggling to hold back her anger. 'Robbing museums, armed raids on archaeological digs – I guess this makes you a recidivist, since doing jail time apparently didn't change your ways.'

'My *ways*?' Berkeley snapped. 'You forced me into this, Nina!'

'Nobody forced you into anything.'

'No? Everything bad that's happened to me in the past two years is entirely your fault. You ruined the opening of the Hall of Records and turned me into an international joke, and then you got me locked up in an Egyptian prison!' His nasal New England accent was still filled with an arrogant superiority despite his misadventures. 'You destroyed my career – I'm doing what I have to do to get by.'

'You got locked up in an Egyptian prison because you were paid by a cult leader to raid a lost pyramid!' Nina hooted. 'As far as I'm concerned, you got off lightly. And if you wanted to "get by", you could always have tried finding, y'know, a job. Not hooking up with a gang of thieves and murderers.'

That last shook the other archaeologist. The lines on his face deepened as he frowned. 'What are you talking about? Nobody's been murdered.'

'Enough of this,' Hoyt interrupted, lighting a roll-up. 'Let's just get the stone, huh? Since they brought it up for us.' He looked out across the frozen lake. 'Axby, Silver, go check that the ice is safe, then winch it up.' Two of his men jogged away.

'What the fuck are you doing here, Hoyt?' Eddie said, regarding the American with undisguised loathing.

'I'm still in the game, Chase. I get hired to do jobs, and get paid big bucks for doing them. Just like you used to – well, except for the big bucks part. You never did get paid for Vietnam, did you?'

'Put down that gun and I'll kick what I'm owed out of your arse,' the Englishman growled. Hoyt's only reply was a mocking smirk, his compact FN P90 sub-machine gun still covering its target.

'Eddie, who is this guy?' Nina asked.

'His name's Carl Hoyt,' her husband replied. 'He's a backstabbing, murdering shithead I had the bad luck to work with about eight years ago.'

'A mercenary?' He nodded. Nina faced Hoyt. 'Who are you working for? And what do you want?'

Hoyt's oily smirk widened slightly. 'Client confidentiality, darlin' – I can't tell you that. But we're here for the stone, that's all. We got the first one already, and we want to complete the set.'

'You're trying to find Valhalla, aren't you? Why?'

'What part of "confidentiality" didn't they teach you at archaeology school?' The mercenary looked around at a shout from the crane. 'Raise it up!' he called back. The runestone resumed its rise out of the frigid water.

'So what're you going to do with us?' Eddie demanded.

'We're not going to do anything,' Berkeley said, before Hoyt could answer. 'All we want is the runestone.' He stepped closer to the fire, leaning forward to warm his face.

Nina considered kicking him into the flames, but the sight of the guns forced her to settle for shooting her rival a scathing look. 'So you waited for us to find it, then came in to steal it?'

Berkeley straightened, responding to Nina's jab with considerable indignation. 'Believe it or not, Nina, I was perfectly capable of translating the runes and deciphering the location of the second stone on my own.' He huffed, plumes of breathy arrogance blowing from his nostrils into the cold air, then addressed Tova. 'Sorry about this, Dr Skilfinger, but I'm only doing what I have to do.'

'What you have to do,' Tova echoed bitterly. 'So you think you had to kill Arvid to take the first stone?'

Again Berkeley was thrown by the accusation. 'What do you mean?'

'Oh, didn't your friends tell you, Logan?' said Nina, her voice acidic. 'They killed a security guard at the museum when you stole the runestone. You're an accessory to murder. Forgot to mention that, did they?'

The archaeologist rounded on Hoyt. 'Is this true? Did your people – did they *kill* someone?'

'Afraid so,' he replied, though without a trace of remorse on his hard face. 'He came at us out of nowhere. We didn't have any choice.'

'That is not true!' Tova protested. 'The police said he was shot in the back!'

'While he was going for an alarm,' the mercenary told Berkeley, still with no more concern than if he had been discussing the weather. 'But it happened, and wishing won't make it un-happen. We're here to do a job, so let's get on with it, huh?' He raised his gun slightly for emphasis. 'Dr Berkeley, you might want to go check on the stone before we bring it ashore. Make sure these guys actually know their shit and found the right one.'

Berkeley blinked in momentary confusion, still shaken by the revelation. 'What? Oh, yeah, right. Is the chopper ready to load it?' He gestured at the EC175.

'Soon as you get it to 'em,' Hoyt replied. Berkeley nodded, then started for the lake.

'And what about us?' Nina asked loudly, making sure the retreating man heard her. 'Are you going to kill us too?' Berkeley paused, looking back at Hoyt for an answer.

The mercenary's face tightened. 'You don't give us any trouble, we won't give you any trouble. We just want the stone.'

That satisfied Berkeley, and he continued out on to the ice. The crane had by now lifted the runestone fully out of the water. Nina watched its ascent, fury and frustration churning inside her. She gave Eddie a sidelong glance. His expression was one she had seen many times before: guarded, giving little away about his thoughts – but she knew that behind the mask, he was taking stock of their captors, searching for weaknesses. Getting ready to attack.

All he needed was an opportunity . . .

There was not going to be one. As if reading his mind, Hoyt stepped back, then ordered his men to widen the cordon around the prisoners. 'Don't do anything dumb, now,' he said, the remark aimed directly at the Englishman.

'Wouldn't want to steal your thunder,' Eddie replied. If he had been hoping to provoke Hoyt, the attempt failed; the mercenary merely smirked again, keeping his P90 fixed on his one-time comrade.

Nina turned her attention back to the lake. Berkeley opened his case and took out an expensive camera, snapping several pictures of the ice-crusted runes before signalling to Hoyt's men. One stopped the winch, the other climbing into the crane truck's cab and gently revving the engine. Ice crunching beneath its wheels, it began its ponderous return to the shore.

Berkeley walked ahead of the vehicle, leading it to the larger helicopter. Hoyt nodded to some of his men. 'Help him get it loaded,' he ordered. They hurried off. Nina saw a subtle shift in Eddie's stance as he watched the remaining men spread out to keep their prisoners covered. The odds had shifted – only slightly, but she knew from past experience that he was a master at exploiting any advantage.

But there was still nothing he could do. The gunmen were standing too far away for him to tackle without being cut down.

The sun was finally gone, the sky's twilight glow fading to leave the campfire as the brightest source of illumination. More lights came on inside the EC175 as Hoyt's men extended a sturdy winch arm out from the cabin, ready to receive the runestone. The monolith itself had now made landfall, the crane truck lumbering to the waiting aircraft and backing up to it. More chains were attached, these connected to the chopper's winch. With Berkeley issuing instructions and warnings to be careful, the heavy stone slab was slowly brought into the cabin.

Matt watched the transfer ruefully. 'So we put in all that work bringing the thing up, and these guys just swoop in like seagulls and steal it?' He eyed Hoyt, lowering his voice to say to Eddie: 'There's got to be something we can do, mate.'

'There isn't,' came the curt reply.

Hoyt gave Eddie a sneering look. 'Nobody to help you out this time, Chase. Although with the way you show your gratitude, that's probably a good thing!'

The Englishman scowled. 'Shut up.'

'Why?' Hoyt came closer, though he still kept his gun fixed on Eddie. 'Oh, I get it. You didn't tell anyone what really went on in Vietnam? Can't say I'm surprised – if anyone knew what happened to the people you were supposed to be protecting, you might have had trouble getting work.' He glanced at Nina. 'She's your wife, yeah? Amazed she's still alive with you looking after her. You tell her about it?'

Eddie glared at him, avoiding Nina's questioning gaze. 'Nothing to tell.'

'Oh, I dunno. She might wanna find out what you're really like.'

'I know what he's like,' Nina said.

'You know what he *did*, though? Might change your—' He broke off at a shout from the helicopter, backing away from Eddie before turning. The runestone was now secured in the Eurocopter's cabin. The driver moved the crane truck well clear of the aircraft and got out. Berkeley signalled to Hoyt that everything was ready, then clambered into the helicopter. Its engines started up, the rotors beginning their slow rise to take-off speed. The Jet Ranger also whined to life.

'You've got what you came for,' said Nina. 'Are you going to let us go?'

Hoyt turned back to face the prisoners. A nasty smile creased his fleshless face. 'Nope.'

'Didn't think you would,' Eddie growled.

'That was just for Berkeley, to keep him on side. We need him to translate the stone and figure out how to find Valhalla, but I knew from the first minute I met him he wouldn't have the stomach for anything more. Like getting rid of witnesses.'

Panic ran through the group. The men surrounding them stepped closer, bringing up their guns. Tova gasped in terror.

Despite the fear coursing through her, Nina managed to summon up some defiance. 'You're just going to mow us down?' she asked, hoping that Eddie was planning some way to fight back. But he seemed oddly calm. Not *accepting* of the situation – more waiting for the right moment to act. She couldn't see what he meant to do, though. 'I think Logan'll hear that even over the chopper.'

'No he won't,' Hoyt replied. 'Garrow?'

One of the gunmen reached into his coat, taking out a chunky black metal cylinder. He slid it over his P90's muzzle, locking it into position with a sharp click. 'Silence is golden,' the mercenary leader said with a smirk.

One of the Norwegians cried out in horror as Garrow raised his weapon. Nina tensed, muscles tightening as her fight-or-flight reflex kicked in, but she could do neither. Beside her, Eddie's gaze flicked over the men surrounding them, but he still didn't seem about to take any action . . .

'Do it,' said Hoyt, nodding at Garrow. The P90 rounded on Nina—

A whipcrack sound, and a hole the size of a coin appeared in Garrow's forehead – as the entire back of his coat's hood blew outwards in an eruption of gore.

Now Eddie moved, lunging at the dead man as he collapsed and snatching the gun from his nerveless fingers. Hoyt's other men were still frozen in shock by the unexpected attack – then one of them broke through his paralysis and swung to cut down the Englishman.

Eddie was faster. The stolen P90 bucked in his hand as he swept it around and pulled the trigger, the suppressor reducing the gunshots to dull clacks. The mercenary and the man next to him fell backwards as the spray of automatic fire stitched bloody lines across their chests.

'*Run!*' Eddie yelled. He tracked Hoyt, but the American dived behind a truck before he could shoot. 'Get to cover!'

Nina had already responded, seizing Tova by the wrist and pulling her past the fire to drop down behind another crippled vehicle. Matt ran in a different direction, scrambling into the little shelter containing the submersible's controls.

Mikkel was also quick to respond, pushing Peder behind a 4x4. But some of the team were as stunned as the mercenaries, left gawping as the bodies fell around them.

It cost them their own lives. One of Hoyt's men finally snapped back into motion and opened fire on the group as it splintered, slicing down two of its members and turning to find more—

A burst of Eddie's bullets ripped into his stomach. He fell, screaming.

The Englishman was now the mercenaries' primary target. Another gunman rounded on him—

A second sniper round punched through the man's chest and exploded out of his back.

Eddie had already realised from the supersonic crack of the first bullet that the unseen shooter was on the far side of the lake. One of the mercenaries was slower on the uptake, head darting from side to side as tried to find the source of the gunfire. Two shots from the silenced P90 brought an abrupt end to his search.

Eddie ducked behind a truck, giving his weapon's translucent plastic magazine a momentary glance to check the remaining ammo – about half of the original fifty rounds – before rising to locate Hoyt.

The American was running for the larger helicopter. 'Take off, take off!' he yelled to the pilot. 'Get the stone out of here! The rest of you, give us cover!' More members of his team jumped out to join the battle.

Berkeley looked on, horrified. 'What happened?'

Hoyt leapt into the cabin. 'Chase grabbed a gun and started shooting,' he lied, before turning his attention back to the pilot. 'Go on, go! Take off! Get the—'

He ducked as bullets hit the fuselage, aluminium splinters spraying around the cabin. Berkeley shrieked, the men outside diving flat. The mercenary leader didn't need to look to know who was shooting at him. 'Chase,' he growled, before yelling: 'Kill him!'

Eddie hurriedly took cover against the front of the truck as the mercs from the EC175 shot back. Bullets tore through sheet metal with harsh clanks, the 4x4's windows shattering. But he knew the front wheel and engine block would protect him; the 5.7mm bullets of the P90s were designed to penetrate flesh and body armour, not thick steel and cast iron.

The gunmen closer to him were a bigger concern. The survivors had regrouped. Fear of the sniper was keeping them down, but a glance warned Eddie they were now moving through the camp to hunt down the remaining expedition members. He spotted Nina and Tova in the firelight, sheltering by another vehicle. 'Nina! They're coming towards you!' he shouted. He was about to shoot at the approaching mercenaries when one of them zeroed in on the sound of his voice and opened fire, forcing him to jerk back.

Another whipcrack, and a scream. The sniper was still finding targets. The other mercs scrambled into cover.

One hunkered down behind the pickup holding the submersible. He pressed against its flank and edged forward to get line of sight on his targets.

He spotted Nina and Tova, who were moving in a crouch towards the lake in response to Eddie's shout. His P90 came up, glowing cross hairs lining up on the redhead as his finger curled around the trigger—

The pickup jolted against him as he fired. The shot missed Nina's head by inches, smacking into the truck behind her. She yelped and threw herself back.

The mercenary cursed. It felt as though someone was moving around the pickup bed, causing the vehicle to rock on its suspension. He raised his gun to kill the interloper—

A gleaming steel claw clamped around the P90's barrel and squeezed.

The mercenary flinched in surprise, instinctively pulling the trigger – and his gun exploded as the bullet hit the crushed metal, the blowback of trapped gases ripping the weapon apart. He fell on to his back, screeching as red-hot shrapnel sizzled in his arm and chest.

In the shelter, Matt worked the remote controls to open the submersible's claw and drop what was left of the ruptured P90. He had switched on the ROV's cameras to get a view of what was happening outside, and spotted the gunman taking aim at Nina just in time to extend one of the manipulator arms, rocking the pickup. 'Too bloody close,' he gasped.

Nina stayed low, not willing to risk moving into the open again. Beside her, Tova had closed her eyes, whispering fearfully in Swedish. 'Hey, it's okay, it's okay,' said Nina, trying to reassure her companion – and herself. She crawled to the back of the truck, looking over the diving gear propped against its tailgate for any movement beyond the nearby fire.

One of the mercenaries stared straight back at her.

She gasped and hurriedly retreated – as a bullet hit the ground in front of her, sending up a spray of snow. Tova screamed, curling into a tight ball against the side of the truck. Nina heard the crump of footsteps in the snow. The mercenary was coming for them.

The fear returned. She had nowhere to go, no weapons . . . .

No. She *did* have a weapon. *Knowledge*, of what was in the tank leaning against the truck.

She lunged forward again and knocked the cylinder over, twisting the valve at its head fully open. A shrieking jet of compressed gas blasted out – and the crackling campfire suddenly became an inferno.

The high oxygen content of the nitrox fanned the flames enormously, as if she had thrown a can of gasoline on the fire – and the force of the gas jet itself blew them outwards from the blazing pile of wood like a flamethrower. Before the mercenary could bring up his gun, the fireball had swallowed him.

Nina cringed back from the wave of heat. For a moment, all she could hear was the piercing hiss of the nitrox cylinder and the roar of flames, drowning out even the noise of the helicopters – then a horrific scream rose above all else. Completely shrouded in fire, the mercenary ran blindly past her towards the lake.

But there was no water there to extinguish the flames, only ice. He threw himself on to the surface, skidding for a few feet before coming to a stop, writhing and shrieking in helpless agony. The sight was so shocking that those on the shore could do nothing except stare – until the heat of the man's burning clothes and skin weakened a stress line in the ice. The mercenary abruptly vanished with an icy splash, as if some lake monster had dragged him under, leaving wafts of steam swirling in the cold air.

'Jesus!' Nina gasped. 'Fire *and* ice – paging Robert Frost!'

Matt was also watching the grisly spectacle on his monitor, rotating *Nelson*'s camera pod to track the running man to his doom – until something rose to obstruct the image.

Despite his injuries, the mercenary behind the pickup was not out of the fight. The exploding gun had shredded and scorched his sleeve, his wounded hand dripping with blood . . . but being ambidextrous was apparently one of his talents, as he raised the other to yank a savage-looking knife from a sheath.

Matt swung the robotic arm again, but the man easily jinked past the metal limb. Face contorted with rage, he advanced on the shelter. 'Aw, hell,' gulped the tubby engineer as he followed him with the ROV's cameras, only to realise too late where he was going. The man on the screen lashed out at the canvas flaps – and the knife ripped through the real ones. 'Aw, *hell!*'

He stumbled back into the corner of the little tent as the injured gunman pushed his way inside. 'Try to kill me with a fucking *robot?*' the mercenary snarled. He raised the knife. 'Let's see how tough you are when you're facing me for real!' He stepped closer—

'Matt!' Eddie's voice, close by. '*Down!*'

Matt dropped – and bullets puckered the fabric wall above him. The mercenary spun back, arms flailing as rounds tore into his upper body.

Matt released a shuddering breath of relief. 'Thanks, mate,' he called out.

'No problem,' came the reply.

'How did you know I'd ducked?'

'I didn't, I just hoped you had.'

'Oh.' The Australian blanched.

Eddie allowed himself a small smile – he had seen Matt's silhouette against the canvas in the glow of the heater – before becoming deadly serious once more. He shifted position to look back at Hoyt's helicopter. The EC175 was almost at take-off revolutions, kicking up a stinging vortex of snow and ice crystals. The mercenaries from it had spread out, but were no longer advancing. Instead they were holding position in whatever cover they could find on the frozen shore, hiding from the sniper – while protecting Hoyt and his prize. Even Eddie's brief glance was enough to draw fire, forcing him back as more bullets hit the truck.

The second helicopter was still squatting on the ground, waiting for its passengers. 'Nina!' he shouted over the racket. 'How many more of them are there?'

'I don't know!' she yelled back. 'Only one or two, I think!'

One or two too many. The only thing keeping them at bay was the threat of the sniper – and the fact that the helicopter carrying the runestone hadn't come under attack suggested to Eddie that their unseen guardian was on the move. It wouldn't take the mercenaries long to realise the same thing.

He checked the P90 again. About a quarter of its bullets were left, twelve or thirteen rounds. He would have to make them count . . .

The Eurocopter finally left the ground, engines straining under the extra weight of the stone slab. Even so, it would be beyond the sub-machine gun's effective range in under thirty seconds.

Now or never—

Eddie dived out of cover, throwing himself flat and bringing up the P90 to blaze away at the ascending helicopter on full auto.

The bullets found their target. One of the aircraft's windows cracked as an armour-piercing round tore through it, another shot visibly sparking as it struck the solid block of the engine beneath the thin aluminium fuselage. He couldn't see the results of the other impacts in the darkness, but he could tell from nothing more than the feel of the gun's recoil that they were tightly grouped – most, if not all, had hit.

But they had done nothing.

The chopper was still climbing, tipping into forward flight as it ascended. No smoke, no sprays of oil or hydraulic fluid. He hadn't hit anything critical. And now he was out of bullets, exposed on the ground as the mercenaries moved—

They weren't coming for him. Instead, they ran for the second helicopter, using the encampment and vehicles for cover against the sniper. Eddie scrambled back behind the truck. The P90 was empty. The dead mercenaries had dropped their weapons, but he would be exposed to their comrades' fire if he tried to retrieve one.

He still had to find some way to fight. Hoyt's men weren't fleeing. They were going to take off and hunt down the survivors from the air.

He needed a weapon . . .

What he found was far from ideal, but desperation left it as the only option.

Bent low, he scurried to the truck that had brought the underwater lifting gear. The unused inflatable buoyancy units were still in its rear bed, along with their air cylinders. He hauled one out. A glance towards the Jet Ranger warned him that the last mercenaries were piling aboard – and in the firelight he saw the barrel of a sniper rifle protruding from an open door.

The same gun that had disabled the expedition's vehicles was about to be turned on its members.

He ran for the crane. 'Get everyone behind the trucks!' he shouted to Nina. But he knew that would not give them much protection once the chopper was airborne. He only had one chance to stop it – and even that was slim.

But he had to take it.

Eddie reached the crane, hitching the IBU to one of the dangling hooks before darting to the winch control and disengaging the brake. He started the motor, then ran back and snatched up the bright orange bag, more of the cable unspooling behind him. He stayed low behind the other vehicles for as long as he could – but knew he would have to cross open ground to reach the helicopter.

'Hope this fucking cable's long enough,' he muttered, crouching behind the last 4x4 to draw in a breath . . . then sprinting for the chopper.

Ice and grit blasted his face as the Jet Ranger went to full take-off speed. It rocked on its skids as the rotors took its weight. He arced towards it, coming in from behind.

The rifle swung at him—

The Englishman dived to the cold ground and rolled as a bullet ripped through the air above him. Another gunman leaned out, P90 tracking him – and firing. The tail rotor buzzed above Eddie's head like a circular saw as he scrambled under the helicopter's rear boom, the vortex pummelling him. The gunfire stopped as the mercenary lost line of sight on his target, but he was already shouting a warning to his comrades on the other side of the cabin.

More guns came up—

Eddie slammed open the valve and hurled the IBU through the open door.

It hit one of the mercenaries hard, the steel cylinder knocking him back – then the tough orange bag snapped open with mousetrap speed as it filled with air.

One end wedged against the door frame – and the dazed

mercenary suddenly found himself being forced back into his seat with a pressure that grew more crushing with every moment.

The helicopter took off. One of the men on the other side opened fire on the camp, bullets cracking off the vehicles as the archaeological team took shelter behind them.

A second gunman on Eddie's side, Silver, leaned out further and took aim—

The rapidly swelling airbag shoved him as he fired. The bullet blew a little crater out of the snow mere inches from Eddie's skull as he rolled again.

Silver tried to line up another shot – only to realise with horror that he was being squeezed out of the cabin. The other mercenary tried to scream as the pressure on his chest increased, but could only manage a choked gasp.

The helicopter climbed. Forty feet, fifty, the men still firing at the camp—

Silver finally lost his grip as the expanding flotation bag drove him through the open door. He plummeted to the ground, shrieking all the way before hitting the frozen earth with a bone-splintering crack.

The trapped man coughed out a violent spew of red over the shiny orange PVC as a rib broke under the pressure, a jagged shard piercing one of his lungs. One of his companions twisted in his seat to puncture the bag with a burst of gunfire—

The cable snapped taut.

The crane truck's back end jumped upwards as the ascending helicopter hauled at it, but the vehicle was too heavy for the already fully laden aircraft to lift. The chopper tipped sharply backwards. The pilot battled to regain control, jamming the cyclic stick forward in a panicked attempt to level out.

It was too late. The Jet Ranger spun back towards the camp, engine howling . . .

Nina's eyes bugged in horror as she realised it was coming straight at her.

'*Run!*' she screamed, grabbing Tova. Matt also burst from the shelter and sprinted for the lake, the other team members scattering as the aircraft plunged towards them . . .

Its tail boom crumpled as it hit the ground back end first, then the main rotor carved into the frozen surface like a monstrous scythe. The blades shattered, ripping away from the hub and sending debris flying in all directions. Nina threw Tova flat as shrapnel whipped over them. The chopper's shattered carcass tumbled through the camp, disintegrating in flames as it hit a truck. Wreckage mowed Mathias down as he ran. One of the Norwegians was also struck, screaming as a chunk of mangled metal ripped into his leg.

The helicopter's remains finally came to rest. Nina raised her head. The truck hit by the aircraft was crumpled like wet cardboard, a trail of fire leading from it to the burning wreck. It didn't seem possible that anyone aboard could have survived the crash, and she was in no hurry to offer assistance if someone had. 'Are you okay?' she asked Tova. The Swede shakily brushed her hair from her face and nodded. 'Stay here – I'm going to check on the others.'

She started back into what was left of the camp. Stunned figures slowly rose in the firelight; Matt, Peder, Mikkel, two of his team. But she didn't see the one she was most concerned about. Where was Eddie?

'Nina!' A shout quelled her rising fears. Relieved, she turned to see her husband trudging towards her. 'You all right?'

She ran to Eddie and embraced him. 'Oh God! You're okay, you're okay!'

'So are you,' he said, holding her tightly and kissing her. 'Jesus. Fucking Hoyt . . .' He lifted his head. The EC175 was heading rapidly away to the west.

'And Logan,' said Nina. 'That son of a *bitch*! What the hell is all this about?'

The question prompted memories, which in turn led to deductions – none of which she liked. She stepped back. 'You know something about this,' she said, trying to maintain a semblance of calm. 'Who is Hoyt, and how do you know him? And what's he got to do with the runestone?' He didn't answer. The veneer cracked. 'Dammit, Eddie!' she yelled, fury erupting. 'Why won't you tell me what's going on?'

He looked away. 'Because I made a promise,' he said, conflict clear in his voice. 'But . . . he didn't.'

'Who?' She followed his gaze – and was startled to see a man approaching across the frozen lake. He was carrying a long rifle. The sniper. 'Who is he?' she demanded.

'He's someone I met eight years ago. In Vietnam,' Eddie told her, moving to meet the new arrival. Nina followed. As the figure drew closer and was lit by the glow of the fires, she was shocked to see a familiar face.

It was the leader of the Russians who had tried to kidnap Tova.

Her shock grew when the two men came face to face . . . and shook hands. 'Oh my God,' she gasped, confused – and suddenly frightened. 'That's why you let him go in Stockholm. And the bomb – he gave it to you, didn't he? You're working together!'

Eddie's uncharacteristic silence was more unnerving than any reply.

16

Vietnam

'Fuckin' finally,' Chase muttered as the narrow path he and Natalia had followed since crossing the river joined up with a broader, more well-trodden track.

'How far are we from your friends?' she asked.

The Englishman slung the rifle and shifted the Bouncing Betty and its detonator to the crook of his arm, then examined the map. 'Less than half a mile. Should only take us about ten minutes to get there.'

'Good.' Natalia cautiously checked that the track was clear. 'Will they still be there?'

'I bloody hope so.' Chase was confident that Castille would have waited for him, and doubted Sullivan would have let him stay in the jungle alone. He regarded the muddy ground. The track, which headed roughly north–south, had been used by at least one vehicle, the chunky tread pattern of off-road tyres standing out in the mud. Since the camp from which he had rescued Natalia was to the south, there was a good chance the 4x4 belonged to their pursuers.

The prints didn't have the sharp edges he would have expected if they were recent, though. They were several hours old. He raised his head, listening intently. No engine noises were audible over the jungle chorus.

'Are we safe?' Natalia asked.

'Think so. But if you hear anything coming, duck into the bushes.' He turned to head north. 'Okay, not far now.'

They made their way along the track. The sound of the river gradually returned; the rendezvous point was an abandoned building on one of its meanders. Before long, Chase slowed. 'What is it?' asked Natalia, nervous.

He ushered her into the cover of the surrounding vegetation. 'I heard voices. We're nearly there, so it might be my mates . . . or it might not.'

Senses fully alert, he moved carefully through the undergrowth, Natalia a few paces behind him. The rotted skeleton of a wooden structure came into view ahead. He whispered for her to stay where she was and remain silent, then put down the landmine and detonator before hefting the AKS and creeping silently to the edge of his cover.

The remains of the building stood on the shore beside an equally mouldering wooden platform extending out into the river. Parked on the track nearby was a mud-spattered but otherwise new Toyota Land Cruiser. Four figures stood beside it, talking.

Chase's heart leapt with relief: one of the men was Castille. His friend had waited for him, just as he'd hoped. The Belgian had changed into civilian clothes, drab camouflage gear replaced by a gaudy shirt emblazoned with cheerful patterns of brightly coloured birds. Beside him was Sullivan, the New Zealander wiping sweat from the top of his bald head. To the Englishman's surprise, the third member of the group was Ivor Lock, looking out of place and uncomfortable in the humid heat. The expensive

4x4 was probably his, then; he must have been concerned enough on learning that his daughter had not been among the rescued hostages to come and wait for news in person.

The fourth man was Hoyt.

Cold anger rose in Chase at the sight of the cigarette-smoking American. Whatever his reasons for ransacking the Russian laboratory and trying to take Natalia, he undoubtedly now meant to cover his tracks. Of the group, he was the only one with a weapon at the ready, his AK-47 hanging at his hip. Sullivan's gun was shouldered, and Castille's propped against a tree.

Hoyt's plan was clear. If Natalia showed up, he would kill everyone else and take the young German.

Chase wasn't going to let that happen.

A brief glance back to make sure that she was still hidden, then he stepped out of the bushes – with his gun pointed at Hoyt. 'Don't move!'

The four men looked round in surprise. Lock flinched at the sight of the gun, Castille and Sullivan reacting with confusion – but Hoyt immediately grasped his own weapon. 'I said don't fucking move,' Chase snarled. 'Drop it!'

The American froze, but the rifle remained in his hands. 'You're missing your mag there, Chase,' he said, eyeing the AKS-74U.

'It's still chambered.'

Hoyt's gaze flicked down to his older Kalashnikov, and its fully loaded magazine. 'One bullet against thirty?'

The AKS did not waver. 'I only need one.'

'Reckon you do, at that.' Hoyt spat his cigarette from his lips and reluctantly lowered the AK to the ground by its strap.

Chase glanced at his friend. 'Hugo, grab his gun.'

Castille did so, though with a bewildered expression. 'Edward, what is going on?'

'That's a very good question,' said Sullivan. 'What the hell's this about, Chase?'

Lock had questions of his own. 'Where's my daughter? Did you find her?'

'Natalia's fine.' Chase considered calling her out of cover, but decided to wait until the situation was resolved. 'Hugo, have you got anything you can tie that arsehole up with? I don't want him causing any more trouble.'

'What trouble?' Sullivan demanded.

'This bastard's the reason we got into a firefight at the camp,' the Englishman explained as Castille, keeping a wary eye on Hoyt, went to the Land Cruiser. 'He wasn't just there to rescue the hostages. He was there specifically to get Natalia – and steal all the research on whatever the fuck the Russians were doing to her. He knew what they were up to all along.'

'What?' gasped Lock. He rounded on Hoyt. 'What were they doing to my daughter?' The mercenary remained silent.

'When we went into that cabin to get her, first thing he did was start taking all their notes,' Chase went on. 'One of the Russians was already in there. I told Hoyt to watch him while I helped Natalia, but instead he shot him in cold blood. Then he pointed his gun at me and told me to carry her out of there.'

Sullivan looked at Hoyt as if expecting a denial, but the American still said nothing. 'Why did you do it?' he asked. Hoyt's only response was a disdainful sneer.

'Edward,' called Castille from the rear of the Land Cruiser. 'There is nothing to tie him with – but look.' He held up what Chase recognised as Hoyt's pack, opening it. 'You are right. It is full of papers, disks, a computer . . .'

Sullivan unshouldered his own gun and pointed it at Hoyt. 'All right, you. I want some answers.'

'I got nothin' to say,' Hoyt replied.

Chase lowered the AKS and joined Castille. 'Did you get the other hostages out all right?'

The Belgian nodded. 'We came here from the camp last night and put them on the boat. Lomax and Rios went with them – they are all safe in Da Nang now. I waited for you, and Hal stayed with me. Hoyt arrived a few hours later.'

'And decided to stick around until I got here with Natalia,' Chase added, glaring at the prisoner. 'Hal, how long have you known this twat? What's his background?'

Sullivan was concerned by the revelations. 'I haven't known him long, but he was recommended to me by someone I thought I could trust. All his references were excellent.'

'They usually are when you're a spook.'

'Where is my daughter?' Lock asked, impatience rising over his concern.

'She's safe – I'll fetch her once we've got him secured. Hugo, take the strap off his AK – we'll tie his hands with it.' Chase crossed back to Hoyt. 'You going to tell us who you're really working for?'

'Go fuck yourself,' Hoyt replied.

Chase gave him a crooked smile – then punched him hard in the face. Hoyt fell to the ground, a bright fan of blood spraying from both nostrils. 'Never heard of 'em. They got a website? Go-fuck-yourself-dot-com?'

'Mother*fucker*!' Hoyt spat. He wiped his mouth, wincing as he touched his now broken nose. 'You just made a big fuckin' mistake.'

'You made a bigger one,' said Sullivan. 'I don't appreciate being lied to, or being used. So either you give us some answers, or I'll leave you here for the Vietnamese and their Russian friends to find. *After* I've let Eddie get his licks in.'

'Speak up,' said Chase, kicking Hoyt hard in the side when no reply was immediately forthcoming.

The American clamped a hand to his bruised ribs. 'You cocksucker! All right, okay,' he hurriedly added as Castille joined the group and drew back one leg to deliver a blow of his own. 'But if I talk, I get to walk out of here, okay?'

Sullivan reluctantly nodded. 'You've got my word. *If* I believe you.'

'Okay.' Hoyt took a deep breath. 'Right. This is what's happening. The Russians have a biological warfare department they call Unit 201. It's been active since the Cold War, and it's one of their biggest secrets – only people at the very top levels of the Russian government and military know about it. The Ruskies at the camp? They're part of 201.'

'Biological warfare?' said Castille uneasily. 'Why did they kidnap the aid workers?'

'They don't give a fuck about the aid workers. They're only interested in the German girl, Natalia.'

'Why do they want her?' Sullivan demanded.

'Natalia's family,' Chase remembered. He quickly glanced back at the surrounding vegetation to make sure she was still hidden; there was no sign of her. 'Her grandad – he was Russian, and he was a biowarfare scientist. He tried to defect to the West with his research, but didn't make it. That's the connection, isn't it? They want her. Or rather, they want what's *in* her.'

Castille and Sullivan were both confused, but Hoyt nodded. 'Yeah. They think they can use her DNA or whatever the hell it is they're after in their experiments.'

'Well, since you started gunning 'em down, then stole their work and set everything that was left on fire, I'm guessing you don't work for the Russians,' said Chase scathingly.

'You're goddamn right I don't,' Hoyt replied vehemently.

'Thing is, though, Unit 201 is like a fucking fortress. It works out of a maximum-security bunker at one of their nuclear bomber bases. It's impossible to get in. So the only way we could get our hands on their work . . . was by getting them to come *out*.'

'You set them up,' Chase realised. 'You told them about Natalia so they'd try to get what they were after from her.'

Hoyt wiped his nose, then gave the Englishman a twisted smile. 'You ain't quite so dumb as you seem, Chase. Yeah, we set them up. We fed Unit 201 information about Natalia, and they took the bait. She was working in a country friendly to Russia, so it was easy for them to get permission to do whatever the hell they wanted to get her. When they made their move, we were ready.'

'You little bastard,' snarled the New Zealander, baring his teeth. 'How long have you been planning this?'

'Long enough. But it was worth it. We drew 201 out of Russia to somewhere we could reach them. And once they were out in the open, well . . .' Another unpleasant smile. 'We took their research, we destroyed everything they'd been working on, we killed some of their top scientists – about the only way things could have gone better would be if their head honcho had been there too so I coulda blown the fucker away as well.'

'You didn't get everything you were after, though,' said Chase. 'You didn't get Natalia.'

Hoyt snorted. 'We will. You think this is over, Chase? You dumb Limey fuck. We're only getting started——'

Chase slammed his boot deep into Hoyt's stomach, leaving him gasping and writhing. 'So are we.'

Jaw clenched in anger, Sullivan stood over Hoyt, pointing his rifle at the treacherous mercenary's head. 'I want answers, Hoyt. You kept saying "we" – who are you working for? Who's your employer?'

Hoyt stared up defiantly at the three men. Sullivan's finger slowly tightened on the trigger—

The sharp crack of a gunshot echoed around the riverbank.

But it didn't come from Sullivan's gun. The mercenary leader flinched, confused shock rising on his face . . . then he toppled and crashed to the rotten wooden decking. Blood gushed from a wound in the centre of his back.

Chase and Castille whirled – to find the smoking weapon now aimed at them.

'You want to know Hoyt's employer?' said Lock, the slim chrome-plated Glock 26 pistol in his hand rock-steady. 'That would be me.'

243

17

Russia

'So, how long are you planning to ignore me?' asked Eddie.
Nina refused to turn her head towards him, keeping her gaze fixed on the dawn-lit steppes of southern Russia as they rolled past far below the small business jet. 'I'm not ignoring you. I'm just so *mad* at you right now that if I looked at you, I might have trouble stopping myself from punching you in your goddamn lying face.' She jabbed an angry finger at the man on the other side of the cabin. 'How long have you been working with your Russian friend over there?'

'He's not my friend,' Eddie insisted, exasperated. 'The only reason I was working with him was because . . . I had to.'

'You *had* to,' she echoed sarcastically. 'You *had* to let him go after he tried to kidnap Tova.' The Swede, who was in the row of seats behind them, sleepily raised her head at the mention of her name. 'You *had* to try to sabotage the expedition. You *had* to plant a goddamn *bomb* on the runestone!' She finally looked round at her husband as her voice rose to a shout. 'And you still won't tell me *why* you had to do all of this? Why not, Eddie? Why won't you tell me what's going on?'

The conflict was clear in his voice. 'Because . . . because I made a promise. I told you, I can't say any more.'

'But I can,' said the Russian.

It had taken considerable cajoling by Eddie to persuade Nina and Tova that the Russian was not a threat, but neither woman was willing to trust their mysterious – and until now taciturn – benefactor. At the lake, he had radioed for a helicopter of his own to fly Nina, Eddie and Tova away from the scene of the battle, though Nina had insisted that he also alert the Norwegian authorities so Matt and the other survivors could be taken to safety. A jet waiting at a small airport had then flown into the night to deliver them to a destination deep inside the vast former communist country.

Beyond that, however, he had not been forthcoming with further information. 'So, you've decided to talk now?' Nina said. 'Why?'

He smiled. 'I do not like it when a husband and wife fight. It reminds me too much of my parents. So. What do you want to know?'

She eyed him coldly. 'Everything. Starting with: who the hell are you?'

He straightened, giving her a salute. 'I am Colonel Grigory Alekseyevich Kagan, commander of operations for *Sekcija dvesti odin* – or as it is called in English, Unit 201.'

'And just what *is* Unit 201?'

'On a normal day, if I told you I would have to kill you. It is a state secret. Today, though . . . I believe that you need to know. So I will tell you, and not kill you.' Another sly grin. 'For now.'

Nina was not amused. 'So? Get on with it.'

Kagan turned to Eddie. 'She is impatient, yes? Red hair, it is like fire in a woman. I like it.'

'Just tell her, Yuri,' the Englishman grumbled.

'Grigory. As you wish.' He looked back at Nina. 'Unit 201 was created during the Cold War. It is a biological counter-warfare agency.'

'*Counter*-warfare?' said Nina.

'Yes. Over fifty years ago, the Soviet Union discovered something deep within the earth, a poisonous substance – something first found more than a thousand years earlier by the Vikings.' Nina and Tova, now fully awake, exchanged surprised glances. 'At the time, the Soviet leaders thought to turn it into a weapon. That was a mistake. As they found out, it was too terrible to use, ever. So Unit 201 was created to make sure that no one ever did. It worked on ways to deal with the substance, but it was also authorised to take . . . direct action.'

Nina's eyes narrowed. 'Direct action like killing anybody who might find more of it?' Behind her, Tova stiffened in resurgent fear.

Kagan shook his head firmly. 'We are not murderers. We would not have killed you, Dr Skilfinger. But our enemies had already stolen the runestone, and your research. They would use them to find the second runestone, and from there, Valhalla. We could not allow that to happen, so our intention was to use what you had learned to find and destroy the second stone before they reached it. My apologies.'

Nina was already making connections. 'According to the text on the runestone, the Vikings would only travel to Valhalla to prepare for Ragnarök – the final battle. The end of the world.'

'It will be the end of the world if our enemies find it,' said Kagan, nodding.

'But who *are* your enemies?' asked Tova.

'I am afraid, Dr Wilde, that they are from your country,' the

Russian told Nina, who reacted with shock. 'In 1961, a Russian scientist tried to defect to America, taking this terrible weapon with him.'

'Natalia's grandfather,' Eddie said quietly. Kagan nodded again.

Nina regarded her husband quizzically. 'Who's Natalia?'

Kagan answered for him when it became clear he was unwilling to reply. 'A young woman, an innocent. Eight years ago, we learned that the Americans had taken an interest in her. Her DNA, her very blood, could give them what they needed to recreate this scientist's work. We found her in Vietnam—'

'You *kidnapped* her,' Eddie cut in. 'And all the people with her.'

'We had to do it. We could not let the Americans get her. Our plan was to use her DNA to create a neutralising agent. She and the others would then have been released – the story would be that the Vietnamese police had rescued them. But then,' he gave Eddie a sharp look, 'you and your mercenary friends interfered.'

'We were hired to find them,' Eddie told Nina. 'Me and Hugo, and some others.'

'But you did not know who had hired you, did you?' Kagan clucked his tongue. 'Or that one of your team was a spy working for our enemies. And because of that, two of Unit 201's best scientists were killed, their research destroyed. And an innocent woman—'

Eddie interrupted again, much more forcefully. 'I know what happened.'

The pilot's voice came from a loudspeaker. Kagan listened, then told the other passengers: 'We will be landing soon. The Academician will explain everything.'

'Good,' said Nina, peering back out of the window. The snowy landscape was indeed getting closer. 'It's about damn time somebody gave me a proper answer.' She directed this last at Eddie, who looked apologetic, but still said nothing.

Before long, the plane crossed over a wide river with towns on both sides, descending towards a long runway beyond the settlement on the east bank. Their destination was not inviting. The surrounding land was a flat expanse of frozen marshes, criss-crossed by concrete taxiways. As the business jet landed and slowed, Nina saw lines of parked aircraft: large, lumbering old beasts whose brutally functional designs, very different from the sleek modernism she associated with American military aircraft, gave them an almost alien feel.

Eddie looked past her. 'It's Engels airbase.'

Kagan reacted with suspicion. 'How do you know that?'

''Cause Russia's only got two active nuclear bomber bases, and the other one's way, waaaay over in the far east.' He indicated some of the planes, these ones long and menacing jets resembling winged hypodermic syringes rather than the hulking turboprops they had just passed. 'And the Tu-160 is a nuclear bomber.'

'You know a lot about the Russian military, Mr Chase.'

Eddie grinned. 'Part of my old job. We never knew when we might be sent to blow up all your planes, so we had to be prepared.'

'You will not be blowing any of them up today,' said Kagan sourly.

Nina sighed. 'Oh God. Someone always has to tempt fate, don't they?' Her husband's grin widened, while the Russian's expression became even more disapproving.

The jet trundled along the taxiways, finally powering down outside a squat concrete blockhouse with a rack of large metal tanks along one of its side walls. The travellers disembarked. Nina couldn't read the Cyrillic text painted on the side of the grim and ugly building, but numbers were the same in Russian and English: *201*. 'Follow me,' said Kagan, leading the group towards a broad and very solid-looking set of sliding metal doors.

Three uniformed men came out to meet them, the leader – a stocky officer with dark hair and a rather feeble moustache – engaging Kagan in a brief and somewhat agitated conversation in Russian. The commander made a dismissive gesture before turning to his guests. 'This is Captain Slavin,' he announced. 'He is in charge of security here at the bunker.'

Eddie frowned at the new arrival. 'I remember him. He was in Vietnam.' It was the man who had encountered him and Hoyt in the cabin. The look of surprise on Slavin's face told the Yorkshireman that the recognition was mutual.

'He was,' Kagan confirmed. 'But he has found that his place is standing guard rather than intelligence work. Is that not right, Kolzak Iakovich?'

There was a condescending tone to his words, which Slavin did not appreciate. However, he did not rise to the bait. 'Sir, Academician Eisenhov waits for you and your guests,' he said instead, his English rendered almost comical by his placing of emphasis on the wrong syllables.

Nina held in her amusement, but Eddie couldn't resist. 'Thank *you* ve-ry *much*, we're look-*ing!* forward to meet-*ing!* him.'

Slavin scowled and gestured towards the doors. 'This way.' He re-entered the building, his two subordinates marching behind him.

Tova hesitated; Kagan gave her a reassuring smile. 'It is all right. Please?' She reluctantly followed the three men into the bunker, Nina and Eddie behind her. They found themselves in a large steel-walled elevator. Nina shivered at the sight of a biohazard warning symbol, a claw-like trefoil of black on yellow, with a long and stern warning sign beneath it. Kagan came in after them and pushed a button. The doors closed, shutting out the cold daylight with a deep clang. There was a distant rumble of machinery building up to speed, then the elevator jolted and began its descent.

'How deep down are we going?' Nina asked.

'The facility is thirty metres underground,' Kagan replied. 'It is designed so that in an emergency, it can be completely sealed off from the surface. And if necessary, sterilised.'

Eddie regarded him dubiously. 'What do you mean, sterilised?'

The Russian indicated the warning sign. 'If there is a biohazard alert, any contaminated section of the bunker can be locked down and everything in it incinerated by acetylene jets. You saw the gas tanks outside the bunker.'

'Have you ever had to do that?' Nina asked, nervously scanning the elevator's ceiling for said jets.

'Not here,' replied Kagan. 'But there was once an . . . incident, in another place. It is why Unit 201 was created – to make sure it never happened again.'

The elevator came to a stop. The heavy inner doors rumbled open again, another equally thick set parting beyond them. Unlike the weathered barrier on the surface, these were polished metal. The walls and floor of the area past them were covered by stark white tiles. Slavin's boot heels clicked on them as he stepped out. 'The Academician is in his office,' he announced, ushering everyone out.

'There's your gas jets,' Eddie said quietly as he and Nina emerged into a wide lobby area. She followed his gaze to see a squat black dome in one corner of the ceiling. Other domes overlooked the rest of the bunker's interior, covering every square inch.

Slavin led them down a broad central passage. There were rooms on each side, all accessed via thick metal sliding doors. Some had windows; Nina glanced in as they passed to see various laboratories, though only a couple were in active use. The occupants gave the new arrivals curious looks from behind goggles and hazmat suits. More doors obstructed the corridor itself every few dozen metres, the Russian officer using a keycard to open them. As well as the panel for the card lock, each door also had another control board containing a lever behind a glass shutter, ominously bordered by yellow and black warning stripes and marked with the biohazard symbol. She realised the latter system's function: anyone activating it would seal the section behind them and fill it with fire.

Side passages branched off between the laboratories, but the group continued along the main corridor until they reached its end. The last door was, incongruously, made of dark, thickly varnished old wood rather than metal. Slavin knocked respect-fully upon it. A muffled reply came from within. He opened it and stood back to let the others through.

Even with the out-of-place door as prior warning, Nina was still taken aback by the room they entered. It was much warmer than the bunker outside, almost stifling. Far from the harsh, sterile tiling of the rest of the facility, this was panelled in wood, overstacked bookshelves occupying much of the wall space. Soft music came from a portable CD player; she belatedly recognised it as Frank Sinatra's 'The Best Is Yet To Come'. Small potted plants were dotted seemingly at random on tables and shelves. There was a musty scent, one that immediately brought back memories of academia, of libraries and lectures.

The room's occupant perfectly matched his surroundings. The old man was seated in a well-worn wing-back chair, a little round table by its right arm bearing a steaming cup of tea. His suit was slightly too large for his age-shrunk frame, giving him an oddly childlike appearance. She guessed him to be well into his eighties. One of his eyes was milky, but the other was still a piercing blue.

Kagan spoke to him in Russian. The old man nodded, then waved a gnarled hand at the other chairs facing him. 'Please, sit,' Kagan told the visitors.

Eddie waited for Nina and Tova to do so before joining them. 'Nice place,' he said. 'Love how it totally matches the decor outside. Bit hot, mind.'

Their elderly host chuckled throatily. 'When you are as old as me, you too will keep your room hot!' His command of English prompted an exchange of surprised looks from his guests. He spoke in Russian; Slavin's two men departed, though the captain stayed in the room, watching the three Westerners balefully. 'Dr Wilde, Dr Skilfinger, Mr Chase: I am Academician Dmitri Prokopiyevich Eisenhov, the director of Unit 201. I have to admit that my feelings are mixed about meeting you, but I am glad that Grigory Alekseyevich,' he waved a finger towards Kagan, 'was able to bring you here alive and well.'

'Not everyone in my team was so lucky,' Nina said, anger over events at the lake returning. 'Nobody is giving me straight answers about what the hell is going on. I think it's time that changed.' She looked directly at Eddie as she spoke; he shifted uncomfortably.

Eisenhov nodded. 'You are right. It is time, Dr Wilde.' He switched off the music, then leaned back. 'In the Cold War, the Soviet Union chose to use Novaya Zemlya in the Arctic as a test site for nuclear bombs. To prepare, they surveyed the islands. They found something.' His one clear eye turned towards Tova. 'A Viking runestone, marking a deep cave. It held a warning of what was found inside.'

'A warning of what?' Tova asked, intrigued.

Eisenhov spoke in Russian to Kagan, who went to a filing cabinet and took out a folder. He handed it to the old man. 'Of death,' said Eisenhov, extracting a large and yellowed photograph. 'Of the end of the world.'

He held out the photo. Tova took it, the two women examining the image. Bleak, treeless tundra stretched away into the distance behind a rocky hole in the ground, nothing but blackness visible within. In front of the sinister chasm was a runestone, much like the one from the bottom of the Norwegian lake.

'We in Russia know of the Norse legends,' Eisenhov went on. 'The Vikings are part of our history too. But we did not believe there was any truth to their stories of gods and monsters – until we explored the pit.'

Tova peered intently at the photo, but it was too grainy for her to make out any details on the runestone. 'I cannot read what it says . . .'

'I can tell you,' said Eisenhov. 'They say the pit is the home of Jörmungandr – the Midgard Serpent.' At the group's surprise, he continued: 'And it is, in a way. I once saw it with my own eyes, a long time ago. It is not a real serpent, but I know why the Vikings would think it was. It was an impressive – and frightening – sight. But it is not the serpent of which we should be afraid. It is its venom.'

'The eitr,' said Eddie. As in Stockholm, what now felt like an age ago, Nina was surprised by his knowledge – though now her feelings were also spiked with anger that he had been keeping secrets from her.

'The eitr, yes,' Eisenhov echoed. 'A black liquid, just as the legends said. A terrible poison. There was a vast reserve beneath the earth, a river flowing underneath the surface to . . . we did not know where. It was too dangerous to explore, and we did not have the technology to follow it. But we knew from the runestone that the Vikings found another place where it emerged. They believed that when Ragnarök came, the serpent would emerge from one of these pits. The Viking warriors would divide into two armies, so that wherever Jörmungandr emerged, they would be waiting.'

'So the Vikings found two sources of the eitr,' said Nina, 'and you discovered one of them in the Cold War. But why is it so dangerous? You say it's a poison, but humans have come up with some pretty horrible poisons of their own. How is this any worse?'

'If you had seen what it can do,' the old Russian replied with a sad sigh, 'you would not ask that question. I *have* seen. It has been over fifty years, but the nightmares have not gone away.'

His sincerity sent a chill through Nina, but she still had to know more. 'So what can it do? What *is* it?'

To her shock, it was Eddie who gave her an answer. 'It's a mutagen. If it doesn't kill you, it attacks your DNA, changing it. Like a cancer. Natalia, the woman I rescued in Vietnam? Her grandfather was experimenting with it. He deliberately infected her grandmother with it, while she was pregnant. It caused tumours that killed her grandmother, then her mother.' His tone became even more grim. 'And it would've eventually killed her too.'

'Serafim Zernebogovich Volkov,' said Eisenhov, spitting out the name. 'A traitor and a monster. If he had lived, his name would be as cursed as Mengele. He tried to take the eitr and his work to your country.' His gaze snapped almost accusingly back to Nina. 'It was only by luck that he was stopped. He chose the wrong day to return to Novaya Zemlya.'

'What happened to him?' Tova asked.

'Ever heard of the Tsar Bomb?' said Eddie. Both women shook their heads. 'Biggest H-bomb in history.'

'What's that got to do with— *Oh*,' Nina said, realising. 'Nuclear test site. Right.'

Eisenhov made a satisfied sound. 'Khrushchev ordered the activation of what became known as the Tsar Protocol. The bomb was dropped on the thirtieth of October 1961, completely obliterating everything on the ground and sealing the pit for ever. Nobody will ever be able to open it again.'

Nina was still astounded. 'Using a hydrogen bomb, though? That sounds like overkill.'

'You would not say that if you had seen what I have seen,' Eisenhov replied.

'Which was what?'

He did not answer straight away, as if summoning up the resolve to speak. 'Two months before the Tsar Protocol was activated,' he said at last, 'a sample of eitr was being transported to a missile testing site. There was an accident on the way. The eitr was spilled in a civilian area. It had ... terrible effects. On people, but also on animals, plants, even insects – anything living. Most of the people who were exposed died within days, or even hours.' He paused, moistening his dry lips with his tongue. 'They were the lucky ones. Those who survived ...'

'What happened to them?' Nina demanded, after Eisenhov said nothing for several seconds.

He took a long, slow breath, then opened the folder again. 'You may not want to see these pictures. They have been a state secret for half a century, seen only by those at the highest levels of government. All the men who saw them . . . wished they had not. But they understood at once why Khrushchev ordered the pit to be obliterated. Even at the height of the Cold War, no Russian ever again suggested using eitr as a weapon. Do you still want to see them?'

'No,' whispered Tova. 'I do not.'

'I don't want to either,' said Nina. 'But . . . I think I *have* to. If this is an IHA matter, a global security threat, I've got to know what we're dealing with.'

Eisenhov nodded. 'You are a brave woman, Dr Wilde. Very well. But remember that I warned you.' He reached forward again to hand several photographs to her.

Eddie leaned closer to look as she turned them over. 'Oh, Jesus.'

Nina couldn't even speak as she stared at the first picture, horror and revulsion freezing any words in her throat. The image showed the upper body of a man lying on the ground, contorted in unimaginable agony at the moment of his death.

The cause was obvious. Parts of his face and neck appeared almost to have exploded from the inside, vile cancerous growths within the flesh having swollen to burst through his skin before themselves rupturing into oozing, diseased slurry. Bloodstains soaking through his clothing showed that the terrifying contagion had spread throughout his whole body.

Eisenhov's voice seemed to come from a long way off. 'Exposure to more than a mere few millilitres of the eitr causes DNA to mutate and grow uncontrollably. The effect begins almost immediately. Death was the result in every case.'

Nina forced herself to talk. 'And in smaller doses?'

'There are pictures.'

She reluctantly looked at the next photograph, afraid of what it would show her.

Her fears were justified.

Eddie closed his eyes, shaking his head. 'Shit,' he whispered.

The picture showed a woman in a hospital bed, ugly lumps on her skin revealing that she too had been contaminated by the eitr. Her abdomen was covered in blood from a deep longitudinal incision – a Caesarean section, the umbilical cord still connected to the just-birthed child.

A child that was barely recognisable as human.

Nina fought the urge to vomit. The baby's limbs were hideously malformed, one leg a withered, twisted stump, an arm bloated and covered with tumours and pustules. Ribs pushed through skin, a length of some intestinal organ hanging limply out of a hole beneath the distended stomach. But most appalling of all was the face, a gelatinous mass of twisted features trying to scream without a mouth, the one visible eye bulging in anguish . . .

The pictures slipped from her shaking hands to the floor as she squeezed her own eyes tightly shut, unable to bear the sight any more.

'It did not live for long,' said Eisenhov in a quiet, saddened voice. 'Fortunately.'

Tova gasped in horror as she glimpsed the fallen photographs, hurriedly looking away. Nina tried to speak again. 'Wh—' Her mouth had gone bone-dry. 'What . . . what about the mother?' she finally managed to say.

'She died soon after,' the Russian told her. 'The child was born a month after she was exposed to the eitr. Only a few drops, but it was enough to do that to her, and to turn her baby into a monster.'

'It's not a monster,' Eddie said angrily. 'It was still a baby. It didn't ask to be born like that. *You* did it, with your fucking experiments!'

'Experiments that we knew had to be stopped and never restarted,' Eisenhov replied, contrition clear even beneath his mask of stoicism. He gestured to Kagan, who collected the photographs. 'Every kind of life in the area of the accident was affected. In the smaller forms, plants and insects, mutations spread quickly. Most died, but some survived long enough to breed – and passed down further mutations to the next generation. We saw that there was a danger of the contamination spreading beyond the quarantine zone. So the entire area was . . . sterilised.' He glanced up at the ceiling. Another of the domes lurked beside a light fitting.

'You killed everything?' Nina asked. Eisenhov nodded. 'Including people?'

'It had to be done,' he said, sickened. 'And may God have mercy on us. But we could not let the mutations spread. When Khrushchev learned what had happened, he immediately ordered all research on the eitr to be destroyed. Even the hydrogen bomb is not so terrible a weapon as the poison from inside the earth itself.'

'The blood of Jörmungandr,' said Tova. 'The poison of the Midgard Serpent.'

'So the legend's true, in a way,' Nina realised. 'The eitr brings life, or at least changes it – maybe it was even responsible for kick-starting evolution billions of years ago by causing mutations on a massive scale.' She knew from her discoveries at Atlantis that a meteor had brought life to the primordial Earth – but the eitr might have been what caused that life to explode into endless new forms. All birthed from poison, just as the Norse legends said. She looked at Eddie. 'That's what this girl's grandfather was trying to do, wasn't it? Take *control* of evolution, try to force it down the paths he wanted?'

'Volkov!' Again Eisenhov practically spat the name. 'The man was insane – experimenting on his own wife and child! And when Khrushchev ended the project, he tried to sell his work to the Americans.'

'But you nuked him first,' said Eddie. 'Good.'

'Yes. He burned for his greed, and now he burns in hell, where he belongs.' Kagan returned the photographs to the old man, who put them back in the folder and closed it. 'But once we had seen for ourselves the terrible things that eitr could do if unleashed on the world,' Eisenhov continued, 'we knew we had to make sure that never happened. So Unit 201 was created.'

'To find a way to neutralise it?' asked Nina.

'That is one of our purposes, yes,' Kagan told her. 'Our scientists have created chemicals that may work.'

'May?' Eddie repeated. 'That doesn't sound too hopeful.'

'There is a problem,' said Eisenhov. 'We have no way to test our theories – because we have no eitr to test them upon! All the samples were incinerated, and the pit was sealed by the Tsar Bomba. Khrushchev was right to stop the experiments, yes, but he went further – he ordered everything destroyed. And we were too quick to obey.' He shook his head. 'If we had kept some of the research, we would have precious information that could have helped us. Instead, we had to recreate everything from memory alone. And even after fifty years, and now with computers and genetic sequencing to help us, we do not know if that is enough.'

Kagan eyed Eddie. 'But if we had found someone who had been contaminated by eitr, a person whose DNA we could test and compare to an uninfected sample . . .'

Eddie jabbed a finger at him. 'Don't you even fucking start.'

Nina looked between the two men. 'What?'

'He means Natalia – and he's going to blame *me* for them not getting what they were after!'

'If you had not interfered eight years ago,' said Kagan, 'we would have let her go, and returned here with everything we needed.'

Eddie jumped to his feet. 'Maybe if you'd just fucking *asked* her, instead of acting like spooks and coming up with some fake kidnapping bullshit, she would have let you take a blood sample!'

Eisenhov raised a hand, speaking sharply to Kagan before addressing the others. 'Enough, please. What is done is done. We cannot change it – we can only try to correct our mistakes. And to stop others from making the same ones.'

'Which is Unit 201's *other* purpose, right?' said Nina. 'You knew from the runestone at the test site that there's another source of eitr out there, somewhere. So you've been trying to find it – before anyone else does.'

'Yes, yes,' Eisenhov replied. 'But we have not been successful. The runes said that the Vikings reached the pit on Novaya Zemlya from Valhalla – but they did not say where Valhalla was.'

'But the two runestones that Hoyt's nicked do,' Eddie pointed out. 'And Berkeley's translating them. He took longer than Tova to work out that the second stone was under the lake – but he got there eventually.'

'We must find Valhalla,' Kagan insisted. 'We must destroy the eitr before the Americans reach it.'

'And what if your anti-eitr doesn't work?' asked Nina.

A change in Eisenhov's attitude caught the attention of all three visitors, the old man stiffening in his chair. He took in a deep, slow breath, considering his next words very carefully. 'If it does not,' he said, 'then Unit 201 has failed. If that happens, the military takes over.' He looked up, his gaze aimed not at the ceiling but the sprawling airbase thirty metres above.

'Meaning what?' said Eddie. The sudden tension in his voice suggested to Nina that he already had a horrible idea of the answer.

'The Tsar Protocol was never rescinded,' Eisenhov told the group. 'It remains active to this day. The Soviet Union had several secret . . . doomsday programmes. After it fell, Russia maintained them. The Tsar Protocol was one.'

Despite the heat, Nina felt an icy cold run through her body. 'Wait – if you find the other pit, and you can't neutralise the eitr . . . you'll *nuke* it?'

Eisenhov nodded solemnly. 'Wherever it may be. Even if it is in the United States – even if it is in Washington itself. That is the Tsar Protocol. Nobody can be allowed to control the eitr. It *must* be destroyed. No matter what.'

Tova stared at him, wide-eyed. 'That is insane,' she whispered.

Nina saw that Slavin, standing quietly by the door, had a similarly shocked expression. Knowledge of the Tsar Protocol had clearly been limited only to the highest-ranking members of Unit 201. He spoke urgently, gesturing towards the exit to indicate that he should leave, but Eisenhov shook his head. He replied to the younger man, then addressed the Westerners. 'Kolzak Iakovich thinks that what I have just told you is, how do you say, above his security clearance,' he said. 'But I need every possible idea for how to deal with this situation. I do not want the Tsar Protocol to be activated again. But if we fail . . .' He let his grim words hang in the air.

'You're willing to risk war – an all-out nuclear war – over this?' Nina said, appalled.

Eisenhov held up the folder. 'You have seen what eitr can do, and this was only a small amount. Can you imagine it unleashed over an entire civilian population? Those who do not die will be left as monsters, their children cursed for generation upon generation. Nobody must ever be allowed to possess such a terrible thing. *Nobody*.'

'But if we find the second pit and destroy the eitr, that does not need to happen,' said Kagan.

'So long as your gunk does what it's supposed to,' Eddie pointed out.

Eisenhov spoke in Russian, and Kagan helped him stand. The old man shuffled to one of the bookcases. He reached under a shelf, groping for a moment, then there was a soft click followed by the hum of an electric motor. The entire bookcase retreated backwards and slid sideways out of sight behind the wooden panels to reveal a gleaming metal safe door set into the steel wall.

Eddie nodded in approval. 'We need one of those at home,' he told Nina. 'Good place to keep all our porn.'

'All *your* porn, I think you mean,' she replied.

'Yeah. Yours wouldn't fit in something that small.'

'I don't have *any* porn,' she insisted. But the exchange had eased her tension, slightly. She watched as Eisenhov placed one palm flat against a black glass panel: a handprint scanner. A soft chime sounded. The elderly Russian then squinted at a keypad in a recess, moving in front of it to block the view of the room's other occupants as he tapped in a code. Another chime – then a deep metallic thunk came from within the door as thick locking bars retracted, and it slowly swung open.

Inside were numerous files and metal containers marked with Cyrillic text. Eisenhov reached for one of them, a steel cylinder roughly a foot high and eight inches in diameter. The metal was clearly thick; it was a strain for him to lift. He held it by its curved carrying handle and turned to face his audience. 'This is our best hope,' he said. 'Its official name is Article 3472, but we call it "Thor's Hammer". In Viking legend, Thor killed the great serpent. If we are right, this will do the same to the eitr.'

Tova looked uncomfortable. 'I do not want to sound negative, but Thor also died. Jörmungandr's poison – the eitr – killed him.'

'Then I hope we do better,' said Kagan.

Nina regarded the cylinder. 'So what does Thor's Hammer actually do?'

'It is a chemical compound,' Eisenhov explained, 'that should neutralise the eitr completely. Once introduced into the source, it will break down the mutagenic agents and make them harmless. It is,' he searched for the right English word, 'an autocatalytic reaction. Once it begins, it will spread through the eitr until it is all destroyed. If, as we believed at Novaya Zemlya, there are underground channels through which the eitr flows, then if they are all connected it may wipe out all the eitr in the world. We do not know – but we can hope.'

'So when you find the other pit, you just pour that stuff in, and *foosh*! All done?' said Eddie. 'Sounds easy enough.'

'Not quite,' Kagan told him.

'Yeah, it never bloody is.'

'Thor's Hammer is as deadly as eitr,' said Eisenhov. 'We are using a poison to destroy a poison. It must be handled with great care. If it touches you, it will kill you.'

'Thanks for the heads-up,' said Nina in a scathing tone. 'But none of this matters if you can't find the second pit, does it?'

'Which is why I asked Grigory Alekseyevich,' the old man nodded at Kagan, 'to bring you here. We need your help. Now that our enemies – your enemies too – have both runestones, they will sooner or later find Valhalla – and when they do, they will find the second Ragnarök pit. You are our only hope of stopping them. If we do not, then . . . the Tsar Protocol will be activated. And the world will be thrown into war.'

'Will you help us?' Kagan asked.

Nina looked at her companions. 'Do we have a choice?'

'We should help 'em,' said Eddie firmly. 'I don't want Hoyt or anyone like him getting hold of that shit. Because they're the kind of people who'd actually *use* it.' His expression became sorrowful. 'I saw what Agent Orange did in Vietnam, and that was nothing compared to this stuff. And I saw what *that* did to Natalia. I made her a promise – that I'd do everything I could to stop anyone from carrying on with her grandfather's work. And,' he went on, managing a faint smile, 'you know how I like to keep my promises.'

Kagan was not impressed. 'If you had not made that promise, we would not be in this situation. Unit 201 would have done what it went to Vietnam to do – and Natalia would still be alive.'

'I don't need any fucking lectures from you,' Eddie snapped back at him – then his expression suddenly changed from anger to dawning realisation. 'Wait a minute . . .'

'What?' Nina asked.

Her husband was silent for a moment, thinking. Then: 'You went to Vietnam,' he said to Kagan. 'Unit 201 went to Vietnam *specifically* to get hold of Natalia in a way that meant nobody'd suspect you were involved, right?'

'That is right,' Kagan replied, uncertain where the shift of direction was leading.

'So how did you know she was there?'

'Through intelligence reports,' said Eisenhov. 'The Americans had become interested in finding Volkov's granddaughter. We realised there was only one possible reason why they would do that, so we resolved to act first. The Vietnamese secret police helped us locate her – though we did not tell them why we wanted to do so, of course.'

'But if the Americans knew about Natalia already, they could have picked her up any time – she lived in Germany, it's a US ally. It would have been a lot easier for them to operate there than in Vietnam . . . but it was the other way round for you. So they waited until she was in a country that was one of *your* allies – somewhere you could get away with kidnapping her.'

Kagan's next words were wary. 'You are leading somewhere, Chase. What are you saying?'

'Hoyt told me that his people deliberately fed you information to get you out of Russia – out of *here*.' Eddie gestured at the bunker's walls. 'But if Unit 201 is so secret, how did they know who to feed it to? Who gave the information to you?'

'The intelligence officer—' Kagan began, before abruptly breaking off and whirling to face Slavin. 'The information came through you! What was its source?'

Slavin blinked, wide-eyed and perspiring. 'The source . . .' he began, before reverting to Russian and delivering a halting explanation. Neither Kagan nor Eisenhov appeared convinced.

'Hoyt let you live,' Eddie continued, also rounding on Slavin. 'He shot the scientist in Natalia's cabin, but when you came in, he let you go. He already knew you, didn't he? You're a fucking mole!'

'*Sookin syn!*' snarled Kagan. His hand darted into his jacket to draw a gun.

Slavin was faster, snatching the pistol from his uniform's holster. He pointed it at Kagan—

'*Nyet!*' cried Eisenhov, stepping forward – as Slavin fired.

The bullet hit the old man in the chest. He convulsed, face filled with shock, then sagged to his knees before crumpling on to his front. The steel cylinder dropped from his hand and rolled across the floor before coming to rest near the shocked Nina's feet.

'Yes, I was working for the Americans,' said Slavin, almost panting with barely contained panic. He glanced at the fallen container. 'I still am – and now I will give them Thor's Hammer!'

18

Vietnam

Chase stared at Lock. The American's gun was unwavering. 'What the *fuck* is going on?' the Yorkshireman demanded.

'Where's Natalia?' said Lock.

'On a bus to fucking Saigon.' Chase narrowed his eyes. 'You're not really Natalia's dad, are you?'

'No, I'm not.' Lock glanced at Hoyt, who was painfully levering himself upright. 'Hoyt! She can't be far away. Go find—'

'Natalia, *run!*' Chase yelled. 'It's a trap, get out of—'

Hoyt snatched up Sullivan's fallen Kalashnikov and clubbed Chase with the wooden stock. The Englishman fell. Hoyt flipped the rifle around and took aim – but Lock's shout froze his finger on the trigger. 'No! Not yet, we need him to tell us where she is.' He gestured with the Glock for Castille to kneel beside his friend. 'I'll cover them. You call in the others.'

'What others?' Castille asked as Hoyt, after giving Chase a poisonous look, headed for the Land Cruiser.

'You're not the only people I have working for me in this godforsaken country.'

'Then why did you need us at all?'

''Cause we're deniable,' Chase said with a groan as he sat up. 'If things went wrong, he didn't want the Russians knowing he was on to them.'

Lock nodded. 'If you hadn't caused trouble, Natalia would have been taken away with the rest of the hostages. But instead, you had to be the hero.'

Chase managed a sarcastic grin. 'That's kind of my job.'

'Your *job* was to do what you were hired to do, nothing more.'

'And your job is, what? Use Natalia as a guinea pig so you can restart her grandad's experiments?'

'More or less. With the added bonus of having stolen the Russians' research,' he glanced towards Hoyt's pack in the back of the Toyota, 'while setting them back by years. The eitr has the potential to be an extraordinarily powerful weapon in the right hands . . . or a horrible threat in the wrong ones.'

'And yours are the right hands, of course,' said Castille scathingly.

'Obviously.'

'So who are you exactly?' Chase demanded. 'Another fucking spook, aren't you? God, I hate spooks.'

'And I'm sure the feeling is mutual. But yes, I'm the deputy director of the Biochemical Safety Agency.'

'Never heard of it.'

Lock smiled. 'You wouldn't have.'

'But this must be a major intelligence operation if a big-shot like you is out here in the sweaty arse-crack of nowhere to run it personally. You Yanks are taking a massive risk doing something like this in *Vietnam*, of all fucking places.'

The smile became sly. 'It's not exactly sanctioned. But I have a high degree of operational autonomy – and sins are always forgiven when a mission is successful. And this *is* an important mission, make no mistake. You want the Russians to get their hands on the eitr, Chase? Or the Chinese or – God forbid – the Iranians or North Koreans?'

'I don't want *anyone* to have the fucking stuff,' Chase replied. 'And Natalia doesn't either.'

Lock shook his head. 'What she wants doesn't really matter. This is way too important to leave up to civilians. Or their consciences.'

Hoyt put down a radio. 'They're on their way, five minutes out.' He gestured towards the track leading north.

'Good. When they arrive, send them after her – I doubt she'll have gotten far.'

'What about these two?' The tall mercenary moved his AK-47 back to Chase and Castille.

Lock thought for a moment. 'Make use of them. Chase, you're going to call her back here.'

'The only thing I'm going to call is you, a twat,' Chase replied defiantly. Despite the danger of the situation, Castille couldn't help but smile.

Hoyt stalked back to the group, gun raised. 'Watch your fuckin' mouth.'

'You'll call for her, Chase,' said Lock. 'Because if you don't, I'll shoot your friend.' He aimed the Glock at Castille. 'Just because I wear a suit rather than a uniform, don't think I won't do it.'

Chase eyed Sullivan's body. 'I don't,' he growled.

'Good. You've got ten seconds.'

'Edward, don't do it,' Castille said – though with fear in his voice.

Chase looked up at Lock and Hoyt, adrenalin driving away the pain. He was certain they intended to kill him and Castille whether or not he did what Lock asked. But from his current position, there was nothing he could do except make a futile attempt to tackle one of them, which would get him shot before he'd covered even half the distance . . .

It was either that or watch Castille die, then wait for a bullet of his own. He was not going to surrender Natalia to them, no matter what.

'Five seconds.'

He shared a brief glance with Castille, communicating his intentions in an instant: *fight to the end*. The Belgian understood, also preparing to move.

'Four. Three.'

Chase tensed—

'Don't shoot! Please, don't hurt them!'

All heads snapped round at the sound of Natalia's voice. 'No, run!' Chase cried as she emerged from the bushes – only to freeze as he saw what she was holding.

The landmine was balanced precariously on her outstretched left hand. The detonator had been screwed back into position, and the wire removed from the safety pin hole. Her right hand was held palm down just above the trigger's rusted prongs.

The three mercenaries all regarded the weapon with alarm. 'Is it live?' Castille asked cautiously as the young woman moved towards them.

'It was when I took the detonator out,' Chase replied, grim-faced.

'But the detonator is now back in.'

'Yeah, I noticed!'

Lock was more interested in Natalia than in what she was holding. 'I told you she wouldn't go far. Natalia, if you want your friends to live, you'll do exactly what I tell you.'

'Let them go,' she replied, voice trembling. 'Or I use this.'

He moved his gaze to her hands. 'What is that? A landmine?'

'Hell *yeah*, it's a landmine,' Hoyt muttered. 'It's a goddamn Bouncing Betty!'

Concern finally crossed Lock's face as he registered the other American's nervousness. 'How dangerous is it?'

'It'll kill us all if it goes off.'

Lock stiffened. Natalia stepped closer. 'Don't move,' she ordered. 'Drop your guns or I will blow us all up.'

'Put it down or I'll shoot them,' he countered.

She lowered her right hand until the prongs touched her skin. 'I'll do it, I will do it! Let them go!'

'You won't kill yourself. Or them.' Lock relaxed slightly, smugness creeping into his expression. 'I may not be your father, but I still know a lot about you. You're a peacenik – you wouldn't kill anyone. You couldn't.'

'You do not know me at all,' she said. Though her voice was still shaky, Chase recognised the same resolve behind it as when she told him of her hatred for weapons of war. 'I know why you want to use me – you, and the Russians. You want to start Serafim Volkov's work again. Yes, I know all about him,' she added on seeing Lock's surprise, 'and what he did to my grandmother, and my mother – and to me. I will not let you do that!'

Lock's response was to move the Glock away from Castille, aiming at her legs. 'Put it down, Natalia, or I'll put *you* down.'

'Don't!' said Hoyt. 'If she drops it, it'll go off!' His boss hesitated.

'You think that because I believe in peace, I am a coward?' Natalia went on, stopping ten feet from the four men. 'You are wrong. I will not allow you to use me to make a weapon. I already know that I will not live to be old, because of my grandfather's experiments – but I would rather die to save lives than in pain in a hospital bed.'

'You'd be killing Chase and his friend too,' Lock said.

'We're fine with that,' said Chase. Castille raised a forefinger, about to express his own opinion to the contrary, but the Englishman continued: 'If it stops you arseholes from getting your hands on a bioweapon, then it's worth it. So if you don't drop your guns . . . then Natalia, blow us up.' He gave her a look to assure her he was serious, then turned back to Lock. '*You've* got ten seconds.'

The American's gun was still pointed at Natalia, but was no longer rock-steady. 'Hoyt!' said Lock. 'Do something!'

'Do what?' protested the mercenary. 'If that mine blows, we're all dead!'

'It might be a dud!'

'You wanna bet your life on that?' To Lock's dismay, Hoyt cautiously lowered his AK-47 to the ground.

Chase smiled coldly at Lock. 'Four. Three . . .'

'God *damn* it!' Lock spat. He dropped the Glock.

'Smart lad,' said Chase, standing and collecting the fallen gun. Castille did the same with the AK, gesturing for Hoyt to back away. 'Natalia, stay still until we've dealt with these two.'

'Okay,' she said, the tremor returning to her voice.

'Edward, we have to get out of here,' Castille said. He glanced towards the northern track. There was not yet any indication of approaching vehicles, but the river's noise masked out other sounds.

'We'll take the jeep,' said Chase, quickly checking the Glock before pointing it at its former owner. They would have to go south; a risk, as it took them back in the direction of the Russian camp, but it would be preferable to running head-on into a truck full of what he expected to be well-armed mercenaries. He waved for Lock to join Hoyt. 'You two dickheads, get your hands up and move back. Now!' The two Americans reluctantly obeyed.

Castille climbed into the Land Cruiser and started the engine. Chase went to the young German. 'Okay, Natalia, I'll take the mine. Move your hand off the top, it's okay.'

Both her hands shook as she offered the weapon to him. He splayed his left fingers, palm up, and carefully took its weight. She gasped in relief as it finally left her grip. 'Okay, get in the jeep,' he ordered. She hurried to the Toyota.

Chase kept the gun trained on Hoyt and Lock as he backed off the wooden deck. Natalia got into the front passenger seat; he went to the open tailgate.

Castille regarded the Bouncing Betty with disbelief. 'Why are you bringing that?'

'I'm not bringing it, I'm using it!' The sound of another engine, approaching quickly from the north, had just reached the Englishman. He crouched and put the landmine in one of the muddy ruts, then jumped into the back of the Land Cruiser and yanked the tailgate shut. 'Okay, *go!*'

Castille set off in a spray of mud, the 4x4 fishtailing across the sodden trail before finding grip and jumping forward. Loose items skittered about the rear cargo area as he accelerated, Chase amongst them. He grabbed one of the folded seats to brace himself and looked back. Lock and Hoyt were already running towards the track – and waving furiously, not at him but at a second Land Cruiser that had just come into sight.

Its driver reacted to their warning, braking hard. But the sheer weight of the big SUV and its occupants sent it slithering onwards through the mud, the rutted surface channelling it directly at the waiting landmine.

Lock and Hoyt both flung themselves flat as the Toyota's front wheel hit the Bouncing Betty—

Even though he was now outside the weapon's effective range, Chase instinctively ducked – but there was no explosion.

A feeble puff of smoke came from the detonator. Then Castille rounded a bend in the track, but Chase still managed a short laugh at the sight of a mud-stained Lock looking up in a mixture of relief and fury before being lost to view. 'Christ! All that faffing about, and we could have used the bloody thing as a football if we'd wanted.'

'It did not blow up?' asked Natalia.

'Nope – although I wish it had, 'cause now we've got a whole truckful of those arseholes coming after us!'

'Oh, *merveilleux*,' sighed Castille. 'I do not suppose you have a plan, Edward? No, of course not,' he added.

'I'll come up with something. Just keep going.' He looked at Natalia. 'That was good thinking back there – a hell of a bluff,' he told her with admiration. '*I* was convinced, so I'm not surprised they bought it too.'

'So did I!' Castille said with a grimace.

'I was not bluffing,' she replied quietly.

He was not sure how to respond to the admission, but had no time to do so as he saw headlights in the rear-view mirror. The second Land Cruiser was powering after them. 'Hugo, put your foot down,' he said, pocketing the Glock and reaching over the rear seat for the Belgian's AK-47. 'Here they come.'

274

19

Russia

'Get behind me,' Eddie told Nina and Tova, his eyes fixed on Slavin's gun.

Tova obeyed, but Nina stayed beside him, crouching to check on Eisenhov. 'He's still alive – we've got to help him.'

She reached out to apply pressure to the gushing bullet wound, but Slavin jabbed his pistol at her. 'No! Up! Stand up! Or I shoot you too.' She reluctantly straightened.

'You were working for the Americans,' said Kagan, disgusted. 'All these years, you were a spy for them! Why?'

The Russian officer was sweating, almost hyperventilating in his near-panic. 'I – I lost money gambling,' he gasped. 'I had to borrow from gangsters to pay for it. If the Americans had not helped, they would have killed me!'

'So you became a traitor?' said Nina.

'A *traitor*?' Slavin said, nearly screeching. He stepped closer and stabbed the gun at her again. 'To what? This country is *run* by gangsters, bottom to top – everyone is corrupt! If you do not have money, you are no one!' He glanced at the fallen steel canister. 'But I will *have* money – I will sell Thor's Hammer to the Americans. And then I will disappear.' With his free hand, he fumbled for a radio on his belt. '*After* I shoot the spies who have killed Dmitri Prokopiyevich!' He spoke in frantic Russian into the handset.

'He is telling them we murdered the Academician,' Kagan warned the others.

'Shut up!' Slavin stepped over Eisenhov and pointed the gun at his commander. 'I have wanted to do this for a long—'

Eisenhov jerked one leg sideways to hit Slavin's ankle with his foot. It was only a light impact, but enough to make the already agitated officer flinch and look down.

His gun twitched away from Kagan—

Eddie kicked the armchair at Slavin. Its broad back hit the Russian, sending him reeling. Before he could recover, Eddie used the chair as a springboard to dive at him. Both men crashed against a bookshelf, volumes cascading down.

The Englishman took a particularly hefty tome to the top of his head. 'Fuck!' he yelped, quickly shaking off the pain, but the distraction gave Slavin an opening. He drove his elbow into Eddie's stomach, knocking him back, then spun and brought up his gun—

Nina snatched up the steel container by its handle and smashed it against his outstretched hand with all her strength.

Slavin shrieked as two of his fingers broke, only for his wail to be abruptly cut off as Eddie drove a punishing punch into his face. The Russian tumbled back over the armchair, blood spurting from his burst lip.

Kagan retrieved the gun, then hurriedly checked on Eisenhov. '*Nyet!*' he gasped, mortified. The scientist wasn't breathing. Tova put her hands to her mouth in horror.

'Slavin would have killed us if not for him,' Nina reminded them. 'He saved us.'

Though dismayed, Kagan nodded as he stood. 'He was a good man – a hero.'

Eddie kicked Slavin. 'Unlike this twat. What do we do with him?'

Alarm bells sounded. 'Watch him,' said Kagan, picking up the radio. He spoke rapidly into it, only for his face to fall as he listened to the reply. 'This is not good,' he told the others.

'What did they say?' Nina asked.

'They believed him – they think we are spies, that we killed the Academician!'

'But you are in charge here!' Tova protested. 'Can't you tell them that we did not?'

Kagan glared at Slavin. 'He is in charge of security at this bunker. They are his men, they are all chosen and promoted by him. Everyone is corrupt, indeed!' He thought for a moment. 'We must protect Thor's Hammer,' he said, indicating the container. 'We cannot allow him to give it to the Americans.' He stepped on Slavin's injured hand, making him scream. 'To get past his men, we will have to use him as a hostage.'

'Or a shield.' Eddie hauled the anguished Russian to his feet. 'Is there any way out except for the lift?' Kagan shook his head. 'You lot weren't big on health and safety in the Cold War, were you?'

'You will not get out,' rasped Slavin. 'The bunker is locked down.'

'I can override the lockdown when we get to the elevator,' insisted Kagan.

'*If* we get to the elevator,' Nina said. 'We're at the opposite end of the bunker, and there are all those security doors to get through – as well as however many of his guys are waiting for us outside!'

Kagan gave her a grim smile. 'Let us find out.' He grabbed

Slavin from Eddie, twisting his wounded hand behind his back and pushing the gun to his head. 'You will tell your men to stay back, or I will kill you.'

'If you shoot me, they will shoot you,' Slavin growled in reply.

'Then let's hope nobody shoots anyone, huh?' said Nina.

Kagan nodded. 'Let us hope. Chase? Check the door.'

Eddie eased it open a crack. A man outside shouted in Russian. 'What did he say?'

'He wants us to let Slavin go, and surrender,' said Kagan. He called out in his native language, then told Eddie: 'Open it.'

'You sure?'

'I said I have him at gunpoint, and to pull back if they want him to live.'

'Hope he wasn't a shitty boss, then.' Eddie took a breath, then swung the door wide.

They were not greeted by gunfire. 'Okay, that's a start,' said Nina. She peered nervously around the two Russians to see several uniformed men, weapons raised, at an intersection thirty feet down the main corridor. 'Although it's still not exactly a great one.'

Kagan barked an order in Russian; when nothing happened, he ground the muzzle of his gun against Slavin's head. His sweating prisoner reluctantly nodded, and the soldiers slowly backed away. 'Dr Wilde, Dr Skilfinger – stay behind me.'

Pushing Slavin ahead of him, he advanced through the door. Nina and Tova followed, Eddie joining the slow-moving line behind them. Kagan spoke to the Russians again, only to be interrupted by Slavin – whose frantic gabble broke off with a cry of pain as the other man crushed his hand. '*Govno!*' Kagan growled, before telling the others: 'He told them to shoot us – if they can do it without hitting him.'

Eddie looked ahead. 'They'll cut us down from the side corridors. We'll never make it fucking plodding along like this.'

Slavin managed a pained chuckle. 'You think you can force me to run, Grigory Alekseyevich? Even with a gun to my head?'

'Then we'll have to do something else,' said Eddie. He spotted a fire extinguisher clipped to a bracket a few paces ahead. 'Kagan, are you a good shot?'

The Russian nodded. 'Yes.'

'A *really* good shot?'

'Yes, yes!'

They reached the extinguisher. 'Okay – then shoot *this*!'

Eddie yanked it from its clips and flung it down the corridor. It bounced off the hard floor with a loud clang, skittering into the intersection—

Kagan whipped the gun away from Slavin's head and fired. The bullet hit the pressurised metal cylinder – which exploded. The blast knocked the soldiers down, a freezing cloud of carbon dioxide leaving them blinded and choking.

'Run!' Eddie yelled, racing past the others towards the junction. 'Come on!'

Kagan shoved Slavin forward, but the traitor deliberately stumbled, dropping flat to the floor. Kagan hesitated, then ran after Eddie. Both women followed him, Tova skirting the fallen man while Nina trampled on his hand, making him scream again.

Eddie held his breath and ran into the cloud. It was already dispersing, shadowy shapes resolving into the Russian soldiers. He kicked the closest of the staggering figures in the head, then snatched up his AK-103 assault rifle. Another savage kick downed a second trooper, then he was through the swirling mist.

The corridor ahead was empty. 'It's clear, go!' he shouted. Behind him, Kagan emerged from the cloud, Tova and Nina in his wake.

Eddie increased his pace. One of the security doors was ahead. 'Kagan! Can you open it?'

'Yes, my card will override it,' came the reply.

'Then bloody do it, quick!' He turned to cover the rear as Kagan reached the door. The carbon dioxide had now mostly cleared – revealing one of the soldiers back on his feet, bringing up his AK—

Eddie fired first, sending the man crashing to the floor. Bright red blood stained the white tiles. Tova screamed, clutching her hands to her ears as the Kalashnikov's clamour echoed off the walls. The other soldiers hurriedly retreated down the side passages, Slavin scrambling after them.

Kagan found his keycard and jammed it into the slot. A warning buzzer sounded, but he stabbed a four-digit code into a keypad and the door heaved itself aside. He pulled out the card, gun raised as he scanned the corridor beyond. 'Okay, it is clear!'

'Go!' Eddie said, backing towards the door. Kagan went first, the women right behind. The Russian waited for Eddie to come through, then hit a button on the door's control panel. It slammed shut. 'Can Slavin open that?'

'Yes,' Kagan told him. 'We must hurry.' He ran down the central corridor to the next junction, peering around the corner to check the adjoining passages. 'Clear.'

The group hurried through the intersection and headed for the next security barrier. Nina glanced through the window into one of the laboratories as they passed. Confused scientists, locked in their workspaces when the alarm sounded, stared back, reacting with horrified shock when they saw what she was carrying. Unlike the Tsar Protocol, Thor's Hammer was clearly no secret to Unit 201's staff.

Kagan entered the code into the next door, which opened. Again he checked that nobody was lying in wait on the other side before going through. 'Two more doors, then we reach the elevator,' he said.

Nina followed him. 'Shit! Here they come!' she cried, looking back to see the first barrier opening again. Someone poked their head around it, jerking back as Eddie fired.

'Hope the fucking lift's still at the bottom,' he said, coming through and hitting the button. The door rolled shut – as a bullet hit the other side with a piercing clang. 'Okay, we need to pick up the pace!'

They ran past more labs, some occupied, others dimly lit and empty, and reached another security door. Kagan entered the code again. The door opened – followed a few seconds later by the one behind them.

Eddie fired two more shots to deter their pursuers, then darted through the narrowing gap as Kagan closed the barrier. More bullets twanged off the other side. 'Only one more,' said the Russian.

They quickly reached the last door, Kagan using his card to open it. The barrier behind them opened almost in sync. This time, Slavin's men were already in position and ready to shoot. Nina shrieked as a bullet shattered a tile just behind her. Eddie switched his AK-103 to full auto and unleashed a deafening burst of fire down the corridor, one of the crouched figures taking a bloody hit to the shoulder and falling with a wail. His comrades retreated into cover.

'Chase!' shouted Kagan. 'The elevator, we are almost there!'

Eddie backed through, the door closing behind him. He looked down the passage. The elevator was twenty metres away, at the far end of the lobby area. There was one more intersection to cross, but beyond that it was a straight run past the final labs. He quickly moved to the junction and glanced down each of the side passages.

No one there. 'Clear here,' he said, looking back at the elevator as Kagan ran past him. Still nobody in the lobby.

Wait . . .

Overhead lights in the reception area were casting shadows on the floor at the end of the corridor.

Moving shadows—

'Back, get back!' he yelled, pulling Nina into one of the side passages. 'They're waiting for us! Tova, down here!'

Tova fearfully rushed after them. Kagan skidded on the tiled floor, then reversed direction – as several soldiers leapt out from hiding and brought up their AK-103s.

The Russian dived after his companions as gunfire exploded tiles into shrapnel behind him. He hit the floor hard – and hurt, a red slash marking where debris had caught his calf. Nina and Tova pulled him into cover as Eddie sent a couple of shots at their attackers to force them back.

Nina checked the wound. 'It doesn't look too deep. Kagan, can you walk on it?'

'Help me up,' he said through clenched teeth. 'I will try!'

'Try fast,' said Eddie. He looked up the new corridor. 'Where does this go?'

'Only to offices,' said Kagan, grimacing as he put weight on his injured leg. 'It is a dead end— No, wait!' He pointed with sudden excitement at a doorway a few metres from them. 'We can go through this laboratory – there is a door on the other side just across from the elevator!'

'Is anyone in there?' Nina asked, remembering the scientists she had seen in the other labs.

'No, it is empty. Quick, quick!' He hobbled to the door and inserted his keycard, then readied his gun as the barrier slid open.

'Is it clear?' Eddie demanded from the junction.

Nina checked. The long room was in shadow, the only light

coming through a window beside another door at the far end. Boxed-up equipment lurked on workbenches, but there was no movement. 'Think so.'

'Okay, go. I'll be right behind you.'

Kagan went through the door, Tova following. Nina hesitated as she heard the clatter of running footsteps. Slavin and his men were through the last security door. 'Eddie, come on!'

He backed up. 'I'm coming, don't bloody worry!' The soldiers approached the intersection. Eddie fired two shots, shattering more wall tiles, and the footsteps hurriedly halted. He ducked through the door and hit the button to close it.

Tova helped the limping Kagan through the dimly lit laboratory. Nina quickly caught up. Through the window, she saw the elevator. 'Jesus, we'll be completely exposed.'

'It is the only way out,' Kagan reminded her grimly. 'Chase! How many bullets do you have?'

Eddie had been counting his shots. 'About ten.'

The Russian grimaced again. 'It will have to do.' They reached the other exit, and he raised his keycard once more. 'We only need to hold them off until the doors open—'

A shrill, piercing alarm filled the room, lights snapping on. But these were not the glaring overheads illuminating the rest of the facility; they were instead a sickly yellow. 'What's that?' said Eddie.

Kagan's expression was one of utter, trapped horror. He shoved the card into the lock, but the only response was a warning rasp and a flashing red light. '*Govno*,' he gasped, stumbling back. 'The alarm – they have started the sterilisation procedure!'

'What?' Nina cried. She checked the ceiling. The lab was overlooked by two of the sinister black domes – which split as she watched, their casings opening up like hardened flowers to expose a cluster of metal nozzles pointing outwards. 'Oh my God! Stop it, use your override!'

'I cannot!' Kagan replied. 'Once it is activated, there is no way to stop it.'

'There's got to be a way!' She grabbed his card and jammed it back into the lock, but the buzzer sounded again.

Outside the window, some of the Russian soldiers appeared, peering warily through the glass – followed by Slavin. The sweating officer now wore a nasty, triumphant smile. 'How long do we have?' Eddie asked.

Kagan regarded the nearest set of nozzles. 'The gas must build up pressure before it is lit – about thirty seconds.'

Eddie whipped up his AK and fired a burst at the window – aiming directly at Slavin. The Russian jerked back in fear as bullets smacked against the glass, but quickly recovered his composure, his smirk widening as he saw that the window was cracked, but not broken. 'Shit!'

'Shoot it again!' Tova cried.

'It won't make any difference,' he said, looking around. 'But . . . that might!'

Amongst the boxes and equipment on one of the benches was a squat red cylinder topped by a pressure valve. Eddie couldn't read the Cyrillic text on its label, but the symbol of a flame in a warning triangle beside it was immediately understandable. He swung the heavy container on to a small trolley, then pushed it to the window. 'Everyone get behind that bench.'

'What are you doing?' Nina asked.

'Remember that fire extinguisher? Same thing – only the bang'll be a bit bigger.'

'If you blow it up, it will kill us!' protested Kagan.

'It *might* kill us – but that'll *definitely* kill us,' Eddie replied, pointing at the nearest dome. 'Come on, get down!'

Nina hunched behind the bench, clutching the steel canister. A new sound became audible over the alarm: a rumble coming from the nozzles, slowly but steadily rising in pitch. 'Oh God,' she whispered as the others joined her. 'It's starting!'

'You ready?' Eddie called out as he crouched beside Nina, taking aim around the side of the workbench at the gas cylinder. Slavin's eyes widened as he realised what the Englishman was going to do. 'Cover your ears!'

They did so – as Slavin made a hasty retreat, barging soldiers out of his way.

Eddie pulled the trigger—

The Kalashnikov barked once – and the container exploded.

A room-shaking blast shredded the far end of the workbench and hurled blazing equipment across the laboratory. Broken ceiling tiles dropped around the crouching fugitives like hailstones. 'Jesus *Christ*!' Nina screamed as a sharp-edged piece hit her.

Eddie didn't even bother checking the results of his handiwork, simply grabbing her and jumping up to run for the window. Either it was broken – or they were all dead. 'Go, *go*!'

Even with his leg wound, Kagan found a burst of speed as he and Tova followed the couple. The lab was littered with burning debris – but amongst it was shattered glass. The weakened window had been blown apart.

Still holding the AK, Eddie hurdled through the opening with Nina. Those soldiers who had not reacted quickly enough to follow Slavin lay on the floor, faces cut, uniforms ripped and smouldering. Slavin himself was sprawled on the far side of the lobby area. The thought of shooting him flashed through the Englishman's mind, but survival outweighed it – they were not safe yet. 'Get to the lift!'

He pushed Nina ahead of him as Tova scrambled through the

broken window. She started to run for the elevator, but Kagan yanked her with him to one side—

High-pressure acetylene gas gushed from the nozzles, electric igniters sparking – and the laboratory was engulfed in jets of white-hot flame.

The swelling fire surged through the remains of the window. Tova screamed, Kagan pressing her against the closed metal door and shielding her with his body. One of the soldiers managed to scrabble clear of the blaze, but the luckless man beside him was instantly incinerated. Eddie and Nina dived away from the inferno, landing by the elevator.

But the danger was not over. The nozzle clusters began to rotate, searing jets blasting like deadly lighthouse beams over every square inch of the laboratory – and out into the lobby. More soldiers fled, another man being hit by the fire and instantly bursting into flames. The back of the door glowed red as burning gas washed over it, Kagan's hair scorching as heat rose behind him—

The jets stuttered, then cut out. Every part of the lab had been sterilised by fire almost half as hot as the surface of the sun, even stainless steel warped and ceramic tiles cracked by the pitiless heat. What pieces of equipment had not been smashed by the explosion were melted or burned to charcoal.

Smoke poured from the lab. 'Is it just me, or is it warm in here?' said Eddie, coughing as he stood. He tried to open the elevator doors, but they were locked. 'Kagan, get the lift open!'

Kagan hobbled to him. Tova followed, trying not to look at the burning remains of the dead soldiers. The Russian put his card into the reader and entered his override code; after a moment, the doors rumbled apart.

Eddie ducked through, keeping the AK raised to cover the soldiers, but they all seemed shell-shocked, more concerned with escaping the flames than hunting down their targets. Slavin raised his head; on seeing the Englishman, he made a frantic dash for a side passage. Eddie tracked him, but before he could shoot, Kagan had closed the doors.

The car began its ascent. 'What do we do when we get to the top?' Nina asked.

Kagan leaned against a wall to take the weight off his injured leg. 'I will tell the base commander what has really happened. I know him – I am sure he will believe me over Slavin.'

'Won't Slavin already be talking to him, though?' Eddie asked. He pulled out the AK's magazine to check his remaining ammunition; including the one in the chamber, he was down to his last three rounds. 'It's no good you being mates with the guy if he's already told his security forces to shoot us!'

'We will see what they do when we reach the surface. If they will listen to me, we may have a chance.' He closed his eyes, grimacing as he straightened. 'If they will not . . .'

'We have to shoot our way out of an airbase in the middle of Russia?' Nina finished for him. 'Oh boy.'

Tova put her head in her hands. 'How could this happen to us?'

Eddie reseated the magazine. 'I wanna know how it could *keep* happening to us! Kagan, are you ready?'

The Russian opened his eyes again. 'I am.'

'Great. Let's see what's waiting for us.'

20

Vietnam

Chase quickly checked Castille's AK-47. The magazine was fully loaded. He looked through the Land Cruiser's rear window at the pursuing 4x4 – and saw Hoyt leaning from one of the side windows with a Kalashnikov of his own. '*Down!*'

He ducked as the American's AK chattered. The bumpy track threw most of Hoyt's shots wide, but one still struck the tailgate and shattered the window. Natalia screamed.

Chase kicked out the broken glass and fired two shots of his own. He knew his chances of hitting even the other Land Cruiser, never mind its occupants, were slim, but his main goal was to force the driver to fall back. A plan was already forming in his mind, but he would need more of a gap to pull it off . . .

'Hold on!' Castille warned. The track ahead jinked to avoid a large rock. He braked, flicking the steering wheel to swing out the Land Cruiser's rear end on the muddy surface before applying more power and spinning the wheel hard in the opposite direction. The 4x4 kicked up a spray of wet earth as it performed a power slide around the obstacle.

Chase saw his chance and fired another pair of shots. He

couldn't tell if they had hit or not, but they had the effect he'd hoped for. The driver flinched, distracted at a crucial moment – and braked too hard as he turned. The second Toyota slewed sideways, its back end ripping through the undergrowth before hitting the rock, caving in the rear passenger door.

The Englishman braced himself again as Castille took their own vehicle around another curve. Their pursuers were lost to sight behind the trees. 'Nice driving, Hugo! I didn't know you were into rallying.'

'I grew up in the country,' Castille replied. 'There is a lot of mud when it rains!'

'Wow, that's about the most interesting thing I've ever heard about Belgium.' In the mirror, Chase saw his friend make a sarcastic face. 'Okay, Hugo, I've got a plan, but you probably won't like it.'

'You want me to slow down so you and Natalia can jump out, and then carry on to decoy them away from you?'

'Well, that saves me explaining! So you *do* like it, then?'

Castille snorted. 'No, not one little bit! But,' he added, giving Natalia a quick smile, 'it is the best chance we have to get you away from them. Edward will take care of you, you do not have to worry about that.'

'I know,' she replied quietly. But there was something behind her words that made Chase give her a questioning look: resolve, or . . . resignation? He wasn't sure.

And there was no time to think about it further. 'Here, here,' he said, pointing ahead. The track began to rise up a hill, the ground to the left dropping away quite steeply at the entrance to a valley. He realised it was the same one into which he and Natalia had been swept by the mudslide the previous night. 'We'll jump out behind those bushes there. Natalia, are you ready?' She gave him a worried nod.

Chase clambered over the back seat and was about to slide across to the door when a thought stuck him. He reached back into the cargo area to snag Hoyt's pack, heavy with the laptop and research notes stolen from the Russians. 'Just making sure those twats don't get their hands on this stuff,' he told Castille.

The Belgian had an unhappy expression. 'It sounds as if you do not think I will get away from them.'

'I hope you do, but . . . fight to the end, Hugo.'

'Fight to the end,' Castille echoed. He held up one hand; Chase clasped it firmly in a gesture of brotherhood, then slung the pack from a shoulder and moved to the door. 'I hope to see you again soon.'

'So do I,' Chase replied, heartfelt. He opened the door, then took a firm hold of the AK. 'Just here. Natalia . . . go!'

Castille slowed the Toyota to a jogging pace. Natalia jumped out, Chase behind her. They stumbled as they hit the ground, but recovered. Natalia scrambled behind the bushes, while Chase thumped a fist on the window to tell Castille they were clear. With a wave, the Belgian accelerated.

Chase slithered down the hillside after Natalia. 'Stay low,' he warned her. He could already hear the second Land Cruiser rapidly approaching.

He brought up the Kalashnikov; a sharp-eyed passenger might spot their footprints. Thumps and creaks from the straining suspension became audible over the engine's roar as Lock and Hoyt's 4x4 pounded along the track. Chase felt Natalia tense beside him. The Land Cruiser drew level . . .

And rushed past without a pause, charging into the jungle after Castille.

Chase waited several seconds, then crawled up the slope and peered after it. The vehicle was out of sight behind the trees. He returned to Natalia. 'All right, they've gone.'

'I hope your friend will be okay,' said the young German. 'If they catch him, they will—'

'Hugo's pretty tough,' Chase said firmly. 'It'll take more than an arsehole like Hoyt to bring him down. He'll be fine, he's not scared of anything. Well, except helicopters,' he added.

'Helicopters?'

'He had a bad experience with one once. Long story, and right now we need to get moving.'

'Where are we going?'

'Good question. We'll figure that out once we've got away from here – they might realise we're not in the car any more and turn round. Come on.' The pair made their way down to the valley floor and headed deeper into the trees.

Castille powered the Toyota along the track, bumps and ruts hammering at his vehicle. The hill was getting steeper, and he was uncomfortably aware that he might be heading towards – or even right into – the encampment from which he had helped rescue the aid workers, leaving him trapped between two forces.

He pushed that concern aside; there were more immediate ones. Slowing to let out Chase and Natalia had given his pursuers back their momentum. The second Land Cruiser's headlights reappeared in his mirrors. The rising terrain would slow him – and bring Lock's men back into weapons range.

All he could do was stay ahead for as long as he could. He gritted his teeth, determined to give his friend and the woman he was protecting as much of a chance to escape as possible.

The path dropped into a dip, a large muddy puddle across it. Castille knew that the water would both slow him and make the 4x4 trickier to control, but he kept his foot on the accelerator. The other Land Cruiser was still homing in, Hoyt leaning from its window once more.

Gunshots cracked through the jungle. The Belgian ducked, bracing himself as he reached the puddle . . .

Despite his efforts, he was thrown forward by the deceleration as a huge wave of spray exploded from his vehicle's tyres. The water was deeper than he had thought. The steering wheel squirmed in his hands like an eel. He gripped it harder, trying to haul the off-roader back into line with the track – but it skidded towards a sodden ditch to one side.

'*Merde!*' Castille cried as he realised he was past the point of no return. He let go of the wheel, bringing up both arms to protect his head—

The Land Cruiser lurched sideways as its front wheel dropped into the ditch. Castille was slammed against the door, then pitched painfully into the steering wheel as the 4x4 came to an abrupt halt.

He slumped back in his seat. His arms had cushioned the impact to an extent, but he still had a piercing pain in his forehead, and felt blood running from one nostril.

Noise from behind, the growl of an engine – and shouts. Castille tried to push himself upright. The Land Cruiser had come to rest at an angle, two wheels in the ditch. He grabbed the door handle, only to find to his dismay that it wouldn't open, blocked by the bank. Grunting in pain, he scrambled over the central console to the passenger door.

It opened before he reached it.

'Don't fuckin' move!' Hoyt shouted, thrusting his rifle at the Belgian. Castille drew back. The American looked into the 4x4 as other men yanked open the rear passenger door and the tailgate. 'Shit! They're not here!'

Lock strode from the second Toyota. 'What? Where are they?'

'They musta bailed out somewhere back along the track.' He

glared at the mercenary team's driver. 'You stupid son of a bitch. If you hadn't hit that rock, we wouldn't have lost sight of them!'

Lock raised a hand. 'Enough, enough!' He gestured at the overturned Land Cruiser's lone occupant. 'Get him out of there.'

Hoyt and another man dragged Castille out of the 4x4, throwing him into the muddy water. 'All right – Castille, is it?' said Lock. 'You're going to take us to where you let out Natalia and your buddy.'

Castille wiped blood from his nose. 'That is funny – I thought I was going to tell you to, ah . . .' He thought for a moment. 'To go and fuck your whore mother. If you will excuse the crudity. That is more Edward's area.' Lock's face twitched in anger.

'Funny guy,' said Hoyt, unamused. He kicked Castille hard in the stomach. 'You want to stay alive, you show us where they went. Otherwise I'll shoot you right here, and we'll go find their trail on our own. Either way, we'll get 'em. You got ten seconds to decide.'

Castille caught his breath. 'Do what you must, *abruti*. I will never give them up.'

'Your choice.' Hoyt aimed the gun at his face—

All heads turned at an unexpected sound.

'The *fuck*?' said Hoyt in disbelief as the shrill electronic warble of a police siren cut through the jungle's background chatter. Castille looked up the track – and saw three vehicles approaching. In the lead was a Ford Ranger pickup in white-and-blue police livery, the lights on its roof flicking to life. Behind it was a mud-caked Nissan Patrol 4x4, and following that a larger six-wheeled truck in military green. Men in its rear bed peered over the top of the cab to see what was going on: *uniformed* men, all armed with Kalashnikovs.

Some of Lock's men raised their own weapons, but their

leader was already hurrying back to his Land Cruiser. 'It's TC2 – they called in backup, dammit!' he snarled. 'Come on, let's get out of here!'

Hoyt looked back down at Castille, the gun still fixed on him. The Belgian tensed – then Hoyt turned and ran after his boss. The other mercenaries piled into the Land Cruiser, which reversed rapidly before making a mud-spraying handbrake turn and powering away back down the track. The police pickup sped after it, the Patrol pulling over into the undergrowth near Castille's vehicle to let the lumbering troop truck past.

Castille staggered to his feet – and decided on the part he was going to play. 'Thank God, thank God!' he said in French, giving the men getting out of the SUV a smile of relief, part of which was because none of them were either of the guards who had been watching the kidnapped aid workers when Sullivan's team moved in; they would almost certainly have recognised him. 'They drove me off the road – they tried to kill me!'

The four men – Castille guessed they were members of TC2 – regarded the bloodied figure warily. He knew what they were thinking: they were searching for Westerners, so any Caucasian in the area would automatically be a suspect or even a target . . . but the group of *other* Caucasians had been holding him at gunpoint before they fled, and garish shirts were not exactly camouflage gear. One of the Vietnamese spoke, in halting French: 'Who are you? What are you doing here?'

'I am so glad to see you,' Castille went on, coming to them and exaggeratedly wiping his brow. 'My name is Hugo, Hugo Castille. I drove past those men at a jetty a kilometre or so up the road, and they started chasing me and shooting at my truck! I crashed,' he gestured at the overturned Toyota, 'and they robbed me – they were going to kill me!'

'You are French?'

'No, I am *Belgian*,' he replied in haughty protest.

'And what are you doing here?'

'I am a tourist. I was exploring the jungle – I did not know it was going to be dangerous!'

The French-speaking man translated this into his native language for the benefit of the others. One of them, apparently the leader, regarded Castille unreadably from behind a pair of oversized mirrored sunglasses, then issued a curt command. 'We are going to look in your truck,' the first man said.

Castille covered his concern; he didn't *think* there was anything inside that would expose him as a mercenary, but he didn't know exactly what Lock had brought with him. 'Of course, of course,' he said, smiling again. 'And if you could help me get it out of the ditch, that would be great!'

The Vietnamese ushered him to the Land Cruiser, the leader standing back to keep an eye on the foreigner while the other three men rummaged through its interior. To Castille's relief, Lock had not concealed any more weapons inside it. The man in the sunglasses spoke again, Castille getting a translation: 'Show us your papers.'

'I have them right here,' he said, reaching into his top pocket to produce his passport, visa and other documents.

The man plucked them from his hand and leafed through them. 'You are staying in Da Nang?'

'Yes, the Red Leaf hotel.'

A nod. 'The men who chased you – what were they doing when you saw them?'

Castille thought fast. 'There was a boat at the jetty – I think they were about to get on board.'

'A boat?' He passed this on to the others, who exchanged calculating looks.

'Yes. There were more people with them.'

That caught the man's attention. 'Who? Did you get a good look at them?'

He shook his head. 'They looked European or American – I remember, because I was surprised to see so many other white people out here. I thought they were tourists, but then those men tried to kill me.'

'Did you see a girl? A blonde girl?'

'I do not know.' Castille shrugged. 'Perhaps. I am not sure.'

The leader received another translated report. He frowned, sunglasses still fixed on the Belgian, then spoke once more to his subordinate. 'Why did you come down this road?' the other man asked.

Castille shrugged again. 'I saw the turning on the highway and thought it looked interesting. As I said, I wanted to explore the jungle.'

'There is nothing to see here. Turn around and go back. If you want to visit the jungle, go to the Bach Ma park. This is a military area.'

'But there was nothing on my map . . .'

The man glowered at him. 'If you do not, we will arrest you.'

'Then I will turn around and go back,' Castille hurriedly assured him. 'But what about those men?'

'We will catch them. Now go.' The four Vietnamese returned to the Nissan.

'Are you going to help me get my truck out of the ditch?' Castille asked. The slamming of doors gave him an answer. 'No? Oh well.'

He clambered back into the Land Cruiser as the other 4x4 drove past. 'Edward, I hope you have got her a long way from here,' he said, restarting the engine.

★

Chase pressed on through the jungle. 'Once we get to the river, we can find that crossing point and go back to the village,' he said over his shoulder. 'We'll ask your friends to look after you while I . . .'

He realised Natalia was no longer following him. She had not fallen or been forced to sit to catch her breath; instead, she had simply stopped walking, staring blankly at the ground. Everything about her bowed stance suggested utter defeat. 'What is it?' he said, going back to her. 'What's wrong?'

'Everything,' she replied, voice filled with misery. 'Everything is wrong.'

'Yeah, I know. But we need to keep moving. It's not safe to stay here.'

'But that is the point!' she cried, raising her head to regard him with despairing eyes. 'It is not safe anywhere! Not for me. That man at the river, the one who pretended to be my father – he is working for the Americans, yes?' Chase nodded. 'And the men who kidnapped me are Russians. Do you think they will stop looking for me?'

'I'll make sure they don't get you.'

'For how long? A week? A month? A year? Are you going to be my bodyguard for ever?' Tears rolled down her cheeks. 'Eddie, these people will find me wherever I go. If they think they can use me to continue my grandfather's experiments, they will never give up. They will keep sending people after me until they get what they want – and they will kill anyone who tries to stop them. They will kill *you*, Eddie.'

'They can fuckin' try,' he growled.

'Do you think you are invincible?' She held out her hands almost pleadingly. 'They will come for me, and they will kill you, and then they will use what is in my blood to kill even more people. I do not want that to happen. I – will not *let* that happen!'

'I won't let it happen either,' Chase insisted. 'And the first thing we need to do to make sure of that is get out of here. Come on.'

He reached for her hand, but she pulled away. 'No. I will not let anyone die because of me. Not you, not my friends in the village, not anyone! And I do not want you to have to kill people to protect me. Even if they are doing . . . bad things. It would still be because of me that they were dead, and I cannot live with that.' Her voice dropped to a whisper. 'I cannot live.'

Chase understood her meaning, but refused to accept it. 'Don't say that. I can still get you out of here.'

Natalia shook her head. 'No. This . . . this is where it has to end.' She slowly turned, taking in the verdant jungle around them. 'It is beautiful here, isn't it? The Americans tried to kill it with Agent Orange, but it grew back. Nature will recover.' Then she looked back at him, suddenly firm. 'But what my grandfather was trying to do was against nature. He wanted to *corrupt* nature, to make monsters. And that is what the Americans or the Russians will do if they find me. They will fill the world with monsters, and poison everything living. There is only one way to stop them.'

Now it was Chase's turn to shake his head. 'No, there isn't.'

'You know I am right, Eddie!' She walked to him, more tears swelling. 'I am going to die young, no matter what – my grandfather's curse has seen to that. But that does not mean I have to die like my mother and my grandmother. I can *choose* how I die – and I choose to die to save other people. Including you.' There was a long pause, then she drew a decisive breath. 'Give me the gun.'

He stared at her, appalled. 'I'm not going to let you fucking shoot yourself!'

'Then *you* will have to shoot me.'

'No!' he protested. 'No, that's fucking crazy.'

Almost angry, she jabbed a hand back along their path. 'Your friend, the Belgian . . .'

'Hugo.'

'Hugo, he was willing to give his life to protect us. And you are willing to give your life to protect me. Am I wrong?'

'No, but there's a difference between *giving* your life to protect someone, and *risking* it—'

'The only difference is if you are lucky. But you cannot be lucky for ever. We all die in the end. And this is where I am going to die.' She gestured at the surrounding trees, her anger replaced by an almost peaceful acceptance. 'Once I am dead, if you burn my body there will be nothing for them to take. My grandfather's work will be ended.'

'This is insane,' he said, shaking his head again. 'Natalia, I'm not going to kill you. I promised to protect you!'

'But I am just one person. If I am dead, many more lives will be saved.'

'You don't know that.'

'Once these people have the eitr, do you think they will not use it? Why else would they want it? And,' she added, 'one of the lives that will be saved is yours. If I am gone, they will have no reason to kill you.'

'I wouldn't bet on that,' he muttered.

'But you know I am right, Eddie,' Natalia continued, desperation entering her voice. 'And it is what I want to do. Please!' She wrapped her hands around his. 'I will not let anyone else die because of me. You have to do it. You have to!' She squeezed his hands, then let go and turned away, getting down on her knees. 'You . . . you know how to make it not hurt, don't you?' she said quietly.

'Yeah, I do,' he replied. 'But—'

'Then do it. It is the only way to end this.' She raised her head, and closed her eyes.

He stared down at the young woman. 'Are you sure this is what you want?'

'Yes,' came the reply.

He was silent for a long moment. Then he slowly raised the gun.

'Please,' whispered Natalia. 'Do it.'

Chase hesitated – then pulled the trigger.

21

Russia

The elevator came to a stop. Eddie and Nina went to one side of the doors, Tova and Kagan the other as they parted. A freezing wind gusted in.

To everyone's relief, it was not accompanied by bullets. Kalashnikov raised, Eddie cautiously exited. Nina followed. The business jet had gone, though a constant low drone told them that another aircraft was idling on one of the base's long taxiways. But the only movement was of snow flurries swirling across the flat expanses between the concrete lanes. 'Okay, there's nobody here – yet.'

Kagan limped to the racks of gas tanks at one end of the blockhouse and indicated a group of concrete buildings across the runway. 'We need to reach the base headquarters.'

Eddie judged the distance. 'Christ, they're over half a mile away.'

Nina, however, was looking at something closer. 'Maybe these guys'll give us a ride!' she said, pointing in alarm. A military UAZ jeep was tearing along one of the taxiways. On seeing the group, its driver made a sharp turn to angle across the snow-covered grass directly towards them. She turned to Kagan. 'Good, or not good?'

A man leaned out of the 4x4's side and raised an AK. 'Take a guess!' said Eddie. 'Get back!'

They retreated – only to come face to face with Tova as the elevator closed. 'What is happening?' she asked.

'No, keep them open – oh, shit!' Eddie yelped as the weather-scoured metal doors slammed shut. 'Now Slavin and his guys'll come up behind us!'

'Sorry, I am sorry! But you said there was no one here,' the Swede protested.

'It's okay, it's not your fault,' Nina told her. 'What do we do?'

Eddie had an idea. 'Get behind the bunker,' he said, gesturing in the opposite direction from the approaching UAZ.

Nina, Tova and Kagan scurried for cover – but Eddie hared into the open, running across the taxiway. 'Eddie!' Nina yelled, stopping. 'What are you doing?'

'Giving 'em a warm welcome!' he shouted.

A glance back. The two men in the 4x4 had seen him, the bounding jeep changing direction to intercept. He adjusted his own course; he needed the vehicle to pass close to the bunker—

The passenger's AK thudded. Eddie heard bullets sear past him, little puffs of snow marking their impacts on the frozen ground. He reached the edge of the concrete and dropped flat on the grass, scrambling around to bring up his own rifle.

The gunman fired again, a three-round burst this time chipping the taxiway only feet from the Englishman. He flinched, then raised his head and took aim. With only three bullets left, he had to make them all count . . .

He pulled the trigger.

The shot crazed the jeep's windscreen. The driver made a

rapid stop, the 4x4 slithering on the snow to end up almost side-on to Eddie. Both men scrambled out to take cover behind the unarmoured vehicle.

Just as Eddie had hoped.

He switched his aim – to the gas tanks along the bunker's side, about fifty feet from the stationary UAZ. He aligned the sights on a valve on the nearest tank, held his breath to steady the rifle – and fired.

The shot clanged off the tank just below the valve. The sights were slightly off. Eddie muttered a curse, raising the gun to compensate – just as the two soldiers opened fire.

This time, their aim was much better.

'Shit!' Eddie gasped, dropping his head as bullets smacked against the concrete. The shooting stopped, but he knew they had not given up – they would be switching their rifles from burst-fire to single-shot mode for greater accuracy.

He raised his head again, lining up the sights on the tank for his final shot. In the corner of his vision, he saw one of the soldiers taking aim . . .

He took the shot.

The acetylene tank blew apart, the shockwave throwing the soldiers to the ground. A fireball roared out from the side of the bunker. Both Russians felt the hellish heat sweep over them, and simultaneously made the same wordless decision to jump up and run as quickly as they could away from its source.

Eddie was also back on his feet – running for the UAZ, the front end of which was now adorned by spots of flame where its paint had caught light. He waved for the others to join him. 'Anyone order a taxi?' he shouted.

Nina led the others out from behind the bunker, giving the blaze around the remaining acetylene tanks a very wide berth. 'I am *so* never putting you in charge of any barbecues,' she said as she reached the jeep. Her husband, already in the driving seat, grinned.

Tova gave the UAZ an unhappy look as she helped Kagan aboard. 'But it is on fire!'

'Second-hand cars've always got *something* wrong with 'em,' said Eddie. He put the jeep into gear and made a sharp turn to head away from the bunker. 'Okay, where are we going?'

Kagan was thinking out loud. 'We will never reach the commander to explain the truth – he has issued orders for us to be shot on sight. The orders can only be countermanded from above . . . I need to speak to my superiors in Moscow,' he announced, now focused. Nina started to take out her phone, but he shook his head. 'All the cell towers in the area will have been shut down when the base was put on alert. I need a secure line.'

'Where can we find one?' she asked.

'The main communications centre – but we will never get to it alive. Or . . .' He pointed off to one side. 'Or there!'

Nina looked round – and did a double-take when she saw what he was indicating. 'On a *plane*?'

Standing on one of the taxiways was the silver bulk of a Tu-95MS Bear bomber, the thrum of its eight massive propellers at idle the source of the droning rumble. Ladders led up into its long fuselage, a couple of small trucks waiting nearby. 'It's got a radio link?' Eddie asked.

Kagan nodded. 'There is an emergency frequency that will connect me to the Kremlin – my superiors can order the base commander to arrest Slavin. It will take only a few minutes.'

'If we even *have* a few minutes,' said Nina in alarm, seeing several other jeeps charging across the great expanse of the airbase.

'Better than nowt,' Eddie told her, swinging the UAZ on to

the grass to head for the bomber. In the wing mirror, he saw figures piling out of the bunker's elevator. 'Shit! Slavin and his lads just got to the surface.'

'Keep down,' Kagan warned. They all hunched lower. A few shots cracked after them, but none hit.

'We're out of range,' Nina said in relief.

Eddie dampened her mood. 'We won't be for long,' he warned, glancing back at the pursuing vehicles.

Kagan checked his gun's magazine. 'I only have seventeen bullets. It will not be enough to hold them off.'

'We need more guns . . .' Eddie looked again at the Bear. They were approaching the huge bomber from behind – and he saw windows at the very end of the fuselage beneath the tail, a turret mounted below it.

A turret from which jutted the long black barrels of two AM-23 autocannons.

'And we've *got* more guns,' he concluded.

'Where?' Nina asked, not seeing any in the UAZ.

'There.' He pointed at the turret.

'You're kidding.'

'Nope!' One of the ladders led into the tailgunner's compartment. He looked under the wings. Pylons were loaded with sleek grey shapes: the Bear was fully armed with Kh-101 cruise missiles. He hoped the cannons were combat-ready too. 'Nina, Tova – go up the front ladder and get Kagan to the radio. I'll hold 'em off with the guns.'

Kagan shot him a sharp look. 'You are going to kill Russian soldiers?'

'No, just scare 'em – unless they're stupid enough to keep coming!'

He brought the smouldering UAZ on to the taxiway, the jeep bouncing hard over the edge of the concrete. Two men with thick parkas over grubby overalls were working on the landing gear. They looked round in surprise as the 4x4 skidded to a halt, then hurriedly backed away as Kagan pointed his gun at them. He limped for the steep metal steps leading into the forward fuselage, Nina and Tova going with him.

Eddie, meanwhile, clattered up the aft ladder. A confused face peered down through the hatch at him, asking a question in Russian.

The Englishman reached the top and replied with a punch. 'Sorry, mate,' he said, pulling himself up into the cramped compartment and dropping the dazed airman out of the opening. The fall was about twelve feet; the man hit the runway hard and yelled in pain, but no bones were broken. 'If I were you, I'd shift your arse!'

He turned to survey his surroundings. The tailgunner's station was cut off from the rest of the bomber's interior, a lonely, claustrophobic and noisy eyrie whose sole saving grace on the Bear's long patrols would be a spectacular vista beyond its panoramic windows. The current view of the flat and bleak expanse of Engels was less inspiring, but Eddie was more concerned with targets than scenery. The incoming jeeps were barrelling down the taxiway towards the Tu-95.

He squeezed into the gunner's seat. 'Think in Russian,' he said to himself as he looked over the instrument panel. The controls all had Cyrillic labels, but he didn't need to be a linguist to work out the function of the red button on the handgrips beneath the swivelling gunsight mount. The twin cannons were currently pointed skywards in their failsafe position; he rectified that by the crude but effective method of flicking every switch he could see until the guns lowered with a hydraulic whine.

An experimental push on the handgrips was matched by the turret's tracking to match the movement. Eddie squinted through the gunsight, aiming at a spot on the runway a short distance in front of the racing 4x4s. 'Hope they're loaded . . .' he said as he pushed the button.

They were.

The chainsaw snarl of the twin 23mm cannons ripping through twenty rounds per second was almost deafening. Eddie winced as the noise pounded his ears. Flames from the muzzles obscured his view – but through the flashes he saw concrete shattering as the storm of explosive shells chewed across the taxiway. The incoming jeeps swerved to avoid the line of destruction as he guided it towards them, one losing control as it turned too hard on the wet surface and flipped on to its side.

Eddie took his thumb off the firing button just before the shells hit the overturned vehicle. The guns went silent, leaving his ears ringing. The remaining jeeps were now heading away from him – but, he realised, they weren't all fleeing. Some were curving around the bomber, intending to come back in from beyond the turret's arc of fire. He unleashed a few more brief bursts in the hope of discouraging them, then spotted a set of bulky headphones and put them on. 'Nina! You in the plane yet?' he said into the microphone.

She was – and was holding Kagan's gun on the shocked flight crew as the Russian pulled the communications operator from his rearward-facing seat. He donned the man's headphones, then cocked an eyebrow in surprise and gestured at another headset. 'It's for you.'

Tova passed the headphones to Nina, who wedged the steel container securely behind Kagan's seat before fumbling them into position with her free hand. 'Eddie?'

'No, it's Leon fucking Trotsky,' said a familiar Yorkshire voice. 'Of course it's me!'

'We heard shooting – was that you?'

'Yeah, I scared off those jeeps, but they're going to come back at us from the sides, where I can't aim the guns. Is Kagan there?'

'I hear you,' said Kagan as he examined the radio's controls.

'Tell the pilot to pull up the steps and start taxiing before we get swarmed. How soon can you get your bosses in Moscow to call 'em off?'

'Two or three minutes. I will have to go through procedures to confirm my identity.'

'Then bloody get on with it!'

Kagan relayed the order to the pilot, who protested briefly before Nina's jab of the gun at him convinced him to change his mind. He made a rapid check of the instruments, then released the brakes and eased the four throttle levers forward. The rumble of the propellers rose in pitch and volume, the entire airframe trembling as the Bear started to move. The forward stairway retracted into the plane's belly, the ladder to the tailgunner's compartment falling away with a clang as the ejected airman scrambled out of its way.

Eddie looked out of the side windows. Some of the jeeps had almost overtaken the trundling bomber, closing in once more. 'They're going to try to block the runway,' he reported. 'Don't let the pilot stop – for anything.'

'What if they shoot at us?' Nina replied.

'They will not,' Kagan cut in. 'This plane is fully armed with missiles – it is too valuable to damage.'

'Hope they've been told that,' muttered Eddie. He looked back towards the bunker. Some sort of large truck or tracked vehicle was heading from the base's outer periphery towards the burning blockhouse, presumably to collect Slavin and his men, but the drifting smoke from the gas explosion made it hard to identify.

In the forward compartment, Kagan began to send his radio message. Nina turned her attention back to the Bear's crew. As well as the pilot and co-pilot up front in the cockpit, there were four other men in the cabin, and all looked as if they were considering playing the hero. 'Hey! Handski upski,' she snapped, seeing one man's arm creeping towards a compartment beside his seat. He retreated. Through the porthole next to him, she saw two jeeps overhauling the bomber and turning to rejoin the taxiway ahead of it. 'Oh, crap. Eddie, they're getting in front of us!'

'Tell the pilot to go faster,' came the reply. 'If they get aboard, we're fucked. How's Kagan doing?'

Kagan was still speaking into the microphone in Russian, breaking off to say: 'I have made contact and given them my pass codes. Once they confirm who I am, they will put me through.'

'I hope your bosses aren't having a coffee break,' said Nina. Keeping a wary eye on the men behind her, she moved up the cabin to stand behind the pilots and looked through the cockpit windows. Off to starboard, two UAZs hopped over the kerb from the frozen grass on to the concrete. They immediately swung in front of the aircraft, a man leaning from one of the jeeps and gesturing furiously for the bomber to stop. The pilot's hand tightened on the throttle levers as if to pull them back. 'Ah-ah,' Nina warned. The middle-aged man glared over his shoulder at her. 'Kagan! What's Russian for "go faster"?'

'*Idti bistryeye*,' he called out.

'What he said,' she told the pilot. He reluctantly pushed the levers further forward. The Bear picked up speed. One of the UAZs hurriedly moved clear, but the other held station, the soldier still gesticulating – then he stopped and pulled inside.

Only to lean back out a moment later – holding a Kalashnikov.

'Shit!' Nina cried, ducking as he opened fire. Bullets clunked against the bomber's nose, punching through the aluminium skin and smacking into structural members beneath. Tova shrieked and dropped to the deck as one of the windows crazed. 'They won't shoot, huh?' Nina yelled.

The pilot pulled back the throttles, prompting an angry shout from Kagan, followed by: 'Dr Wilde! Put the gun to his head!'

'What? I'm not gonna shoot him!'

'He doesn't know that – they don't speak English!'

'You hope,' she said, before hesitantly pushing the gun's muzzle against the back of the pilot's skull. '*Idti bis . . . istry* – that thing he said again!'

Even with her mangled Russian, the pilot got the message. He moved the levers forward once more. The plane picked up speed, closing on the UAZ.

The soldier kept firing. This time, one of the bullets ripped through the pilot's console – and hit the pilot himself, blood spurting from his left shoulder. He cried out, letting go of the control yoke to clasp his right hand to the wound.

The co-pilot had also taken his hands off the controls, shielding his head as he ducked. More shots hit the plane, another window cracking—

Nina lunged and jammed the throttle levers forward.

The Bear roared as all four engines surged to full power. The communications officer, left standing in the gangway after being yanked from his seat, stumbled and fell. Eight enormous propellers spun up to maximum speed, the great bomber charging along the taxiway—

Straight at the UAZ.

The gunman saw the silver machine's hefty forward landing

gear bearing down on him and yelled for the driver to swerve, but his companion had already seen the whirling propellers on each side in his mirrors and realised the jeep had nowhere to go. He bailed out, bouncing hard off the cold concrete and flattening himself on the ground as the bomber swept overhead. The other man stared stupidly at him for a moment before throwing himself from the careening 4x4.

Driverless, it veered to one side as the Tupolev caught up—

The twin contra-rotating propellers on the port inboard engine nacelle scythed through the UAZ, shredding its bodywork like paper. What was left of the jeep was spat out from under the wing and flung off the taxiway, chunks of mangled metal cartwheeling through the snow.

Warning buzzers sounded, a red light flashing on one of the control panels. The co-pilot grabbed his own set of throttle controls and pulled them sharply back, shouting in panic at Nina. 'He says an engine is damaged!' Kagan told her.

'We can't stop!' she replied, pointing her gun at the co-pilot and gesturing for him to reapply power. He looked helplessly at his commander for advice, but the older man's eyes were clenched shut in pain. With no choice, he grudgingly opened three of the throttles again, leaving the damaged engine at idle.

Eddie's voice sounded in Nina's headphones. 'What the fuck was that? Did we hit something?'

'We're experiencing turbulence,' said Nina. She looked back at Kagan. 'Have you gotten through to your bosses yet?'

'I am . . . on hold,' he admitted, slightly sheepish.

'Oh, great!' She looked ahead once more. The Bear was approaching a parked line of its sister aircraft, beyond them several of the threatening stiletto jet bombers she had seen on arriving. In the distance, but drawing ever closer, were bright lights marking the end of the taxiway. A glance through the side windows revealed jeeps still keeping pace with the aircraft, but after what had happened to their comrade's vehicle, the drivers were not inclined to play roadblock. 'Eddie, we're going to run out of runway soon. Are there any more of them chasing us?'

In the tailgunner's compartment, Eddie saw another clutch of vehicles coming from the airbase's main buildings. 'They've sent out everything short of the fucking bin lorry. What's happening with Kagan?'

'He's still waiting.'

'What, have they put him on hold?'

'Ah . . . actually, yes.'

'Oh, for fuck's sake! How long before we reach the end of the taxiway?'

'A minute, maybe?'

'Shit.' He surveyed the view behind the bomber again. The tracked vehicle had now apparently picked up Slavin and was tearing across the open ground in pursuit, headlights glaring. The long main runway ran parallel to their current route, stretching away into the distance. 'Okay, tell 'em to turn on to the runway – we've got to keep moving for as long as we can. But we need some way to hold 'em off . . .'

The first of the parked bombers swept past. He grinned, and swung the gunsight around. The cannons followed his movement. 'Did you just *cackle*?' Nina asked.

'Remembered my training,' he replied, lining up the sight and pushing the red button.

The guns blazed again, even the headphones doing little to muffle the din. But Eddie didn't care, walking the line of fire along the rank of bombers. A stream of 23mm rounds blasted holes in the fuselages of the stationary Tu-95s, aluminium shreds scattering like confetti.

'Chase!' demanded Kagan. 'What are you doing?'

'Keeping 'em busy!' he shouted back over the noise. 'Don't worry, a friend of mine once told me Russian planes are easy to fix.' The bulbous radar dome beneath the chin of one of the Bears disintegrated as he concentrated his fire upon it. 'Bit of work with the tin snips and a hammer, that'll knock right out.'

'*Chase!*'

'Just talk to your fucking bosses, all right?' He switched his aim to the Tu-95's forward landing gear. The leg collapsed under the onslaught. The Bear's front end dropped to the ground, the fuselage smashing flat like a dropped egg and breaking the aircraft's back.

Most of the more distant pursuers abruptly slowed. The message had got through: *back off or I take out your entire fleet.* The UAZs hounding the hijacked Tupolev came back into view, veering away. Eddie stopped firing. Turning the AM-23s on them would result in a massacre, and he had no enmity towards the base personnel.

More bombers rolled past, the old turboprop behemoths followed by newer and even larger swing-wing Tu-160 jets. Eddie was sorely tempted to put a few dozen explosive rounds into each to make life easier for NATO, but held his fire; even if they survived long enough for Kagan's superiors to call off the hunt, they were already in enough trouble with the Russian government – and diplomatic immunity would only extend so far.

Eddie's voice came through Nina's headphones. 'They've pulled back.'

'Good,' she replied, looking ahead. 'We're almost out of road!' The end of the long concrete taxiway was now only a few hundred yards away. She gestured with the gun for the co-pilot to follow a connecting lane around to the main runway. The Tupolev swung on to its new course, the nosewheel tyres squealing in protest at the fast turn.

Kagan spoke in urgent Russian, briefly holding a hand over his microphone to say to Nina, 'I am through,' before continuing.

'Thank God,' she replied. 'Eddie, Kagan's got through to his bosses.'

'Great,' he said. 'Let's hope *they* don't get put on hold when they try to call the base!'

The pilot gasped in pain. Nina saw blood spreading across his shirt. She searched for some way to help him. A white box marked with a red cross was attached to one of the sickly green-painted cabin walls. 'Tova, do you know first aid?' The Swede nodded. 'Grab that and see if you can help him. I'll make sure nobody tries anything stupid.'

Tova collected the medical kit and came into the cockpit. The co-pilot appeared briefly confused that his hijackers were also willing to help his injured comrade, but turned his attention back to the view outside as the Bear approached the main runway. 'Go on to it,' Nina told him, accompanying the command with a hand signal. He worked the controls to turn the bomber. 'Kagan, what's happening?'

'I have told them about Slavin,' he replied. 'They are going to tell the base commander to cancel the shoot-on-sight order and hold everyone until the truth can be determined.'

'How long will that take?' The base's main runway, almost two miles long, swung into sight ahead.

'Not long – Unit 201 has a high—'

The Bear shuddered as its flank was hammered by a series of explosive impacts.

Holes ripped open in the fuselage. The communications officer was practically cut in half by shrieking metal, his blood splattering the back end of the cabin as shrapnel tore through him.

'Holy *shit*!' Nina yelled as she crouched. 'What the hell was that?'

The co-pilot screamed into his headset. Nina didn't need to understand his language to know that he was begging whoever was firing on the bomber to stop. It had no effect, another fusillade hitting the wing. Black smoke belched from the outermost engine nacelle.

Astern, Eddie swore as he shoved the gunsight as far over as it would go, but to no avail – the Tu-95's turn had put their attacker out of sight. But he knew what it was – and *who*. 'It's Slavin!'

The Russian officer had commandeered a ZSU-23-4 – a tank-like anti-aircraft system armed with four 23mm autocannons much like those the Englishman was controlling. In his desperation, he was willing to destroy the entire aircraft to silence anyone who could expose his treachery. The guns would cut the Bear to pieces – and there was nothing anyone could do to stop him.

Unless . . .

More pounding blows shook the bomber. Eddie twisted to look through a small side porthole, glimpsing the ZSU under the port wing. 'Go! Full power, get us moving!' he shouted into his headset.

'We will never be able to take off!' Kagan protested.

'I don't want to take off – I want to get past him so I can fucking *shoot back*!'

In the cockpit, the Russian urgently relayed the order to the co-pilot. The man hesitated, but more explosive rounds shredding the side of the fuselage immediately erased his doubts. He pushed all the throttles to maximum power.

The wounded Bear surged forward. The trail of smoke from the damaged engine was joined by flames – then an explosion ripped open the nacelle.

Nina risked raising her head and saw the squat ZSU carving towards the runway ahead of them. More fire flashed from its cannons, tracers streaking at her like meteors. She ducked again as the Tupolev took more hits, impacts tearing along the hull. Another set of warning lights flashed on the instrument panel. 'Eddie! This thing's going to rip us apart!'

'Just tell them to keep going – it's only got light armour, so if I can hit it, it's dead!'

'*If* you can hit it! And we're a much bigger target!' She looked up again. The ZSU was about four hundred yards away, but rapidly growing as the bomber bore down upon it.

'Just tell me how far away it is – and where to aim!'

'It's on the left, about – I dunno, a hundred feet from the runway and getting closer. We're about three hundred yards away – *whoa!*' She dropped behind the pilot's seat as cannon shells punctured the radome below the cockpit. A shrill wind blasted into the cabin.

The co-pilot shouted at her, but she waved for him to keep going. 'Two hundred yards, we're almost—'

The ZSU unleashed another ferocious burst of fire.

An entire section of the Tupolev's port wing blew apart as shells ripped through a fuel tank. A hot gale rushed in through the holes in the hull.

The Russian weapons officer opposite Kagan shouted in panic. Nina looked back to see red lights flashing urgently on his control panel. 'The wing is on fire – and so are the missiles!' Kagan yelled.

'Then tell him to drop them!' She stumbled back down the gangway.

'It's against protocol!'

'*Screw* protocol!' She reached the weapons station. The Cyrillic was impenetrable, but the symbol beside a rank of switches under the blinking lights was self-explanatory. A stylised missile with a downward-pointing arrow behind it, surrounded by an irregular multi-pointed star: *explosive release*.

She glanced forward, seeing the ZSU whip out of sight as the Bear rushed past it. 'Eddie, I'm sending you some bombs!'

Before the weapons officer could stop her, she stabbed at the switches.

A series of rapid cracks came from the burning wing pylon – then the three cruise missiles mounted upon it dropped away and tumbled along the runway like skittles.

Eddie's view of the runway's edge had been blotted out by a huge cloud of swirling black smoke. If he didn't destroy the ZSU, it would tear the crippled Bear apart, but he couldn't see his target—

Flashes of pale grey on the ground – and he realised he didn't need to.

Each Kh-101 was fully laden with fuel and carried a warhead weighing a full metric ton. The 23mm rounds were more than enough to detonate them.

He fired—

The missiles exploded, their combined blast ripping a huge crater out of the runway. Eddie was thrown back in his seat as the detonation pummelled the Bear's tail. But the bomber was already haring away from the explosion.

The ZSU was not.

Slavin was in the commander's cupola, looking out from the top of the turret. His triumph at seeing the Tupolev's wing erupt into flames changed to terror – then the shockwave pounded his head into a bloody pulp against the unyielding open hatch cover behind him. The ZSU was flipped end over end, the burning wreck slamming down on its back in the snow.

'I got him, I got him!' Eddie shouted into the headset. 'Slow us down!'

Nina desperately searched for somewhere to secure herself. 'We can't!' she cried. The co-pilot had already yanked back the throttles and stamped on the pedal to apply the wheelbrakes, but with half a wing missing the Bear was unbalanced and veering towards the side of the runway. One of the overstressed nose-wheel tyres exploded, the metal rim screeching along the concrete in a shower of sparks. '*Hang on!*'

She grabbed the back of the bombardier's seat as the plane careened on to the frozen grass—

The forward landing gear was ripped away on the rough ground, followed a moment later by the aft legs. The Tupolev slammed down on its belly.

Eight mighty propellers carved deep channels into the soil before the stress ripped the blades out at their roots. The burning port wing was wrenched from the fuselage, cartwheeling away from the plane before the fuel still inside it exploded in a colossal fireball. The rest of the Tu-95 continued onwards, skidding across the snowy plain in a trail of churned earth and mangled aluminium before finally grinding to a standstill.

Nina groggily raised her head. Tova, sprawled in the pilot's footwell, moaned softly. Kagan had managed to partially fasten his seat belt just before the crash, while the aircraft's remaining crew were in varying states of confusion and relief at having survived the destruction of their plane.

The sight of gleaming steel amongst the scattered debris on the cabin's corrugated floor snapped Nina back to full, horrified

ANDY MCDERMOTT

awareness. 'Oh, shit!' she gasped, scrabbling to it. The container holding Thor's Hammer had been jolted from its resting place, and was now lying on its side.

Kagan saw it too. 'Is it broken?' he said, fumbling to unfasten his restraints.

What Nina could see of the container appeared undamaged bar a few scratches. She hesitantly nudged it over to examine the other side, paying close attention to the seal around the lid. 'Oh, thank God,' she whispered. It had remained intact.

A crackle came from her headphones. 'Nina, are you okay? Nina! Can you hear me?'

'I'm here, I'm here,' she assured Eddie. 'Are you okay?'

'I'll live,' he replied. 'Got a problem, though.'

'What is it?' she asked, worried again. If the bomber was on fire, or Kagan's superiors had not yet got their message through to the base commander to stand down . . .

'The plane's landed on its belly, so I can't get out! Don't suppose you've got a hammer up there to smash open the window?'

Her relieved laughter echoed incongruously through the wreckage.

22

Vietnam

Finding wood dry enough to burn in the depths of the jungle had been difficult, but Chase had managed it. The pyre he constructed in the centre of a small clearing was not large, but still enough to support the young woman's body.

He used the gunpowder from some of his remaining bullets to help start the fire. The flames spread quickly, wood popping and snapping. Dark smoke swirled up through the trees as the blaze grew, swallowing the motionless figure atop it.

Chase watched the grim sight, his face set and expressionless. When he was sure that the corpse was completely consumed by flames, he picked up Hoyt's backpack. One by one, the pieces of stolen Russian research it contained were thrown on to the bonfire. Papers curled into ash, discs melted. The laptop was the last item to be destroyed, acrid grey smoke belching from the vents in its casing as plastic sizzled and melted. There was a muffled bang and a sputtering gush of sparks as its batteries ignited. He withdrew from the stench – both of technology, and of charred flesh.

More time passed, the sky reddening as the sun dropped, but

the Englishman did not leave. Instead, he added more wood to the pile, keeping the fire strong. Natalia had told him that nothing could be left for the Americans or Russians, and he knew she was right. This was the only way to end things.

But by doing so, he was giving away his position, sending a beacon into the sky that would lead his enemies right to him.

He pushed a last chunk of broken branch into the flames, then sat on a mouldering log, wondering what had happened to Castille. The smoke might also lead his friend to him – if he were still alive – but who else would he find waiting?

His macabre vigil resumed. He couldn't leave until he was sure that the body was totally incinerated. If any part remained intact, there was still the danger that the Russians or Lock's people might analyse it and discover the secrets it contained . . .

A bird chattered in alarm. Chase looked around, raising the gun. He saw nothing, but had a gut feeling that the disturbance had been caused by something more than an animal. 'All right!' he shouted, crouching behind the log. 'I know someone's out there. Come on, show yourself!'

A pause, then: 'Chase!' Lock's voice. He couldn't see the American, but estimated that he was about forty yards distant behind some bushes. That meant Hoyt and his men were also nearby . . . 'If you hand over Natalia, I'm willing to let you live.'

'Come and get her,' Chase shouted back, checking the other approaches to his position. If Hoyt hadn't already sent his team to surround him, he would be in the middle of doing so. He was not surprised to spot movement in the undergrowth. 'Oi, you behind the bush! Yeah, I see you.'

'And I see you,' said another voice, closer. Hoyt. Chase spun to see the skull-faced mercenary rounding a tree twenty yards away, an AK pointed at him. 'Don't move. Drop the gun.'

Chase did so, then put his hands up. Hoyt cautiously

advanced. 'Move in,' he called to the others. Four men in dark clothing rose from the undergrowth and closed on the Yorkshireman. Hoyt's gaze flicked suspiciously from side to side. 'Son of a bitch,' he said. 'This was another goddamn decoy, wasn't it? Where's the girl?'

'She's here,' said Chase, letting an angry bitterness into his voice.

'Where?'

'Are you fucking blind? Right in front of you.'

Hoyt looked at the fire, still wary – then his eyes widened in shock. 'What the— Mother*fuck*!' he gasped. 'Boss, get over here!' He turned back to Chase, his expression for once completely devoid of its usual arrogance. 'What the *fuck* did you do?'

'What she asked me to,' Chase replied.

Hoyt stared at him, still stunned, then yelled to the nearest of his men. 'Bonnell, watch him! If he moves, shoot him!' The mercenary guarded Chase as his leader ran to the pyre.

Lock made his way through the trees. 'What's going on?' he demanded. 'Where's Natalia?'

Hoyt put one hand to his head in dismay. 'She's . . . she's here, on the fucking fire! She's fucking *dead*!'

Lock froze. 'What?'

'He's burned her! And – son of a bitch!' He snatched up his empty backpack, fruitlessly shaking it out. 'He's burned all the research I took from the Ruskies too. Jesus!'

The goateed man's jaw dropped open as he looked at the shape in the flames. 'Holy Christ. What did you do, Chase? What the *hell* did you do?'

Keeping his hands raised, Chase slowly straightened. 'Natalia knew she was going to die young anyway, thanks to that shit her grandfather infected her with. And she told me she'd rather go out how she chose than like her mum and her grandma. She wanted to save lives. And by stopping you from getting hold of what's inside her, she has done.'

'So you *killed* her? You actually put a bullet in her?'

He looked down at the ground. 'Yeah. I shot her.'

Hoyt shook his head, something almost approaching a smile of admiration on his lips. 'I underestimated you, Chase. Never thought you'd be stone-cold enough to do something like that.'

'It's not like I enjoyed it,' Chase said angrily. 'Unlike you. Fucking psycho.'

Lock shook his head. 'No, no way. I don't believe this. It's got to be a trick. Put that fire out and check the body. And see if you can recover any of the research.'

The other mercenaries used the butts of their rifles to knock apart the base of the pyre branch by branch, then kicked and scattered the burning wood. Hoyt probed the laptop's remains with a stick. 'This thing's toast. So is all the rest of it.'

'What about Natalia?'

One of the men gagged as the flames faded and he got his first clear view of the burnt body. Lock's face twisted in disgust, but he leaned closer to look at the blackened skull. 'Okay, definitely human . . . and one hell of an exit wound.' A chunk of the dead woman's face was missing, a ragged hole in the bone running from above her right eye down into her left cheek. 'Dammit, everything's been burned . . . Wait.' His gaze flicked to a dark stain on the ground beside the fire. 'Got some hair in the blood spatter here.'

He picked up a twig and very carefully used it to snag the dirty strands, then tipped his prize into a cupped hand. 'Has anyone got water?'

One of the mercs produced a canteen. Lock poured a few drops on to his hand, then delicately ran the hair through it before using his fingertips to wipe away the caked blood. 'It's blond.' He brushed the hairs from his palm and turned to Chase. 'Jesus, you actually did it. You burned everything.'

'To stop you,' said the Englishman, stone-faced.

'We're on the same side, Chase! America and Britain, the special relationship! Remember that?' Lock stalked towards him, the mercenaries following. 'We bake the cake, and you get our crumbs. That's the way it works. We had a chance to set back the Russians by years and give our own work a huge boost,' he stabbed a finger at the empty backpack, 'but thanks to you, we've got nothing!'

'Good! Natalia told me all about what her grandfather did – and nobody should have that fucking stuff. Not you, not the Russians, not anybody.'

'That's not for you to decide.'

'No. It was for *her* to decide.' He looked past Lock to the remains of the pyre. 'She decided what she wanted to do. And I helped her. God fuckin' help *me* for doing it.'

'Funny you should mention God,' said Hoyt. 'You'll be seeing him soon enough. If Natalia's dead and 201's research is gone, then we're done here. The only thing left for us to do is clean up after ourselves.' He glanced at Lock, who nodded. 'This is all your own fault, Chase. If you'd just done what you were being paid to do rather than play the bleeding-heart hero, you'd be on a plane out of here by now. Instead, well . . . we've already got a funeral pyre. No sense wasting it.'

He brought up his gun. Chase tensed. 'Do I get any last words?'

'Only if they're quick,' said Lock. 'And if I don't like them, you'll never get to finish your sentence.'

Hoyt sneered. 'Well, what you got to say?'

Chase took a deep breath, trying to control his fear. 'Just that . . . at least I kept my promise.'

The tall American snorted sarcastically. 'I've heard better.' His finger curled around the AK's trigger—

'Nobody move! Drop your guns!'

Hoyt spun at the unexpected voice, his team doing the same – to find weapons aimed at them.

Men emerged from the undergrowth. Most were Vietnamese, but the man who had shouted was not.

Chase recognised him immediately. It was the commander of the encampment, the lean, pale-eyed Russian. With him was the sweaty younger man with the weak moustache who had found Chase and Hoyt in the cabin. 'I said, drop them!' the leader called again, firing a shot over the group's heads for emphasis.

Hoyt looked to Lock for instructions, his expression suggesting that he was willing to risk shooting his way out of the situation, but his boss urgently shook his head. The mercenary reluctantly lowered his gun. 'Put 'em down,' he told his men. Rifles thudded to the wet ground.

The new arrivals advanced, collecting the fallen weapons. The Russian stood before the suited man. 'Mr Lock. I did not expect ever to meet the deputy director of the BSA in person.'

'It wasn't part of the plan,' Lock growled.

The Russian half smirked, then cast an unfriendly eye over Hoyt and his men before turning to Chase. 'I do not know if I should thank you, or shoot you.'

'I'll take the first one,' said Chase, not sure what was going on but looking for any opportunity to take advantage of it. 'Who're you?'

'My name is Grigory Alekseyevich Kagan. I am the field commander of a Russian special operations unit. I am sure you have an idea of its purpose by now.'

'Yeah, I got the gist,' Chase said with disapproval. 'Why would you want to thank me?'

'Because you did not deliver Natalia to these men. By keeping her from them, you have done a great favour not only for Russia, but for the whole world. And once we have her back, we can make sure they never get what they were trying to obtain.' He looked back at Lock. 'I would guess that you will be out of a job soon, no?'

To everyone's surprise, Lock began to laugh. 'Oh, you stupid son of a bitch,' the American said between chuckles. 'You haven't realised what he's done, have you?'

'What do you mean?'

Lock gestured towards the fire. 'See for yourself.'

Puzzled, Kagan moved closer – then whirled to face Chase in horrified disbelief. 'What have you done? *What have you done?*'

'What she asked me to do,' Chase replied.

'She asked you to kill her?'

'Yes.'

'*Why?*' It was almost a shout.

'To stop all you arseholes from restarting her grandad's work. She made me promise that I wouldn't let that happen. And now it won't.'

'But we were not trying to restart it! We were trying to *end* it!'

The sudden smug look on Lock's face told Chase that things were not as he had thought. 'Wait, how do you mean?' he asked the Russian.

Kagan spoke slowly, trying to control his emotions. 'How much do you know about the work of Serafim Volkov – Natalia's grandfather?'

'She told me that he wrote a letter telling his wife what he'd been doing – about that eitr stuff, and his experiments. And that your lot used the biggest fucking nuke ever made to seal up the pit where you found the eitr.'

'She told you a great deal.' He shook his head. 'But not

everything. The Tsar Bomba destroyed the eitr pit – but we knew from the Viking runestone that somewhere there was another. Unit 201 was created to discover ways to neutralise the eitr if it was found. But we did not know if they would work, because we had no samples – until we learned about Natalia. The mutations in her body should tell us the nature of eitr, and with that knowledge we would be able to destroy it.'

'So you *kidnapped* her? Why didn't you just ask her?'

'We did not think she would believe our motives.' Kagan jabbed a finger at Lock and Hoyt. 'She thought we were like the BSA, trying to turn the eitr into a weapon. But we were not. We have seen what it does – and we will not let it be used again. So when we learned that Natalia was in Vietnam, we arranged for her to be brought to us, in a way that gave us total deniability. She and her friends would have been released unharmed, once we finished our tests.' A glance at the fire, his expression now almost despairing. 'We were not going to hurt her. But you – you have *killed* her! For *nothing!*'

'Oh, fuck . . .' whispered Chase.

Now it was Hoyt's turn to laugh. 'God damn, Chase! You were supposed to rescue her, and you fuckin' *murdered* her! You really fucked up, didn't you?'

The Englishman rounded on him angrily. 'Killing you'll be worth something, though.'

'Enough!' barked Kagan. He rubbed his temple, then stepped back to regard his prisoners. 'Natalia is dead, and all our research is destroyed – but that means neither side has it. No one has gained an advantage. But . . .' He faced Lock once more. 'If I were to kill you, here and now, you would cease to be a threat.'

The American was no longer smiling. 'If you kill me, someone else will take my place. This won't end.'

'It will for you. And I know that your agency is, what is the phrase? *On the bubble* for its funding, that is it. With you dead and the BSA humiliated, the US government may shut it down completely. And that can only be a good thing for the world.'

Kagan's sweating comrade spoke to him urgently in Russian, regarding Hoyt and Lock nervously. Kagan's reply was impatient. 'He thinks killing you will cause an international incident, and that it is a bad idea,' he added, addressing the Americans. 'But you tried to kill *us* with no such concerns, so . . .' He thought for a moment, then gave an order in Vietnamese. The men accompanying the Russians raised their weapons to firing position.

For the second time in a matter of minutes, Chase found a rifle aimed at him. 'You're going to kill me too?'

'I am sorry,' Kagan replied, with seemingly genuine regret. 'You thought you were doing the right thing – for Natalia, and for the world. And what you decided to do . . .' He locked eyes with the Englishman for a moment. 'I think you did not want to do it, no?'

'You're fucking right I didn't want to.'

Kagan nodded. 'But this must end. With Lock gone, the Americans will likely shut down their work on the eitr.'

'But they'll shut it down anyway, surely?' Chase indicated Lock. 'He failed! He had a plan to get Natalia and steal your research, but he blew it. He comes away with nothing, but you're no worse off.'

'Two of our best scientists are dead!' snapped Kagan. 'He did not destroy Unit 201, but he still damaged it.'

'But you're still in business. Lock won't be! You were right, he'll be out of a job once his bosses realise that he fucked everything up, and caused an international incident by doing it. He might have hired mercs for deniability, but just by being here, right now, he's blown that excuse.' He regarded Lock, who now appeared as fearful of the prospect of being at the heart of a diplomatic storm as of the guns pointed at him. 'Nobody's won here. Everyone's lost. And killing us won't get you any extra points.'

Kagan did not reply at once, again staring thoughtfully at Chase before turning his gaze to the funeral pyre. 'You have done a very good job,' he said. 'It will be almost impossible to extract DNA from a body so burned.'

'You just said this needs to end. Well, this ends it. Natalia wanted to make sure nobody could get anything else from her – you or them.' He lowered his head. 'Just leave her alone. Let her rest in peace.'

The other Russian spoke again, asking a question. Kagan considered it for a long moment, Chase hyper-aware of the Vietnamese covering the group, all with fingers poised on their Kalashnikovs' triggers . . .

'Nyet,' Kagan finally said, shaking his head once more. 'No, you are right, and so is the Englishman. Lock has failed – and that will embarrass Washington if we make good use of it.'

'You son of a bitch,' snarled Lock.

Chase made a sarcastic sound. 'You'd rather he killed you?'

Kagan had a brief exchange with one of the Vietnamese, then turned back to Lock. 'My associates from the Vietnamese secret police will take you and your men to Da Nang for . . . questioning.' His tone made it clear that the interrogation would be more than verbal. 'They are still angry that several of their friends were killed when the camp was attacked. I think they are keen to find out who was responsible.' Hoyt's facial muscles tensed. 'As for you, Mr Lock, I am sure they will let you go in a few days. After making an official complaint to the US ambassador and the United Nations.' Lock's expression was much like his countryman's.

'And what about me?' Chase asked.

'You? What was your name – Chase?' The Englishman nodded. 'Your job here is over, Mr Chase. You should go home. There is nothing in this country for you now.'

Chase looked past him at the remains of the pyre. 'There's one thing that I need to do.'

'What is that?'

'Bury her. I'm not going to leave her body in the jungle to rot. She deserves more than that.'

Kagan nodded. 'Very well. But once you have done that, you should leave. The jungle can be dangerous, especially at night, no?'

'Yeah, I'd noticed.'

Kagan issued more orders, the Vietnamese herding the mercenaries into a group and marching them away at gunpoint. Kagan and his subordinate did the same with Lock and Hoyt, both still complaining angrily. The Russian reached the edge of the clearing, then paused, looking back at Chase. 'Sometimes . . . sometimes we have to do bad things for good reasons,' he said. 'But knowing that you have done the right thing does not make you feel any better.'

'No,' Chase replied. 'It doesn't.'

'She has found peace,' Kagan went on, with a tip of his head towards the fire. 'I hope that some day, so do you.'

The Englishman did not reply. Kagan turned and followed the others into the jungle.

Chase remained still for a minute, waiting until the sounds of movement had faded. Then he picked up a large piece of broken branch and began to gouge a hole out of the damp earth.

The sun had almost set by the time Chase finished his task. Hands dark with mud and ash, he looked down at his work, face solemn. The shallow grave was marked by a crude cross, two pieces of branch bound together by a length of vine. The logical part of his mind knew that the marker would not last long – jungle decay and the ceaseless gnawing of insects would see to that – but he felt better for having built it. At the very least, the dead woman deserved some form of remembrance.

He lifted his head at a distant, but familiar, shout. 'Edward! Edward, can you hear me?'

'Hugo!' Chase called back. 'I'm here!'

Castille appeared a few minutes later. 'Edward!' he said, with a huge beaming grin at the sight of his friend. 'I saw the smoke. Are you okay?'

'Yeah, I'm fine,' Chase replied, managing a smile. The two men embraced. 'What about you? You managed to get away from 'em, then.'

Castille pursed his lips. 'It was a close thing! Hoyt would have killed me if the police had not arrived.'

'So much for there never being a copper around when you need one.'

'I know. I was quite surprised!' Castille released the Englishman. 'Where is Natalia? Is she safe?'

There was a lengthy pause before Chase finally answered. 'No,' he said quietly. 'She . . . didn't make it.'

He stepped aside to reveal the grave. Castille did not seem – or want – to believe his own eyes. '*Mon dieu!* What happened?'

'I don't want to talk about it.'

'But – but I thought that surely you were clear . . .' He took in the churned ground, seeing the footprints. 'They were here? They caught you?'

'Hoyt and Lock – and then the Russians. They had a bit of a stand-off.'

Castille surveyed the whole clearing. 'There is no blood, no spent casings. They did not fight?'

'No.'

'Then where are they? Why did they leave?'

'They didn't get what they were after.'

'But what happened to Natalia? Did they kill her? Hoyt and Lock – or the Russians?'

Chase shook his head. 'Like I said, I don't want to talk about it. What I do want to do is get out of this fucking jungle. How far away's your jeep?'

'About a kilometre, not far from the rendezvous point.'

'Great. Let's go.'

He started to walk away, but Castille remained still, staring at the grave. 'Edward,' he said. 'What really happened here? I am your friend, you can tell me – you know that.'

'Yeah, I know.' Chase gave him a small, sad smile. 'I made Natalia a promise. And . . . I kept it.' He sighed. 'That's all I want to say for now. Maybe sometime later, when things are different, I'll tell you everything. Right now, though? I need a shower.'

Castille decided not to press the issue any further. 'Yes, you do,' he said instead, with overstated lightness. He started walking towards the edge of the clearing, Chase alongside him. 'But then, you are English. You *always* need a shower.'

'Oh, fuck off, Hugo.' The Yorkshireman gave him another small smile, then hesitated as they reached the trees, glancing back at the grave. 'Goodbye, Natalia,' he whispered. Castille gave him a look of deep sympathy, but remained silent out of respect for his friend's wishes. Then Chase turned away, and the pair set off into the jungle.

'You do realise that we will not get paid for the mission,' said Castille.

'Yeah, I know. Think we could get any money for the jeep?'

'Hmm. I am sure Bluey knows someone who would buy it,

no questions asked. So what are you going to do when you get home?'

'Who says I'm going home? There's fuck-all there for me now, just a big pile of solicitor's letters from Sophia. You know what? Fuck her. She wants her divorce, she can have it. There's more important things in life.'

'Then what are you going to do?' Castille asked.

'What I'm best at. Troubleshooting, like Mac said. The fist in the glove. I reckon I could do that.'

'Well, you can always rely on me to help, Edward. We will fight to the end.'

'Yeah, I know.' Chase clapped his friend on the back. 'Fight to the end.'

23

MOSCOW

'Well, that was . . . fun,' said Nina with a grimace as she put down her phone.

'Seretse not happy, was he?' said Eddie, lying on the hotel suite's bed.

'He was not. I think being shouted at by a member of the UN Security Council kinda ruined his day.'

He sat up. 'So what's going to happen? About us, I mean?'

Nina ran a hand through her hair, tired. 'As much as he'd probably love to fire both our asses, there's not much he can do. It seems Kagan's bosses pull a lot of weight at the Kremlin – they still want Unit 201 to find and destroy the other source of eitr before Hoyt or anyone else can find it, but they need us and Tova to do that. So I'm guessing Seretse's conversation with the Russian representative went something like: "Two people from the IHA just shot up our nuclear bomber base and caused billions of roubles in damage! But don't fire them, because we're still working with them. And we won't tell you why, only that it's important. I just needed to vent by yelling at you."'

'Yeah, I can see that'd be like someone pissing in his orange juice. I suppose now we've got to *find* the bloody thing.'

Nina glanced towards the door connecting the room to the adjacent suite. 'All we can do for now is wait and see if Tova manages to come up with a location for Ragnarök.' She sat beside her husband. 'Which gives us a chance to talk about something else.'

He waggled his eyebrows. 'You want to try for a kid right here?'

'As fun as that would be, no.' Her face became more serious. 'What happened in Vietnam, Eddie? What *really* happened? Hoyt, and Kagan, and that guy Slavin from the bunker – you met them all there. And you knew about the eitr, and about the pit the Russians found.' Her eyes narrowed. 'And you lied to me about it.'

'I know, I know. I'm sorry.' He sat up. 'But I couldn't tell you about any of it because . . . because I made a promise.'

'To whom?'

He shifted uncomfortably, still conflicted after eight years, before answering. 'Natalia. The girl I was hired to rescue in Vietnam.'

Nina moved closer, intrigued. 'What was the promise?'

'Unit 201 had kidnapped her to run secret tests. That stuff in the jar, Thor's Hammer – that's what they were trying to create, using her DNA. My job was to bring her and her friends back safely, but Hoyt and his boss had set the whole thing up as a way to lure Unit 201 out of the bunker. They had it all worked out – Slavin told 'em where the camp was, and then their plan was to nick all the research, burn everything else and try to kill as many of the scientists as they could . . . and also take Natalia.'

'They wanted to use her like the Russians?' she asked. 'Use

her DNA to work out the composition of the eitr?'

Eddie nodded. 'Yeah. Only they wanted to be able to create the stuff, not destroy it.'

'But they didn't get her, obviously. Neither side did. So what happened?'

'I got to her before Hoyt. The Russians chased us through the jungle, but I managed to get her clear. There was a village not too far away where she had friends, so we went there. On the way, she told me all about the eitr, and her grandad and his experiments. And that's when I made her a promise.'

'Which was?' she prompted.

He was silent for a long moment before answering. 'She made me promise that no matter what, I wouldn't let anyone use her to restart her grandfather's experiments. So I burned the research that Hoyt stole from the Russians. But . . . there was still something else they could have used. So I did what she asked me to, and made sure they couldn't get it.'

'What did you do?'

Another, longer pause. 'I can't tell you.'

'Why not?'

'Because of what I promised Natalia.'

'You made a promise to me too,' said Nina, not liking his uncharacteristic evasiveness. 'When we got married. You know you can trust me, with anything.'

'I know, I know,' he said. 'But this is . . . different. I don't want— I *can't* say. Not to anyone.'

Nina picked up on his hurried correction. To her, it suggested that the reasons for his silence were as much personal as professional. He was keeping more than the secrets of the Soviet research to himself.

But he would not tell her what else he was hiding, not today. After six years together, she knew when his defences were up.

Instead, she changed tack. 'What about Natalia, then? Did you get her back home?'

To her surprise, that made him even more defensive. 'I don't want to talk about it,' he said, brusque.

'Why not?' she demanded. No answer. 'Eddie, what happened to her?' Another silence. 'Did . . . did she die?'

Eddie stood, walking to the window and staring out across Moscow. 'We saved the other hostages, but Natalia . . .' He faced her, expression grim. 'I didn't get her out.'

'Oh . . .' She got up and joined him. 'Eddie, I'm sorry.' He nodded, but said nothing.

The moment was broken by a knock at the connecting door. Kagan opened it and stepped through. 'Good job we weren't in the middle of trying for a baby right now,' said Eddie, some of his usual irreverence returning.

'They didn't teach you what "come in" meant in your English classes?' Nina asked the Russian.

'There are times to wait with politeness,' he said. 'This is not one of them.'

'What've you got?' said Eddie.

'First, Thor's Hammer is safe. All of Unit 201's research from Engels has been transferred to a new secure location.'

'I hope the staff's been vetted better than it was at the bunker,' Nina said in a barbed tone.

Kagan glared at her, but continued: 'Our intelligence services have been trying to locate Hoyt and Dr Berkeley. So far, there has been no indication that they have left Scandinavia.'

'Berkeley might still be translating the runestone,' said Eddie.

'That seems likely. But since he led Hoyt's people to the lake in Norway, we have to assume that he will succeed. Once he does, he will have the route to Valhalla. We *must* get there before them, but . . .' He glanced back towards the adjoining suite. 'Dr

Skilfinger does not think she has enough information to find it.'

'What has she got so far?' Nina asked.

'It is best that you ask her that,' Kagan replied, though his doleful look implied that the answer was not what he'd hoped for. He went back into the other suite, Eddie and Nina following.

Tova looked up from her laptop as they entered. 'Hello,' she said, with a weary smile.

'Hi,' said Nina. She regarded the pages of notes, printed and handwritten, spread out across the desk beside the computer: every scrap of information they had concerning the runestones. 'Have you found out anything useful?'

'I am afraid not much,' Tova admitted with a sigh. 'If I had been able to read just a little more of the text on the second runestone, it might have been enough to tell me the name of the river on the stone taken from the museum, but . . .' She gave them a helpless little shrug. 'It is not enough.'

'Well, tell us what you've managed to find out anyway,' said Nina.

'Anything you have learned may help us,' Kagan added.

Tova shrugged again. 'I will try.' She gathered together some of her notes, running a fingertip over them. 'Okay. The text that I saw on the runestone in Norway was mostly the same as on the other, but one section was different. This is the part that I believe would have told the Vikings which river to follow, but I did not have time to read it properly before Eddie made us move away.' She gave the Englishman a brief sidelong glower.

It was Eddie's turn to shrug. 'If *somebody*,' he said, eyeing his wife, 'hadn't gone back for a closer look and made me chuck away the bomb, Hoyt and Berkeley wouldn't have got away with the stone.'

'Can we play the blame game some other time, thanks?' Nina complained impatiently. 'Tova, what *did* you manage to get?'

'I remember that it named Fjarriheim,' said the Swede. She opened a map of Sweden and indicated a point roughly halfway up the country's length. 'That is an old archaeological site, here. From there it said to go north – no, to "strike" north, which to me suggests travelling a long distance – until they reached some mountains.'

'That doesn't narrow it down much,' said Eddie. Coloured contours on the map marked the rugged spine of Scandinavia, Sweden's mountain ranges running along the border with Norway.

'No, but there was something that may help. I am not completely certain, but I think one of the words I saw in the runes would translate as "saddle". It may be an Old Norse name for a particular mountain.'

'Is there anywhere in Sweden that fits the bill?' Nina asked.

Tova shook her head. 'Not that I have found.' She gestured towards a laptop. 'I have researched as much as I could, and checked the IHA database, but there is nothing that matches.'

'Perhaps the name is a description,' said Kagan. 'It is a mountain that looks like a saddle.'

Eddie laughed sarcastically. 'Should be easy to find. It'll be right above the mountain that looks like a horse.'

'I do not think it will be that simple,' said Tova, with a slight smile. 'But the Vikings often did use descriptive names for features like mountains and lakes. If only we had just a few more words from the runes!' She turned to Kagan. 'You said there was a runestone at the place on Novaya Zemlya. Was it translated?'

'There were translations and pictures,' said the Russian, 'but no more.'

'Why not?' asked Nina.

'They were destroyed with the research on the eitr on the orders of Khrushchev. Eisenhov might have been able to remember some of what was written on the stone, but he is dead, and no one else at Unit 201 is old enough to have seen it.'

'Someone else saw it, though,' said Eddie, with an urgency that immediately caught Nina's attention. 'Volkov. Natalia's grandfather.'

'Yes, but he is also dead,' Kagan pointed out with a dismissive tone.

'Yeah, I know – but before he died, he wrote a letter to his wife, telling her about what he'd found.'

Surprise filled Kagan's face. 'He wrote a letter? How do you know about this?'

'Because Natalia told me about it – and she told me what it said on the runestone!'

That produced an electric response in the room. 'You know what the runestone said? Why did you not tell us this earlier?' Kagan demanded.

''Cause I only just remembered! Tova reminded me, when she said about the Viking names for lakes. Natalia told me that after the Vikings left Valhalla, they went to a lake.'

'Which lake?' Nina and Kagan said simultaneously.

'Christ, calm down, I'm trying to think! It was eight years ago, and it wasn't exactly the main thing I was bothered about at the time. Let's see, they left Valhalla, and went across a rainbow bridge—'

'Bifröst,' cut in Tova. 'It was also in the runes on the first stone as a landmark on the route to Valhalla.'

'Must be on the right track, then. But after that, they went through, er . . .' He frowned, trying to uproot the memories, before snapping his fingers. 'Lightning! That was it. The lake of lightning.'

Nina looked back at Tova. 'Does that mean anything to you? The lake of lightning?'

The historian's eyes widened. 'Yes, there was a place – let me check!' She turned back to the laptop and began typing. Very soon, she had results. 'Here, here! There is a lake called Blixtsjö – it means literally "lightning lake", and it took its name from Old Norse. It is on a river that in Viking myth was sometimes called Leipt.'

The name sparked Nina's memory. 'That's one of the primal rivers of the Norse creation mythology, isn't it?'

'Yes, that is right. There were eleven rivers that flowed from the spring of Hvergelmir, and Leipt was one of them. It got its name because it was supposed to streak like lightning. I always thought it *was* just a myth, but after what we have seen . . .'

'Where's this lake, then?' Eddie asked.

'Let me look . . .' More typing, then, after rapidly reading through the results, Tova returned her attention to the map. 'It is . . . here!'

She pointed out a thin, sharply winding lake in the highlands of central Sweden. Eddie took a closer look. 'It's pretty much north of Fjarriheim.'

'In the mountains,' Nina added. 'If one of them looks like a saddle . . .' She commandeered the laptop, accessing the IHA database to bring up a satellite image of the lake and its surroundings. 'I can't really tell from this, though.'

'All that money the IHA spent on this stuff, and you'd be better off using Google Earth,' he joked.

'I'll bring it up at the next budget meeting. But look, the lake's fed by a river at its north end, and it goes up into the mountains. Tova, what did the Valhalla Runestone say about following the route?'

Tova didn't need notes to recite the relevant part of the ancient inscription. 'Up the river you must travel, until great

Bifröst is reached. Across, follow the stream to the falls. At their summit is Odin's hall, now of the slain.'

Nina pursed her lips. 'So if this is the right river, then somewhere up it is Bifröst – the rainbow bridge. But a bridge to where?' She scrolled the satellite view, following the river northwards, but saw nothing except forests and mountains around it.

'If Valhalla is there, we must find it,' said Kagan. 'Berkeley and Hoyt have the same information that we do. They might be on their way already.'

'But how do we find it?' asked Tova.

'The old-fashioned way,' said Nina. 'We go there and look. I'll contact the IHA to make arrangements with the Swedish government, and get us some suitable transport. Kagan, what's the situation with your bosses at the Kremlin? Are they going to make trouble for us over what happened at the airbase?'

The Russian gave her a grim look. 'The President is very angry – at you in particular, Chase,' he went on, turning to Eddie. 'You destroyed some very valuable military aircraft.'

Eddie grimaced. 'Great, a world leader with nukes is personally pissed off at me . . .'

'It wouldn't be the first time,' Nina reminded him, smiling ruefully.

'But,' Kagan continued, 'he knows the importance of Unit 201 and its work. He is willing to accept your United Nations diplomatic immunity and not punish you for what you have done – as long as you help Unit 201 to find the other source of eitr.'

'An offer we can't refuse, eh?' said Eddie.

'Slavin did say something about gangsters,' Nina remarked, to Kagan's clear displeasure. 'But under the circumstances, I'll take it. Okay, if you go deal with your bosses, we can get moving. Tova, I'm sure you'll be wanting to go back to Sweden anyway, but beyond that . . . it's up to you if you want to come with us. After everything you've been through, I can entirely understand if you've had enough.'

Tova considered this for a moment. 'No, I . . . I will come with you,' she said. 'If Valhalla really exists, if this river really is the way to it, then I want to see it for myself.'

'Thank you. I really appreciate everything you've done to help us.' Nina straightened, gazing down at the map. 'Okay. Let's go and find the hall of the slain.'

Eddie gave her a look of dark humour. 'Just hope we don't end up as residents.'

24

Sweden

'There's the lake!' said Tova excitedly, looking over the helicopter pilot's shoulder.

Nina, in the front passenger seat, had a better view. Blixtsjö was a zigzagging ribbon running through the tree-covered hills. They were approaching from the south, looking along its length – and she saw at once why the Vikings, and later the Swedes, had given it its name. From the summit of one of the hills below the aircraft, it would indeed resemble the shape of a lightning bolt. One of the nearby mountains also matched the description in the runes, its bowed summit appearing somewhat like a saddle.

She looked beyond the lake. The landscape rose higher, snow-capped peaks and ridges standing out between forest-filled valleys as far as she could see. It was a beautiful sight, but her appreciation was now far more archaeological than aesthetic. Hidden some-where amongst the endless trees was Valhalla.

If they were right. They were following a route that had been pieced together from the deliberately incomplete writings on one ancient runestone, a few barely remembered scraps of information from another, second-hand recollections of Viking inscriptions that had been melted to glass over half a century earlier – and her husband's recollections of what Natalia Pöltl had told him, also second-hand, eight years before. The pieces did seem to make up a coherent picture, but there were no guarantees that it was the *correct* picture . . .

She put her doubts aside. It was all they had, whereas Berkeley and Hoyt possessed both runestones, and in theory everything they needed to lead them to Valhalla. The disgraced archaeologist had already proven that he could follow the clues left by the Vikings; she *had* to take the gamble that Tova was as good as or better than her former IHA colleague. It was the only chance they had of finding Valhalla first – and with it, the location of the second source of eitr.

The helicopter descended. On the lake's western bank was the little village of Blixtholm, and Nina saw a reception committee waiting on the frozen shoreline. 'There are the snow-mobiles,' she said. 'Remind me to thank Melinda for arranging everything so quickly.'

The pilot landed the chopper on the lake. The ice creaked loudly enough to be heard even over the noise of the rotors as it took the aircraft's weight, but to the relief of all aboard it showed no sign of cracking. All the same, the four passengers collected their belongings and made their way to land with a degree of haste. The helicopter departed in a whirlwind of sparkling ice crystals.

While Nina, Tova translating, spoke to the man who had delivered the snowmobiles, Eddie went straight to a box amongst the gear waiting for them. 'Remind *me* to thank Melinda,' he said with a grin.

'What is it?' Kagan asked.

Eddie opened the box, which was covered with stickers denoting it a United Nations diplomatic package. Inside was a rectangular metal case about eighteen inches long. He lifted the lid to reveal a gleaming steel handgun, the long, thick barrel reinforced by a hefty rib along its top. 'Oh yeah,' he said with a Christmas morning grin. 'It's been a while.'

Nina let out a disapproving sigh when she saw the weapon. 'Jeez. When did you get another one of those?'

'Picked it up two months ago,' Eddie replied, taking out the Wildey automatic and checking it admiringly in the morning sunlight.

'And you didn't tell me?'

'No, 'cause I knew you'd throw a fit. I mean, I lost the last couple before I even had a chance to fire them.'

'That's not why I threw a fit, and anyway I *didn't* throw a fit,' she complained. 'I don't like you having them because firstly, they cost two thousand dollars and you keep losing them –'

'See? Fit-throwing.'

'– and secondly, it's illegal to have them in New York City!'

Eddie pulled back the slide. 'That's why I kept it at work.'

She spluttered. 'You – you kept a *gun* at the United Nations?'

'It's not technically part of the city, is it?'

Nina held a hand to her ear. 'You hear that distant popping sound? That was Seretse's head exploding. And for God's sake, put it away before someone calls the cops.' The helicopter's arrival had inevitably attracted curious onlookers from the village. 'If you lose that one, you're never, *ever* having another, not at two grand a go. Seriously.'

Eddie grinned again, then slid one of the two magazines in the case into the pistol. The slide snapped back into place, chambering the first .45 Winchester Magnum cartridge. 'I just got fed up with being caught out without a gun. If I'd put a couple of bullets through Hoyt when I had the chance, we'd all be a lot better off.' He took a leather shoulder holster from the box and put the second magazine into a clip on one of its straps, then took off his winter coat to don it.

Kagan opened his own coat to reveal his SR-1. The Russian gun was considerably smaller than the Wildey. 'You seem to like overkill, Chase.'

'Overkill's my middle name,' the Yorkshireman replied.

'No it isn't,' said Nina. 'It's Jeremy.'

He made a disgruntled sound. 'Thanks for reminding me, *Persephone*.'

Tova gave her a look of surprise. 'Your middle name is Persephone?'

Nina blushed faintly. 'My parents were . . . well, obsessed with mythology. I'm lucky they didn't call me Melpomene or Eris or something.' The Swede laughed.

'I suppose if I knew anything about Greek gods that'd be hilarious,' said Eddie. He slipped the Wildey into the holster and put his coat back on over it. 'Okay, I'm set. Everyone else ready to go?'

Kagan refastened his own coat. 'Yes. But I would feel more confident if I knew exactly what we are looking for.'

'I wish I could say,' Tova told him. 'All I know is that if my reading of the runes is correct, somewhere up the river from here, we will see Bifröst – the rainbow bridge to Asgard. But what that means, I do not know.'

'I just hope we'll know it when we see it,' said Nina.

It did not take long to fix their gear to the back of the snowmobiles. Eddie switched on a GPS unit attached to the handlebars of his machine, then started the engine. 'All right! Let's give it some James Brown.'

'What?' said a puzzled Nina.

He put on a strained, rasping voice. 'Yow! Take me to the bridge!'

Both Tova and Kagan remained mystified, while Nina rolled her eyes. 'That was your best James Brown? I don't feel good.'

'Tchah! So, the plan – we just head north up the river until we see something that looks like it might be a rainbow bridge? And then we wander about until we find Valhalla?'

'That's pretty much it, yeah,' Nina told him, feeling faintly absurd at hearing the vagueness of their mission put into words.

He shrugged. 'It's not exactly the D-Day landings, but . . . we've found stuff in the past with less to go on.' He revved the engine, sending the snowmobile out on to the frozen lake in a spitting spray of ice. 'See you somewhere over the rainbow!'

Eddie turned north, speeding towards the gap in the trees marking the mouth of the river. Nina, Tova and Kagan started their own machines and followed his trail.

The journey upriver was scenic . . . at first. Before long, though, the monotony of unbroken mile after mile of conifers became wearing. The chainsaw buzz of the snowmobiles' two-stroke engines and the constant vibrations from the ice – which was far from smooth, the pressure ridges that had formed as the flowing water froze leaving it in places as striated as a washboard – also did nothing to ease the journey.

Nor did the group see anything that could possibly have been described as a rainbow bridge. They passed rocks and boulders of ever-increasing size the higher they rode into the hills, but none were large enough to span the river. Eddie gave one formation a hopeful look as he passed, but there was nothing of note about it. 'Bollocks to this,' he muttered, bringing his snowmobile to a stop and checking the GPS.

'What is it?' Nina asked, pulling up alongside him. Kagan and Tova followed suit.

'Just seeing how far we've gone. Christ! Only thirty kays? Feels more like a hundred and thirty.'

'It cannot be much farther, though,' said Tova. 'The runes said it was two days' travel from the lake on foot. Even the Vikings could not travel very fast over land like this.'

Eddie took out a map and used the GPS coordinates to find their position. The river was now heading roughly north-west, towards the mountains forming the spine of Scandinavia. 'Okay, in about ten kays the river forks, and the runes didn't say anything about that, did they?' Tova shook her head. 'So if it's here, we can't be too far from it.'

'Is there anything on the map?' asked Kagan.

'Just a big load of bugger-all. Nearest town I can see marked must be at least twelve kilometres from here. Looks like the terrain gets steeper, but there's not that much detail.' He folded the map again. 'Worst comes to the worst, we can ride up until we hit the fork, then come back and see if we missed something.'

Tova looked downhearted. 'I was so sure this was the right river, though.'

'We're not done yet,' Nina reminded her. 'Ten kilometres is a long way.'

Eddie rolled his buttocks from side to side on the saddle. 'Yeah, especially on these bloody bumps. It's like riding over the world's longest cattle grid.'

'If the Vikings could handle it, I'm sure you can too,' Nina said with a grin as she set off again.

The juddering journey resumed. It did not take long for the explorers to see that Eddie's reading of the map had been correct; the landscape grew steeper and more rocky, the waterway narrowing. They continued up it, at one point almost doubling back as they rounded a hairpin bend before curving back to the north-west. A couple of kilometres further, and the banks rose higher, turning the valley into a ravine. Nina caught up with her husband. 'If the sides get much taller, we won't be able to see anything,' she called.

'Yeah, I know,' he replied, looking up at the overhanging trees before turning his gaze back to the ice ahead. 'Whoa, slow down. There's a load of rocks in the river.' He eased off the throttle as the group approached a cluster of snow-covered shapes rising above the surface.

Tova also reduced speed, changing course to avoid the obstacles. 'If the Vikings were on foot, they would have gone away from the river here. Perhaps we should do the same.'

'Might be an idea,' said Eddie. He craned his neck to check the ravine's top. The western side was noticeably higher than the eastern. 'Dunno if we'll get the snowmobiles up there, though.'

Nina, however, was now looking ahead. 'Guys! You think that might be our bridge?'

The others followed her gaze. Crossing the top of the ravine was a huge slab of rock, a chunk of mountain that had been torn away and carried downhill by a glacier in aeons past, before eventually being dumped when the ice retreated. Shaded stripes ran lengthways through it, the various strata exposed. Some of the layers glinted in the sunlight.

The snowmobiles stopped. 'Yeah, it's a bridge,' said Eddie, 'but it's not a rainbow one. It's a bit grey. Unless the Viking who made the runestones was colour-blind?'

'I guess,' Nina said, disappointed. 'It's quite pretty, though. There must be a lot of quartz in it to get that effect with the light.'

'Damn, and I was hoping it was full of diamonds.' He was about to set off again when he noticed Tova staring up at the slab with an expression that suggested she had someone's name on the tip of her tongue but couldn't quite remember it. 'Tova? What's up?'

'The rainbow bridge,' she said, more to herself than in response to his question. 'No, Eddie is right, it is not a rainbow. It is, it is . . .' She suddenly flinched, excited. 'It is *not* a rainbow bridge! The translation, it is wrong!'

'What do you mean?' Nina asked.

'The translation of the runestone – not just the one that was stolen from the museum, but many others. The description of Bifröst is usually translated as "the rainbow bridge", which we think of as being many colours, yes? But there is another possible translation, which is . . . oh! What is the word in English?' She frowned and closed her eyes, thinking hard. 'The word, the word . . .' She snapped them open. 'Shimmering! It can also mean "the *shimmering* bridge"! The light changes as you look at it!'

Nina regarded the rock again. The quartz crystals indeed shimmered, reflected sunlight subtly shifting as she moved her head. 'That would definitely fit. But if you're right, and that really is Bifröst, then . . .'

'Then Asgard is on the far side – and so is Valhalla!' Tova cried in delight. 'It is real, it is up there!'

Kagan was more sceptical. 'We do not know for sure. You may be seeing what you want to see.'

'I want to see a nice pub with a roaring log fire, but it's not happening,' said Eddie. 'We've got to check it out, at least. If there's nothing up there, we can just come back and carry on.'

'Yeah, we need to look,' Nina agreed. She brought her snowmobile around.

Although Kagan was still dubious, they headed back downriver to the foot of the ravine. Eddie took the lead, revving his engine in controlled bursts to bring his vehicle up the steepening slope.

Nina, Tova and Kagan followed his tracks between the trees. The snowmobiles lurched and bumped over obstacles hidden under the snow. 'Bollocks,' Eddie said after fifty metres. 'It's getting really rocky. Probably a good idea to leave the snowmobiles and go the rest of the way on foot. If anything breaks, it'll be an absolute pain in the arse to fix out here.'

Nina was feeling faintly seasick from being thrown about. 'Yes, definitely,' she agreed, stopping and dismounting with relief. She gazed back the way they had come as the others also switched off their engines. The frozen river weaved away into the distance until it was swallowed by the forest, the sun reflecting dazzlingly off the ice. The stillness and sudden silence made the starkly beautiful sight seem almost like a painting. There was definitely a mythical quality to the snow-draped landscape; she could easily imagine the Vikings of old marching through it.

But would they have been heading for Valhalla – a real, physical place, not just a legend? She looked up the slope. Nothing was visible but raw nature: trees, rocks, snow. If the great hall were here, it was well hidden.

'Everyone ready?' she asked, though addressing the question mostly to Tova.

The Swede nodded. 'Yes. I cannot wait to see what we find! If the rock bridge really is Bifröst . . .'

'Then let's see if it is, eh?' said Eddie as he took a backpack from his snowmobile and donned it. 'What about you, Kagan? You don't look too excited.'

'My leg is hurt, so I had hoped not to walk very far,' the Russian grumbled as he collected his own gear.

They proceeded up the hill. The going was slow, the thick snow and uneven ground making each step an effort. But before long they reached the top of the slope and the glistening slab of quartz came into view. Another few minutes, and they reached it.

Eddie assessed the bridge. 'Shouldn't be too hard to get across,' he said, brushing away snow to check the rock beneath. The great span was shaped roughly like a spearhead, the narrow end on the far side of the ravine. 'Seems pretty flat under the snow. Looks solid, too.'

'I will let you test that,' said Kagan, with a faint smile.

Eddie took a coiled rope from his pack. 'Tie the end to that tree,' he said, fastening one end around his waist and handing the other to the Russian. 'And don't use a bloody granny knot!'

The line was quickly secured. Eddie set out over the crossing. Nina watched his progress anxiously – the drop to the ice below was at least thirty feet – but despite a couple of heartstopping moments when he almost stumbled, he was soon on the other side. 'Piece of piss!' he called. 'I'll fix the rope so you can get across.'

With the guideline in place and pulled taut, the others quickly followed him. Nina, last to cross, surveyed her surroundings as she set foot on solid ground. 'So, if that really was Bifröst we just crossed, then technically . . . this is Asgard. The home of the Norse gods.'

'That is true,' said Tova, thrilled at the prospect. 'If the Old Norse myths are euhemeristic, then Thor, Odin, Loki, Freyja . . . they all came from here. This is the land from which they ruled.'

'There's not much *to* rule, though,' opined Eddie. 'Except pine trees.'

'It might not always have been forest,' Tova said, a little defensively. 'There have been warmer periods in the past. It may once have been able to support farming.'

'Tova, where do we go from here?' said Nina, keen to move on.

The Swede checked her notes. 'The runestone said, "Across, follow the stream to the falls." There must be a stream nearby.' She pointed ahead. 'This way, I think.'

'You've been right about these things so far,' said Nina reassuringly.

'So what are we actually looking for?' Eddie asked as they began their trek into the forest. 'Valhalla's some sort of hall, but I doubt we're going to find a building just standing in the middle of the woods.'

'I do not know,' admitted Tova. 'It depends on how much of the *Eddas* are based on truth, and how much Snorri created himself, or took from sources that had already added their own details to the mythology. In the *Poetic Edda*, Valhalla is described as a hall with five hundred and forty rooms.'

'Big place. The heating bills must be a bugger.'

She smiled. 'In the *Prose Edda*, though, the huge golden hall that King Gylfi sees when he arrives in Asgard may be an illusion created to impress him. So there is no way to know what was real.'

'Until we find it,' said Nina. 'But if the runestones were describing a real place, we can't be far from it now. Is there anything else mentioned in the *Eddas* or other sources that might be useful? Like a landmark?'

'There is a tree, or a grove of trees, called Glasir,' Tova replied. 'It depends on the translation whether it is just one tree or many. But Glasir is supposed to mark the entrance to Valhalla. There has been speculation that it is connected to Yggdrasil, the world-tree, which would make it an ash.'

'So we just need to watch out for an ash tree, then,' said Eddie. 'Not that I know what an ash tree looks like. Anyone else?' Nina and Kagan shrugged.

'I do,' said Tova, before adding, 'I think.'

He smiled sardonically. 'I'd look it up on my phone, but I don't think I'll get much of a signal out here.'

'I think it'll just be a case of "not one of these",' Nina joked, gesturing towards the conifers surrounding them.

Eddie grinned, then continued onwards. After a few minutes, he spotted something ahead. 'Ay up.'

'You've seen an ash tree?' said his wife.

'No, but that matches what Tova said, don't you think?' A hundred yards away, the forest was split by an ice-filled stream bed that had cut deeply into the ground. 'What was the translation? Something about following a stream to a waterfall?' Tova nodded.

'The water is frozen, though,' said Kagan as they approached. 'Which way do we follow it?'

'I'm not an expert,' Nina said with gentle sarcasm, 'but I'm fairly sure that water doesn't run uphill.' She looked up the slope towards the stream's source. 'Over there.' In the distance between the trees, the group saw the rocky line of a cliff.

They followed the icy waterway. 'Oh, that is beautiful,' said Tova as they reached the cliff's foot. There was indeed the base of a waterfall there, but like the stream it was frozen, cascading water turned to overlapping sheets of icicles.

Eddie was more interested in the surrounding rocks. The falls had cut quite deeply into the cliff, exposing step-like strata on each side. 'Shouldn't be too hard to climb up,' he said, clambering on to the lowest level. 'I'll find a good route, then you follow me.'

He began his ascent. As he had predicted, it was not a difficult task; there were a few places where he had to haul himself up to higher ledges, producing grunts of exertion and muttered obscenities, but before long he was at the top. 'Okay, it's pretty straightforward,' he announced. 'Just watch out for that ledge about halfway up – there's a lot of ice on it.'

'Got it,' said Nina, beginning her own climb. 'What can you see up there?'

'Loads of future Billy bookshelves. Which way are we supposed to go?'

'The runes said to the summit,' Tova called to him. 'You must be close.'

'All right. I'll have a look around.'

'Don't get lost,' said Nina.

He smiled, then disappeared from view. She kept climbing. It took her longer than Eddie to reach the top, taking care negotiating the ledge he had warned her about, but she pulled herself up on to level ground with nothing more than a slight shortness of breath.

She glanced down to see how Tova and Kagan were doing. The Russian was following the archaeologist, his injured leg only slowing him slightly. Beyond them, the stream had carved a path through the forest – providing another view back along the frozen river. If anything, the sight was even more captivating than it had been from the rock bridge.

Nina finally turned away, finding with mild surprise that her husband was out of sight. 'Eddie? Where are you?' The dappled light through the trees made his tracks in the snow surprisingly hard to follow.

'Over here,' came the reply from a dip about fifty yards away. She headed for it. Eddie came into view below as she approached its edge. 'Have a gander at this.'

'At what?' she asked. There was nothing immediately unusual in sight; a large bowl-shaped depression had a long hump at its centre, snow-laden trees atop it. But his expectant half-smirk told her she had missed something. She followed his path down the slope, looking in all directions. Was there an opening in the ground, or a group of stones that might once have been part of a structure? Nothing presented itself—

The answer suddenly appeared with such obviousness that she couldn't believe she hadn't seen it immediately. 'You got it now?' Eddie asked.

'Yeah, I got it,' she said, laughing. 'Talk about not seeing the wood for the trees.'

The forest surrounding them was made up entirely of evergreens – but the trees on top of the mound were devoid of leaves beneath their coatings of snow and ice. Wiry branches spread out to form roughly spherical shapes, in contrast to the distinctive cones of the conifers. 'So you think that's an ash tree?' said Eddie.

'I think that's an ash tree,' gasped Tova, hurrying up behind Nina.

'An ash grove,' Nina corrected. She counted at least a dozen of the interlopers. A few small evergreens had managed to take root amongst the group, but otherwise the ashes seemed to have been in possession of the hillock for a long time. 'Is this it? Have we found Valhalla?'

'I do not know. Come on, we must search!' Tova rushed past Nina down the slope.

'If there were any buildings here, they're long gone,' Eddie said as Nina followed the Swede.

'I don't think we're looking for an actual building,' she replied. 'I think we're looking for *that*.' She pointed at the hump.

He was less than impressed. 'You think *that's* Valhalla? '

'No, but Valhalla is under it!' said Tova. 'The Vikings often put their dead in burial mounds – the largest in Sweden is called Anundshög, in Västmanland. It is big, over nine metres high.' She led the way around the little hill. 'Perhaps that is even where the name came from; "Valhalla" means "the hall of the slain", but if whatever was built here was buried to hide or protect it, then it would have looked just like a burial mound.'

'It'd match the runes,' Nina noted. 'They said Odin's hall was *now* of the slain.'

'You mean Valhalla might just be a nickname?' Eddie asked dubiously.

Nina smiled. 'You've heard of Emperor Caligula?'

'The mad, pervy one? Course I have.'

'Caligula was a nickname – it was a type of soldier's boot. His real name was Gaius Germanicus.'

'No wonder he changed it. But if this place was so important to the Vikings, why would they bury it? What were they trying to protect?'

'The eitr,' said Kagan as he caught up. 'They were afraid of it, because they knew how deadly it was – but they also knew some people would still be crazy enough to look for it.'

'That might be where the myth of Loki comes from,' Nina said thoughtfully. 'He was a Norse god like Thor and Odin, but he betrayed them and sided with the serpent and the wolf at Ragnarök. Maybe he was like Hoyt – he wanted to use the eitr as a weapon.'

'So they hid the map to the eitr pits so that only Vikings they trusted would know how to find it?' said Eddie.

Tova nodded. 'The only time they would need it would be when Ragnarök was upon them.'

'Kind of an "open in event of doomsday" thing?'

'It'd explain why they went to such lengths to hide it,' said Nina. 'You don't want your people deciding to go out there on a macho whim. If you think the Midgard Serpent's about to surface, though, *that's* when you gather the troops and follow the secret path to Valhalla. It's a mobilisation point. Once you're here, the next stop is the serpent's pit – the source of the eitr.'

'Novaya Zemlya,' Kagan said. 'Or . . . the other place. We have to find it – before Hoyt and Berkeley do.'

'We've got to get inside first,' Eddie pointed out. He looked up at the mound. 'And we might have to do a lot of digging – this thing's big, it must be at least forty feet high. We'll need to find a door.'

Tova stopped. 'A compass! Does anyone have a compass?' Phones were produced in unison. 'Ah, of course. But we should go to the west side of the mound. Which way is it?'

Eddie checked his compass app. 'Keep going this way around it. Shouldn't be far.'

'Why the west side?' Nina asked.

The Swede set off again, her pace quicker than before. 'The entrance to Valhalla is supposed to be on the western side, guarded by a wolf.'

'A wolf, eh?' said Eddie, suddenly on alert and checking the surrounding forest. 'Good job I brought the Wildey.'

'I don't think it'll still be on guard after over a thousand years,' said Nina. She now almost had to jog to keep up with Tova, who had picked up a stick and was scampering along the edge of the barrow, poking at the snow. 'What are you looking for?'

'They may have left a marker, even a runestone, just as they did in the Arctic,' Tova replied. 'Are we at the west side yet?'

'Pretty much,' Eddie answered.

'Then there could be something that would show the way in. Help me look for it, please.'

The others joined in her search. Nina soon found something under the snow that seemed promising, but a tap with her boot revealed nothing more than a lump of broken wood. Disappointed, she continued around the mound. If Valhalla really was buried beneath it, it could be a very large structure: she guessed the barrow's total length at close to three hundred feet. If there was no marker, then Eddie would be right – it would require a lot of digging to open it up . . .

She approached a tree, a small conifer rather than an ash. Its trunk was tilted at an angle, and as she drew closer she saw why: the ground dropped away on its far side, almost as if a trench had been cut into the earthen slope. She reached its edge and looked down into it. The overhanging tree, some of its roots exposed where the unstable soil had slid away, had shielded it from most of the snow.

Even though it was thickly carpeted with ice-crusted dead leaves and partially hidden by scrubby bushes, she could tell that the cutting, with its level floor and steep sides, was not natural.

A dark opening, about five feet high and framed by gnarled ash roots, lurked at its end. Her heart raced. 'Tova! Over here – I think I've found it!'

The group hurried to her. 'This must be it!' Tova cried, hopping down on to the frozen detritus. She peered into the opening. 'There is something back there – it may be a gate!'

'Whoa, whoa!' Eddie shouted as she moved to enter. 'Hold on a minute!'

Tova stopped with a questioning look. 'What is wrong?'

'Don't you remember? It had different names depending on what translation you read. One of them was a gate . . . and the other was a *death-barrier*! Don't just run in there.'

'I really wouldn't,' Nina added. 'We've learned that the hard way. Eddie, you've got a flashlight, haven't you?'

He climbed down into the trench and took a powerful torch from his backpack, then shone it into the hole. The beam revealed dirty, dull grey metal. 'Looks like lead,' he said, sweeping the light across its surface. More details appeared. The obstruction was one of a pair of double doors. A rough image of a wolf, head lowered aggressively, had been pounded into the lead. Lines of small holes ran across the barrier at head, stomach and knee height.

'What are those?' Kagan asked.

'I dunno, but I'm not going to poke a finger inside to find out.' He fixed the torch on a larger vertical slot in one of the doors, then raised it to illuminate its interior. 'I think they're made of wood – the lead's just armour. I can't see anything on the other side, though. It's blocked off.'

Nina moved alongside him. 'You know what would fit into that? The sun compass that was set into the runestone, if you turned it sideways on.'

'"The two parts together brought, shall alone open the death-gate of Valhalla,"' said Tova quietly.

'The compass must be some sort of key. No idea how, but it can't be a coincidence that it's the right size. Eddie, let me have the flashlight.'

'Careful,' he warned as she took the torch and stepped closer to shine it into the slot. 'You might set something off.'

'I'm not going to touch it,' she assured him, leaning as close as she dared to peer into the opening. As Eddie had said, the barrier was made of fire-hardened logs behind the lead sheathing. But there was more lead inside, plates of the dull metal on each side of the slot. The temptation was strong to prod one to see if it moved, but she resisted. 'I think there's a mechanism, but I don't—'

She was interrupted by Kagan's bark of 'Quiet!' The Russian turned, expression intense. 'I can hear something. I think it is a plane!'

The others froze, listening. The snow-cloaked stillness of

the forest surrounded them . . . then was broken by a harsh mechanical buzz.

Distant – but getting closer.

'It's not a plane,' Nina whispered, trying to pinpoint its origin. 'It's too low.'

'It's coming from the river,' said Eddie grimly. The hearing loss he had sustained from years of gunfire and explosions had affected his sensitivity to higher-frequency sounds, but the droning noise was all too clear. He jumped out of the trench and ran back up the slope towards the waterfall. 'Come on!'

Nina and Tova followed, Kagan loping along as quickly as he could. The group reached the top of the cliff and looked back at the frozen river.

Several vehicles were racing along it.

Nina didn't need binoculars to know who was in them. 'It's Berkeley and Hoyt,' she gasped. 'They've found us.'

25

Tova stared at the convoy in dismay. 'It – it might not be them,' she said, with very little conviction.

'No, it's got to be,' Eddie growled. He counted seven vehicles: two snowmobiles in the lead, followed by a trio of large 4x4s, and another pair that took him a moment to identify as icerunners – two-seaters resembling steroidal bobsleds, driven by noisy pusher propellers on their tails. 'Nobody else'd come out here in force like that.'

'Damn you, Logan,' Nina snarled. Even if the off-roaders only had four occupants each, that still meant they were facing at least eighteen people.

They watched as the vehicles headed for the ravine. Rather than halt so their passengers could reach the rock bridge on foot, however, they continued on through the narrow valley, the roar of engines echoing from its sides.

'Perhaps they are not stopping,' said Tova, again sounding unconvinced by her own suggestion.

Nina shook her head. 'They'll have had access to satellite maps, just like us. They probably think it'll be easier to reach Valhalla if they go farther upriver and double back.' She turned to Eddie. 'What do we do?'

'They might not have seen the snowmobiles,' he said, 'so there's a chance they don't know we're here. If they don't . . .'

A moment of thought, then he jogged to a nearby tree and jumped to grab a large branch, pulling until it snapped from the trunk. 'There's some rocks overlooking the entrance, over there,' he said, pointing to a spot about a hundred metres west of the barrow. 'Get behind 'em and stay low.'

'What are you going to do?' demanded Kagan.

'Cover our tracks. I'll come up after you when I'm done.' Hefting the branch over one shoulder, he returned to the entrance as Nina and the others headed for the rocks.

Before long, the rumble of engines cut out. Nina checked her map; from the direction of the sound, the vehicles had probably stopped on flatter ground about half a mile to the north. Assuming that Berkeley had accurately pinpointed Valhalla's location, that meant Hoyt's forces were only around fifteen minutes away on foot.

She looked over her cover at the mound. Eddie was using the evergreen's branch like a carpet sweeper, swinging it from side to side as he paced backwards along the group's tracks to brush away their footsteps. But it did not take much effort to spot that *something* had disturbed the snow, even if the bootprints themselves were no longer clear. If Hoyt's team spent any time searching the area, the game would be up.

Eddie finally backed to the top of the depression. He swept over the tracks at the slope's brow, then yomped to the others. 'Did the best I could, but it's not great,' he said. 'Any sign of 'em?'

Kagan had produced a compact set of binoculars and was scanning the trees to the north. 'No, but I do not think they can be far away now.'

'Yeah, I know. Unless they all get eaten by a troll.' Tova managed a small smile at Eddie's joke.

Silence descended once more. Minutes passed. Tension rose

amongst the little group. The arrival of the intruders was inevitable – it was just a question of when, and from where . . .

'I see them,' Kagan hissed, locking his binoculars on a particular spot. 'About a hundred and fifty metres.'

Nina picked out new colours amongst the white and brown and green. Men in bulky winter gear, most with hoods up to protect their heads from the cold, were tramping through the forest.

Coming towards them. Berkeley's deductions had been accurate.

Kagan kept watching. 'I count . . . nineteen, maybe twenty.'

'Let me look,' said Eddie. Kagan gave him the binoculars. 'I see Hoyt – and Berkeley. He's got a GPS or something, he's checking it . . . he just pointed at the mound.' He passed them back to the Russian and opened his coat to draw the Wildey. 'Just want it ready,' he told the concerned women. 'I'm not going to start shooting. Yet.'

Voices reached them as Hoyt's team drew closer. Berkeley led the way, wearing a bright yellow padded jacket that stood out from his more muted companions. Behind him was Hoyt, hood down and a cigarette between his lips. A P90 sub-machine gun was slung over his shoulder. Most of the other men were similarly armed.

'Pity you didn't bring that sniper rifle,' Eddie told Kagan. He watched as the rest of the group followed Berkeley through the snow. The archaeologist divided his attention between the GPS and his surroundings – then lowered the device and broke into a clumsy jog, pointing excitedly at the ashes.

'This is it!' he called. 'Look at the trees!' He reached the mound and glanced around, then spotted the cutting at the foot of the tilted tree. 'Over here!'

Eddie drew in an anxious breath, his hand tightening around

the gun. 'If they see our footprints, we're in deep shit. We'll have to run for the waterfall and try to get back to the snowmobiles.'

Nina felt a chill that no amount of warm clothing could prevent as Berkeley reached the trench and hopped down into it. Hoyt did the same, waiting for an unarmed man, face hidden by his hood, to join him before heading for the darkened opening.

They reached the brushed snow above the edge of the trench . . .

And continued past it. The prospect of discovering what lay in the darkness was too enticing to resist. A couple of the other mercenaries followed them, the remainder spreading out around the foot of the mound. Cigarettes were lit, food and drink produced from pockets and packs.

'They don't know we're here,' said Nina with relief. 'They aren't expecting trouble.'

'Maybe not, but they're still ready for it,' Eddie replied. He borrowed the binoculars again. Flickers of light came from the darkness as Berkeley shone a torch over the lead barrier. 'Okay, they're having a look at the doors . . . Berkeley's checking out that slot.'

'Let me see,' Nina demanded, plucking the binoculars from his hands. He made a 'tchah!' sound, but she ignored it, intent on discovering what was going on below. Berkeley continued his examination of the slot, then, after exchanging words with Hoyt and the other man, signalled to one of the armed mercenaries in the trench behind them. 'Now what's he doing . . . Oh, crap.'

'What is it?' asked Tova.

'He's got the sun compasses!' The mercenary took a box from his backpack, the two dark stone discs inside. Berkeley extracted them and, with great care, brought them together back-to-back. He flinched as they suddenly clapped against each other with a clink that was audible even from her hiding place. 'They *are* magnetic – he's just fitted them together. And I was right, they're exactly the same size as the slot. Dammit, they really are a key!'

She watched helplessly as Hoyt shone the light on the opening in the door and Berkeley, looking extremely pleased with himself, gently eased the combined compasses into it as if inserting a coin into a slot machine. 'He's putting it in, and . . .'

'And?' prompted Eddie after a few seconds.

'And nothing!' Nina exclaimed. Berkeley's expression slipped to annoyance, then confusion. He used his fingertips to edge the disc back out, then tried again with more force. 'It's not doing anything.'

Another attempt had the same lack of result. Frustrated, Berkeley removed the compasses, holding them as he began an animated discussion with Hoyt and his companion. It went on for a good minute, the archaeologist repeatedly gesturing at the doors and becoming visibly more dismayed each time.

'He's really not happy,' Nina reported. 'I think Hoyt wants to bust the doors open.'

'But – but that will destroy the site,' Tova protested.

'I don't think he cares,' said Eddie.

The group looked on from their hiding place as Berkeley reluctantly caved in to Hoyt and his companion, and called out to the mercenaries. A man whom Nina recognised as one of the team from the Norwegian lake flicked away a cigarette and picked up a large case he had brought, taking it into the trench. 'Son of a . . .' she spluttered when she saw what was inside.

'What is it? Kagan asked.

'It's a chainsaw! They're going to open the doors with a frickin' *chainsaw*!'

Eddie chuckled humourlessly. 'Now that's my kind of archaeology.' Both women glared at him. 'Joking, obviously. Well, mostly.'

Nina scowled, then looked back through the binoculars. Berkeley aimed his light at the doors, pointing to a particular spot. The man with the chainsaw nodded and pulled the cord to start it. The machine's snarl shattered the quiet, a few birds that had been roosting nearby taking panicked flight.

The others in the trench retreated as the man stepped up to the doors and raised the saw. 'God *damn* it, Logan,' Nina said, wincing at the first screech of metal slashing through metal. 'You don't—'

A scream made everyone, mercenaries and their hidden observers alike, jump. The chainsaw revved violently as its user staggered back into the light – and sliced into his leg, blood spouting against the side of the trench. 'What the fuck just happened?' Eddie said, startled.

Through the field glasses, Nina had a clear view of the shocking sight. The horrific gash in his thigh was not the only injury the mercenary had received. Blood was also running down the front of his coat – from a foot-long wooden shaft buried in his abdomen. He screamed again, falling on his back. 'Jesus!' she said as Hoyt rushed up and threw the chainsaw clear. 'Eddie, you were right – it *was* booby-trapped. Looks like it shot an arrow out of one of those holes.'

More of his comrades ran to help the screaming man. 'Everyone get away from the doors!' Berkeley shouted, hurriedly scrambling clear.

The wounded mercenary was hauled out of the trench, leaving a trail of blood through the snow. 'Who's got the fuckin' medical kit?' Hoyt demanded. One of his men retrieved something from a pack. 'No, that won't be enough! He's gonna need morphine! Someone go back to the trucks and get the proper fuckin' thing!' Two of the mercs raced away back along the group's tracks. 'Put a tent up – we need to get that thing out of him!'

A pop-up tent was quickly unfolded, several men gingerly carrying their still-wailing fellow inside. The rest of the team looked on, more with curiosity than concern. Hoyt stormed over to Berkeley and began haranguing him. The archaeologist's protest of 'I *told* you not to do it!' carried clearly across the hollow.

Hoyt's companion joined the argument, seeming to side with the former soldier. Berkeley held up the sun compasses. 'I tried them, what more can I say?' he said angrily. 'The runestones clearly said they had to be put together to open the door. Well, I did, and they didn't work. The site is over a thousand years old – maybe the lock's broken, I don't know!' He listened with growing displeasure as the third man lectured him, jabbing with his forefinger. 'Okay, okay, if that's what you think is necessary! But I did everything I could.' Cradling the compasses in one arm, he stalked off.

'I do believe he's going to sulk,' said Nina, almost amused.

Eddie watched Berkeley move away from the rest of the group. 'You know . . .'

'What?'

'Everyone else is watching the wounded guy – but look, some of them are just standing there having a smoke. If they were proper soldiers, they'd be worried about their mate, but it's like this lot barely know each other.'

'We did kill many of Hoyt's men in Norway,' Kagan pointed out. 'He would have had to recruit more, fast.'

Nina could tell her husband had something in mind – and also that it would involve a large degree of risk. 'What are you thinking, Eddie?'

'I'm thinking,' he replied, his square face breaking into a crooked smile, 'that most of these guys don't know each other too well . . . and that they're all dressed pretty similar, and most

369

of 'em have got their hoods up.' He tugged at the thick fleece surround of his own hood. 'Like this.'

She stared at him. 'You're not serious.'

'Why not? I should be able to get down there without being seen so long as they're all watching Harold Spearguts in the tent. My coat's pretty much the same as anyone else's, so if nobody gets a good look at my face I can walk right up to Berkeley and,' he held up the hulking Wildey, '*persuade* him to give me the sun compasses.'

Tova was horrified. 'But if they realise you are not one of them, they will kill you!'

'And if we don't do something, they'll just blow the bloody doors off and stroll in to take whatever's inside.'

'We cannot let them do that,' said Kagan firmly. 'It will lead them to the other source of eitr.'

'It won't help us get into Valhalla, though,' Nina objected. 'The compasses didn't open the lock even when he put them together . . .' She trailed off as a new possibility occurred to her. 'He put them together *wrong*. That's why they didn't do anything. The lock isn't broken – the key just didn't touch it!'

'What do you mean?' asked Tova.

'I mean, the compasses are magnetic – but there are two ways you can put magnets together. They can attract each other . . . or *repel*. Berkeley combined them so they'd attract each other, which is the obvious thing to do. But the mechanism inside the lock is on each side of the slot. The only way the two pieces of the key would touch both parts at the same time is if they're repelling each other!'

'Like poles attract, unlike poles repel,' said Eddie, nodding. 'Or is it the other way round? I can never bloody remember. But it doesn't matter; all you need to know is which sides repel each other.'

'It fits what the runestone said. It *has* to be how the lock works.' Nina looked back at the mound. Berkeley was now standing on his own under a tree, stabbing at a tablet computer with one ungloved hand. Hoyt had gone to the tent, while the third man peered into the barrow's entrance before turning away to join him. The rest of the mercenaries were holding station, either anxiously observing the progress of the injured man's first aid, or hanging back, waiting to see what happened.

She moved her gaze to the trench. Everyone was heeding Berkeley's warning and keeping well clear. 'If we took the key from Logan, we could get inside without anyone seeing us.'

Tova was not keen on the idea. 'But how will we get to the doors? Even if they do not realise Eddie is not one of them, they will spot an extra three people – especially as two of them are women!'

'Through the trees,' said Kagan. He indicated the ash grove on the barrow. 'We go around the hill until we are out of sight, then cross over its top and drop down to the doors. If we are careful, they will not see us.'

'Can we do it?' Nina asked Eddie.

He regarded the scene with a soldier's trained eye. 'Yeah. I think we can. There's enough cover above to get to the entrance, so long as nobody attracts their attention.'

'This is crazy,' said Tova unhappily.

'You don't have to come with us,' Nina assured her. 'You can wait here if you want.'

The prospect was just as unappealing. 'On my own? But what if something happens to you?'

'Then you run for the snowmobiles and burn it out of here as fast as you bloody can,' said Eddie.

'You should go now, if you are afraid,' Kagan added. 'It will be safer.' There was a calculated air to his suggestion that caught Nina's attention, but she couldn't tell what lay behind it.

'Tova, we need you,' she countered. 'This is Valhalla, it must be – it's exactly where the runestones said it would be. Which means that inside, it tells us how to reach the second eitr pit, and we need you to translate the runes. And also,' she went on, professional excitement rising, 'it's Valhalla! It would be the greatest Old Norse archaeological discovery ever – and it would be your find. The hall's been sealed for hundreds, maybe even thousands of years. Don't you want to know what's inside?'

The Swede held a brief internal battle between instinct and intellect. The latter won, though with considerable trepidation. 'Yes, okay . . . but what if they see us before we get in?'

Eddie held up the Wildey. 'They'll wish they hadn't.' She was not reassured.

'You'll come with us?' Nina asked, getting a nod in reply. 'Then let's go.'

Crouched low, they moved away from the rocks and circled around the top of the hollow. The mercenary group was soon lost to sight behind the conifers. 'Okay,' said Eddie, once he was sure they were concealed, 'you all go up on to the hill and wait above the entrance. Don't do anything until I've got the compass. If anything goes wrong, leg it.'

'We're not leaving you,' insisted Nina.

'I'll either be right behind you, or dead.'

'I'd really rather it wasn't the second one.'

'Yeah, me too!' He grinned. 'Okay, I'll go and have words with Berkeley.' He headed down into the hollow, angling around the foot of the barrow. Nina and the others climbed the mound to make their way through the stand of ash trees.

Eddie slowed his advance as he drew closer to the entrance. The injured man's screams had fallen to moans, but he was still conscious and in pain. That meant the men sent to collect the medical kit had not yet returned. When they did, all attention would be on them . . .

He kept that thought in his mind as he moved through the evergreens surrounding the island of ashes. Movement ahead; he paused, sliding behind a tree trunk to observe. Vivid yellow stood out against the woodland colours. Berkeley.

The archaeologist was still occupied with his tablet computer. Eddie leaned out a little further. A couple of the mercenaries were visible from his position, but they were looking towards the tent. Nothing about their stances suggested that they were on alert.

He set off again, hood up, head low. Sidelong glances revealed more of Hoyt's men as he rounded the barrow. Keeping the gun out of their sight, he closed on Berkeley. He was now only thirty feet away, near enough to hear the scientist muttering to himself as he stabbed at the screen. Another brief turn of the head to check on the mercenaries—

One of the men by the tent was looking right at him.

Cold adrenalin surged through Eddie's body, his hand tightening around the gun – but then the mercenary turned away. All he had seen was another anonymous figure in a thick coat. The Englishman felt a rush of relief, and hope. This might work . . .

He reached Berkeley. The scientist was typing notes on the tablet, frustration clear as he tapped repeatedly at the screen like a woodpecker; the cold was affecting the device's sensitivity. He let out a steaming huff of annoyance as he jabbed at one of the virtual keys to no effect, then turned as a reflection in the screen told him he was not alone. 'Yes, what?'

'Ay up, Logan,' said Eddie, pushing the Wildey's broad barrel against his chest. 'How's things?'

Berkeley twitched in surprise and fear. 'Chase!' His eyes flicked towards Hoyt and his men.

'Say a fucking word and I'll shoot you,' said the Englishman, his expression deadly. 'And that's not a bluff – I will put a bullet through your fucking heart if you try to warn them. Got that?' Berkeley started to speak, then thought better of it and nodded instead. 'Good. Where's the compass?' Berkeley tipped his head down. The dark discs of the conjoined compasses sat in the crook of his arm. 'Okay, let's walk to the entrance, nice and casual. You're going to open the door for us.'

'It – it doesn't work!' the archaeologist hissed. 'The key, I mean. I put it in the lock, and nothing happened!'

'Well, it's a good job Nina's smarter than you.'

'She's here?' He looked around nervously, as if expecting her to materialise from behind a tree and punch him.

'No, I came out here all on my own 'cause I like collecting pine cones. Of course she's here, you fucking dipshit. Now move.'

Keeping the gun shielded from sight, Eddie set off behind Berkeley. The mercenaries were still staying well clear of the entrance, but the pair would have to pass less than twenty feet from one of them to reach the trench. He tensed as they drew closer. The man looked round . . .

And dismissed Berkeley with a glance, returning his attention to the tent. Eddie pushed the gun into the archaeologist's side. 'Keep going,' he whispered.

He raised his head to check the top of the mound. At first glance he saw nothing except ash trees, but then a more focused search revealed Kagan, barely visible as he peered around a small snow-covered bush. The Russian had been well trained to make the most of any available concealment.

Eddie glanced back at the mercenaries. Nobody seemed

interested in the two men. He guided Berkeley ahead of him as they reached the cutting. On the hillside above, Kagan started to emerge from his cover—

'Berkeley!'

The Russian froze – as did Berkeley at Hoyt's shout. Eddie stopped right behind him. He turned his head just enough to see the tall American glaring at them from by the tent. 'Answer him,' he rumbled, keeping the gun pressed against the scientist's body.

Berkeley hesitantly looked back at the mercenary leader. 'Wh-what? What is it?'

'What the hell are you doing?'

'Come up with something good or I'll shoot you,' Eddie growled, when his prisoner didn't immediately respond.

He swallowed, but managed to stammer out a reply to Hoyt. 'I was – I was going to check the damage done by the chainsaw. If it's broken the lock mechanism, we might be able to open the doors without triggering any more booby-traps.'

'Why bother?' Hoyt replied impatiently. 'We're just gonna blow 'em open anyway.' Eddie tensed again, worried that the American was going to call them back, but then a shout from the woods drew everyone's attention. The men who had been sent to collect the morphine had returned. 'Just don't get yourself shot,' the mercenary leader said with a shrug before turning away.

'That's good advice,' Eddie told Berkeley. 'Do as you're told, and you won't. Okay, move.' He shoved the other man forward again. Above, Kagan emerged from the trees and crept down the slope to drop into the entrance. Nina and Tova did the same, the latter with considerable fear. But nobody was watching the barrow, all eyes on the returning mercenaries.

'Hello again, Logan,' Nina said coldly as Eddie brought

Berkeley into the shadows. 'Give me those.' She grabbed the sun compasses from him.

'Nina!' Berkeley exclaimed. 'What is this, what's going on? Why is your maniac of a husband pointing a gun at me?'

'You're lucky *I'm* not pointing a gun at you, you son of a bitch!' She took off her gloves and, with some effort, prised the two magnetised discs apart. 'Your buddies in Norway were going to kill us after you left.'

He shook his head. 'No, that's absurd. Why would they do that?'

Nina turned one of the compasses around and pressed it against its companion. As she had hoped, they repelled each other, almost squirming in her hands as she forced them together. 'What, hasn't the fact that they're all carrying machine guns tipped you off that these are not nice people? You asshole.' She gave him a disgusted look, then faced the doors. 'Okay. Let's hope this works . . .'

Eddie regarded the lines of holes running across the barrier. 'Yeah, let's bloody hope! Tova, you stand behind me. And I'll stand behind this berk.'

Berkeley was clearly unaware that the truncation of his name was also a British insult. 'What, you – you're going to use me as a human shield?' he protested.

'We finally found something you're good for,' Eddie told him. 'Stand there and shut up.'

'But what if you set off another trap?'

'Then we're both going to be pincushions,' said Nina. 'And yes, shut up.' Still holding the two compasses together, she raised them to the slot and carefully slid them inside. They scraped against the edges of the opening as the magnetic force tried to drive them apart. 'Okay, nearly there . . .'

Everyone held their breath, watching anxiously – Berkeley

most of all – as she pushed the compasses fully into the hole—

Clang!

The dull ring of stone on metal echoed through the entrance as the discs finally had room to separate – and sprang apart, hitting the lead plates on each side of the slot. A muffled thumping came from inside the door, the mechanism being released . . .

And with an ear-splitting shrill the doors began to open for the first time in over a millennium.

'Jesus!' Eddie said, wincing. 'My ears might be bad, but I heard *that*!'

'And so will Hoyt's guys!' Nina realised in alarm. 'Get inside, quick!' She moved to the gap between the two-foot-thick doors, but it was widening with agonising slowness.

'But we do not know what is in there!' said Tova.

'We know what's out here – blokes with guns!' Eddie shot back. He shoved Berkeley forward, looking down the cutting. A man ran into view at its end, shouting in alarm when he saw the intruders.

The doors finally parted enough for Nina to fit. She squeezed through, finding herself in darkness; the only thing revealed by the narrow line of daylight was a filthy stone floor. 'Come on!' she shouted, backing away to give the others room. Eddie held Berkeley back so Tova could enter, then pushed the American inside before following himself. Kagan brought up the rear, gun raised.

The mechanism ground on, the doors opening wider. More mercenaries appeared and ran along the trench. 'Shut the fucking things!' Eddie yelled, throwing Berkeley to the ground and slamming his back against one of the barriers. The doors slowed, but didn't stop. 'Kagan, get the other one!'

The Russian barged against the other door. The two men pushed, boots scrabbling for grip. With a deep and echoing creak, the barrier's movement finally stopped – but even shoving with all their might, they couldn't force it back. 'Shit!' Eddie yelled. 'Nina, Tova, help us!'

Tova ran to add as much weight as she could to Kagan's side. It was enough to tip the balance – but only slightly, the doors inching shut. Too slowly. The men outside were closing fast, drawing their weapons.

Nina went to help Eddie, but knew it would be futile—

Her eyes had adjusted enough to make out more of the interior – and the mechanism opening the lead-covered doors. 'Eddie!' she cried. 'Give me your gun!'

'You can't take 'em all on!' he protested.

'I'm not going to! Quick!'

The conviction in his wife's voice overcame his doubts. Still straining against the door, he passed her the Wildey. Nina whirled, falling a huge cylinder of roughly carved stone suspended by a thick skein of rope.

She pressed the muzzle against the trembling line – and pulled the trigger.

The deafening boom and pounding recoil made her stagger backwards. The .45-calibre round shredded the rope – and the great block slammed to the floor, shattering the flagstones and knocking her on to her back with the sheer force of the impact.

But with the counterweight gone, the doors were now free to move. 'Push, *push*!' Eddie yelled, driving himself backwards. Kagan and Tova did the same. The gap closed . . .

'Shoot 'em, shoot!' Hoyt bellowed from outside. 'Don't let 'em shut it!'

Guns cracked, bullets smacking through the lead sheeting and splintering the logs beneath. Eddie flinched as splinters caught the side of his face. He ignored the pain and kept pushing as more shots ripped into the doors.

The two sides met with a deep thump – and the rattle of a mechanism resetting. Some of the mercenaries charged against the doors, trying to ram them back open. Eddie lurched at the impact—

More jolts, these from within the barrier – and screams came from outside as the reactivated booby-traps fired a fusillade of bolts at point-blank range. Muffled sounds of panic reached him as the other mercenaries fled. 'I think they got the point. Well, points.'

'I'm sure you've used that one before,' Nina said as she took out a flashlight and switched it on.

'I'll have words with my scriptwriters.' He made sure the doors were secure, then saw that Tova was still pressed against them, curled up in a tight ball. 'Tova, are you okay?' he asked, worried that she had been hit.

Nina joined them. 'Tova?' She crouched beside the older woman, who was trembling. 'It's all right, we're safe for now.'

Tova reluctantly lifted her head. Her face was tightly drawn, as she struggled to stop herself from crying. 'I – I'm sorry, but . . .' She swallowed, trying to lubricate her fear-dried throat. 'I am scared! Everyone is trying to kill us, but you do not seem bothered!'

'Oh, believe me, I'm bothered,' Nina assured her.

'But you do not show it!'

'You get used to it after a while.' Eddie reached down to help her up.

Tova stood. 'I do not want to get used to it,' she said quietly. 'This is not what I want to do.'

Eddie and his wife exchanged concerned looks, then Nina saw something in the torchlight. In the back of one door were two slots down at knee level – and in each was one of the sun compasses. After releasing the lock, they had fallen down through the door's innards so they could be collected. 'Looks like we might need these again,' she said, picking them up and letting the magnetised discs clap back together.

Kagan straightened, eyeing a ragged bullet hole beside his head. 'You okay?' Eddie asked.

'Yes, but . . . that was close,' he said. 'We must go. They will blow up these doors soon enough.'

'Yeah.' The Englishman crossed to Berkeley, who was still lying on the floor. 'All right, arsehole,' he said, hauling him to his feet, 'let's move.'

'They were shooting at us!' Berkeley said in shrill outrage. 'They could have hit *me*!'

'Oh, you noticed?' Nina replied scathingly. 'These are the people you're working for, Logan. You really know how to pick 'em.' He opened his mouth to object, but she had already raised a warning finger. 'Shut up. We don't have much time.'

She turned her light down the tunnel. The floor and walls were stone, braced by thick logs. More broad beams supported the ceiling, but from the amount of dirt that had fallen on to the paving slabs and the shrivelled roots clawing down from above, it was clear that the sheer weight of the soil and trees concealing the Viking hall had taken its toll over the centuries.

But that it was here at all was incredible. Despite the adrenalin and fear running through her, Nina felt an undeniable thrill of discovery as she led the group deeper into Valhalla.

26

'So,' said Eddie as they advanced down the tunnel, 'what are we looking for?'

Even with her misgivings, Tova was still a professional. 'According to the mythology, there is a large main hall roofed with golden shields. I would say it is the most likely place to find anything.'

Ahead, the entrance tunnel ended at a junction, new passages heading left and right. 'Which way?' asked Kagan.

Tova shook her head. 'I do not know.'

'Nor do I,' admitted Berkeley.

Nina glowered at him. 'Colour me surprised.'

Eddie produced a flashlight, and shone it down the right-hand passage. 'We should've brought that chainsaw.' Gnarled roots hung down to the floor like a curtain, one of the ash trees above having broken through the ceiling beams. 'Let's try the other way.'

The group went left. A low doorway led into a side room, but Nina's torch beam revealed only mouldering sacks covered in dirt. Whatever supplies the Vikings had left behind had long since rotted or been consumed by burrowing animals and insects. A short way on, the tunnel made a sharp turn to the right – and Eddie, leading, stopped immediately after rounding it. 'Buggeration. Don't think we'll get through this way.' The ceiling had collapsed, broken beams jutting from tons of fallen soil. More ash roots clawed their way into the space.

'There is something up there,' Kagan said, pointing. Eddie moved the beam to find the remains of a large bird near the top of the dirt pile.

'It is an eagle,' said Tova, dismayed. 'It must have come in through a hole looking for food, and been trapped.'

Nina felt brief sympathy for the majestic predator, but it was not the only thing caught in the tunnels. 'We'll have to go back. Come on.'

They quickly retraced their steps. Eddie glanced towards the entrance. The mercenaries had wisely decided not to try to force open the doors again, but he knew that Hoyt's next attempt would involve explosives. 'We'll need to snap off some of those roots so we can get through,' he said as they continued. 'Kagan, give me a hand. Berkeley, you can make yourself useful too.'

'Why should I help you?' the American whined.

''Cause I'll beat the shit out of you if you don't.'

Berkeley blanched. 'Since you put it like that . . .'

Tova took Eddie's torch as the three men reached the roots. Berkeley broke off a few smaller branches, while Eddie and Kagan concentrated on one of the larger limbs. They both had to strain, but with a splintering crack it broke away. The gap it left was not wide, but Eddie was able to squeeze through to yank at the thinner obstructions beyond. He tossed the broken roots aside and hunched lower. More dried talons scratched at him as he forced his way past, but he was soon through. 'There's another corner,' he announced, illuminating the passage beyond as Nina started to follow. A short walk to the left turn, and: 'This way's clear.'

'Can you see anything?' she called.

'Looks like more rooms and tunnels off to the side. This place'd better not be some sort of maze.'

Tova sounded uncomfortable, and not solely because she was pushing through the roots behind Nina. 'Some of the descriptions of Valhalla say it is surrounded by a labyrinth.'

'Hopefully not the euhemeristic ones,' said Nina, joining her husband. Tova emerged, followed by Berkeley and finally Kagan. The Russian was about to continue down the passage, but Nina held up a hand. 'I don't like the sound of that.' Distant shouts came from the entrance; from their tone not pain or warnings, but orders.

'Then we'd better shift,' said Eddie, setting off. 'Tova, where's the route to the eitr pits most likely to be?'

'At the centre,' she said. 'If Valhalla was built like a traditional Viking hall, its ceiling would be highest there. The main hall has a ceremonial function; that is where it will be.'

'So it'll be on our left,' said Nina. The left wall of the long tunnel appeared unbroken, in contrast to the several exits on the right. At its far end was another T-junction. 'And we know how big the barrow is, so . . . it's got to be round that next corner.'

They hurried down the passage. Nina was first to reach the turn, going left. 'This must be it!' she cried.

'Yes, it has to be,' Tova gasped in agreement. Berkeley was equally impressed.

About forty feet away, another tunnel heading east intersected the one they had entered. Facing it in the left wall was a set of large double doors, framed by elaborately carved oaken pillars. Other doorways on the opposite side of the passage led into more small rooms, but the group ignored them as they made their way to the majestic entrance.

Eddie looked down the broad eastern passage. 'They closed that off deliberately,' he said, playing his torch beam over a sturdy barricade blocking the tunnel. More roots had wormed through the ceiling beams, loose earth piled at the barrier's foot.

'That would have been the main entrance,' said Tova. 'They must have closed it up when they buried the hall, so the only way in was through the death-barrier.'

'And the only way to get through *that* without being killed was with the compasses,' added Nina, holding up the two discs. 'They wanted to make sure that only people they considered worthy – true Viking warriors on their way to Ragnarök – could get in.'

'So does that make us Vikings?' Eddie asked with a grin as they reached the doors. 'I mean, you *have* got red hair . . .'

Nina smiled back, then examined the carvings. 'These are beautiful,' she said, admiring the workmanship. Intertwining patterns of leaves, branches and what appeared to be snakes – or *a* snake, singular, she realised as she followed the seemingly endless curves of the stylised reptile's body – ran up the pillars. Above the doors, the lintel was decorated with representations of horsemen, longships – and at the very centre, a face. A bearded man, features partially concealed behind his helmet's faceguard.

Tova saw it too. 'Is that . . . could that be Odin?'

'I think it could be,' Nina replied. The stern visage, a deep scar running down over one closed eye, glowered down at them as if challenging them to enter the room beyond.

Berkeley had momentarily forgotten his status as a prisoner. 'There's much more detail than I would have expected,' he opined. 'And the helmet seems like a more elaborate version of the Ringerike find, so yes, undoubtedly someone of very high status. Wouldn't you agree, Dr Skilfinger?'

'Yes, yes, I . . .' Tova began, before trailing off and giving him an odd look. Nina also shot him a disapproving glare.

'Okay, so it's a nice antique,' Eddie said impatiently. 'But is it likely to be booby-trapped?'

'I would not think so,' said Tova. 'The death-barrier was the trap – anyone who passed it would be assumed to be a warrior, and so worthy to enter.'

All the same, the Englishman shooed the others back and lifted the corroded iron latch at arm's length. But there was no rattle of deadly mechanisms from the other side. He cautiously opened the door. His torch revealed shapes in the darkness beyond, faint glints of metal reflecting back, but nothing moved. 'Odin sesame . . .' he said, pushing harder.

The oak door swung wider, revealing the chamber beyond.

The great hall of Valhalla.

Nina and Eddie panned their lights around the room as they entered, the others close behind. As Tova had suggested, the vaulted ceiling was high, a good forty feet above the floor at its peak. But unlike the passages outside, there was more to the roof than simple dark wooden beams. 'Wow!' Nina said, awed, as her flashlight beam was reflected back at her with a much warmer tint. 'Look at that.'

'Amazing!' Berkeley said, staring in wonder. The entire ceiling was covered by overlapping golden plates, the effect resembling a snake's scales. Each plate was at least four feet in length and nearly as wide.

'It is as the poem *Grímnismál* described it,' Tova told them, wide-eyed in wonderment. 'A roof made of golden shields – and look! The rafters are like the shafts of spears.' Unlike the squared-off, axe-cut beams in the tunnels, these had been carved into more rounded cross-sections.

Eddie lowered his torch to illuminate tables and benches, the source of the metal gleams draped over them. 'Looks like chainmail,' he said, going to the nearest table.

Tova joined him. 'They are called byrnies – shirts of chain armour. Also just like *Grímnismál!*'

Kagan moved deeper into the room, but almost stumbled over something. Nina shone her light down at his feet. 'Good thing you didn't kick it too hard, or you might have needed a tetanus shot.' The obstruction was a large double-bladed axe, the head speckled with rust.

'They're all over the place,' Eddie reported, sweeping his beam across the flagstones. The floor was noticeably cleaner than outside, the golden scales on the roof holding back the soil, but it was instead strewn with straw . . . and discarded weapons: knives, swords, axes and even spears. More such items lay on the tables. 'Christ, so they just chucked the stuff down wherever and hoped that the sword fairy'd pick up after them?'

'Like you and your socks,' Nina joked. Taking care not to step on anything, she headed down the great hall. The room was well over a hundred feet long, and almost three quarters as wide. As she advanced, she spotted something on the far wall. 'Tova, look at this.'

The Swede joined her as they approached a stone dais, on which stood three ornate thrones, dark carved oak decorated with silver and gold detailings. But it was not the chairs that had caught the attention of the archaeologists; rather, what was on the wall behind them. More runes were carved into granite slabs, around them running a now familiar symbol: the snaking form of Jörmungandr, the Midgard Serpent. 'What do they say?' Eddie asked.

Tova examined the inscriptions. 'These are definitely very old, from possibly as long ago as AD 200. It is the early runic alphabet of twenty-four characters, not the sixteen from after AD 800. Let me see if I can translate them . . .'

'Actually, I may be able to speed things along,' said Berkeley haughtily. He raised his tablet computer, only to flinch as Eddie pointed the Wildey at him. 'Whoa, whoa! It's a translation app. It's a lot faster than doing it the old-fashioned way.'

'For you, perhaps,' said Tova, offended.

Eddie looked at Nina, who shrugged. 'We know his program works, otherwise he wouldn't be here,' she pointed out.

'Don't try anything,' Eddie rumbled as he ushered Berkeley to the dais.

Now it was the rogue archaeologist's turn to take offence. 'I'm as interested in this as anyone. Well, okay, maybe not you. Although I have no idea *what* you're interested in. Apart from swearing and violence, obviously.'

'Hegelian dialecticism, mate,' the Yorkshireman replied, to Berkeley's surprise. 'All right, see if your iPad can do better than a real person.'

Still aggrieved, Berkeley switched on his tablet and brought up an app before aiming its camera at the runes. Nina sidled up to her husband. 'Since when are you interested in Hegelian dialecticism?' she whispered.

He chuckled. 'Since never – I don't even know what the fuck it means. It was a question on *Jeopardy*, that's all.'

Nina sighed. 'For one brief moment, I thought I'd got you interested in philosophy. Oh well . . .'

'Look at this,' said Tova. She indicated part of the runes. 'These do describe the route to one of the eitr pits, I have read that much already.'

'I agree; these are definitely directions,' Berkeley added. Nina went to him and regarded his tablet's screen. The app was similar to programs she had used herself; the user photographed ancient text, and it employed pattern recognition algorithms to identify words, which were then translated into English. The computer was working through the runes line by line. Such software lacked nuance; the translations were blunt and often awkwardly phrased, and could not compete with the work of a human expert, but were effective enough at uncovering the gist of the original text. 'Almost a step-by-step guide. Look, here – it starts by telling you to travel across Bifröst and back down the river to the lightning lake.'

'But are those the directions to the eitr pit the Soviets already found, or the other one?' Nina asked.

'I don't know yet. It'll take a while for it to translate the whole thing.'

Eddie glanced back towards the entrance. 'Yeah, you just take your time, mate. No rush.'

'I think I can be faster,' said Tova. She was examining one of the blocks of runes, running her finger over the ancient text – but rather than doing so line by line, she was skipping quickly through it, picking out key words. 'I know where these directions lead.'

Nina and Berkeley hurried across to her. 'Where?' Nina asked.

Tova tapped on one particular word. 'Here. This says "Helluland". It is the Old Norse name for—'

'Baffin Island!' Berkeley interrupted. He raised his tablet and took a snapshot of the text. 'Of course, it makes sense. There's archaeological evidence that Vikings had reached there even before Leif Erikson. Tanfield Valley, Kimmirut—'

Tova shot him an annoyed glare. 'Those finds are not conclusive. But . . .' she read on, 'this may help confirm them. The runes say where to land on Helluland, and from there,' excitement filled her face, 'it tells us the way to Jörmungandr's western lair!'

'That is what I feared,' said Kagan. He strode to the group of archaeologists, and before anyone could react snatched Berkeley's tablet from his hands and dashed it to the floor. The screen cracked, shards of glass scattering.

'Hey!' Berkeley protested. 'What – what are you doing?'

'My job.' The Russian shoved the two women aside, Berkeley already having retreated in shocked fear, and drew his gun. 'Get back.'

Nina grabbed the startled Swede and pulled her away as Kagan aimed at the carved runes and fired at almost point-blank range. Gritty splinters spat at them as the bullet shattered a palm-sized chunk of the ancient stone. 'Jesus!' Nina yelped. 'Why the hell did you do that?'

'This is the best way to make sure that nobody finds the eitr,' Kagan told her. 'We destroy the runes and the sun compasses. That way, *nobody* will be able to follow the path of the Vikings.'

Nina interposed herself between him and the carved text. Kagan lowered his gun, but did not put it away. 'And you're going to do that by shooting them to pieces?'

'We have no explosives, so it is either that or hit them with axes. And we do not have much time – Hoyt and his men will soon blow up the gate. Now move.'

'But this is Valhalla!' Tova protested. 'It is the most incredible Norse site to be discovered in centuries. Nina, you can't let him destroy it.'

'I don't intend to,' Nina assured her.

'You must,' Kagan insisted. 'You are the director of the IHA – you know what is at stake here! This is a matter of global security, not archaeology. We have to destroy the runes. Quickly!'

Nina looked to her husband for support, but he shook his head. 'Sorry, but he's right. We can't let Hoyt get hold of this shit. It's too dangerous.'

'Dammit, Eddie!' she cried. 'If we translate the runes, we give

Unit 201 a chance to use Thor's Hammer on the eitr and neutralise it!'

That gave Kagan pause for thought, but Eddie was unswayed. 'And if it doesn't work, they'll nuke the fucking place! That'll do a world of good for global security, won't it? Especially if it turns out the other pit's in Norway or Scotland, or even the States.'

Kagan's moment of doubt passed. 'It must be done.' He brought his gun back up – aiming at Nina. 'Move aside.'

She flinched, but held firm. 'No. There has to be another way.'

The Russian was unmoved. 'I will shoot through you if I have to—'

Eddie's own gun snapped up, finding a target: Kagan's head. 'Oi! What the fuck do you think you're doing?'

Kagan tensed, but held his position. 'Chase, we have to do this. You know I am right!'

'Yeah, I know, but *hello*! You're pointing a fucking gun at my wife! I don't care how right you are, I'll fucking shoot you if you don't—'

The whole chamber shook at the piercing boom of an explosion.

A couple of the golden shields on the roof broke loose and dropped to the ground with echoing clangs, clods of soil falling between the newly exposed beams. 'Shit!' said Eddie. 'They're in.'

Shouts echoed through the tunnels outside – along with the muffled clamour of footsteps. 'What do we do?' Nina asked. She swept her torch around the walls. The wooden doors through which they had come were the only apparent exit.

'If we give up and let them photograph the runes, they might let us go,' Tova suggested fearfully.

'Hoyt's not going to offer us any deals.' Eddie hustled to one of the tables near the doors and tipped it on to its side. The chainmail vests slid off and fell to the floor. He grabbed a couple and draped them over the thick old oak as extra protection. 'He's got no reason to let us live. Kagan, we'll have to hold 'em off as long as we can. Have you got a spare magazine?'

The Russian overturned another table. 'One only.'

'Make every shot count, then. Some of 'em got hit by the booby-trap – if they start running out of people, they might fall back.' The noises from the tunnels grew louder; the intruders had spotted the broken roots and knew which way to go to follow their quarry. 'Nina, you and Tova find cover and stay down.'

'Wait, what about me?' Berkeley quailed as the women crouched behind the wooden thrones.

'They're your friends, what are you worried about?' Nina said.

'Then maybe I should just walk out of here.'

'Or maybe you should shut the fuck up and keep your head down,' barked Eddie.

'Or, yes, that.' Berkeley scuttled to hide behind one of the benches.

'Nina, put your light down and point it at the doors,' the Englishman told her, doing the same with his own torch. The twin beams illuminated the entrance. They were not blindingly bright, but he hoped they would produce enough dazzle to confuse anyone entering the large room, even if only for a moment.

He readied the Wildey. A moment was all he needed.

Footsteps in the hallway outside. Low voices; the mercenaries had seen the light coming through the part-open doors. He knew from his own training what Hoyt and his men would be thinking. There was only one way in – but anyone taking it would be completely exposed. Would they try to reconnoitre first . . . or gamble on the shock tactics of a sudden frontal assault?

The voices dropped to urgent whispers. One issued an impatient command. Eddie couldn't make out the words, but knew who had spoken them: Hoyt. Whatever the mercenaries planned, they were about to do it. He watched intently for any movement through the gap.

Someone shifted in the shadows. Not at the door, but several yards back down the barricaded passage. Eddie caught the faint gleam of gunmetal as a man brought up his P90 to shoot out the lights . . .

The Englishman fired first, the Wildey's retort like cannonfire. Tova shrieked and covered her ears. The man outside flew backwards with a thumb-sized hole in his sternum – and an exit wound the size of a clenched fist in his back. 'Holy *fuck!*' someone gasped.

'Hoyt!' Eddie shouted as the gunshot's echoes faded. 'That was your warning – pack up and fuck off.'

A pause, then a humourless laugh came from the tunnel. 'Chase, God damn. You're like fuckin' lung cancer – we think we've got rid of you, but then you pop back up and make life shit.' He gave an order, but too quietly for Eddie to make out. 'Y'know, we've had our differences, but we could reach a deal here. There's a lot of money to be made.'

'Go to hell,' barked Kagan. 'We will not let you find the source of the eitr. And your spy Slavin is dead.'

More muttering. 'Is that Kagan?' said Hoyt. 'It's getting like a damn high school reunion around here. Although there's someone who'll never get to attend, ain't there, Chase? A cute little German girl?'

'Bastard,' Eddie growled, before raising his voice. 'We smashed the runes, Hoyt! You'll never find the other eitr pit.'

'I reckon I'd like to see that for myself.'

'Stick your head round the door and have a look.'

Hoyt did not reply at once, instead whispering to somebody. When he spoke again, Eddie was instantly on alert: there was anticipation in the American's voice, even though he was trying to hide it. The mercenaries were about to make their move. 'I think I'll pass on that, Chase. But how about you—'

He broke off as someone kicked open one of the doors. Eddie snapped the Wildey around, but the man had already jerked back behind the wall.

A hand whipped into view, lobbing an object into the room. Eddie caught the briefest glimpse of something small and pale with a metal tube sticking from it as it flew overhead.

A glimpse was all he needed. It was a chunk of plastic explosive, the tube a detonator. It weighed little more than thirty grams – but an ounce of explosive was more than enough.

'Down, get *down!*' he screamed, throwing himself flat as the bomb arced down—

The detonation blasted a table apart and scattered discarded weapons and chainmail in all directions. Even prepared and protecting his senses as best he could, Eddie was still dazed.

Kagan had been slightly slower to dive for cover. He paid the price, a sharp chunk of pulverised wood stabbing through his coat into his shoulder like a dagger. Further away, Berkeley howled as the blast slammed the bench against him. Even at the far end of the room, Nina and Tova were knocked down and left stunned. The sun compass skittered across the dais.

Eddie forced his way through the pain and disorientation to open his eyes. He couldn't see much – his torch had been sent spinning away, only dim outlines of the room's furniture visible. The Wildey was still firmly in his right hand, however. He raised it and lifted his head—

Men were rushing into the room, weapons up and ready.

He swung his gun towards the pack, searching for Hoyt, but knew he was already too late. Bright lights pinned him. 'Drop it, motherfucker!' someone bellowed.

Defeated, Eddie turned the gun upwards. But before he could release the Wildey, someone pulled it from his hand. Blinking in the glare, he looked up to see Hoyt smirking at him. 'Nice gun,' said the mercenary leader. 'Get up. Move over there.' He gestured towards the far end of the room.

The injured Kagan was dragged to his feet, other mercenaries advancing through the chamber with their lights and guns aimed at Nina, Tova – and to Eddie's surprise, Berkeley. The group was soon surrounded on the dais.

'Search 'em,' ordered Hoyt. As his men patted down the prisoners, the American pulled out the Wildey's magazine and tossed it into the shadows, then racked the slide to eject the chambered round. It clinked on the stone floor. 'They armed?' he asked as he threw the gun away. The responses from the mercenaries were all in the negative.

'What about the runes?' said another man, also American. Eddie felt a sudden twinge of recognition. He knew the voice, even after eight years.

Hoyt shone a light over the wall. 'Looks like they tried to smash 'em.'

'Let's hope for their sakes that they didn't destroy anything crucial.' The mercenaries stepped apart to let the speaker on to the dais.

Ivor Lock pulled down his hood, surveying the runes before turning to the prisoners. 'Hello again, Chase.'

27

Eddie stared disdainfully at the new arrival. The passage of almost a decade had not changed Lock much; his hair and the goatee beard had greyed, and his face was fuller, but otherwise he was the same as in their last encounter. 'Ivor Lock. Should've known. Hoyt doesn't have the brains to do anything without you having your hand up his arse like a glove puppet.'

Hoyt smirked – then punched the Englishman hard in the stomach. Even with the padding of his cold-weather clothing, the blow still made him double over. 'Funny fucker.'

Edie saw a glint of brass on the floor – the cartridge Hoyt had ejected from the Wildey. But he was pulled back upright before he could reach for it. Lock, meanwhile, had moved on to Kagan. 'And you, working with him. The situation's reversed from the last time we met, though. I've got *you* outnumbered. Mind you, from what I've heard, you're pretty much the last man standing at Unit 201.'

Kagan gave him an icy glare. 'You have heard wrong.'

'Oh, I don't think so. You think Slavin was our only source? Money talks, my friend. We may not have been able to get anyone into your inner circle, but we still know what's going on. Shame about old Eisenhov, huh?'

Kagan tried to rush him, but was yanked back by two

395

mercenaries, one of whom twisted the wooden shard stuck in his shoulder. He gasped in agony.

'Thought you'd have been fired after the enormous fuck-up you made of Vietnam,' said Eddie, trying to draw attention back to himself. If they were to have any chance of escaping alive, he would need the Russian's help.

Lock's mocking expression became harder as he turned back to Eddie. 'I'll admit, things were a little tough when I got back to Washington. But one failure doesn't end a career; in fact, I'm doing better than ever. The BSA was spun off into the private sector at the end of the Bush presidency and became Xeniteq. I was appointed chief operations officer, and after a few years ended up as CEO. Turned out that once I was freed from the shackles of the public sector I had a talent for business. Who knew?' A smug smirk. 'Same work, same client – Uncle Sam – but a lot more money. And I never forgot about the potential of the eitr, so when the Valhalla Runestone was found,' he glanced at Tova, 'I realised we had a chance to pick up where we left off.' He went to Berkeley. 'Logan, you're still in one piece.'

'It was a close thing,' said Berkeley, relieved. 'I'm glad your men's aim was good, though. When they threw that bomb into the room – well, if it had landed any closer, I could have been killed!'

'You think they even knew where you were?' said Nina. The thought had clearly not occurred to her former colleague.

'Ignore her,' said Lock. He shone his flashlight over the carved text on the wall. 'Did you find anything out from the runes?'

'I'd started a translation on my tablet. Unfortunately, this guy objected, rather strongly.' Berkeley indicated the broken device on the floor, then glowered at Kagan.

'You're not kidding,' said Hoyt, fingering the bullet impact in the stone.

Lock took a closer look. 'Damn it, there are some lines missing,' he muttered. 'Logan, had you translated this section?'

'I'm afraid not,' Berkeley replied. 'Dr Skilfinger had read it, though.'

'Had she now?' With a wolf-like smile, Lock faced the Swede. 'Dr Skilfinger, if you would be so kind as to fill in the blanks?'

Tova hesitated, looking to Nina for support before replying. 'No. I know what you are looking for, and I will not help you find it.'

Hoyt adopted a sarcastic tone. 'Well, hey, guess that's it. We'd better pack up and go home.'

'But it'd be such a shame to have come all this way for nothing,' said Lock. 'All right, Dr Skilfinger, let me rephrase that. Tell me what the damaged section of the runes said . . .' He reached into his coat, drawing out a handgun – which he pointed at Nina. 'Or I'll kill Dr Wilde.'

Eddie lunged at him, only to be hauled roughly back by Hoyt and one of his men. The mercenary leader jammed his gun into the Englishman's side. 'Stay still, or you go before she does.'

Lock gave the scuffle only the briefest glance before returning his attention to Tova. 'Well? I'll give you ten seconds to tell me, or I'll shoot your friend – and don't think I won't do it. Chase here will confirm that for you.'

'If you hurt her, I'll fucking kill you,' Eddie snarled.

The American ignored him. 'Ten seconds, Dr Skilfinger. Nine.'

Berkeley finally broke through his bewilderment. 'Wait – Ivor, what are you doing? You're not, ha, you're not *really* going to kill her, are you?'

'I thought you'd be happy about that, Logan,' Lock replied. 'Seven. Six. Dr Skilfinger, tell me *now*.'

'Tova, don't tell him anything,' said Nina, trying to suppress her rising fear.

Lock thumbed back the pistol's hammer. 'I *will* kill her. Three, two, one—'

'No, wait!' Tova cried, close to panic. 'It was part of the route to Helluland! I do not know exactly what those lines said, I did not read all the runes, but they lead to Helluland!'

The gun remained locked on to Nina for a long moment . . . then was lowered. 'Helluland,' Lock repeated. 'Where is that?'

'It's – it's Baffin Island, in Canada,' Berkeley replied, shocked. 'But . . . Jesus, you really were going to shoot her! Ivor, what the hell?'

Nina's heart was still racing. 'For God's sake, Logan! Haven't you figured it out yet? They're the bad guys!'

Berkeley shook his head in desperate denial. 'No, no, they can't be – they're working for the US government!'

'No, they're working for *themselves*. They didn't come to Valhalla out of any interest in Norse history – they came because they want to use eitr to make a biological weapon. You think they'd have brought along a private army just to make sure you didn't get scooped in the *International Journal of Archaeology*?'

He gaped like a fish before rounding on Lock. 'Okay, okay,' he said, trying to recover some scrap of authority. 'Ivor, what's all this about? Is she telling the truth?'

Lock regarded him with dismissive disdain. 'As a matter of fact, yes. Is that going to be a problem for you, Logan?'

It was clearly not the response Berkeley had been expecting. He looked in confusion between his patron and Nina. 'Wait, you mean . . . you're telling me the lair of the Midgard Serpent is *real*? Eitr actually exists?'

'It does,' said Kagan. 'The Soviet Union discovered one of the pits. And for the past fifty years, Unit 201 has been trying to ensure that nobody makes that mistake again.'

'Yes, it's real,' Lock told the astounded Berkeley. 'And now it's almost in our hands.' He examined the runes once more. 'So this is some sort of route guide, then? I'm sure that with the benefit of modern technology, we can skip a few steps and just work out where it ends. All we need is someone to translate it.'

'Logan, don't do it,' Nina said. 'These people are killers – and they're trying to get their hands on something they can turn into a WMD. I've seen photos of what it does, and I wish I hadn't. You can't help them. You mustn't.' Her voice became more earnest. 'I know we've never exactly got on – to be honest, I've always thought you're kind of an asshole.'

'My wife, the diplomat,' Eddie muttered.

'But,' she went on, 'I've never believed that you're actually a bad person underneath it all. And I don't think they do, either.' She shot Lock and Hoyt a disparaging look. 'Otherwise they wouldn't have kept all this secret from you.'

'The runes, Logan,' said Lock. 'Can you translate them or not?'

'Of course I can translate them,' said Berkeley, his old pride briefly resurfacing. 'Given time and resources, it won't be a problem. But the question really is: *should* I translate them?'

'No, the question is: why *wouldn't* you?' said Lock, with a clear undercurrent of threat.

Berkeley picked up on it loud and clear. 'Because, well,' he said with some hesitancy, 'I didn't hear any denials when Nina said you were planning to use the eitr to make a weapon of mass destruction.' Lock's expression darkened, but Berkeley pressed on. 'So I'm starting to reach the conclusion that . . .' He looked at the mercenaries around him, almost as if registering for the first time that they were armed. 'That it might not be a good idea for me to do it. No offence,' he hurriedly added.

There was a lengthy silence – then, to everyone's surprise, Lock shrugged, almost smiling. 'That's your decision, of course, Dr Berkeley. And I respect it.'

Berkeley blinked. 'You do? Oh. Well, good.'

'I don't agree with it, though. But it doesn't matter, because now that we have her,' he indicated Tova, 'we don't need you any more.'

Hoyt grinned. 'About time. Guy's been a pain in the ass ever since we brought him aboard.'

He gestured to two of his men, and before Berkeley realised what was happening, they had grabbed him by his arms and pulled him away from Lock. 'What are you— Hey! Let me go, what the hell are you doing?' the archaeologist protested.

Lock ignored his squawks. 'Someone photograph the runes,' he said. One of the mercenaries opened a pack and took out a high-end digital SLR camera, then began to take pictures. 'Dr Skilfinger, you're going to translate them for us.'

'I will not,' she replied.

'Yes, you will. Because we haven't just got you – we've got Dr Wilde too. If you don't do what I say, then . . .' He made a *boom* sound.

'Don't do it,' Nina told Tova. 'We can't—'

She cried out as Lock backhanded the side of her face. 'Shut up,' he growled. 'You talk too much – you're as bad as your husband. Get them back to the trucks, we're taking them with us.'

Nina pressed a hand against her aching cheek, filled with both fury and outrage at being humiliated. 'You *fucker!*'

Only the gun pressed hard into his abdomen stopped the

enraged Eddie from hurling himself across the dais at Lock as his men dragged Nina and Tova towards the exit. 'Nina, don't give these shitheads anything!' he shouted. 'I'll come and get you, I promise!'

Hoyt laughed. 'Yeah, we all know what a promise from you means, Chase. A bullet in the back of the fuckin' head, just like you gave Natalia!'

Even as she struggled, the words caught Nina's attention – as did Eddie's suddenly mask-like expression. Hoyt saw her shocked reaction. 'Whoa, wait!' he called to the men hauling her. 'She stays for a minute.' They stopped, holding Nina as their comrades took Tova from the chamber.

'What are you doing?' Lock asked.

A malevolent smile oozed across Hoyt's bony visage. 'I think Chase has been keeping secrets from his old lady.' Keeping the gun aimed at Eddie, he released him and stepped back. 'So, you never told her about your little adventure in 'Nam?'

'I know about Vietnam,' Nina said defiantly. 'You were trying to use a German girl to get your hands on the formula for eitr. Eddie protected her.'

Now it was Lock's turn to laugh. 'That's one hell of a definition of protection. I think you're right, Hoyt – she doesn't know.'

'Know what?' she demanded.

'Don't you get it?' said Hoyt. 'He *killed* her! He fucking *executed* her and burned her body, to stop us from getting samples of her DNA. That's what a promise from him gets you! Just can't protect your women, can you, Chase?'

The men holding her eased their grips, but Nina was too stunned to try to break free. 'Eddie? What are they talking about? Did you . . .' She couldn't bring herself to say the words.

His mask was still in place, but it couldn't hide the dismay and conflict behind it. 'What's the matter, Chase?' said Hoyt gloatingly. 'Oh, *now* all of a sudden you don't have any smart-ass comments? Ain't that a thing.'

Nina shook her head. 'No. I don't believe it.'

'It . . . it is true,' said Kagan, with a heavy sigh. 'I saw her body with my own eyes. I am sorry.'

She looked back at her husband. 'Eddie?' she asked, voice almost plaintive.

'I did what she wanted me to do,' he said, struggling to meet her gaze.

The silence that followed was broken by the man with the camera. 'Okay, I've got them.'

Lock nodded. 'We're done here, then.'

'What about them?' Hoyt asked, with a flick of his gun at Eddie, Kagan and Berkeley.

Lock shone his flashlight at the ceiling. The beam glinted off the golden shields, but he was more interested in the wooden rafters, tracing the lines of the supports down to floor level. 'This all looks very flammable, don't you think, Hoyt?'

Hoyt grinned evilly. 'Yeah, a real fire hazard.' Pistol still pointed at Eddie, he took out his cigarette lighter and descended to the great hall's floor. He crouched by a table, scraping some of the loose straw into a pile and setting it aflame. 'Guys? Light 'em if you got 'em!' Some of the other mercenaries spread out across the chamber to start fires of their own.

Nina watched in horror. 'What are you doing?'

'Consider it a Viking funeral,' Hoyt replied. He watched as his fire grew, taking hold of the ancient, bone-dry wood of the table. 'Burn, baby, burn.' More flames rose around the chamber as furniture and beams caught light.

'But – but you can't just burn it down!' Berkeley protested. 'This is Valhalla, one of the greatest discoveries—'

Lock cut him off. 'I don't know how many people at the IHA or in Russia know about this place, but if Dr Wilde found it, somebody else could too. I don't want to risk anyone else discovering the runestones before we reach the eitr pit.'

Hoyt turned to Berkeley. 'Besides, thought an archaeologist'd love the chance to be a part of history. You're gonna—'

Eddie lashed out with his elbow at the man holding him, knocking him back. He lunged at Lock, but the mercenary recovered and clubbed him down with his rifle. 'Eddie!' Nina cried as he fell.

'I'm okay, I'm okay,' he groaned. He pushed himself up on to his knees . . . and surreptitiously grabbed the Wildey's ejected bullet, tossing it away with a flick of the wrist. It clinked off the stone floor to land in one of the spreading fires.

Lock was shaken by the attempted attack, but quickly covered it. 'That was stupid, Chase. What were you hoping to achieve? You really think you can punch your way out of here?'

'Worth a try,' Eddie replied, preparing himself. When the heat of the fire caused the round to cook off and explode, he had to be ready to take his only chance.

When it cooked off. Any moment now . . .

Nothing happened. He glanced at the fire. The glinting brass case was visible amongst the flames, but the blaze wasn't hot enough to ignite it.

The other fires were rising higher, though. Smoke billowed up into the vaulted ceiling. Hoyt suppressed a cough. 'Think we need to get moving, boss.'

'I think so too,' Lock replied. Covering Eddie with his gun, he backed down the steps of the dais. The soldiers of fortune followed his example. 'Get Dr Wilde out of here.'

Nina's captors hauled her towards the doors. 'You bastards!' she yelled.

'What about these assholes?' asked Hoyt, indicating Eddie, Kagan and Berkeley.

'Shoot them,' Lock decided. Berkeley moaned in fear.

'No!' cried Nina as the mercs raised their guns – but then she was dragged out of the great hall, her shouts lost beneath the growing crackle of the fires.

Eddie helplessly watched her go, then looked back at the cartridge. It was now barely visible within the fire, but still hadn't exploded – and might never do so. 'If we leave them alive in here,' Lock continued, 'they might find a way out if part of the roof collapses.'

'I ain't complainin',' said Hoyt. He raised his gun. 'Okay, Chase! I spent three years in a Vietnamese jail 'cause of you. But now, it's finally payback time.'

Eddie tensed—

Crack!

The cartridge detonated, kicking up a shower of sparks and burning straw – and the mercenary nearest to Eddie screamed as the .45-calibre bullet tore into the back of his calf.

Everyone whirled to face the unexpected threat—

Eddie sprang up like a runner off the starting blocks and charged across the dais. The mercenaries' weapons whipped back around to track him, but he had already hurled himself off the platform and dived behind one of the overturned tables.

Hoyt opened fire, his men following suit. Bullets ripped into the thick wood. Eddie shielded his face as splinters stabbed at him – but the 5.7mm rounds from the mercenaries' P90s struggled to penetrate the dense oak planks. 'Go around it, get him!' Lock yelled.

Kagan grabbed Berkeley and hauled him into cover behind a throne as one of Hoyt's men ran to the table. Eddie searched for anything he could use as a weapon—

He found plenty.

The merc reached the table, ready to shoot the figure hunched behind it – only to find that his quarry was ready for *him*.

A rusty axe hacked deep into his shin, breaking bone. The man screeched in agony, gun forgotten as his injured leg gave way and he collapsed on to his knees. Eddie yanked the axe back – and struck again, slashing the ancient weapon across his throat. A jet of blood sprayed across the stone floor as the merc toppled, the wound gaping like a second mouth beneath his chin.

'Jesus *fuck*!' Hoyt yelled as Eddie snatched up the dying man's P90 and ducked back into cover. 'Take him down, shoot that motherfucker!'

Lock hurriedly retreated from the clamour of automatic fire as the other men opened up on full auto. This time, wood was no match for the onslaught. 'Shit!' Eddie yelped as he dropped flat, the old table juddering as ragged chunks were ripped from it. His shelter would only last a couple more seconds—

Another sound filled the room – a deep, dangerous crack from above.

The fire had reached the roof beams. One of them sheared in two with a noise like a shotgun blast, golden shields jolting loose around it and clanging to the stone floor. Earth and stones cascaded down after them, a mercenary reeling as he was struck on the shoulder. Another beam, flames licking hungrily up its length, broke free from the apex of the vaulted ceiling and swung down to pound a bench into matchwood. The shooting stopped as the gunmen scattered.

'Get out, get out!' yelled Lock. 'The whole place is coming down!'

'What about Chase and the others?' Hoyt demanded. 'They're still alive!'

'Just make sure nobody gets out the front entrance!' Covering his mouth and nostrils with his sleeve, Lock ran from the great hall.

Hoyt glared at the table shielding Eddie, then reluctantly followed his boss. 'Everybody out!' he shouted, firing a few last rounds to make sure the Englishman didn't dare raise his head to shoot back. Dragging the wounded man with them, the others hurried after him.

Eddie peered around the table to see the last of the mercenaries leaving the chamber. He jumped up. 'Kagan! Are you okay?'

The Russian rose from behind the thrones, Berkeley emerging fearfully after him. 'My shoulder is hurt,' he said through gritted teeth, 'but I will live.'

'Not for long if we don't get out of here.' Eddie flinched back as a hunk of burning wood dropped from above and smashed on the dais. The smoke was getting thicker, rasping at the back of his throat. 'Come on.'

'But they'll be waiting for us!' Berkeley objected, before coughing.

'You want to stay in here?' Eddie started for the exit – then veered off to recover his Wildey. 'Not losing this one too,' he said, on Kagan's quizzical look. 'Nina'd never shut up about it.' He set off again. The Russian collected a flashlight and followed.

'Wait, wait!' Berkeley yelped, hurriedly reversing direction.

'What the fuck are you doing?' demanded Eddie. Another ominous crack and a shower of dirt from above warned him that the roof was about to collapse.

'My tablet!' The American picked up the broken computer, shaking out the shards of broken glass.

'What? It's buggered!'

'The *screen's* broken – but we can still recover the memory!'

Berkeley replied as he also scooped up the discarded sun compass, then raced after Eddie. 'It's got the directions to the site on Baffin Island! They can still be translated.'

Eddie was about to ask him why he cared, but decided there were more important concerns. A clutch of shields clashed to the floor like oversized cymbals as other burning roof beams gave way. He weaved around the wreckage, slowing to let Berkeley catch up. 'Come on, fucking leg it!'

He looked back – and realised as Berkeley overtook him that he would be the last person ever to see the great hall of Valhalla. Hidden for over a thousand years, destroyed in minutes. The entire chamber was now ablaze as the fire greedily swallowed tinder-dry fuel. Flames rose around the dais, the three thrones and the runestones behind them disappearing into the smoke.

But there was no time for regrets – and besides, he told himself as he turned away, that was Nina's department, not his. He had tried to keep his promise to Natalia by stopping anyone from ever finding this place, and failed. Now, his only hope was to prevent Lock and Hoyt from escaping with what they had discovered.

And above that, he had to save his wife.

He shoved Berkeley though the doors as a massive splintering *crack* shook the entire hall. The backbone of the great vaulted ceiling had broken. The roof sagged, shedding a cascade of golden shields into the swelling fires – then the middle of the long room was crushed by a giant hammerblow of falling soil and trees. A searing wind blew smoke and cinders through the doors as Kagan and Eddie struggled to shut them.

They finally closed with a thud. More loud crashes came from inside the hall, shaking the walls. Eddie staggered back, eyes stinging. 'Bloody hell!' he said between coughs. 'Guess the Vikings didn't have a god of sprinkler systems.'

Kagan groaned as he pulled the wooden shard out of his shoulder. Blood oozed from the tear in his coat. 'How are we going to get out? They will be watching the gate.'

'I think I know a way,' said Eddie. 'Give me the torch.' He holstered the Wildey, then, with the P90 in one hand and Kagan's flashlight in the other, he jogged down the passage and cautiously looked around the corner.

There were no torch beams in sight, and under the circumstances he doubted that any of the mercenaries were lurking in side rooms to ambush them. A quick sweep with his light revealed smoke swirling through cracks in the wall. The stones were not flammable, but the same couldn't be said about the beams bracing them. 'Okay, it's clear.'

He hurried down the long corridor, the others behind him. The smoke thickened as they approached the far end; a section of wall had partially collapsed where falling rubble in the main hall had piled up behind it. 'My God,' said Berkeley in dismay. 'The whole place is going to come down. We've lost everything!'

'Your mates got the only thing they came here for,' Eddie said, checking the next turn. Again nobody was waiting for them – though there was a glow of daylight coming from the passage leading to the death-gate.

'They're not my "mates",' Berkeley snapped back. 'They used me – they were going to kill me!'

'They still might if you don't keep your voice down.' Eddie weaved through the hanging tree roots and advanced to the intersection, Kagan and Berkeley following. With greater caution than before, he peered around the corner at the gate.

The mercenary team's entrance had been literally explosive. The two lead-sheathed doors were ripped open as if someone had punched through a sheet of aluminium foil, mangled metal curled back from the edges of a ragged hole. Broken wood littered the floor. But Eddie was only concerned about what was outside. He squinted against the glare of sunlight on snow, eyes adjusting to reveal figures in the cutting. 'They're waiting for us. Definitely can't get out that—'

'Chase, look out!' Berkeley yelped, suddenly shoving him into the open. Eddie whirled, the torch raised like a club – the thought flashed through his mind that the renegade archaeologist was betraying him to regain favour with Lock – but then he saw both the other men jumping clear as the ceiling beams above them sagged, then snapped. Hard-packed earth spewed down where they had been standing, a section of the stone wall toppling into the passage.

'Run!' shouted Kagan as another beam split with a whipcrack sound. Eddie needed no further prompting. The trio rushed across the intersection – and bullets smacked against the wall behind them as one of the mercenaries spotted movement in the shadows.

The gunfire ceased as they reached cover on the other side, but more sounds of tormented wood came from overhead. 'Don't stop!' Eddie yelled. 'Keep going!'

'This is a dead end!' Kagan objected.

'No, there might be a way out – if we can get to it!' He shone the light forward. The next corner was just ahead—

The ceiling behind them completely gave way. Hundreds of tons of frozen soil and ash roots plunged into the empty space, the shock of the impact kicking flagstones up from the ground and sending all three men tumbling. Blinding dust swallowed them.

'Whoa!' said Hoyt, shielding his eyes from flying grit as a dark cloud belched out of the entrance. Above it, an ash tree swayed before falling with a savage crackle of breaking branches. Others thrashed wildly as the entire top of the barrow sagged. 'God *damn*! The whole place just caved in.'

Lock watched from further away, mercenaries guarding the zip-cuffed Nina and Tova behind him. 'I don't think anyone'll be getting out of there. And nobody else will find the runestones before we get to Baffin Island, that's for sure.'

Nina stared at the sight in horror. Smoke began to gush from the heart of the broken mound. 'Oh my God. Eddie . . .'

Lock turned to her with an obnoxious smile. 'May I be the first to say sorry for your loss, Dr Wilde. But,' he went on, seeing her expression change to fury, 'it seems appropriate, somehow. Valhalla is the last resting place for heroic warriors, and Chase was that if nothing else.'

'You're givin' him too much credit,' said Hoyt, joining them. 'Guy was an asshole.' Nina fixed him with a glare of hatred, but was filled with too much rage and grief to speak.

'All right,' Lock said, addressing his men, 'let's get back to the trucks. Dr Skilfinger, I hope you don't suffer from travel sickness, because you're going to get right to work on translating the runes. Otherwise, Dr Wilde will be joining her husband in the land of the honoured dead.'

'You are a monster,' Tova told him bitterly. 'Nina, I am so, so sorry.'

Again Nina was too overcome with emotion to answer. All she could do was look back at the remains of Valhalla as the mercenaries led her away into the snowy forest.

28

Inside the ruins, there was nothing but darkness. Silence had descended, the roar of flames snuffed by tons of earth. Everything was still, no movement, no sound . . .

'Buggeration and *fuckery!*'

Eddie stood, shaking off soil and broken wood. His head throbbed where part of the fallen ceiling had struck him, and he had acquired an entirely new collection of bruises all over his body. But he was alive.

And sightless. There was a moment of near-panic at the thought that he was blind, but he quickly overcame it when he realised he had simply lost the torch. He crouched and swept the floor with his hands, soon finding the plastic casing, but a sad little tinkle of glass told him that he wouldn't be getting any more use from it.

The air was thick with dust, caking his lips. 'Kagan?' he said, suppressing a cough. 'Where are you?'

'I am here,' the Russian rasped from somewhere to his right.

'Are you okay?'

A pause as the other man sat up with a grunt. 'I am not worse than I was,' he concluded.

'That's about the best we could hope for, I suppose. Berkeley?'

'Chase?' came the quavering reply from the darkness. 'Oh my

God, we're trapped! The entire roof must have come down! The air – there won't be enough air!'

'Don't wet yourself,' Eddie told him, closing his eyes for several seconds before opening them again. He slowly turned on the spot, picking out indistinct shapes in one direction. 'We're in a passage that'd already collapsed, we found it when we came in.'

'And how's that going to help us? That just means we're *doubly* trapped!'

'If I could see you, I would fucking slap you right now,' Eddie said with a sigh as he carefully advanced towards the dim light. 'There was a dead eagle; if it got in, there must be a way out. We've just got to find it.' He felt stone slabs give way to dirt underfoot; he had reached the cave-in. The light was coming from above, a faint blue-grey wash that he realised was being filtered through a layer of snow. 'I think I can see it.' He scrabbled to the top of the irregular slope.

There was indeed a hole, as he had thought. It was less than a foot wide, but as his eyes adjusted he saw that its sides appeared to be loosely packed earth. He scraped experimentally at the opening. Some small stones came away, but most of the soil was frozen. 'Don't suppose anyone packed a pickaxe, did they?'

'Can't you get through?' Berkeley asked, worried again.

'Should be able to, but it'll take a fair bit of work.' The thought that every moment he was stuck in Valhalla saw Nina and Tova being taken further away was at the forefront of his mind. 'Pass me the torch, I might be able to chip the— No, wait, forget that,' he said, reaching into his coat. 'I've got something better.'

He took out the Wildey. 'You are going to shoot your way out?' the dubious Kagan asked.

'I like the idea, but no.' He took his spare magazine from the holster strap and loaded it to ensure dirt couldn't clog the feed, then turned the hefty weapon around and began to hack away at the soil with the grip. 'Nina always said she couldn't see the point of having a gun like this. Shame – if she was here I could gloat at her.'

'Smug superiority, the perfect building block for a marriage,' said Berkeley sarcastically.

'Works, doesn't it? I don't see any wedding ring on your finger.' Eddie kept up the attack with his makeshift pick. Larger chunks broke away, the bottom of the hole widening. 'Okay, let me see if I can reach up . . .'

He stretched his arm through the opening, fingertips exploring its sides. He found hard stones, cold soil . . . then felt a sudden chill. A quick scrape, and he withdrew his hand to find ice crystals encrusting his fingernails. 'I reached snow,' he told the others. 'The hole can't be that deep – we can get out!' With renewed vigour he raised the Wildey again and resumed his assault.

The trek through the forest to the waiting vehicles took about fifteen minutes. 'Come on, hurry up,' Lock called impatiently to his men, some of whom had been slowed by carrying their injured comrades. 'Ragnarök's waiting for us.'

'You know Ragnarök's an event and not a place, right?' Nina said.

'Pedantry will get you nowhere, Dr Wilde,' he replied as he went to one of the trio of 4x4s. The large Volvo XC90 SUV had been converted to an all-terrain vehicle; its wheels were mounted on a roof rack, replaced by compact Mattracks caterpillar track units fitted to each of the hubs. 'Hoyt, you come with me – make sure Dr Skilfinger stays out of trouble.'

Hoyt pulled Tova with him to the off-roader. 'What about her?' he said, nodding at Nina.

'Better that we keep them apart. I'm sure she'd spend every minute of the journey trying to convince Dr Skilfinger not to translate the runes.'

'We could just gag and hogtie her, then throw her in the trunk.'

'Try it, and I'll bite your damn fingers off,' Nina growled.

'Just put her in one of the other SUVs,' Lock said impatiently. 'I want to get out of here. The sooner we leave Sweden, the sooner we can find the eitr.' He opened the Volvo's door and climbed into the driver's seat.

'Treynor, Tarnowski, keep an eye on Red,' Hoyt ordered two of his men, gesturing for them to put Nina in the back of the second 4x4. 'Wake, you drive 'em. Wounded go in the other SUV, everyone else packs up and grabs a vehicle. We're moving out.'

The mercenaries divided amongst the various transports. The still of the forest was soon shattered by first the rasp of the snowmobiles, then the piercing buzz of the two icerunners as their propellers wound up to full speed. Lock was first to move; Nina gave Tova a last despairing glance through the window as his XC90 set off, then her own SUV pulled away behind it.

Engines roaring, the convoy headed back down the frozen river.

'Yes!' Eddie gasped as he squeezed free of the hole and rolled on to his back in the snow, panting from the exertion. 'I'm through.'

Berkeley peered up from below. 'Well, come on, then! Help me out!'

The Englishman's grateful breaths were cut short as he heard a distant rumble through the trees. 'Shit!' he said, sitting up. 'You'll have to get yourself out – Lock's already moving.'

'What are you going to do?' asked Kagan.

'Go after 'em, what do you think? Chuck the gun up.' He holstered the dirty Wildey, then collected the P90 as Kagan raised it through the hole. 'Once you're out, go back to the snowmobiles and head for that village. I'll meet you there.'

'Good luck,' called the Russian as Eddie ran off, heading for the waterfall.

He descended the rocks as quickly as he dared, jumping from fifteen feet up to a hard rolling landing at the base of the frozen falls. The tracks his group had left on their way to Valhalla led back along the stream bed; he angled away from them on what he hoped would be a direct route to the great stone bridge of Bifröst.

It was not long before the trees thinned out, marking the top of the ravine. The sound of engines grew steadily louder. He saw that the rock crossing was off to his right and headed for it. The rope was still in place between the trees on each side; he took hold of it and made his way over, the coating of ice and snow forcing him to go slower than he would have liked.

A quarter of the way across—

The low thunder of vehicles abruptly rose to a roar.

He looked up the river – and swore as the convoy came into sight in the canyon below. One of the SUVs was in the lead by some distance, an icerunner following with the two other 4x4s trading positions behind. The pair of snowmobiles flanked them, the second icerunner bringing up the rear.

Lock was in a rush. The vehicles were heading downriver much faster than they had come up it. They would be long gone by the time Eddie reached the parked snowmobiles.

He had to get down to the river. But how?

The idea was crazy, he knew the instant it came into his head, but it was all he had.

He gripped the rope with one hand, bringing up the P90 and

putting the muzzle against the line. Bracing himself as best he could on the treacherous surface, he pulled the trigger.

The rope jerked in his grip as the bullet tore through it, flames scorching the ragged strands, but the shot hadn't quite severed it. 'Fuck's sake!' he muttered, repositioning the gun for a second attempt. One shot would be enough to alert the mercenaries to something unexpected; two would confirm it.

No choice. He fired again.

This time, the rope snapped – and he almost fell as the weight of the line, now unsupported, jerked him sideways. With a sharp gasp of fear, he dropped to a crouch to regain his balance.

The convoy was still coming down the icy river. He didn't know if he had been seen or not; he would find out when somebody started shooting at him. Keeping low, he scuttled across the quartz bridge, bringing the slack rope with him. Would it be long enough for his plan to work?

It would have to be. He was running out of time. The lead SUV would pass below in twenty seconds, less, and the other vehicles strung out behind it would only take another twenty or so to go by.

He reached the halfway point. If the drivers stayed on their present course, they would go directly beneath him. The Volvo drew closer, kicking out a spray of ice from its four whirling sets of caterpillar tracks. The surface of the frozen river was thirty feet below. Did he have enough line to reach it?

Not nearly enough to loop it around the hefty rock bridge. And if he tried to descend on the severed rope, he would just swing towards the canyon's side, away from the vehicles. He needed to go straight down . . .

There was only one way to do it. But it meant losing one of his weapons.

Again, no choice—

Eddie turned the P90 vertically, muzzle upwards, and forced its polymer stock as hard as he could into a crack in the rock until it jammed. He twisted the weapon to wedge it in place, then tugged at the barrel. The gun moved, but did not come free.

The first 4x4 roared under him. The other vehicles in the convoy were closing, not wanting to get left behind.

He gathered up the rope – then looped it around the gun and tossed it over the edge.

The rope fell, rippling as it uncoiled to hang with its end about ten feet above the ice. It swayed in the propeller blast as the first icerunner charged past. He grabbed the line with both hands and pulled at it. The stock creaked under the strain, but the gun stayed in place.

For now. In a moment, it would have to take his full weight . . .

The second tracked SUV roared below him, the snowmobiles on each side. The third Volvo was just seconds behind – then, after that, only the other icerunner—

Eddie jumped.

Friction burned his hands as he slid down the rope. He forced back the pain, ready to drop on to the roof of the last SUV – only to realise to his horror that he had left it too late.

The Volvo whipped past, having increased its speed to catch up with its companions. He tightened his grip to slow himself, twisting to locate the icerunner.

Its occupants saw him. The driver gawped in surprise at the dangling figure – then jerked the steering wheel to swerve away from the Englishman.

Eddie let go – just as the P90's stock sheared apart under the strain and the rope cracked away from him like a whip. He dropped, the propeller at the icerunner's rear carving through the air at him—

He landed with a crash on the icerunner's port outrigger. The impact drove the steel skate-like runner at its end deeply into the ice, making the vehicle swing sharply around and throwing both mercenaries against the cockpit's side.

The turn slammed the stowaway against the icerunner's fuselage. Eddie clawed for grip, but the sleek bodywork had no handholds. He slithered backwards towards the screaming propeller—

An air intake gaped like a dumbfounded mouth from the humped engine compartment behind the cockpit. His hand clamped around its edge.

The propeller's suction tore at Eddie's face, trying to drag him into its blades. He flailed his free arm, for a heart-stopping moment finding nothing but air, before catching the outrigger's trailing edge. He pulled himself away from one danger . . .

To find himself looking straight at another.

Both the icerunner's occupants had recovered from their shock at receiving an unexpected passenger. The driver straightened out, bringing the vehicle back in line with the rest of the convoy, while his companion in the back seat retrieved his P90 and unfastened his seat belt, rising and twisting to bring the gun to bear on the intruder—

Eddie lashed out with one leg, kicking the gun upwards as it fired. A three-round burst seared uselessly into the sky. The mercenary jerked back, then shifted position to take another shot – only for the Yorkshireman to use his grip on the intake to lunge forward over the lip of the cockpit. Before the startled merc could respond, he punched him hard in the face, then grabbed his gun hand.

The two men struggled for possession of the weapon. Eddie, on top of the scrimmage, made full use of his advantage. He forced the gunman's arm outwards and slammed an elbow into his opponent's face. The merc's grip on the P90 weakened as he spat blood. Eddie tried to wrench it from him, but was unable to get a solid hold. The gun slipped from both their hands, bouncing off the starboard outrigger. The racing icerunner's slipstream whipped it away to fall to the frozen surface below, left behind in a moment.

'Cocksucker!' snarled the mercenary. He grappled with Eddie, trying to pitch him overboard after the gun. The Englishman's legs were still outside the cramped cockpit; he stamped down hard on the outrigger to brace himself, then straightened and dragged the other man up from his seat. The merc threw a punch, but didn't have enough leverage to do more than jar his adversary.

Eddie's response had far more force behind it. He delivered a savage headbutt, crushing the other man's nose, then hauled him bodily from the cockpit and threw him over the icerunner's side.

There was a brief scream as the merc hit the ice – which was immediately cut off as the outrigger's heavy runner sliced over his neck like a guillotine blade. The man's body tumbled to a stop on the frozen river, his severed head bowling onwards for some considerable distance.

Eddie had no time to come up with an appropriately tasteless one-liner. The driver had drawn a pistol and was bringing it around to shoot over his shoulder. The Englishman yelped and dropped into the newly vacated seat as the other man fired. The bullet tore through his coat just above his right shoulder, shredding the material and scorching his skin.

The driver turned his head to see if he had hit his target, but his view was obscured by his raised hood. He tugged it down with his free hand, then looked again—

His new passenger was no longer sitting in the rear seat, but *standing* in it.

Eddie kicked the mercenary in the head, slamming him face first against the steering wheel, then grabbed the dazed man's gun hand and forced it back around to push the muzzle against its owner's temple. Before the unfortunate merc realised what was happening, the Englishman had squeezed his own finger around the trigger. A gruesome red and grey spray showered the clean white ice.

The dead man convulsed, right foot jerking on the throttle pedal. The icerunner lurched. Eddie had to drop back into his seat to save himself from being pitched out of the cockpit – and in doing so was forced to let go of the mercenary's gun. It followed the P90 over the side. 'Bollocks!' he snarled. He still had his Wildey, but the sheer size of its Magnum rounds meant it could only fit seven bullets in the magazine.

And there were more than seven people trying to stop him from rescuing Nina and Tova.

Still cursing, he tugged at the driver's corpse. Its foot came off the pedal. The icerunner's engine slowed, the shrieking rasp of the propeller falling to a mere snarl as the vehicle lost speed. Eddie stood again, releasing the clasp of the dead man's seat belt and looking ahead as he strained to throw the body out of the cockpit. The other vehicles in the convoy were pulling away – then the rearmost of the three SUVs weaved sharply, silhouettes inside looking back up the river at him.

They knew he was there.

Nina realised something unexpected had happened behind her when the narrow-eyed, bearded mercenary Wake, driving the SUV, did a double-take after glancing in the rear-view mirror – and his sudden swerve to get a better look confirmed it. 'The fuck are you doing?' demanded Treynor.

'Wilson just fell out of the fucking icerunner!' Wake replied, staring through the side window. Both guards and their prisoner followed his gaze.

Even at a distance, Nina instantly recognised the man clambering into the icerunner's front seat. 'Oh, I hope you guys made wills,' she said, heart leaping in elation. Eddie was alive!

'It's that Limey!' said Tarnowski. 'How the fuck did he get out of there?'

Treynor fumbled a walkie-talkie from a coat pocket. 'Hoyt, come in! Boss!'

A pause, then: 'What is it?' came Hoyt's distorted voice.

'We've got a problem! That British guy – he's alive, he just killed Wilson and took his buggy!'

There was a brief silence, then Lock spoke. 'Everyone listen. I don't care what it takes, but I want that bastard dead!'

It didn't take Eddie long to figure out the basics of controlling the icerunner. A pedal controlled the pusher propeller's throttle, and the steering wheel turned the single runner at the vehicle's nose.

Actually *driving* it was considerably harder. There were no brakes; the only apparent way to slow down was to lift his foot completely off the pedal to drop the engine to idle, and hope the icerunner glided to a standstill before it hit anything. Steering was also tricky – even with the outriggers providing extra stability, it still felt as if he were balancing on a knife edge. Anything more than a gentle turn made the vehicle threaten to tip over. 'Great, I'm driving a fucking Reliant Robin,' he muttered as he gingerly increased power.

He looked ahead. What would Hoyt's men do now they knew he was on their tail?

The answer immediately became clear. The last Volvo had returned to its original course, following its companions – but the pair of snowmobiles flanking the SUVs broke away, kicking up sparkling rooster tails of ice as they made tight, skidding turns to come around at him. Their riders readied their P90s as they accelerated.

It was a joust – with automatic weapons instead of lances.

Eddie drew the Wildey, all too aware that he had just seven bullets against a hundred. His only advantage, however slight, was that he could hold the oversized pistol in his right hand while driving, while the riders would have to switch their guns to their off-hands in order to control the throttles on their handlebars.

He increased speed and took aim at the lead snowmobile. They were closing fast – the window to take an accurate shot would be brief. The mercenaries would set their weapons to full auto so they could spray-and-pray, relying on sheer firepower to hit their target. But with only limited ammo, he would have to be accurate.

The snowmobiles rushed towards him. Both riders had indeed switched their guns to their left hands, angling so they could shoot at him from that side. Eddie altered course – and felt the runner on the inside of his turn briefly rise off the ice. If he cut across the mercenaries' paths hard enough to force them to pass on the other side, making their shots harder, he risked losing control, or even flipping the icerunner over entirely.

Instead he straightened out – aiming directly at them.

The leading merc's gun blazed—

Eddie hunched down as bullets whipped past. Most went wide, but one hit the raised engine cover with a crack of fibre-glass, and another punched through the icerunner's nosecone, searing between his legs to clang against the aluminium frame beneath his seat.

He flinched, then recovered, aimed . . .

The Wildey boomed like a cannon.

Firing one-handed from a moving vehicle on a rough surface, he didn't hit the mercenary – but still scored an impact on his ride. The Magnum round shattered the snowmobile's headlight and flicked broken shards up into the rider's face. The man jerked in shock, instinctively pulling back from the debris, and swerving into the icerunner's path.

Collision course—

Eddie yanked hard on the steering wheel in a desperate attempt to avert a crash. One of the outriggers came fully off the surface, the icerunner teetering on just two skids as it slithered across the frozen river. He gripped the wheel and raised himself higher, leaning over the cockpit's side to act as a counterweight.

The mercenary panicked and yanked at his handlebars. The snowmobile slewed around, caught in an uncontrollable skid—

He opened his mouth to scream – but the sound never emerged, as the sharply pointed runner on the raised outrigger punched straight through his chest, snatching him backwards off the snowmobile. The extra weight brought the icerunner crashing back down. The body ground over the rough ice like an anchor, hurling the vehicle into a spin.

The world around Eddie became a blur of white snow and dark trees – and a shape racing right at him, the second snowmobile—

He fired on pure instinct, the Wildey kicking again in his hand. There was a Doppler-shifted rasp as the vehicle flashed past him – then a crunch of impact, followed a fraction of a second later by an explosion.

The dead mercenary was wrenched loose from the runner. Eddie released the throttle pedal and held on to the wheel as the tail end shimmied violently, still leaning out of the cockpit to balance the whirling icerunner. The outrigger skipped over the ice, kicking back into the air once, twice . . . then finally landing and staying down. Now pointing backwards, the vehicle ground to a stop.

Dizzied, Eddie slumped back into the seat. The impaled mercenary was crumpled on the ice about fifty metres away, corkscrewing tracks marking the icerunner's path. Farther away was a mangled heap of burning wreckage. The two snowmobiles had collided and blown up. The second rider had been thrown clear – but not to safety. He too was on fire, smoke billowing from his motionless body.

Eddie waited for the spinning sensation to subside, then looked downriver. The convoy was retreating into the distance.

Taking Nina with it.

Jaw set in determination, he put his foot back on the throttle and brought the icerunner around in pursuit.

29

Nina looked through the Volvo's rear window. Even with three armed and hostile men holding her prisoner, she couldn't help but crow as the icerunner swung back on course after them, leaving the pillar of black smoke from the smashed snowmobiles in its wake. 'Ooh, that looked painful. Do you guys get medical? Is there some sort of Blue Cross scheme for goons? I always wanted to know.'

'Shut the fuck up!' Treynor snarled. 'He's catching up! Can't this thing go any faster?'

'Not unless you want to risk shedding a track,' Wake shot back. The icerunner was quickly gaining on the 4x4; swapping wheels for tracks had traded speed for off-road ability.

'God damn it!' The mercenary thought for a moment, then shoved his handgun into a pocket. 'Watch her,' he told Tarnowski, reaching into the back of the cabin to collect a P90. He released the safety, then lowered his window. A freezing wind rushed in.

'What're you gonna do?' Wake asked.

'What do you think? Take that motherfucker out! Head over to the right so I can get a clean shot.' Treynor turned around awkwardly in the tight confines, kneeling on the seat to lean out of the open window. 'Don't even fucking think of trying anything,' he warned Nina. 'You try to nudge me when I shoot, you'll get the next bullet.'

'I don't think your bosses would like that,' she replied.

Tarnowski sneered. 'I honestly don't think they give a fuck. We got other ways to get your blonde friend to do as she's told besides threatening to shoot you. Just stay still, now.' He gripped her bound wrists for emphasis.

Nina glared at him, then looked away. The icerunner was rapidly closing. Eddie had outfought the two men on the snowmobiles, but the 4x4 was a much more stable firing platform, and Treynor was using both hands to aim . . .

Her heart jumped as she saw that the mercenary had another weapon. There was a knife in a sheath on his belt – and by turning around, he had put it almost within her reach.

But as long as Tarnowski was holding her wrists, there was no way she could take it.

She looked back at the icerunner. It was now close enough for her to make out the figure in its cockpit. Treynor had seen him too. 'Come to papa,' said the mercenary, taking aim.

Eddie readied the Wildey again. Even had he not kept count of his shots, he would have been able to tell by the slight shift in its weight and balance that it was no longer fully loaded. Five bullets left, that was all.

And he wasn't even sure if he dared use them on the rapidly approaching 4x4. The Wildey's rounds were powerful enough not just to penetrate the sheet steel bodywork of a car, but to punch all the way through to the other side. If he landed a shot on the SUV, the bullet might also hit Nina.

The man leaning out of the rear window had no such concerns. He fired a three-round burst. They fell short, kicking up little fountains of ice ahead of the icerunner. It was beyond the P90's effective range.

But it would not be for long.

Eddie moved closer to the right-hand bank, trying to slot in behind the 4x4 so the gunman would lose line of sight, but the Volvo's driver did the same. The ice became rougher as he neared the shore, vibrations through the runners hammering at the base of his spine. No option but to move back towards the centre – if he hit a protruding rock, it could rip off a skid.

A burst of bullets tore past. The mercenary was refining his aim as his target drew nearer. If the Englishman didn't do something, he would be a sitting duck.

Eddie caught sight of the figures inside the vehicle once more. One was noticeably smaller than the others: Nina – and he realised she was looking at him. He brought up his gun hand, but rather than shoot, he gestured with the Wildey, pointing it downwards . . .

Tarnowski turned to watch the approaching icerunner, though he still kept his hold on Nina's arm. 'Ha!' he said as he saw their pursuer wave his hand. 'He daren't shoot at us – not while we've got his woman.'

Nina knew what Eddie was telling her to do, though. 'Not while she's got her head up, you mean.'

'What?' As Tarnowski glanced at her, she dropped as low as she could in the seat, hunching her chin down against her chest. 'Hey, wait a—'

The rear window exploded into fragments.

Eddie saw Nina's shadow slip out of sight, and immediately snapped up his gun and fired twice. One of the bullets went high, the other shattering the tailgate window. But he knew in

427

the tiny fraction of a second when the point of impact was visible before the glass disintegrated that he hadn't hit anyone within, the round landing off to one side.

It had the effect he'd hoped for, though. The vehicle swerved as the shocked driver jerked the steering wheel, throwing the gunman off target as he fired again. Eddie saw his chance and accelerated, swinging the icerunner back behind the off-roader. If he could get close enough before the mercenaries recovered, he might have a clear shot—

Too slow. The XC90 straightened out, then again pulled towards the right bank. The gunman banged a fist angrily against the 4x4's side and pushed himself upright.

He took aim at the Yorkshireman.

Tarnowski had ducked and flinched when the back window blew out . . .

Letting go of Nina.

She saw her chance – and took it, grabbing Treynor's knife with her zipcuffed hands and yanking it from its sheath. Before either of the mercenaries flanking her could react, she plunged the blade into Treynor's side.

He screamed, arching his back in convulsive pain and banging his head against the window frame. Tarnowski tried to grab her, but she spun and slashed the bloodied knife across his palm. He jerked away, clutching his wounded hand.

Treynor writhed, trying to pull himself back inside, but found Nina blocking him. She glimpsed the chrome handle of the door release behind him, lunged for it, pulled—

The mercenary's weight made the door swing outwards – and Nina threw herself against him, barging him into the open. He fell, screaming again as he hit the ice at forty miles per hour and tumbled along behind the Volvo.

'Fucking *bitch*!' snarled Tarnowski. She tried to bring up the knife again, but this time he was prepared for her attack. He grabbed her wrist, then used his greater strength to smash her bound hands painfully against her knees until she lost her grip on the blade. It fell to the floor. He drove a brutal blow with his forearm against her face, knocking her back into her seat. Only the thick quilting of his coat saved her from a broken nose.

'What the fuck is going on back there?' Wake cried, but Tarnowski ignored him, instead reaching over the back seat to grab another P90.

Eddie saw the mercenary fall from the 4x4, a bright red bloodstain on his coat. 'Nice one, love,' he said to himself – only to realise that while the man was down, he definitely wasn't out. Despite the hard landing, he had slithered to a far less damaging standstill than he would have done on concrete or earth.

And he had kept hold of his gun.

Treynor managed to stand, shakily raising the P90 as the icerunner bore down on him. He brought the sights to his eye, locking on to the vehicle's driver—

Eddie jerked his foot off the throttle pedal. The icerunner's tail end shimmied again with the sudden loss of power, threatening to slide out – and he made the threat a reality as he hauled the wheel hard over and threw the vehicle into a spin.

It skidded around through a hundred and eighty degrees, tearing up chunks of ice as its runners scraped sidelong over the surface and almost flipping over – until Eddie again leaned out to bring it crashing back down on all three skids. The icerunner was now hurtling backwards . . .

Straight at Treynor.

Eddie stamped on the pedal. The engine shrieked, the propeller roaring to full speed and turning the mercenary into a red spray as the icerunner ploughed into him. All that was left intact were his legs, from the knees down, which managed to stay upright for a couple of seconds as the decelerating vehicle glided over them before slowly toppling amidst a splattered pool of visceral crimson.

'You're screwed,' said Eddie with a grimace. He eased off the throttle and turned the wheel, bringing the icerunner around after the convoy once more.

The two leading SUVs and the remaining icerunner were now lost to sight behind snow-laden trees around a tight bend in the river. Nina's XC90 had pulled away again during his grisly encounter with Treynor. He accelerated, following it. There were still two mercs to deal with before he could rescue her; one would be occupied with driving, but the other was still a threat. He readied the Wildey. Three bullets left. Not good.

Nor was his situation, he realised, as he saw movement in the 4x4—

'Fuck you! Fuck you!' Tarnowski howled as he let rip with his P90 on full auto through the 4x4's broken rear window. Nina shrieked and brought up her cuffed arms to protect her face as empty cartridges spat from the gun's ejection port and bounced around the car's interior. 'Come on, you motherfucker! Bring it!'

'Shit!' Eddie turned hard as a line of bullet impacts raced along the ice towards him. Shots tore into the bodywork behind his seat. A harsh *clunk* reverberated through the entire vehicle as the engine block took a hit. He dropped the Wildey on to his lap, forced to grab the wheel with both hands to maintain control.

The gunfire stopped; the mercenary had burned through an

entire magazine in mere seconds. But the figure inside the SUV was already reaching for a replacement.

Or for something more deadly . . .

Tarnowski snapped open the catches on a green metal box and threw back the lid to reveal its contents.

Hand grenades.

He snatched one up and without hesitation yanked out the pin and let the spring-loaded spoon ping free. 'One, two . . .' He tossed the grenade through the broken window. 'Eat that, you fuck!'

Eddie glimpsed something small and dark bounce along the ice behind the 4x4. He knew instantly what it was, and ducked as he swerved—

The grenade exploded, scattering shrapnel in all directions and ripping a hole through the ice, broken chunks flying into the air amidst a burst of spray. Steel fragments clacked against the icerunner's bodywork, but did no more than scratch the paint; he was beyond the explosive's lethal range.

He was not beyond the range of its secondary effects, though. A dark lightning bolt lanced through the ice directly ahead with a series of gunshot snaps, water gushing through the crack as his vehicle's weight caused the frozen slab under it to tip downwards . . .

Eddie mashed the throttle, the icerunner surging forward – and riding over the newly formed step with a tooth-rattling bang.

'Jesus!' he yelped as he fought to keep control. The impact had damaged the icerunner's front skid, the steering now worryingly slack. He wrestled it back into line and angled after the Volvo. The 4x4 was coming up to the river's sharp bend, swinging wide to take the apex at speed. The mercenary rummaged in the cargo area for another grenade. Eddie recovered his Wildey, hesitating as he checked that Nina still had her head down, and fired.

This time, he didn't even manage to hit the SUV, the rough ride throwing off his aim. A bullet wasted – and only two left.

Tarnowski flicked his arm. Another dark spheroid hit the ice—

The grenade detonated an instant after impact, blasting a second hole in the frozen surface. The results this time were more severe, cracks racing outwards to meet up with the fractures from the first explosion. The ice sheet splintered, no longer a solid expanse but a broken mess of crazy paving.

Eddie saw the danger spreading across his path and tried to change course. The icerunner was slow to respond, and when it finally turned, one of the outriggers lurched upwards again. With a panicked grimace, he leaned out of the cockpit to counterbalance it. The wayward skid slammed back down on to the ice.

A third grenade – and the whole ice sheet shattered and churned in the Volvo's wake as it rounded the bend, splitting the frozen river from shore to shore.

Eddie was about a hundred metres behind the 4x4. He knew at once that the icerunner would never make it across the broken surface without plunging into the freezing water below. But it wasn't designed to travel over the rock-strewn riverbank either. He couldn't continue the pursuit.

Unless—

He remembered the tight bend from the journey upriver. It was practically a hairpin, doubling back on itself on either side of a low ridge.

A ridge covered in deep snow.

He looked up at it. There was a gap in the trees – maybe just wide enough for the icerunner to fit through . . .

'Oh, what the bloody hell am I *doing*?' he moaned as some subconscious part of his mind made a snap decision and jerked the steering wheel. The icerunner slewed around, aiming for the ridge. He mashed the throttle pedal down, the bloodstained propeller's rasp almost deafening.

Off the ice – and the vehicle jolted savagely as the runners barked over stones on the shore. It hit the slope, hurtling up towards the trees—

The gap wasn't wide enough.

'*Shiiiit!*' Eddie wailed, but it was too late to stop.

Both outriggers sheared off as they hit the conifers' trunks. The icerunner sailed over the top of the little ridge as if leaping from a ski jump, then plunged back down on the far side. He glimpsed the 4x4 approaching from the right, but all he could do was cling on for dear life . . .

The icerunner smacked down on the frozen river. The front skid collapsed, dropping the vehicle on to its belly – and the propeller, now with nothing holding it above the ground, carved through the ice behind the skidding wreck.

'Whoa!' yelled Wake as he saw the channel being sliced across his path. He stamped on the brake. The SUV juddered, its four rubber treads rasping over the ice. Nina and Tarnowski were both thrown forwards.

The Volvo slithered towards the line of black water . . . then stopped, its front tracks halfway over the ragged edge.

Eddie fought to hold himself in the cockpit, arms and legs braced against its sides as the battered icerunner started to roll over—

The blades tore away from the propeller's hub. What was left of the vehicle dropped back upright with a crash and ground to a halt.

He let out a relieved breath, then scrambled from the cockpit on to the ice. The propeller had gouged an almost perfectly straight line about four feet wide across the river.

The SUV sat precariously right on the edge of the ice.

Nina raised her head. She wasn't sure what had just happened, but she'd seen something flash in front of the SUV before Wake jammed on the brakes in panic. The Volvo had now stopped—

The door!

She grabbed for the handle with her bound hands – only for Tarnowski to grab her by the hair. 'Get back here!'

Wake whistled in relief, surveying the lapping water beneath his vehicle's nose. 'Holy shit, that was clo—'

One side of his skull exploded outwards as a .45 Winchester Magnum bullet blasted through it.

Eddie brought the smoking Wildey around to target the mercenary in the rear seat as the XC90's dead driver slumped against the steering wheel. Only one bullet left, but that was all he needed to rescue Nina—

Ice cracked, a broad chunk beneath the SUV's front tracks splintering away from the rest of the surface . . . and the 4x4's front end plunged into the water, the weight of the engine dragging the entire vehicle down into the frigid river.

Nina and Tarnowski fell against the front seats as the SUV pitched downwards into the icy water – which then surged into the 4x4 through its broken windows.

The cold was like a punch to her heart. Her thick clothing did nothing to hold back the paralysing chill. In a moment the river had completely swallowed her, the XC90 dropping towards its bed.

Panic rose – but she fought through it. She had been in a similar situation before. She forced her limbs to move, pushing herself upwards. The back window was broken; she could squeeze through it and swim to the surface—

The SUV shook, a muffled, booming crunch echoing beneath her. It had hit the bottom of the river. Loose items from the rear bed cascaded past her in slow motion, a surreal hail of guns and grenades and survival gear. Then the world began to tilt as the Volvo lazily toppled on to its roof.

Bubbles of trapped air from the engine compartment roiled past her, the water darkening as blood from Wake's gaping head wound swirled through the froth. The inverted 4x4 landed with a muted metallic moan, roof pillars bending under its weight. One of the surviving windows shattered.

Nina was head down, the rear seat now a barrier. With Tarnowski still beside her, there was only one way she could go. She pulled herself towards the open side window—

A hand clamped around her ankle.

The mercenary had realised there was only one easy escape route from the overturned vehicle, and was not going to let his prisoner out first. He dragged her back, driving an elbow into her side as he squirmed past. The blow forced a gulp of air from her mouth, and she unwillingly swallowed cold water, almost choking.

She fought back, slashing at his face, but in the confined space and with her hands still cuffed, she couldn't put enough force into the strike. Tarnowski still flinched as her fingernails clawed at his eyes, though – and in retaliation swung his fist at her head.

Even slowed by the water, the blow still hurt. More air escaped her lungs as she was knocked against the front seats. Panic returned as she felt a growing tightness around her chest – not from the cold, but from lack of oxygen.

The mercenary pulled himself head first through the window frame. Nina turned to the other door, but while it had buckled, the glass was still somehow in place despite several large cracks. There wasn't enough room for her to squeeze under the inverted seats ahead or behind, and now Tarnowski was blocking the only exit.

She was trapped.

Eddie! her mind cried. The very first time they had met, he had dived into a river to pull her from another sinking car.

But he wasn't here to help her now.

So what would *he* do?

She spotted the dark shape of a P90 against the pale roof lining beneath her. Snatching it up, Nina jammed the muzzle against the glass – and pulled the trigger.

The boom of the gunshot underwater felt as if someone had struck a huge bell right beside her head. The effect on the gun was even more drastic. With its powder charge sealed inside the cartridge, the bullet fired as normal – but instantly hit the water blocking the barrel, the massive overpressure rupturing the firing chamber and tearing the weapon apart.

But it was enough.

The bullet only travelled a few feet before water resistance stopped it, but it still shattered the window. Millions of tiny cubes of safety glass sprayed out into the river, glinting in the ghostly blue-green light coming through the ice above.

Hand stinging from the shockwave, Nina dropped the ruined gun and dragged herself to the new exit. Tarnowski delivered a couple of parting kicks as he squeezed out of the other window and headed for the surface. She struggled not to cry out, desperate to retain what little remaining air she had.

Heart thumping, chest tightening, she pulled herself through the opening. The cold gnawed at her muscles, every movement stiff and painful. But she kept going, twisting to look up. The hole in the ice rippled above, clean fresh air just twenty feet away. All she had to do was get out of the overturned SUV—

Something tugged at her coat.

For one horrified moment she thought it was Wake, back from the dead. But it was part of the bent door frame snagging on her clothing. She tried to pull free but no longer had any strength, breathlessness and cold finally overpowering her.

A horrible pressure rose inside her chest, her body desperate to expel the foul air in her lungs. All she could do was writhe in an attempt to tear loose, but even that was hopeless, her muscles so enfeebled in her oxygen-deprived state they could only flinch pathetically. Blood roared in her ears, blackness oozing closer as she looked up at the light for the last time . . .

Someone plunged into the water and surged downwards. The dark shape swelled in her vision, taking on form as it drew nearer – revealing a face.

Eddie!

He reached down to rip her coat free. Wrapping one arm around her body, he pushed with both legs against the SUV to pull her clear, then kicked to haul her back to the surface.

They broke through it together. Nina coughed out river water before drawing in several whooping gasps of air. Eddie supported her, shoving bobbing ice chunks aside. 'Are you okay? Nina, are you all right?' he panted.

'I'm – oh God! I'm okay, I'm okay,' she rasped, coughing again. 'Oh, Jesus!'

He reached the edge of the ragged channel. 'Come on, climb out,' he said, taking hold of the ice with his left hand and using his right to help lift her up in the water.

Nina gratefully slapped one sodden arm down on the surface and weakly dragged herself out, her husband pushing her from below. 'Thank you, Eddie. Thank you. Oh God, I really thought I was going to die—'

'The day ain't over yet!'

Tarnowski had pulled himself from the river on the other side of the channel. Sopping wet, he fumbled inside his coat and pulled out a pistol, tilting it to drain the water out of the barrel before pointing it at the couple. 'You fuckers,' he said, breath hissing through his gritted teeth. 'You goddamn near killed me! Well, right now I don't give a fuck if the boss wants you alive – this is where you—'

A geyser burst up in front of Eddie with a muffled bang – and a hole exploded in Tarnowski's chest, blood and shredded flesh spraying out as he tumbled backwards. The mercenary's gun thunked off the ice and splashed into the water.

Eddie lifted the Wildey into the open air. The big gun's slide was locked back after firing its last bullet, the thick steel of its barrel and frame protecting it from the overpressure that had destroyed Nina's P90. 'If you're goin' to shoot, shoot,' he said, in a strained attempt at a Mexican accent. 'Don' talk.'

'Movie quote?' asked the shivering Nina.

'Yep.'

'Thought so.' She clutched his sleeve, helping him climb on to the ice. 'Oh God, I'm so *cold*!' Her teeth were chattering so much she could barely get the words out. 'What do we do?'

'Get to shore,' he rasped. 'Curl up tight, try to keep warm. Keep your clothes on.'

'Not often you want me to do that,' she said, managing a little smile.

He laughed, which turned into a cough. 'Always a first time. But even if they're soaked, they'll still give you some insulation. I'll see if I can start a fire—'

'I don't think we'll have time,' she interrupted, fear returning.

The forest had fallen silent, but now a shrill buzz grew louder with every moment.

The second icerunner. It emerged from another bend a few hundred yards downriver, propeller wash blasting up a swirling cloud in its wake.

'Shit,' gasped Eddie. He reached to eject the Wildey's empty magazine, only to remember that he didn't have a replacement. And Tarnowski's gun was at the bottom of the river. 'Shit!'

The icerunner roared towards them. The man in the back seat leaned out of the cockpit, gun raised and ready. Eddie and Nina stood and staggered for the shore, but with the cold slowing them, they knew they would not reach the trees before the mercenaries got into weapons range.

The piercing roar rose to a scream—

The noise was coming from more than one engine.

They realised it simultaneously, exchanging a wordless look before diving sideways – as a snowmobile leapt over the top of the ridge and crashed down on the riverbank, kicking up a huge eruption of snow.

Kagan was driving, swerving to avoid both the couple and the dark rent in the ice. He skidded to a stop on the frozen river, unslinging a P90 and unleashing the entire contents of its magazine at the icerunner.

The mercenary in the rear seat fired back, but the Russian's bullets found their target first. The pilot jerked back in his seat as rounds ripped bloodily into his chest. One of the outriggers left the surface as the vehicle veered sharply off course – then the icerunner flipped over, the propeller stabbing into the ice and sending it tumbling towards the trees. It smashed into a towering conifer and exploded, blazing debris scattering in all directions.

'That saves you starting a fire, I guess,' Nina said to Eddie.

Her husband gave her a strained grin, then helped her to her feet. They reached the shore as Kagan brought the snowmobile back to them. 'You caught up quick.' The Russian's vehicle still had some of the team's equipment on its rear rack; he dug through it to pull out two survival blankets. Nina gratefully accepted the silver thermal wrapping.

'I set off as soon as I got out of the hole,' Kagan replied. 'I do not like waiting. And,' he added with a dismissive shake of the head, 'Berkeley was whining like a child! I did not know how much longer I could put up with him.'

'Where is he?' Nina asked.

The answer came with the sound of another approaching vehicle on the ridge. A second snowmobile appeared, this one moving at a decidedly more cautious pace. Berkeley hesitantly guided it through the trees and down to the shore. 'You're alive!' he said, somewhat disbelievingly, as he saw Nina and Eddie.

'Yeah, glad you're okay too,' said Nina sarcastically.

The other archaeologist stopped and, with considerable relief, dismounted. He took in the wreckage of Eddie's icerunner and the burning remains of the other. 'Business as usual, I see. Where did you get that gun?' He eyed Kagan's weapon.

'I found it on the ice a kilometre or so back, by some crashed snowmobiles,' said the Russian. He gave Eddie a look of veiled amusement. 'I cannot imagine how that happened.'

'Yeah, it's funny what people leave lying about,' said Eddie.

'Where's Dr Skilfinger?' Berkeley asked.

Kagan turned sharply to Eddie. 'You did not get her?'

'One fucking thing at a time,' said the Englishman as he huddled inside his blanket. 'No, I didn't get her. They must be a couple of miles ahead of us by now.'

The Russian restarted his snowmobile. 'We have to catch them! They will make her give up the location of the second eitr pit!'

'How many bullets've you got left in that thing?' Eddie asked wearily, nodding at Kagan's weapon. 'I'm guessing the square root of fuck-all. And they've still got two trucks full of pissed-off guys with guns. Besides,' he added, hugging the blanket more tightly around himself, 'if I got back on a snowmobile, the wind chill'd fucking kill me. Me and Nina need to dry off and warm up before we can do anything else.'

'But we know where they're going,' Nina reminded Kagan. 'Tova said that the second site is in Helluland – Baffin Island. We can go there too.'

'But we do not know exactly where,' he protested. 'Baffin Island is *big* – it is bigger than Britain! And they have photographs of all the runes from Valhalla, while we have nothing!'

'Ah . . . I wouldn't quite say *that*,' said Berkeley, raising a forefinger in smug contradiction. He unzipped his coat, taking out the broken tablet computer and the sun compasses. 'We still have these.' He smirked. 'You see? I do have my uses. We can recover the data from its memory and finish the translation, and then we'll have exactly as much information as they do.'

Kagan scowled. 'That will mean nothing if we are behind them.'

Nina huddled against Eddie, as much for comfort as warmth, and gazed down the river after the long-departed convoy. 'Then we'd better get started.'

30

Canada

Nina was cold again, a frigid wind biting at her face, but at least now she could warm up simply by going back inside the ship.

All that was stopping her was the question she knew she had to ask her husband . . . and the answer she was afraid to hear.

The RV *Akademik Rozhkov* was a 3,000-ton Russian oceano-graphic survey vessel, which to the surprise – and suspicion – of its crew had been abruptly ordered to divert from its task in the North Atlantic and sent into the Davis Strait between the two great frozen wastes of Greenland and Baffin Island. It had received new passengers by helicopter: Nina, Eddie, Kagan and Berkeley, as well as a small contingent of men who, while dressed in civilian clothes, were clearly members of some military unit, all being of similar age, build, haircut and taciturn disposition.

The escapees from Valhalla had eventually made it back to Blixtholm to call for the helicopter to return and pick them up, learning while they were there that Lock and his team had done exactly the same thing. So they knew they were not far behind Tova's kidnappers. The difference was that Lock could travel to

Baffin Island directly using Xeniteq's resources, while Kagan had flat-out refused to allow Nina to do the same via the IHA, for fear that a leak would alert the Americans to their progress. Instead, they had been forced to arrange to use Russian resources via the Kremlin, slowing proceedings considerably.

But now they were on their way, and getting closer. Berkeley's translation, rapidly completed once the picture of the runes was recovered from the damaged tablet, had allowed them to track the route the Vikings had taken from Valhalla downriver to the coast, and then around southern Scandinavia to a jumping-off point in western Norway. From there, the ancient mariners had travelled in legs to the Shetland Islands, the Faroes and Iceland, and then on to Greenland. The final steps of the journey were now the critical part: exactly where had the Vikings made landfall on Helluland to reach the eitr pit?

The sky was completely overcast, darkening the day still further as the hidden sun descended. Beneath the clouds, the Baffin coastline was visible off to the west, a line of almost unbroken white rising above the leaden horizon. Nina gazed at it, then drew a deep breath before heading inside. She also had questions to ask of Berkeley, and was as concerned about their answers as she was about whatever Eddie might tell her. Her fear of the latter was that it could change the way she looked at her husband, perhaps for ever. The former could get her killed.

Her, and many others.

She made her way down to one of the survey vessel's labs, which had been assigned to the team. The four Russian soldiers were in a group in one corner, playing cards and swapping what she suspected were obscene jokes. Kagan sat close to Berkeley, watching with bored impatience as the archaeologist repeatedly read through his notes and checked the translation on a laptop. Eddie, meanwhile, sat slightly apart from the others, looking up as she entered and nodding in greeting, but not saying anything. He too knew that the question was coming, but was equally reluctant to face it.

Berkeley saved them from it, for now. 'You look cold,' he said.

Nina rubbed at her cheeks, which had gone numb even from the brief exposure to the chill. 'Well, it is sub-zero outside. Fahrenheit *and* Celsius.'

'I can't say I'm surprised.' He turned the laptop towards her as she sat down beside him. 'If the translation is correct, then based on the directions it gives, we'll be making landfall above the Arctic Circle.'

'You've pinpointed where we're going?'

He looked faintly uncomfortable. 'Well . . . *pinpointed* is a little too precise. I used the sun compass to work out the latitudes the Vikings would have been aiming for, but it's only accurate to one or two degrees, which could give us anything up to two hundred miles of coastline to choose from. And I can't even be entirely sure that I'm reading it correctly, as the Norsemen never left clear instructions. I mean, there are still plenty of historians who would dispute that it's even a navigational instrument at all.'

'Let us hope you are right and they are wrong,' said Kagan, unimpressed.

'Well, I usually *am* right,' Berkeley replied airily.

Nina gave him a stern look. 'Except when it comes to picking sides.'

'All right, all right!' he protested. 'So, yes, I've made some . . . less than ideal choices. But I did my time for that business in Egypt, and I'm helping you fix things now, aren't I?'

'Some results would be nice first. What have you got?'

He glowered, but turned back to the laptop. One side of the screen showed the image of the runes in Valhalla; the other, the computer-generated translation of the text, below which was a more refined version edited by Berkeley himself. He pointed out a section. 'This part here told the Vikings, once they'd rounded the southern tip of Greenland and turned north along its western coast, to travel to two islands at a latitude that I think works out at around sixty-eight degrees north. They then sail due west across the Davis Strait to a large island.' He frowned slightly. 'The runes are phrased rather oddly, but as far as I can tell I haven't made any mistakes in translation. They say something like "You will see three mountains that you will recognise", but I haven't been able to find any indication of *why* they would recognise them.'

'Something in Valhalla?' Nina wondered. 'A picture, or a map?'

'Maybe, but I didn't see anything, and nor did Kagan or your husband. Anyway, from there the description of the route is the same kind of thing as on the two runestones in Scandinavia. Find a landmark, go in a certain direction, et cetera. I don't think the place we're looking for can be more than seven or eight miles from the coast.'

'Tell her about the wolf,' said Eddie, speaking for the first time.

Nina detected an undercurrent of concern in his words. 'What about the wolf?'

'It's nothing,' said Berkeley dismissively. 'Viking poetic licence, I'm sure.'

'The other runes were pretty literal – the lake of lightning, the shimmering bridge, all that,' said the Englishman, rising from his chair to join them. 'It might mean something here too. Tell her.'

Berkeley blew out an irritated sigh. 'Okay, okay. One part of the route is called "the vale of the wolf" – the wolf being, specifically, Fenrir.'

'As in "right there on the side of the bad guys at Ragnarök" Fenrir?' said Nina. 'That Fenrir?'

'The one and the same. Son of Loki and brother of Jörmungandr, biter-off of Tyr's hand . . . and the killer of Odin.'

Eddie raised his eyebrows. 'He took out Odin? I thought he was supposed to be the hardest of all the Norse gods.'

'He was, but Fenrir still killed him. Swallowed him whole, according to the myth.'

'Must have been one bloody huge wolf.'

'Well, you've heard of the Big Bad Wolf, haven't you?' said Nina with a smile. She took a closer look at the screen. Assuming Berkeley's translations were correct, it was hard to see any other interpretation of the ancient text. 'So you go through the vale of Fenrir, up a mountain to the plain of Vigrid . . . and that's where you find the lair of the Midgard Serpent?'

Berkeley nodded. 'That part of the route was fairly straightforward to translate.'

'Lock and Hoyt will have forced Dr Skilfinger to translate it by now,' said Kagan. 'They could be ahead of us already.'

'Only if they know exactly where to land,' said Nina. 'We haven't figured that out yet, and we're working from the same information.'

'They might not need to,' Eddie said. 'They've got the directions, and all the descriptions and clues about what they're looking out for on the way. Stick that into a computer with a good enough landscape map, and it might be able to work out the endpoint. I mean,' he gestured at the laptop, 'we already know from the runes that it's on an island, and if it's at least seven miles long and has three mountains, that narrows down the places you need to check.'

Nina gave Kagan a pointed look. 'The IHA database could have told us all that.'

The Russian shook his head. 'We cannot risk anyone else finding the source of the eitr.' He glanced at a sturdy metal safe on one side of the lab. Inside was the steel cylinder containing the substance that Unit 201 hoped would neutralise the eitr: Thor's Hammer. 'Not until we have destroyed it.'

'Just hope that stuff works,' said Eddie. 'I think the Canadians'll be pretty pissed off about the alternative.'

'What alternative?' Berkeley asked.

'It will not come to that,' Kagan said firmly. 'Academician Eisenhov worked for decades to create Thor's Hammer, so it will work. It *must* work.'

'We still need to know where to pour it,' Eddie said. He went to a large map of Baffin Island taped to one wall. 'So, where do we land?'

'Near three mountains,' said Nina. 'But which three?'

'We also have a terrain database,' Kagan told her. 'We could use that and look for features along the coast that match.'

'Half the bloody coast's got mountains, though,' said Eddie, running a finger down the heavily contoured map.

Nina looked back at the laptop. 'The runes say the Vikings would *recognise* the three mountains. From where?'

'Maybe they resemble a mountain range in Sweden,' Berkeley suggested.

'I don't know – the warriors fighting at Ragnarök were called from tribes all over Scandinavia. For the mountains to be ones they would all recognise, they'd have to be near Valhalla, as it's the only place they would congregate. But I don't remember any particularly distinctive mountains nearby.'

Eddie crossed back to the table and picked up the sun compass. 'There's nothing on this?' he asked, angling it towards the overhead lights to pick out the lines etched into its surface.

'Just the navigational markings,' Berkeley told him.

'The ones that brought us here.'

Nina cocked her head towards her husband. His words hadn't been a flat statement of fact, but almost a question. 'What is it?'

Eddie turned the compass over in his hands. 'One side brought us here,' he said, 'and the other one, that would have directed the Vikings to the place the Russians nuked back in 1961, right?' He tapped the flipside of the dark stone disc, which had its own set of inscribed lines.

'Yes; what about it?' said Berkeley.

'Well, they wouldn't have had both compasses with them, would they? They didn't know which of the two sites was going to be where Ragnarök kicked off – that was the whole reason for them splitting into two forces. So each group,' he dug his fingernails into the thin gap around the edge of the linked discs, 'would only have had *one* compass.'

He strained – and the two pieces popped apart as he overcame the magnetic force clamping them together.

Nina took one of the discs and examined its newly revealed face. She realised she had never actually done so before; there had not been time when she'd separated the two halves at Valhalla, and since then they had remained locked together for ease of handling. There were markings upon it, but far less complex than on the other side. 'Logan, look at this,' she said, showing it to the other archaeologist. 'These might be pictographs!'

Berkeley almost snatched it from her. 'Let me see.' He ran a fingertip lightly over the group of etched lines, then flipped the compass back over to compare its position to what was on the other side. 'Wow, my God. If I'm reading it right, this might represent a landmark on the journey around Greenland.' His gaze flicked back and forth between the disc and the text on the screen. 'They had the compass to give them an indication of their latitude, but this is a way they could confirm they'd reached the right place.'

'Kind of like "turn left at this mountain"?' suggested Eddie.

'Yes, exactly!' He peered more closely at the back of the compass. 'I think you're right, Nina – these are pictograms. They've very crude, but they don't need to show anything more than the most general features. These look like two islands, for example.' He tapped one of the angular little illustrations.

'So which one represents our three mountains?' Nina asked. She took back the disc, Berkeley relinquishing it with reluctance. 'If the islands are a landmark in Greenland, they should appear next in the sequence. So . . . these.'

She pointed at a pictogram. It was little more than a set of upward-pointing chevrons, two small and one large, but she could tell how they would relate to real features of Baffin Island's landscape. The small markings were spaced apart with a curving line that could represent the coastline between them, while the larger was positioned above. 'To me, this looks like two mountains on either side of a bay, with a bigger one behind them, farther inland. What do you think?'

'Fits the bill,' said Eddie, examining the markings. He gave Berkeley a mocking look. 'You had these things all this time, and you didn't think to flip 'em over and see what was on the other side?'

The American narrowed his eyes in annoyance. 'I *did* check both compasses, as a matter of fact. But since I didn't know the significance of the other markings, I can hardly be faulted for not picking up on them. There were usually more pressing matters to think about. Like trying to get out of a burning building!'

'This does not matter,' said Kagan, his impatience returning. 'What does matter is that we now know what we are looking for.' He went to one of the ship's internal telephones and made a brief call in Russian, then turned back to the group. 'If Dr Berkeley's work is correct and the eitr pit is at sixty-eight degrees north, we should reach the area in eleven or twelve hours. I have told the captain to bring us closer to the coast so we can watch for the three mountains.'

Eddie looked at his watch. 'It'll be dark well before we get there. You're not planning to head out across the Arctic in the middle of the night, are you?'

Kagan smiled. 'I want to find the eitr pit before Lock and his people, but I am not *that* crazy. We will need to see where we are going – I do not want to fall *into* the pit! No, we will wait until daylight before we land.'

'In that case,' said Berkeley, standing, 'I'm going to have dinner and go to bed. I want a proper night's sleep before I go trekking across the wilds of Canada.'

'That's the first good idea you've had since this whole thing started,' said Eddie. He ignored Berkeley's glare, instead looking at Nina. 'You want to get some rest?'

There was hesitancy behind the question. Berkeley didn't notice, but Kagan picked up on it, giving the couple a quizzical twitch of his eyebrows. Nina knew full well what Eddie meant, though.

The time had come to answer the question they had both been avoiding.

'Yeah,' she said quietly. 'Yeah, I think that's . . . a good idea.'

'In that case,' said Kagan, 'I will see you before first light tomorrow. If you want to eat, the captain has arranged for the mess to be open for you.'

'Thanks,' said Eddie. He headed for the door, Nina joining him. 'So, bunk beds,' he said. The cabin they had been assigned was far too small for a double bed, and was a tight squeeze even for bunks, making the average prison cell seem spacious. 'Kind of limits what we can do – although I suppose there's the potential to try something acrobatic.'

Nina smiled. 'Sleep'll be enough for tonight.' A pause. 'And some talking, I think.'

'Yeah, I think so too.' He let out a heavy breath as they headed through the ship's passageways.

Neither spoke again until they reached the compact cabin. Eddie shut the door, then gestured for Nina to take a chair before folding himself to sit on the lower bunk. 'Well, then,' she said, feeling suddenly awkward. There was a very obvious question to ask, the words almost screaming inside her head – *did you murder Natalia?* – but she couldn't voice it. Instead, she asked: 'What Hoyt said, about you and Natalia in Vietnam – what actually happened?'

Eddie took a long breath before replying. 'Hoyt's boss, Lock – he was behind everything. He set up the job in Vietnam by pretending to be Natalia's dad, and he planted Hoyt in our team as his inside man. They wanted to get hold of the Russian research on Natalia's DNA, and keep her for themselves. I stopped them from getting either of them – I burned the research.'

'And what about Natalia?' Seconds passed without an answer. 'Eddie?' she prompted.

Another sighing breath. 'Remember that I told you in Russia how Natalia was infected by the eitr?'

'Yes, her grandfather poisoned her grandmother with it.' The thought that a person could do something so utterly reckless and immoral – no, outright *evil* – in the name of science chilled her.

'Natalia knew about it, and had sort of accepted it; it's why she was in Vietnam in the first place, trying to help kids with birth defects from Agent Orange. And she was also a pacifist. Not just in a wishy-washy "ooh, war is bad" kind of way like a lot of people who've never actually seen it for real, but totally against any kind of weapon of mass destruction, and willing to sacrifice herself for what she believed. So when she found out someone might be able to make the same stuff that was slowly killing her from her own DNA and turn it into a WMD, well . . .'

His silence let Nina reach her own conclusions. 'She . . . she *asked* you to kill her? To stop them from using her DNA to recreate the eitr?'

He nodded. 'Yeah.'

'*That's* the promise you made to her, isn't it? To make sure they couldn't turn her body into a weapon?'

'Yeah,' he said again. 'She thought that no matter where she went, sooner or later either the Russians or Lock's people would find her and take what they wanted. She wasn't willing to let that happen.' He looked down at the floor. 'She told me to kill her. She *begged* me to kill her.'

'And you . . . you actually *did* it?'

'I did what she asked me to do.'

'Jesus, Eddie!' Nina exclaimed, shocked by the revelation even as it confirmed her fears. 'Hoyt wasn't lying? You killed her?'

'You wanted to know what happened in Vietnam,' Eddie said, voice flat. 'There you go. I made a promise to Natalia, and I kept it.'

A lengthy silence filled the room. He looked up at her. 'Are you okay?'

'Am I okay?' she echoed in disbelief. 'I don't . . . God, Eddie, I have no idea what to say. I don't even know what to *think*. I never – I never thought you could do something like that. Even if Natalia asked you to do it, and you were doing it to stop Lock from getting hold of a horrible weapon . . . my God. I really don't . . .'

Her voice trailed away as the full enormity of what she had learned sank in. Whatever the justification, even though Natalia had begged him to do it . . . her husband had killed an innocent young woman. The thought filled her head, tendrils winding deeply into six years of memories. Everything he had done since their first meeting would now be recoloured by that knowledge . . .

'Nina?' She blinked in surprise, finding him regarding her gloomily. 'So . . .'

She stood. 'I don't know how to take this, Eddie. I don't even know if I *can*.' The walls of the already claustrophobic little room seemed to be inching inwards. She took a deep breath, trying to empty her mind. 'Okay. Okay. Right now, I don't want to deal with this. We've got a mission we need to complete first. Once that's done . . . I don't know. We'll see. For the moment, I just want to go to bed and try to forget what you just told me, at least for tonight.'

Eddie looked deflated. 'Okay. Nina, if Thor's Hammer works and we neutralise the eitr, I'll tell you—'

She held up a hand. 'I don't want to hear any more, Eddie. Please. I'm not sure if I can take it.'

A mournful nod, then he got up. 'You want the bottom bed?' he asked, gesturing at the lower bunk.

'Yeah, thanks.' There should not have been enough space in the cabin even with Eddie pressing back against the wall for her to pass without touching him, but somehow she managed it. Like the two halves of the sun compass, it was as if they could no longer approach each other without an invisible force driving them apart.

Nina's sleep was fitful at best, the rocking of the ship and the constant rumble of machinery rousing her all too frequently. But while she eventually tuned out these distractions, an insistent banging on the cabin door was something she could not ignore. 'What?' she called blearily.

'I think we are there,' came Kagan's muffled voice from outside. 'Come to the bridge.'

That snapped her to full wakefulness. 'I'll be right there.' She sat up in the bed – only to knock her forehead on the underside of Eddie's bunk. 'Ow! God damn it.'

'That's one way to wake up,' said Eddie as he switched on a light and hopped down to the floor.

'What time is it?'

'Too bloody early.' His backside was right beside Nina as she swung her legs from the bed. She reached up to give it a playful swat – only for her hand to flinch back almost of its own accord as she remembered what he had told her the previous night. Subdued, she rose and got dressed, again managing not to make contact with her husband even in the confined space.

They made their way up to the research vessel's bridge to find Kagan and Berkeley already there. Nina frowned as she peered through the windows to see . . . absolutely nothing. 'It's still pitch black.' At such a high latitude in winter, the nights were very long.

'Yes,' said Kagan, with a faint smile, 'but the ship has radar and night-vision equipment.' He picked up a set of image-intensifier goggles and switched them on. 'Wear these.'

Nina donned the goggles, squinting as she refocused on the glowing green image inside the lenses. The coastline was now clearly visible, even the extremely dim illumination of an overcast night more than enough for the device to amplify. 'What do you see?' Eddie asked.

'I see . . . what we're looking for,' she replied. 'I think.'

Three mountains were visible, two flanking a small craggy

bay with a third, somewhat taller, rising beyond them. Judging distance was hard through the goggles, but the largest of the three peaks was clearly some way inland. The land before it was a crumpled blanket of ridges and troughs, the covering of snow only broken by patches of almost sheer rock. There was not a trace of vegetation.

She passed the goggles to Eddie. 'Logan, let me see the compass.'

Berkeley did so. 'Hurry up, Chase, I want a look,' he complained as the Englishman surveyed the scene. 'Does it match the pictogram?'

Nina compared the green-tinted view in her mind to what was inscribed on the disc. The little pictogram was massively simplified, but it did indeed closely resemble the island's topography. 'Yeah, it does. Two mountains beside a bay, and a bigger one behind them.'

Kagan spoke to the captain. 'We are just past sixty-eight degrees north,' he told the others. 'The Vikings were very good navigators.'

'If this is the right place,' said Eddie, handing the goggles to Berkeley. 'It's a pretty close match, though.'

'The island is called Nektaluk,' the Russian said, going to the bridge's plotting table and pointing it out on a chart. It was one of a ragged group of islands off the main coast, none marked with any signs of human habitation. 'I used the satellite link to get information about it, but apart from its name and position, I could find nothing.' With a faint smile, he added: 'It does not even have a Wikipedia page.'

Eddie regarded the map. 'So it's twelve miles of bugger-all, then.'

'Except maybe for a pit full of the most toxic substance on earth,' said Nina, joining him. The map's contour lines showed the highest point on Nektaluk island as around 550 metres above sea level; she did some rapid mental arithmetic to convert the figure to 1,800 feet. Depending on whose definition was being used, that was not even tall enough to qualify as a mountain in many countries – but in this case, it was the opinion of the ancient Vikings that counted. They had climbed a path up its slopes to find the site of the battle that would decide the fate of the world.

And now, over a thousand years later, she was about to follow in their footsteps.

456

31

Dawn crept sluggishly over the island as the *Akademik Rozhkov* moved closer to shore to send out its boats. Even when full daylight finally arrived, the sun taking its languid time to rise this far north, the day was far from bright; clouds still covered the entire sky.

The weather was unlikely to improve. Nina looked ahead as the rigid inflatable boat carrying the expedition members approached the barren shore. The distant mountain's peak was barely visible, shrouded by the low-hanging clouds, and there were swathes of bleak mist lower down its slopes. The entire vista was a flat, dreary monochrome, not one single patch of colour to break the monotony of white snow and grey rock.

'Could be worse,' said Eddie from beside her. 'At least it's not raining.'

'I'm sure it'll find a way,' she replied. Even wrapped in far thicker clothing than she had worn on the search for Valhalla in Sweden, she was still desperately cold.

'It will not take us long to reach the pit,' said Kagan determinedly, gesturing towards a second RIB off to one side. This was a larger craft, carrying the team's equipment – most prominently two of their four snowmobiles. 'We travel, what? Ten or eleven kilometres?' He looked to Berkeley for confirmation; the American nodded. 'All we have to do is follow the route from the runes of Valhalla, then locate the pit – and deliver Thor's Hammer.'

He glanced down. Between his feet was a case made of high-impact plastic, inside which was the steel canister containing the biological counter-agent. 'Once the eitr is neutralised, then all this is over. We can return home.'

'There are still a lot of ifs, though,' said Nina. '*If* Thor's Hammer works. *If* the pit is there. *If* we've translated the runes correctly. Hell, *if* this is even the right island!'

'You needn't worry about the translation,' said Berkeley snippily. 'I've done my job.'

'If you *hadn't* done your "job", we wouldn't all be here at the arse-end of the world,' Eddie reminded him. 'But it looks like we're in the right place. Question is, have Hoyt and Lock made Tova tell 'em where it is too?'

'They would have had less leverage without me,' said Nina.

Kagan shook his head. 'That will not matter. With so much at stake, they will do whatever they have to. They will have found other ways to force her to translate the runes.'

The rest of the short voyage continued in gloomy silence until the boat reached the shore. The four Russian soldiers jumped out on Kagan's order, hauling the RIB on to the shingle so the rest of its passengers could disembark and unload their gear. While they were doing so, the soldiers splashed through the breaking waves to the second boat and carefully carried the snowmobiles to the miserable beach. The vehicles had been partially disassembled for transport; the men began to put them back together as the boat turned back to the *Rozhkov* for the second pair.

'Are these guys any good, then?' Eddie asked Kagan, regarding the four younger men. 'Where did you get 'em?'

'They are members of Unit 201,' Kagan replied. 'Fortunately, they were away from the bunker on training. I called them back for this mission.'

'Why do I get the feeling they're the only members of Unit 201 left that you *could* call back?' asked Nina. Kagan gave her a pained look, but said nothing.

The second boat returned with the other snowmobiles fifteen minutes later. Berkeley used the time to reread his notes, occasionally glancing up towards the distant mountain. 'Do you know which way we need to go?' said Nina.

'I think so,' he answered. 'I'm having to work a little to put myself into their mindset.'

'Yeah, I bet,' said Eddie. '"Tough Viking warrior" isn't exactly the first thing that comes to mind when I look at you.'

Berkeley huffed, then continued: 'But I think I've figured it out. We need to go north-west, up that hill.' He pointed inland. 'At the top, we should see a landmark they called "the shield stone". Hopefully it'll be obvious what it is.'

'At least we won't have to walk,' said Nina, looking around as the soldiers waded to the returning boat to unload the snowmobiles. The hillside in question started out shallow as it rose away from the beach, but quickly became steeper. However, she was sure the vehicles could handle the climb. 'What about after that?'

'From this shield stone we go along the top of a ridge, and then at the other end we have to cross through the vale of Fenrir. I still have no idea what that means, exactly – I just hope we'll know it when we see it.' He consulted his notes again. 'As long as we can find the landmarks, I don't think we'll have any trouble following the route. It's not as if there are any trees to block our view.'

'There's fog, though,' said Eddie. The wallowing clouds were still hanging over the summit, turning the mountain's peak into a vague shadow amongst the endless grey, and some of the banks lower down had spread. 'Looks pretty thick. We'll need to stick close together if we go into that lot.'

'We will manage,' Kagan assured him. He turned to watch his men bringing the last pieces of cargo from the boat. 'We will be ready to move out in a few minutes, once they have put together the snowmobiles. Are you all ready?'

'I'm set,' said Nina.

'Me too,' Eddie said. 'Standing around on a freezing cold beach isn't my idea of fun. Too many flashbacks to my SAS training.'

Kagan was amused. 'SAS, pah! Cold like this? This is just an ordinary day for every Russian soldier.'

'Oh God, don't set him off,' Nina begged, seeing that her husband's pride in his former service was about to demand satisfaction. 'Once he starts ranting about how much better the SAS is than anyone else, he never shuts up.'

'Then I will not listen to him,' the Russian said with a smirk, moving to join the soldiers.

'Cheeky bugger,' Eddie grumbled. Nina laughed.

It did not take long for the snowmobiles to be assembled and loaded. The drivers took their places, then engines roared to life in unison. Each vehicle carried two people; the four Russian troopers took a pair of snowmobiles between them, Berkeley rode pillion with Kagan, while Nina straddled the last machine behind Eddie. A moment's hesitation, then she put her arms around his waist.

She looked over his shoulder at the terrain ahead. The sight filled her with an odd sense of dread. Even though the journey would in theory be little different from the ride upriver in Sweden, the towering evergreens there had been an omnipresent reminder that life could thrive even in the cold. Here, though, there was nothing but bleak and barren rock and snow. A dead land.

Berkeley pointed up the hill. 'That way!' Kagan set off, kicking up a spray of snow behind the snowmobile's broad rubber track. The soldiers followed.

Eddie gave the case containing Thor's Hammer, secured to the back of Kagan's snowmobile, a dubious look. 'If we find the pit and that stuff doesn't do what it says on the tin, then what happens?'

'I don't know,' Nina replied. 'But I get the feeling Kagan's got a contingency plan. He just hasn't told us about it.'

'Yeah, I got that feeling too.' He opened his coat and drew his Wildey, giving it a rather theatrical check before returning it to its holster. 'Good thing I brought a contingency of my own.'

'Couldn't you have left that ridiculous thing in Valhalla?' Nina sighed, shaking her head. 'Why do you need something so damn huge?'

'If you shoot something with it, it stays down,' Eddie said as he revved the engine and set off.

'Like what? A polar bear?' She meant it as a joke, but suddenly realised they were indeed in the domain of the giant Arctic predators. 'Wait, you don't think we'll run into any polar bears, do you?' she said, nervously scanning her surroundings.

'Just being prepared,' said Eddie with a grin. He caught up with Kagan's snowmobile, and the team began the climb towards the waiting mountain.

It took ten minutes for the expedition to reach the top of the first slope. Once there, Berkeley batted furiously on Kagan's shoulder for him to stop. The Russian halted, the others drawing up alongside. 'There, over there,' exclaimed the archaeologist, pointing.

Off to one side was a large flat boulder, tilted at a shallow angle. 'The shield stone?' Nina wondered. The rock was roughly circular, and did indeed bear a resemblance to a traditional Viking shield.

'It fits the description, yeah,' Berkeley replied. He fumbled his notes from a pocket with a gloved hand and studied them, then looked around. 'There should be a long ridge leading up toward the mountain.'

'That way,' said Eddie. He indicated a snow-covered rise leading higher, curling lines of wind-whipped snow gusting off its exposed top. 'We'll need to watch out, the sides are pretty steep.'

Nina tried to survey the terrain above, but the ridge faded into a grey haze of fog. 'Well, we know from the Vikings' route that there's a valley up there somewhere. Hopefully it won't be too—' She saw Kagan straighten in his seat, alert as a watchdog. 'What?'

'Stop your engine,' the Russian told Eddie, issuing the same order in his native language to his men. The snowmobiles fell silent. 'I hear something.'

There was indeed a low rumbling noise at the lower limits of hearing. Everyone looked for the source. One of the soldiers spoke in excited Russian and gestured to the south. Low-hanging clouds obscured much of the view, but the sound was clearly getting louder.

'A helicopter!' Kagan snapped. 'It is Lock, it must be!' He swore in Russian.

'We don't know that for sure,' said Berkeley, though with little conviction.

Eddie was more certain. 'Who else would it be? They made Tova translate the runes, and they figured out where to go the same way we did. Arse chives! They're going to get there before us!'

'Even if they fly directly to the pit, they will be only a few kilometres ahead of us,' Kagan insisted. 'Come on! We must go.'

He set off again, Berkeley yelping and clinging on tightly with the sudden acceleration. Eddie glared in the direction of the unseen aircraft, then followed. 'See? Good job I brought my gun after all,' he said over his shoulder. 'And a good job they brought those.' Amongst the equipment on the back of the soldiers' vehicles was a set of AK-12s: the most modern iteration of the Kalashnikov assault rifle, which despite the addition of tactical rails and polymer parts replacing wood was still instantly recognisable as a direct descendant of the venerable Soviet weapon.

'And I was worried about polar bears,' Nina moaned.

'Maybe we'll get lucky and they'll crash in the fog,' Eddie said, before immediately shrugging in resignation. 'No, I don't think so either.'

'How long will it take us to get there?'

'No idea – we don't even know exactly where we're going.' He looked up at the mountain, which rose ominously above the fog bank at the higher end of the ridge. 'We've probably got another four or five miles to go. If the weather gets worse . . .'

He let the worrying statement hang. Nina also chose to keep her worries to herself, instead concentrating on holding on to her husband as the snowmobiles swept past the flat rock and began their ascent.

The wind bit savagely at the riders as they climbed the exposed ridge. Nina tried to imagine what the trek would have been like for the Vikings, limited to walking pace and with only animal furs to keep out the cold. After the long sea voyage all the way across the Atlantic, the Norse warriors would surely have suffered losses even before reaching the battle.

And when they got there . . . what were they expecting to

fight at Ragnarök? The thought had been at the back of her mind for some time. Eisenhov had said in Russia that whatever was waiting inside the pit was not a real serpent, but it clearly resembled one enough for the Vikings to believe it was a great monster. They had fought it once before, when the men who had later been transformed by legend into gods, like Odin and Thor, had perished.

So what awaited them on the mountain now?

She considered asking Kagan what else he knew about the Soviet experiments, but he had pulled ahead, the narrowing ridge forcing the snowmobiles to drop into single file and space out to avoid the wakes of snow kicked up by the vehicles ahead. The crosswind picked up as they climbed. 'Fuck, that's nippy,' Eddie muttered, hunching lower over the handlebars.

'You're not kidding,' said Nina. 'She felt almost as cold as in Sweden – *after* getting out of the river. 'At least it can't be as windy at the top, if there's fog up there.'

Eddie looked up the ridge again. The bank of obscuring mist was slowly spilling over the lip of the flatter ground at the top, tendrils at its edge being snatched away by gusts blowing across the mountain's face. But most of the looming grey mass remained squatting in place ahead of them, penned in by rocky slopes on each side. 'Don't like the look of that, but there isn't a way around it. We'll never get the snowmobiles up those cliffs.'

'We have to go through it to follow the directions on the runes,' Nina reminded him. 'If we're on the right track, that'll be the vale of Fenrir.'

'Wolf Valley, eh? Bet you're really glad I brought my gun now, eh?' He gave her a brief grin, then returned his attention to the task of guiding the snowmobile up the steepening ridge.

Several more minutes brought the team to the top. The landscape ahead vanished into a pale nothingness, mist shrouding everything. Kagan again signalled for everyone to halt and stop their engines. Silence descended. 'I cannot hear the helicopter,' he said.

'Can't hear *anything*,' said Eddie. They were now mostly sheltered from the wind by the valley's sides. Any other sounds seemed to be swallowed by the fog.

'If they have found the pit and landed, we must catch them before they leave. Dr Berkeley, where do the runes say we must go?'

Berkeley checked his notes again. 'Through the vale of Fenrir, then there's a rock formation they called "the broken finger" pointing up the mountain. We follow that until we get to a plain they called Vigrid – "the place of battle". If this pit exists, that's where it is. Just a couple more miles.'

'Then we must move as fast as we can.' Kagan restarted his engine.

'Careful in the fog,' Eddie warned. 'If you hit a boulder at fifty miles an hour, you'll be fucked.'

'We know what we are doing,' the Russian told him tersely. He shouted orders to his men, then set off again, considerably faster on the flat than during the climb. The four soldiers followed at equally high speed.

'Fuck's sake,' Eddie growled as he restarted his own vehicle. 'If he flips his snowmobile and breaks open his jar of evil crap . . .'

'Try not to drive through the puddle,' said Nina, cringing at the thought.

They entered the valley. The fog quickly enveloped them, first sapping all colour from the other vehicles and their riders, then leaching away detail to reduce them to nothing more than silhouettes. Even these soon faded – not solely because the fog was getting thicker, but because they were pulling away. 'They're going too bloody fast,' complained Eddie as he eased back the throttle, then made a small but urgent course change to avoid a football-sized rock that materialised in his path. 'See? If I'd hit that, it might have tipped us over or even ripped off the front ski.'

'You've still got your lightning reactions,' Nina assured him. 'Although those Russian guys are probably even faster. I mean, they *are* about twenty years younger than you . . .'

'Tchah!' He made a rude gesture, then looked at the snow ahead. 'What the fuck are they doing?' he said as he saw the weaving skein of treaded ruts split apart into three separate tracks. 'They're spreading out. They won't be able to see each other.'

'I can hardly see them now.' Nina squinted into the fog, experiencing an unsettling moment of disorientation as she realised it was now so dense that it had blotted out all points of reference, stranding her inside a featureless grey void. 'No, wait – I *can't* see them now! Damn, I thought it was London that was supposed to have all the pea-soupers?'

'Nah, London just stinks of diesel,' said Eddie. He peered ahead, but the other snowmobiles were completely lost to sight, even the rasp of their engines muted. Reducing speed still further, he picked one of the three diverging tracks and followed it. 'Hope whoever this is has a clue where they're going . . .'

They both strained to see through the surrounding nothingness. The ground became indistinct a mere twenty feet away, the blank snow making the effect even worse. Occasionally it seemed that there were dim shapes at the very fringe of visibility, but they vanished the moment they were focused upon.

Nina stiffened in her seat at a dull noise from somewhere ahead. 'What was that?'

'What was what?' Eddie asked.

'I just heard – I don't know, a bang or something.'

He brought the snowmobile to a rapid stop, trying to listen over the putter of the idling engine. 'Can't hear anything.'

'It's gone, but . . . I can't hear any of the other snowmobiles either.'

Eddie shut the machine down. Silence fell upon them like a wet cloak. 'Nor can I,' he said after a moment, 'but if we keep following their track, we'll—'

A scream cut through the empty stillness.

'Okay, I heard *that*,' he said, restarting the engine and revving to full power.

'What the hell happened?' Nina shouted.

'They must've crashed. Fucking *told* 'em not to go too fast in this fog!'

It was not long before he slowed again. The track he was following suddenly veered sharply – but there was no sign of a rock or other obstacle. 'Where'd they go?' he asked, turning to follow.

'There.' Nina pointed off to one side. A faint shape resolved itself into the overturned snowmobile as they approached. 'I don't see either of the guys on it, though.'

Eddie stopped a few yards from the other machine. 'Hey!' he shouted. 'Anyone hear me? Are you okay?'

There was no answer. 'Maybe they don't speak English,' said Nina, concerned.

'Oi! Vodka, free vodka!'

'Very funny.' But she was not smiling as she dismounted, and nor was her husband. 'Can you see them?'

'No, but something happened here,' he replied, crouching. The snowmobile's track revealed the spot where it had crashed and rolled over; from the sudden change in direction, the driver had obviously been trying to avoid a collision – but again there was nothing except snow in the machine's path. 'Go to the snowmobile and see if you can spot 'em. I'll check if anyone got thrown off over here.'

Nina went to the crashed snowmobile. The engine had stalled, its cargo spilled out across the snow. There was no sign of the case containing Thor's Hammer. 'It wasn't Kagan and Logan,' she called to Eddie, before turning to check the surrounding area. At first she saw nothing – but then a shift in the drifting fog revealed a faint shape, darker than the surrounding snow and mist. She advanced a few steps, then broke into a jog as she realised it was a person. 'Eddie! Over here!'

The young man lay on his side, one arm splayed out behind his back. Nina reached him – then jumped back in horror.

The Russian was dead. But he had not been killed by falling from the snowmobile. His throat had been torn open, ragged strands of flesh hanging out into a splattered pool of bright red.

Eddie reached her. 'Jesus *Christ*!' he gasped on seeing the hideous display. 'What the fuck did that to him?'

Nina had looked away – and in doing so saw something else. 'Eddie, there are some tracks over here. I think the other guy crawled away.'

'He didn't crawl,' he said, grimly examining the churned snow. 'He was *dragged*.'

'By what?'

An answer came as a new sound reached them: a low growl.

But it was not the mechanical rasp of a snowmobile.

Nina and Eddie turned to find the source of the noise. Something appeared through the fog, advancing on them with a fearless arrogance. A wolf.

But not like any they had ever seen before.

It was huge, at least a foot taller than a normal wolf, its hunched back reaching easily to the height of Eddie's chest. But it was monstrous in more than just size. As it drew closer, they saw that it was deformed, swollen growths bulging beneath the dense fur. One eye was almost squeezed shut by a tumour on the side of its face.

The deformities had not lessened its abilities as a hunter, though. Its mouth and fangs dripped with blood, the fur down its chest stained a deep crimson where it had ripped out the soldier's throat.

'Oh my God,' Nina whispered. 'The Vikings were right. It's Fenrir . . .'

32

The wolf curled back its gore-stained lips and snarled, advancing on the couple. 'Get behind me,' Eddie told Nina, eyes locked on to the predator as he slowly unzipped his coat. 'Don't make any sudden moves.'

Nina cautiously sidestepped around her husband – only to turn in fear at a new sound. 'Shit!' A second wolf, as large and twisted as the first, faded into view through the fog. It too was smeared with the fresh blood of its latest kill – the second Russian soldier. 'Eddie, there's another one!'

Eddie's hand closed around his Wildey. The first wolf was about twenty feet away, padding closer with a measured, almost mechanical relentlessness. He started to draw the gun, looking away from the approaching animal to check the position of its hunting partner. It was further away, head low as it advanced.

He looked back—

The wolf charged.

The gun was out of its holster – but the beast had already leapt with shocking speed, knocking Eddie over. Nina shrieked as she jumped out of the way.

The wolf weighed as much as a man, and was easily as strong, claws raking his clothing as it lunged for his throat. Eddie managed to whip up his right arm and force the creature's head back just as its jaws snapped, twisted teeth mere inches from his face.

He pulled the Wildey's trigger. The huge handgun's boom was almost deafening; he expected the noise to scare off both attackers.

It didn't. The wolf flinched away from the retort and muzzle flash, but then continued its attack with even greater ferocity, bloodlust overpowering fear. The second animal hesitated, only to resume its advance when it saw its companion was not harmed.

'Nina!' Eddie cried, struggling to hold off the writhing monstrosity. 'Get out of here, run!'

Nina stumbled back, caught between the urge to flee and the desire to help her husband. She chose the latter, drawing back a leg to kick the wolf off him—

The other animal made its move, rushing at her. Nina broke off her attempted attack and ducked sideways. Its momentum carried it past her – but it immediately scrabbled around for another try, growling and slavering.

She ran for the overturned snowmobile, but could already hear the wolf closing fast from behind—

Nina dived over the vehicle, landing hard amongst its scattered equipment. The animal veered away to circle the snowmobile for a clear run at its prey.

Eddie yelled as the wolf's claws slashed at him again, ripping through his hood and gouging his jaw. A couple of inches lower, and it would have torn into his neck. 'Fuck off, Cujo!' he growled, clenching his free hand into a fist and punching the animal in the face.

Pinned by the monster, he couldn't put his full force into the blow – but it was still enough to startle it. The wolf let out an angry growl, pulling back before making another lunge.

The momentary retreat gave Eddie the chance to move his arm. He brought the Wildey to bear—

The wolf's huge jaws clamped around his hand. Sharp fangs tore through his coat's thick sleeve. They dug into his skin, about to slash tendons and arteries—

Another Magnum round boomed – and the entire back of the creature's head exploded.

The Wildey was *inside* its mouth – and Eddie had pulled the trigger.

The wolf collapsed on top of him. He pulled open the animal's slack jaws to extract his gun, then shoved the corpse away. 'Who's afraid of the Big Bad Wolf *now*?' he muttered as he got to his feet – only to freeze at a sound from the void.

A long, keening howl.

More shadowy shapes loomed through the drifting fog. The rest of the wolf pack.

They circled, closing in. Eddie turned, tracking them – then remembered there was another, much nearer. 'Nina!'

The gunshot had again caused the second wolf to freeze, but now it resumed its charge at Nina, still on her hands and knees beside the wrecked snowmobile. She desperately snatched up a baton-shaped piece of fallen cargo, about to wield it as a club—

It had a better use.

The baton was a flare. She yanked off the protective plastic cap and slapped her palm against the striker as the snarling predator raced in for the kill. The flare sizzled to life, blazing bright red at its tip.

She brought it up—

The wolf sprang.

It slammed her back against the snowmobile with an almost triumphant snarl – which turned to a shriek as she stabbed the burning flare into its neck. The beast leapt away, jumping and spinning as it tried to escape the searing pain, but the intense heat had set its fur alight. With a horrible wail, it raced away into the fog, flames spreading over its body and turning it into a running torch.

Eddie scrambled across the snow, vaulting the snowmobile to land beside her. 'Are you okay?'

'Yeah, I think so,' she gasped, still winded. She saw his torn and bloodied clothing. 'Jesus! What about you?'

'I'm fine – the blood's from Mr Wool-uff.'

'What happened to it?'

He held up the Wildey, drool still glistening on the polished metal. 'It bit off more than it could chew.' A very brief smile, which disappeared as he looked back at the approaching pack. 'There's more of the fucking things, though.'

'Okay, so shoot them!'

'I will, when I get a clear shot. They're not daft, though.' The other wolves had clearly recognised that their prey was far from defenceless, and changed tactics. They were now circling the couple and drawing away to fade into the fog before darting back into view as if daring them to react. 'I don't even know how many there are. Three, four – I can't tell.' He tracked one of the running shapes, which sensed the danger and retreated into the void, only for one of its companions to appear off to the side, moving in the other direction. 'And I've only got five shots left in this mag – if I miss, it'll take me a few seconds to reload, and that'll give them a chance to come at us.'

'Would this help?'

She had picked up one of the soldiers' AK-12s and flicked off the safety, raising the assault rifle to firing position. He grinned. 'And I thought you didn't like guns.'

'I don't, but sometimes they're useful!' Nina looked down the sights, following one of the wolves as it ran at her – and fired. The gun was set to fully automatic, unleashing a thudding fusillade of bullets. The monster screeched and tumbled to a stop in the blood-speckled snow.

'Over here!' Eddie warned. She spun as two more wolves charged towards the snowmobile from the opposite direction. Another burst from the Kalashnikov brought one of them down, the other felled by a single cannonfire blast from the Wildey.

Nina's dismay at killing the creatures was tempered by the sure knowledge that they had been about to tear out her throat. 'Are there any more of them?' she asked, scanning the emptiness surrounding her.

'Don't know.' Eddie did the same, keeping the Wildey raised. 'There might— *Shit!*'

Movement in the corner of his vision – which resolved into a wolf racing towards him at terrifying speed. He whirled as it made a flying leap over the snowmobile—

The Wildey boomed again, but the animal's momentum carried it onwards. It hit Eddie, bowling him over and sending the gun flying.

'Eddie!' Nina cried, pointing the AK at the wolf – but it did not move, lying on its side with its mouth agape. The snow beneath it slowly turned red.

Eddie stood, wincing at a pain in his shoulder from the collision. 'Aaa-fuckin'-wooo, you bastard,' he told the dead beast, before looking around. If there were any more wolves out in the fog, they had taken the hint and fled. 'Where'd my gun go? If I lose another Wildey, you'll never let me hear the bloody end of it . . .'

'I probably shouldn't tell you that it's over there, then,' said Nina, managing a faint smile as she caught her breath.

Eddie tramped to where she had indicated, finding his gun half buried in the snow. He retrieved it, then came back to her, taking a closer look at the wolf's body. It was just as deformed as the first they had seen, oversized and overmuscled but also misshapen, ugly lumps beneath its skin – and in some cases bursting out through it, lesions visible through the fur. 'Christ, look at this. It's like something out of *The Thing*.'

Nina had seen similar deformities before. 'It's the eitr,' she said, with a shiver that was caused by more than just the cold. 'Just like in those photos Kagan's boss showed us.'

'Yeah. We must be in the right place, then. The stuff's mutated them.'

They both stared unhappily at the corpse, then turned at a noise. Not the howl of wolves this time, but the burr of engines. The other snowmobiles came into view.

The two remaining soldiers halted thirty feet away and jumped off their snowmobile, AK-12s at the ready as they checked for threats. 'My God!' Berkeley exclaimed as Kagan stopped beside Eddie and Nina. 'We heard the shots. What the hell happened here?'

Kagan was more concerned by his comrade's body. 'Kontarsky!' he cried, running to the fallen figure, but after a brief examination he returned more slowly, expression stricken. 'Have you seen Lishin?' he asked Eddie.

The Yorkshireman shook his head. 'One of them dragged him off. Don't know where, but we haven't seen him. He's probably dead. I'm sorry.'

'So am I,' Kagan said quietly. He regarded one of the animals. 'The eitr – it did this to them. It is the only explanation.'

'We know,' said Nina.

'And this would have been from only the smallest exposure. Anything more, and they would not have lived this long. I have never seen the effects with my own eyes before, but . . .' A pause, then he set his shoulders. '*Now* you know why we must destroy the eitr, yes? What happened to the wolves must never get off this island.'

'Can't argue with you there,' said Eddie.

Berkeley shook his head. 'I don't understand. How could these wolves have survived so long? The Vikings called this place the vale of Fenrir, but they can't possibly have lived all this time.'

'These are probably the children of animals that came on to the island a few months ago when the sea was frozen,' Kagan told him. 'The parents would have died after being exposed to the eitr – but their pups lived for a time, even like this.'

'It's horrible,' said Nina.

'Yes. But we can stop it – we *must* stop it.' Another regretful look at the soldier's body, then the Russian returned to his vehicle. 'Come. We must move.'

'Keep it,' Eddie said to Nina as she was about to put down the AK-12. 'We might need it.' He holstered the Wildey and they returned to their snowmobile as the others restarted their engines. 'Oi! This time, don't go so bloody fast!' he shouted. 'We need to stick together!'

'Agreed,' said Kagan. He wheeled around back along his own trail, then powered away, though with more restraint than before. The soldiers followed, Eddie bringing the third snowmobile into line behind them.

The landscape began to climb again, before long lifting them clear of the fog trapped in the valley. Swathes of low cloud still clung to the mountainside, but the peak itself came back into clear view, an ominous, irregular pyramid jabbing at the overcast sky.

Berkeley's translations of the ancient runes required very little interpretation to follow. The 'broken finger' was a long slab of rock that the cold had sheared in two along a fault line, the narrow end pointing uphill. The barren island spread out below as they ascended.

The group was concerned only with what awaited above, however. There had been no sight or sound of the helicopter; the only conclusion was that it had landed.

And if it had . . . then its occupants had found the object of their search.

Berkeley tapped Kagan's shoulder. The Russian pulled up, the other two snowmobiles drawing alongside. 'What is it?' Nina asked.

'End of the line,' said Berkeley. 'We need to look for open ground. Once we find it . . . that's it. We're at Vigrid, where the Vikings were going to face Ragnarök.'

Eddie gazed up the slope. 'It's got to be that,' he said, pointing. Off to one side of the looming peak, a few hundred feet higher than the group's position, part of the terrain levelled out. The wind blew spiralling wisps of snow off its edge.

'Looks like we can ride all the way to it,' said Nina.

'Don't think we should, though. We don't want 'em to know we're coming. If they saw the ship, they might be watching out for company.'

'That rock,' said Kagan, pointing at a boulder not far below the flatter ground. 'We will leave the snowmobiles there and go on foot.' He glanced behind Berkeley as if to reassure himself that the case containing Thor's Hammer was still secured, then set off once more. Eddie kept pace alongside him, the soldiers bringing up the rear.

It took five minutes to reach their destination. Eddie stopped his snowmobile by the boulder and dismounted, Nina slinging her borrowed Kalashnikov from one shoulder. A disgruntled Berkeley watched her. 'Shouldn't I have a gun too?' he asked.

Kagan's only response was a brief barking laugh, while Eddie was more verbose. 'Don't fucking think so, mate.'

'Why not? I know how to handle myself – I've used guns before. Well, okay, I've done some target shooting, but I know one end from the other. And I must have proved I'm on your side by now. Even to you, Nina.'

'Maybe so,' she replied, 'but even if I did want you to have one, the other gun's back down there with those wolves.' She gestured into the grey haze below. 'And I don't know if we got all of them or not.'

Berkeley looked for a moment as if he were seriously considering trekking back down the mountain to retrieve the weapon, then shook his head in resignation. 'All right, okay. But if we find ourselves outgunned when we get up there, don't blame me.'

'That's fine. There are plenty of other things I can blame you for.'

'For God's sake,' he muttered, before changing the subject by taking out his notes. 'Okay. This has to be Vigrid. Once we're up there,' he gestured towards the plateau, 'then we're at the pit. The lair of Jörmungandr. The Midgard Serpent.'

'Well, we already fought his brother the wolf,' said Eddie, gathering his gear from the back of the snowmobile. 'How does that work, by the way? Their dad must have been into some fucked-up stuff.'

'Loki was a trickster,' said Berkeley as the rest of the team collected their own belongings and followed the Englishman up the hill. 'He could take on any form. Actually,' he continued, suddenly brightening as a thought struck him, 'the mutation of those wolves? If that was caused by the eitr, it could explain some other Norse legends. Giants, monopodes, skraelings – they might all have been people or creatures who'd suffered the same sort of mutations.'

'Maybe you can rehabilitate yourself in the archaeological world by writing a paper about it,' Nina said in a cutting tone. Berkeley got the message and fell into a sullen silence.

They climbed the slope. It grew steeper as they approached the lip of the plateau, bare rock exposed where snow could no longer find purchase. The last few dozen yards became a climb.

Eddie was first to the top. He waved for the others to hold position, cautiously raising his head to peer over the edge. 'I can see the chopper,' he reported.

Kagan joined him, the case containing Thor's Hammer on his back. 'What about Lock and his people?'

'There's a guy hanging about, but I don't see anyone else. Although . . .' He brought up a hand to shield his eyes from the blowing snow. 'There's a big crater as well. It must be the eitr pit.'

There was a flurry of movement as Nina, Berkeley and the soldiers all scrambled up to look. 'You are right,' said Kagan grimly. 'It is like the one that was found on Novaya Zemlya.'

The plateau was not quite flat; they had arrived near its upper end, the snowy plain dropping gently by about a hundred feet over its length before falling sharply away down the mountainside. The helicopter, a large Sikorsky S-76 painted in high-visibility red to stand out in Arctic conditions, sat motionless two hundred yards away, below their position. A man stood near it, apparently on guard, but he was looking away from them towards the only other feature nearby.

A gaping hole.

It was a ragged oval dropping into the heart of the mountain, over a hundred feet across at its widest. Steam rose from the opening, condensing as it hit the colder air above before being whisked away by the endless wind. 'There's something warm down there,' said Nina, seeing no snow around its edge.

Kagan nodded. 'The eitr comes from somewhere deep inside the earth. The other pit was hot also.'

'Looks like Lock and Hoyt are already inside,' said Eddie. At one side of the pit, a metal trestle had been set up to hold several ropes descending into the abyss.

'How many of them are there?' Nina asked.

'Chopper that size could carry a dozen people, easy. Great, another fucking private army.'

'So what are we going to do?' said Berkeley.

'No matter what, we cannot let them leave with the eitr,' insisted Kagan. 'We must take out that helicopter. Then we will go into the pit and use Thor's Hammer to neutralise the eitr.'

'If it works,' said Eddie. He observed the scene below thoughtfully. The man was still watching the pit, apparently waiting for those inside to return to the surface. 'They don't know we're here.'

'You sure?' said Nina.

'If they did, Hoyt wouldn't have only left one bloke up here. He's nasty, but he's not stupid. That guy's just keeping an eye on the ropes.'

'What are you thinking?' Kagan asked.

'That we can sneak right up to the chopper without being seen. We'll use those rocks for cover.' He gestured at several stones poking up from the snow between the group's position and the helicopter. 'If he stays focused on the hole, we can get within fifty feet of him before he even realises we're there.'

'And if he looks around before then?' said Berkeley.

Eddie took out the Wildey. 'Then I find out how accurate this is at long range! But I reckon we can do it.'

'So do I,' said Kagan, nodding. He spoke to his men in Russian, then turned back to Eddie. 'They will keep us covered on the way to the helicopter.'

'Make sure they don't shoot that thing on your back, eh?' The Englishman cautiously rose. 'Nina, wait here until it's safe. Keep an eye on him.' He jerked a thumb at Berkeley.

'I don't need to be baby-sat,' Berkeley complained. His sour expression became more concerned as Nina unslung her AK-12. 'Nina, are you sure you know how to use that thing?'

'Ask the wolves,' she replied. Then she reached out and squeezed Eddie's hand. 'Good luck.'

'See you soon,' he said, smiling. 'Okay, Kagan, let's go. There's trouble down't pit!' He grinned, adding: 'I always wanted an excuse to say that.' Everyone looked at him. 'It's a Yorkshire thing . . . oh, never bloody mind. Come on.'

He climbed on to the plateau, keeping low as he headed for the first rock. Kagan followed. The Russian soldiers spread out along the rocky edge to cover them.

'So,' said Kagan, eyeing the Wildey, 'the big gun. Does it impress the women?' He smirked.

Eddie made an irritated noise. 'Everyone's a fucking comedian. I use a big gun because when I shoot someone with it, they fall down and don't get back up, okay? Well, usually they don't.' They reached the rock and hunched behind it. The lone guard was still watching the pit; now that Eddie was closer, he could tell from the man's body language that he was both cold and bored. Presumably Lock and company were not rushing their descent into the depths of the earth. 'Okay, his gun's over his shoulder, so he's definitely not expecting trouble. What's that in his left hand?'

Kagan narrowed his eyes. 'A radio, perhaps? I cannot see it properly.'

'Maybe he's waiting for Lock to tell him they've got the eitr, so he can help pull 'em out.'

'Then we must get there before he does.'

They zigzagged between the rocks. About a hundred feet from the helicopter, Eddie signalled for Kagan to pause. 'There's someone else in the chopper,' he said as they crouched behind a snow-covered boulder. A shadowy figure was visible through the aircraft's windows. 'The pilot.'

'There is another person,' said Kagan. Somebody was in one of the passenger seats.

Somebody blonde.

'It's Tova!' Eddie said. 'They must have brought her in case there were any more runes they needed translating.'

'They will not need her for much longer,' Kagan pointed out ominously.

'We've got to get her out of there. You sort out the guard; I'll—'

He broke off, both men ducking as the mercenary moved. The object in his hand was indeed a radio, the squawk as it received a message carried by the wind to the observers. Eddie couldn't quite make out the words, but he recognised the voice. 'Hoyt! That bastard.' He leaned out, trying to listen to the message. 'Can you hear what he's saying?'

'No, he is too far— Wait, get back.'

Eddie pulled into cover as the mercenary turned and started back to the helicopter, still listening to his leader. Fragments of the transmission reached the lurking duo. '. . . at the bottom,' said Hoyt. 'Make sure the ropes . . . gonna get the stuff. Once we've . . . boss wants us to head straight back up. Tell the pilot . . .'

'They are about to take the eitr,' said Kagan in alarm. He raised his AK. 'We cannot wait – we must stop them.'

'Hold on, hold on,' Eddie told him. The radio message became clearer as the merc neared the helicopter.

Hoyt's words sent a chill through him. 'And the boss says we're finished with Blondie. Take her out and shoot her.'

'Roger that,' said the mercenary, a sadistic smile crossing his face. He clipped his radio to his belt and unslung his rifle as he reached the helicopter. 'Okay, out,' he barked as he opened the door, pulling Tova from the aircraft. Her hands were secured behind her back by flex-cuffs, and she almost fell.

'Fuckers,' Eddie hissed as he saw the Swede's face. Without Nina as leverage, Hoyt and Lock had resorted to much more direct – and brutal – ways of forcing obedience from the archaeologist. Tova's face bore several bruises, her lower lip swollen. Her eyes were puffy and red from exhaustion – and fear. 'I'm going in.'

'Chase, wait—' Kagan began, but the Englishman was already moving.

He scuttled towards the helicopter, keeping out of the line of sight of both its pilot and the mercenary. He couldn't risk a shot at the latter; even if the bullet was dead on target, it might rip right through the man's body and hit Tova as well.

He would have to be more hands-on.

The mercenary dragged Tova to a spot ten feet from the helicopter. 'Oh God,' she gasped, realising what he was about to do. 'No, please! I did what you wanted!'

'It's nothing personal,' said the mercenary, though the relish in his voice gave away that the act of killing was more than pure business to him. 'On your knees.'

'Please, don't!' she wailed.

'Shut up.' He forced her down to the snowy ground, then raised his gun to the back of her head. 'If it wasn't so fuckin' cold, I'd have you facing the other way first. Bit of fun in return for me makin' it quick—'

'Make *this* quick,' Eddie growled as he rose up like a spectre behind the mercenary, clamping one arm around the man's head and the other across the front of his shoulders – and twisting them in different directions.

There was a revolting snap from deep inside the mercenary's neck as bone splintered, muscle and tissue compressing with a wet squish. The man's eyes bugged wide and he opened his mouth to scream in pain, but no air escaped; his windpipe was crushed shut, spinal cord severed below the fourth vertebra. Eddie let him drop. The man crumpled to the ground, completely limp, mouth gaping silently like a goldfish out of water. 'Don't fuck with my friends,' the Englishman told him, then moved to help Tova. 'It's okay, we're going to get you out of here.'

'Eddie?' she said, looking around at him with shocked surprise. '*Oj, herre Gud*, Eddie! You found me!'

'Yeah, we followed the runes. Hate to admit it, but Berkeley knows what he's doing.' He raised her back to her feet, then drew his Wildey and went to the helicopter's door. The pilot had just realised what had happened outside and was fumbling for a radio handset, but the sight of the huge gun made him drop it and freeze without even needing to be told.

Kagan ran up behind Eddie. 'Are you okay?' he asked Tova, taking out a knife and cutting her hands free.

'Yes, thank you! Thank you both,' she sobbed.

Eddie gestured for the pilot to get out. 'How many of 'em are there?' he asked the Swede. 'We know Hoyt's here – what about Lock?'

'Yes, they are both here.' Tova rubbed her wrists where the plastic strap had bitten into her skin. 'They have six men with them. They went down there.' She indicated the pit.

'They're not coming back out,' he assured her, before signalling for Nina and the others to join him. 'All right, you,' he said, rounding on the pilot. 'Got a good reason why I shouldn't blow your fucking head off?'

The man's face twisted in terror. 'I – I – I don't know what is going on!' he gabbled, his accent French-Canadian. 'I was just hired to fly here!'

'By a bunch of guys with guns who were holding a beaten-up woman prisoner. That didn't drop any hints that the job might be a bit dodgy?'

'I don't ask questions, I just fly the chopper!' He stared at the mercenary in horror. A last gurgling sound emerged from the fallen man's mouth, then he went still. 'I'll do whatever you want, just please don't kill me!'

Kagan leaned into the cockpit, examining something taped to the instrument panel. 'I think he is telling the truth. This says he works for an air charter company.'

Eddie nodded. 'Okay, hero,' he said to the pilot. 'What were you hired to do, and where were you going to take 'em from here?'

'They wanted me to fly them to these coordinates,' the Canadian replied. 'They had pictures, satellite photos. When they saw the hole, we landed and they went down into it. They were going to collect some kind of sample, and then I would fly them back to Iqaluit to meet their jet. That's all I know, I swear!'

The man's fear was genuine. Eddie reluctantly accepted his story. 'All right, I'm not going to kill you – unless you piss me about,' he added with a wave of the gun, the pilot's moment of relief instantly vanishing. 'Okay, Kagan, what do we need to do? Can you just dump that stuff down the hole?'

Kagan put down the case and opened it, revealing the steel cylinder. 'No. It will have to be poured directly into the eitr.'

'Yeah, I thought so.' A weary sigh, then Eddie looked towards the pit. Steam was still condensing above it; the air below was both warm and humid. 'How hot's it going to be down there?'

'The Academician told me it could reach over one hundred degrees Fahrenheit inside the pit, even in winter.'

'So it's not just a horrible fucking mutagenic poison, it's a *boiling* horrible fucking mutagenic poison. Fantastic.' He turned as Nina, Berkeley and the two soldiers arrived at a run. 'Ay up. Glad you could join us.' Kagan issued an order to his men, and, AKs at the ready, they moved to guard the pit.

Berkeley grimaced at the sight of the dead mercenary. 'You've, ah, being doing your thing, then.'

Nina was more concerned about Tova. 'Jeez,' she said, seeing the bruises. 'Are you okay?'

'I will be fine,' Tova replied. 'I am sorry.'

'For what?'

'For telling them how to find this place. If I had been stronger, you could have reached here first.'

'It's not your fault,' Nina insisted.

'Just . . . do not let them get away with the eitr. Please?'

'We won't,' said Eddie.

'You've got a plan?' asked Berkeley.

'Go down there, kill every living thing we find, pour the Russian goop into the eitr, head home. Sound good?'

'You should come to more IHA meetings,' Nina told him. 'Your bullet points are way more concise than mine.'

'Only if I get to bring Mr Wildey.' Eddie held up the gun. 'He'd encourage everyone to keep it brief.'

'I'm just picturing Seretse's face if he held a meeting where you had that thing on the desk in front of you.' She turned to Kagan. The Russian had carefully removed the steel canister from its case, and was now taking a chunky military radio from the rest of his gear. 'What are you doing?'

'My orders are to report the location of the eitr pit once we have found it and are ready to deliver Thor's Hammer,' he replied as he switched the unit on, then spoke into it in Russian. A reply came quickly; he began a rapid-fire conversation.

Nina regarded the pit. An object stood out above the snow near its lip – another runestone, worn by the savage weather. 'Tova, did you translate that?'

'Yes,' Tova replied. 'It is a message to any Viking warriors who followed the trail from Valhalla, congratulating them on their strength for surviving the journey – and wishing them courage for the battle against the Midgard Serpent.'

'Doesn't look like they'd find many snakes around here,' said Eddie, surveying the frozen desolation.

'No, but I did not go into the pit. I do not know what is down there.'

'We're about to find out,' Nina said, far from thrilled at the prospect. 'And we've got Lock, Hoyt and six other guys down there as well.'

'We've got surprise, though,' Eddie reminded her. 'If we catch 'em before they come out, we—'

'*Ebat kopat!*' cried Kagan, appalled. All eyes went to him as he spoke frantically into the radio. The reply was stern and unwavering, lengthening his expression of dismay.

'What's wrong?' Nina demanded.

Kagan looked at her, eyes wide. 'I gave them the coordinates of the eitr pit – and now they are going to activate the Tsar Protocol!' Eddie, Nina and Tova exchanged horrified glances.

Berkeley pursed his lips. 'I take it that is . . . not a good thing.'

'No shit,' said Nina. 'They're going to drop a *nuke* on us!'

Berkeley's reaction was as confused as if she had spoken to him in Swahili. 'When you say "a nuke", you mean . . .'

'Yeah, an actual *nuclear bomb!*' She turned back to Kagan. 'Tell them not to!'

'I tried,' said the Russian. 'They will not listen. They know

Lock is already here, so my orders are now to stop them from leaving with the eitr.'

'That's easy enough,' said Berkeley, almost quivering in nervous agitation. 'We get in the helicopter and tell the pilot to fly us out of here.' The pilot nodded in vigorous agreement. 'Lock and his buddies are stranded, and when the nuke arrives, they get fried. Simple!' He took in the hostile frowns of his companions. 'Not so simple?'

'Russia is about to launch a *nuclear attack* on Canada,' Nina said, scathing. 'How do you think NATO will respond to that?'

'When are they launching it?' Eddie asked.

The radio came to life again, the Russian at the other end of the line delivering a curt statement. Kagan went pale. 'They just did.'

'*What?*' Nina gasped.

'They had a Tupolev-160 on combat patrol over the Arctic Ocean. It is – *was* carrying a Kh-102 cruise missile. It is a stealth weapon; NATO's radars will not see it.'

'I fucking *knew* I should have shot up those Tu-160s!' Eddie growled. 'How big's the warhead?'

'Two hundred kilotons. Much smaller than the Tsar Bomba, but it does not need to be so big. It is very accurate.' He glanced towards the steaming pit. 'They will be able to drop it straight down the hole.'

'How long have we got?'

Kagan spoke into the radio, soon getting a reply. 'Thirty minutes. The missile is subsonic – but it is still as fast as a jet.'

'But they haven't even given us a chance,' protested Nina. 'We can still try to use Thor's Hammer. If it works, they don't need to nuke the pit!'

'Can they abort the missile in flight?' Eddie asked. Kagan

nodded. 'Then get back on the blower and tell 'em we'll confirm that the eitr's been neutralised in *twenty-nine* minutes!'

'Preferably less,' said Nina. 'I hate it when we cut things that fine.'

'I don't like to point this out,' said Berkeley as Kagan reopened the channel to the Kremlin, 'but I doubt Lock and Hoyt will let us just do whatever we're going to do.'

'We don't have much choice, do we?'

'There *is* still the helicopter option . . .'

'If that nuke goes off, and NATO realises where it came from and retaliates, there might not be anywhere left for us to go home to!' Kagan finished his brief discussion. 'What did they say?' she asked him.

'If we neutralise the eitr, they will abort the missile,' he replied.

'Okay, then let's wait five minutes and say we've done it,' Berkeley suggested.

Kagan was not impressed. 'One way or another, Russia will destroy the eitr,' he said. 'For the sake of the world, we must make it Unit 201's way.'

Nina turned to Tova. 'You don't have to come with us. Wait in the helicopter – and keep an eye on him,' she said, giving the pilot a suspicious look. She collected the dead mercenary's gun and offered it to her. 'You know how to use one of these?'

'I think so,' Tova replied, hesitantly accepting the weapon.

Eddie glanced at it. 'Safety's off.'

'Then I know so.'

'Take this too,' said Kagan, giving her the radio. 'It is a satellite system,' he explained. 'It will not work in the pit. This way, it will be safe.'

Nina gave Tova a smile of reassurance. 'Don't take off until we get back.'

'You came for me, so I will wait for you,' said the Swede. 'Do not worry, I will watch the pilot. Good luck.'

'Thanks, I think we'll need as much as we can bloody get!' said Eddie. He opened the helicopter's door and shoved the pilot inside, then moved back to let Tova enter.

Berkeley looked hopefully at the aircraft. 'What about me?'

'Make yourself useful,' the Yorkshireman told him. He indicated the metal cylinder. 'Carry that. And don't fucking drop it, or you'll be dead before I have a chance to shoot you!'

The scientist was about to object, but a hard glare from Kagan silenced him. 'We must hurry. Come.' He jogged towards the pit, Nina, Eddie and the reluctant Berkeley following.

Shapes were visible beneath the snow as they neared the opening. Eddie wrinkled his face in disgust at the sight of a dead wolf, the cold having preserved its monstrously deformed and diseased features. 'They must have come up here 'cause it was warmer in the pit. Bad move.'

'Maybe they didn't even go into the pit,' said Nina, alarmed. 'The whole *environment* might be toxic. God knows what we'll be breathing in.'

'If it is like the pit on Novaya Zemlya,' Kagan said, 'the air is not deadly – but it will not be pleasant either.'

Eddie grunted sarcastically. 'We go to all the nice places, don't we?'

They reached the two soldiers, the Russian officer exchanging brief words with them. Nina glanced at the nearby runestone, the final marker along the Vikings' long journey, then down into the pit itself.

There was not much to see, the rising steam making it hard to pick out details. But the exposed rock was dark – almost black, in fact, caked with oily deposits. She stepped closer for a better look, only to cough as hot vapour wafted past her. Kagan had been right; it *was* unpleasant, a stinging, almost acidic sensation rasping at her sinuses. 'I hope you're right about this crap not being toxic,' she told the Russian.

'If we do not succeed, it will not matter if it is or not,' he replied, checking that the ropes were secure before squinting into the depths of the pit. 'Okay, I will climb down first.'

'You ready?' Eddie asked Nina.

'As ready as I can be.'

He smiled. 'Then let's save the world. Again.'

33

Kagan took the lead, one of his men, Maslov, behind him as the group descended into the pit. Eddie was next, leading Nina and Berkeley. The second soldier, Pravdin, took up the rear – whether to provide overwatch for the whole group or simply to keep an eye on Berkeley and the canister was something known only to the Russian-speakers.

They were soon glad of the ropes set up by Lock's team. The slope grew steeper as it descended, the steam condensing where rising hot air met the cold air at the surface; it did not take long for them to drop below the vaporous boundary. Eddie stared in disbelief at what came into view below. 'What the hell is that?'

Berkeley was astounded by the sight. 'I can see why the Vikings thought they'd found a giant snake!'

'Not just one,' said Nina, equally amazed.

Jabbing up at them from below were numerous thick columns, twisting around the edges of the shaft and criss-crossing it like bridges, all intertwined like a knot of serpents. It took a moment for her to realise what they were: *crystals*. She had seen pictures of crystal caves from all over the world; one of the largest was in Mexico, a great underground cavern filled with massive natural spans weighing dozens of tons. But this was on another scale entirely. The crystals were not the milky white of selenite, but instead a menacing, oily black covered by a scabrous pattern resembling snake scales. 'That's the weirdest thing I've ever seen, and I've seen the bookmarks on Eddie's laptop.'

Even with some idea of what to expect, Kagan was still as awed as the others. 'They are formed from the eitr,' he explained as they continued the descent. 'The Academician told me what the Soviet scientists learned about them. They are constantly growing – they rise by several centimetres each week. At Novaya Zemlya, most were cleared to make room for ladders, but new ones soon grew to replace them.'

Nina regarded one of the crystals as they approached. Its upper end had broken off, leaving jagged obsidian shards. 'They look pretty fragile. I'm surprised they've managed to get this high without collapsing under their own weight.'

'They are weakened by the cold air at the top. But inside the pit, they are strong enough to take a man's weight.'

Eddie looked down. 'Yeah, I was afraid you were going to say that.'

They reached the foot of the slope, the shaft dropping away vertically. The ropes led to the top of a particularly large crystal, which stretched across the full width of the shaft at a steep angle. It was about five feet in diameter – but its octagonal cross-section made the flat part of its upper surface considerably narrower.

'So,' continued the Yorkshireman, 'we've got to scoot down that all the way to the bloody bottom?'

'Lock and his people managed it,' said Nina. All the same, she felt queasy looking down. She couldn't see the base of the shaft, her view obstructed by the jagged, multilayered lattice of crystals, but she could tell it was a long way down. 'Even if they can take our weight, is it safe to touch them if they're made from eitr?'

'The crystal form is harmless,' said Kagan. 'Okay, not *harmless*, but it will only kill you if you eat it. It is poisonous, but not a mutagen.'

'Good job I wasn't planning on laying out a picnic,' said Eddie. He held his breath as Kagan put both feet on the crystal ledge and let go of the rope. There was a visible change in the surface, the black scales turning a stressed grey under his weight, but it showed no signs of imminent collapse. 'All right. So how do we get down?'

The Russian surveyed the route. 'We follow Lock and his men. Look, they have left footprints.' He pointed out scuffs and scrapes along the structure. 'If they got to the bottom, so can we.'

'Yeah, but how many of them fell off on the way down?' said Berkeley.

'Hopefully all of 'em,' Eddie said. Still holding the rope, he leaned out over the drop for a better look. 'Normally I'd say we should go across each crystal one by one so they don't break, but since we're on the atomic fucking clock, we'll have to go in convoy.' He drew back and checked his watch. 'Shit, it's taken us nearly three minutes just to get down this far.'

'Then we must move faster,' said Kagan firmly. Bringing up his arms for balance, he started down the sloping crystal. Maslov let him get clear, then stepped down after him. The black span creaked faintly underfoot.

Eddie winced, but once the soldier had moved on after Kagan, he followed them. The surface took his weight, but with an unsettling sense of compression, like a layer of thick linoleum rather than the rigid structure it appeared to be. That slight flexibility explained how the crystals had not cracked apart as they coiled around the walls of the shaft, he supposed. But the scales at least provided grip, making his descent less unsteady than he had expected. Ahead, Kagan reached the far side of the pit and clambered down to another bridge below. 'Okay, Nina, come on.'

She reluctantly let go of the rope and followed her husband. The facet along the crystal's top was wide enough to take her feet, but was tilted at a slight horizontal angle in addition to sloping downwards, making it tricky to negotiate. Maslov reached the lower end and climbed down after Kagan; Nina looked back at Berkeley. 'Logan? You coming?'

'Yes, this makes it *so* easy,' he grumbled, holding up the heavy stainless-steel container by its carrying handle.

She gave him an apologetic look. 'Okay, if I reach back, we can share the weight between us.'

'Nina, let Ivan behind him do that,' said Eddie, but she had already paused and stretched out her arm to the other archaeologist. Berkeley held out the canister, and she took hold of it. 'Berkeley, if she falls because of you, you're following her down with a fucking bullet in your head!'

'Eddie, it's okay,' Nina assured him, before regarding Berkeley again. 'Isn't it, Logan?'

'For God's sake,' he grumbled as he edged down the crystal. 'There are enough ways I might get killed today without adding your psychotic husband to the list. I want to get out of here as much as you do – and I don't want to do that only to have a nuclear bomb land on my head!'

'Okay, all right, point taken!' She kept moving, the container suspended between them.

Eddie reached the bottom, waiting until he was sure Nina was progressing without trouble before climbing down after the two Russians. Kagan was already on the next leg of the descent, the crystal crossing below even steeper than the first. 'Hey, there's a light down there,' said the Yorkshireman, pointing.

'Yes, I saw it,' Kagan replied. The diffuse daylight from the top of the shaft quickly faded into darkness below, but there was an eerie blue-white glow amongst the black shards. 'Lock and Hoyt must have brought it.'

'Nice of 'em.' He stared at the light as he waited for the soldier to move clear. 'Know what this reminds me of? It's like we're inside a giant game of Kerplunk.'

'With us as the marbles,' Nina said nervously.

Eddie helped her down, then Berkeley passed Thor's Hammer to her before descending himself. Pravdin followed him as the Englishman started across the next ledge. 'We've only got twenty-five minutes left,' he warned.

That spurred everyone to move faster. Kagan hopped across to another descending crystal bridge and led the way downwards. Before long, the source of the strange light was revealed. A translucent balloon about four feet in diameter had been propped between two crystals, glowing from within and casting a surprising amount of light over its surroundings. 'Now *here's* your Kerplunk marble,' said Eddie, prodding it as he passed. The inflated sphere was made of the same tough latex as weather balloons. 'Must have a bunch of LEDs inside.'

'There are more below,' reported Kagan.

Nina peered over the edge, seeing additional pools of light further down the shaft. 'Can you see the bottom yet?'

'No, not yet. The pit in Novaya Zemlya was almost a hundred metres deep. I hope this is not much deeper.'

'Yeah, so do I!' The air was becoming uncomfortably hot, forcing her to pull down the zipper of her coat in an attempt to keep cool.

They pressed on, zigzagging downwards. As well as the giant crystals worming up the shaft, smaller ones grew from the walls, stabbing outwards like glass spearpoints. Others hung like stalactites beneath the sloping slabs. Kagan leaned warily to avoid a particularly large example, then issued a warning as he saw something below. 'Be careful. Some of the crystals have cracks. I do not know if they will support us.'

Eddie saw what he meant. He guessed that a piece had broken from a crystal higher up and hit one of the bridges as it fell. Ragged stress lines ran through the black surface like lightning bolts, visible even in the low light. Unfortunately, it was the only obvious way to continue the descent. 'Which way did Lock's lot go? Did they risk crossing it?'

'It is hard to see. Wait . . .' A short pause, then: 'No, they dropped down the other side.' Kagan stepped across to the damaged span, the fractured crystal letting out a faint but alarming creak, then lowered himself to another below it. 'Okay, it is safe.'

Eddie looked back at the two scientists. 'You okay?'

'Just about,' said Berkeley, rubbing sweat from his forehead.

'I didn't mean you. Nina?'

'Surviving,' she told him. 'This damn thing gets really heavy after a while, though.' She raised the steel canister.

'Pass it down,' Eddie told her. 'I'll carry it – I'll get Kagan's other guy to give me a hand. Can't be much—'

'Quiet!' Kagan hissed. 'I can hear them.'

Everyone fell silent. Eddie advanced as quickly as he dared to join the two Russians, who were crouched on a jagged black outcrop. More of the illuminated globes were visible below – and for the first time, he glimpsed the bottom of the pit.

The source of the eitr. He could only see a small slice of it through the maze of crystals, but that was enough to reveal a glutinous, light-sucking ooze. It slowly shimmered and rippled in the globes' unnatural glow, as if simmering from a heat source below.

Voices reached him. 'It's Hoyt,' he rumbled. 'Lock, too.'

'If they are still here, then they have not yet taken a sample of eitr,' said Kagan. 'We can stop them.' He brought up his AK-12.

Eddie did the same with his Wildey, but while he could see movement between the crystals, he knew that he would be unable to get a clear shot. 'Arse. I can't get a good angle from up here. We'll have to go lower.'

Kagan nodded, surveying the confusing network of black shards below. 'There,' he said, pointing at a particular section of crystal. It was the widest they had seen, a hulking hexagonal pillar wedged almost horizontally across the shaft as if toppled by a giant. 'We will be able to take them out before they even know we are here.' He signalled for the rest of the group to advance.

'Not sure if it's safe,' Eddie said dubiously. The wash of light from a globe above revealed stress lines in the great structure.

'It will have to be. We are running out of time.'

The Englishman couldn't disagree – the cruise missile was now little more than twenty minutes away. 'Okay, go on. Nina, stay where you are.'

'No,' Kagan insisted as he climbed down. 'We must get Thor's Hammer to the eitr as soon as we can, and we still have to return to the surface to call off the missile. We cannot wait.' He added something in Russian to the soldier at the rear, who tried to squeeze past Nina and Berkeley, but there was not enough room. 'Dr Wilde, come down.'

Against his better judgement, Eddie nodded to his wife. 'Oh boy,' she said, gingerly climbing to the outcrop.

Kagan completed his descent to the bridge and, gun at the ready, made his way across. Eddie followed, then Maslov. The Englishman reached the bridge's centre and looked down – and at last saw clearly what lay at the bottom of the pit.

The shaft widened out into a roughly hemispherical chamber about a hundred and fifty feet across, the rock encrusted in black condensates. Hundreds of jagged crystal stalactites hung down from above, turning the space into an obsidian torture chamber. The heat was sickening, the stinging in the party's nostrils almost physically painful.

The source of it all filled the bottom of the cavern, lit by more illuminated globes bobbing on its surface.

The eitr pit.

A lake of malevolent primordial ooze churned slowly below, large bubbles swelling at its heart. The great crystal columns rose at all angles from the glistening slime. Some were crowded out, forced against the walls and ceiling only to crumble and shatter as they pressed against unyielding rock, while others stretched up as if in competition to reach the daylight high above. The eitr swirled lazily around their bases – but it was not stirred merely by a heat source below. There was a definite current, a flow heading from one side of the pool to the other. The black poison was briefly surfacing before continuing its journey through the earth's coiling subterranean channels.

But all that was of less concern to Eddie than the people inside the chamber. Lock, Hoyt and their team had descended almost to the surface of the foul lake, using the crystals as walkways. As Tova had warned, there were six other men with them. All were armed, this time with SIG 516 assault rifles rather than sub-machine guns; after what had happened in Norway and at Valhalla, Hoyt was taking absolutely no chances of being outgunned.

They were not expecting an attack, though. Instead, all eyes were on the man closest to the lake. Unsurprisingly, Hoyt and Lock had delegated the dangerous task of actually obtaining a sample of eitr to an underling. The mercenary, wearing protective yellow hazmat overalls and a filter mask over his face, was kneeling on a sloping slab of black crystal just a foot above the rippling oil. In front of him was a steel canister closely resembling the one containing Thor's Hammer, its hinged lid open. The man was operating a pump, carefully sucking up eitr through a snake-like metal hose and depositing it in the container. Which was almost full.

Lock was twenty feet away, higher up. 'How much longer?' he called impatiently.

'Almost done,' the pump operator replied, voice muffled.

'About time. I want this stuff back in our lab by the end of the day.'

Hoyt, further back, held in a cough. 'Sooner we get out of here, the better. We're probably gettin' cancer just breathing this shit.'

'Volkov told the CIA it was harmless,' said Lock.

'Yeah, but that was in the sixties, and they said cigarettes were harmless back then too.' He coughed again, then retreated up one of the spars.

Lock ignored him, watching the cylinder fill up with an expression of near awe. 'The Vikings were right,' he said, almost to himself. 'Life and death in one substance.' The awe turned to expectant greed. 'And we control it . . .'

Kagan made a sound of angry disgust, then glanced back across the bridge. Nina and Berkeley had found enough room to let Pravdin past, and the Russian was now moving to join the other three armed men. 'We will need to take them out quickly,' he told Eddie in a low voice. 'Can you hit them from here with that?' He glanced at the Wildey.

'Piece of piss, mate,' Eddie replied. 'Hoyt's mine, though. That bastard's finally going down.' He lined up his weapon on the oblivious American.

'When I say,' Kagan ordered. 'We must get them all at once.'

The Englishman reluctantly held his finger off the trigger.

'You'll need to be fast – you've got to get two of 'em each before they can react.'

'We will,' Kagan assured him. The officer issued rapid instructions, then took aim with his own weapon. 'We have our targets – we will fire on three. Are you ready?'

'Yeah,' Eddie replied. Below, Hoyt hopped across to another ledge. The Wildey tracked him.

The second soldier finally reached the rest of the team, readying his AK-12. He nodded to Kagan. 'Okay,' said the Russian. 'One, two—'

A loud bang echoed around the shaft – but it was not a gunshot.

Eddie felt the crossing jolt beneath him. 'Shit!' he gasped, instantly realising what had happened. Pravdin's arrival had put too much weight on the unsupported middle of the bridge – and the stress lines were now becoming fractures. Below, Hoyt looked up in surprise at the unexpected sound. 'Move, get off the—'

The crystal sheared apart.

501

ANDY MCDERMOTT

34

Eddie was already moving, about to dive for safety – but Kagan blocked his way, his accumulated injuries making him fractionally slower to respond. The crystal span fell, taking them with it.

Pravdin had realised the danger. He leapt back at the ledge on which Nina and Berkeley were standing—

And fell short.

He clawed desperately at the side of the protruding outcrop. His fingertips found purchase on the scales – only for them to crumble under his weight. The soldier fell with a horrible scream, the sound abruptly cut off as he smashed against another crystal bridge below and tumbled into the eitr, kicking up a viscid splash and a cloud of steam as the black ooze swallowed him.

The other men on the collapsing bridge barely fared better. The great chunk of crystal beneath Eddie and Kagan pulverised a narrower structure as it dropped, the impact slowing its fall – and throwing the Russian clear to land heavily atop a steep ledge on the shaft's side.

Eddie was also sent flying, plunging past Kagan to crash down on a lower crystalline span. He skidded across it, just barely clamping his left hand around a protruding spike in time to stop himself from going over the edge. Maslov landed beside him with a pained cry. Shattered chunks of the demolished bridge pounded both men.

The chaos continued below. 'Jesus *Christ*!' yelled Hoyt as the huge crystal block plummeted into the cavern, disintegrating more black spires in a glass-shattering cacophony as it fell. He ducked behind one of the larger columns as shrapnel scythed past.

One of his men was not so quick to react, looking up in shock at the noise—

The falling slab hammered him flat. The crystal he was using as a walkway exploded into pieces, splashing back into the eitr from which they had been formed. The broken bridge rolled over, demolishing more spars and black stalagmites and crunching over the tops of spikes growing just beneath the lake's surface before coming to rest in a nest of rubble.

Nina watched in horror. 'Eddie!' she cried, darting to the edge of the outcrop to see him sprawled precariously thirty feet below. It was hard to be sure in the pale light of the globes, but it seemed possible to climb down and circumnavigate the shaft's outer wall in a spiral to reach him. 'Hold on, I'm com—'

Another sharp crack, this time under her feet.

The outcrop's edge splintered away. She threw herself backwards, but was already falling—

One hand caught the newly torn edge – and she shrieked as razor-like shards cut into her skin. Her grip faltered . . .

And failed.

Fear punched her heart as she dropped, nothing below but the simmering black pool of eitr—

Berkeley grabbed her wrist.

Nina yelled again as her shoulder joint abruptly took her full weight, muscles and tendons crackling. 'Hold on, hold on!'

Berkeley gasped. He had dived to catch her, lying on his belly with both arms over the edge of the broken outcrop.

'Pull me up!' she wailed.

'I can't – get enough leverage!' He strained to wriggle backwards, but couldn't raise his arms any higher. 'Grab the wall!'

'I'm trying!' She flailed her free hand, trying to find purchase, but the newly exposed surface was glassy-smooth. In the corner of her eye she saw a more ragged piece of broken crystal level with her thigh. She stretched for it – but in the process her Kalashnikov slipped from her shoulder.

She flicked her arm up just as its strap slithered over her fingers, casting it across a gap to clatter on to one of the spans below. Freed of the unbalancing weight, she managed to reach the protrusion and steady herself – but with no footholds she couldn't lift herself any higher. The eitr pool swayed hungrily below her.

The man at the lake's surface had almost fallen into it as the slabs around him shuddered, having to drop the pump to grab the sample container's carrying strap before it toppled into the ooze. 'Keep hold of it, for God's sake!' Lock yelled, clinging to a narrow crystal pillar. 'What the hell just happened?'

'You won't fuckin' *believe* this,' Hoyt snarled, emerging from cover and looking up the shaft. 'It's *Chase!*' He unshouldered his assault rifle.

Eddie felt nothing beneath his feet. He looked around to discover that his legs were hanging out over the side of the crossing. Wincing from the pain of his landing, he pulled them back—

Bullets ripped into the crystal under him.

'Chase, you motherfucker!' bellowed Hoyt as he blazed away with the SIG. Both Eddie and Maslov scrambled along the top of the natural bridge as more rounds chipped away at its underside. 'Come on, you Limey bastard!'

The other mercenaries joined the attack. The cavern echoed with the deafening roar of automatic fire. But even over the noise, Eddie still heard the shrill crunch of fracturing crystal as the bridge beneath him weakened . . .

More gunfire – but from higher up.

Kagan's AK-12 blazed. One of the mercenaries reeled backwards as the Russian's bullets ripped through his torso, flopping into the black lake. The others ducked for shelter behind the snaking pillars.

Eddie seized his chance and leaned over the bridge to take aim with his Wildey. He had lost track of Hoyt's position in the confusion, but the light from one of the floating globes cast a crouching shadow from behind a small crystal spire – which exploded like a bomb as a Magnum round hit it, the bullet continuing through the stalagmite to hit a lurking mercenary in the throat. The last Russian soldier joined the assault, sending bursts of Kalashnikov fire at the mercenaries.

Above, Berkeley was still struggling to pull Nina back up. 'Hold on!'

'Whaddya *think* I'm doing?' she protested.

'There's a – a rock,' he rasped. 'Going to try to – brace myself against it.' The scientist changed tack, squirming sideways rather than backwards. One leg found purchase against a chunk of stone . . .

Bumping the steel canister as it did so.

Berkeley had dropped it when he dived to save Nina. The only thing preventing it from rolling away was a wedge-like stone chip – and now that had been knocked away.

The container clunked across the ledge, picking up speed.

Berkeley let out a stifled shriek as he saw it trundling towards oblivion, but could do nothing to stop it without dropping Nina. 'Thor's Hammer!' was all he had time to gasp before it went over the edge.

Kagan glimpsed the flash of metal above. 'No!' he cried, breaking off from his attack to stare in helpless horror at the canister as it fell past Nina towards the oily lake—

It clipped a small crystal jutting out from the wall, snapping it off at its base – but the impact was just enough to jolt it on to a new trajectory. It hit a span and bounced down it before falling again. This time, it made a solid landing on another crystalline bridge in the chamber with a noise like the ringing of a dull bell.

Lock heard the sound and looked up to find its source. 'Sons of bitches,' he muttered on seeing the container. 'Slavin was right – they were working on a counter-agent.' He raised his voice. 'Hoyt! Don't let them get near that canister!'

'Only thing they'll be getting near is the Pearly Gates,' Hoyt shouted back. He changed his hold on the SIG, bringing his hand to the attachment mounted beneath its barrel.

An M203 grenade launcher.

He lined it up on the bullet-scarred span above. 'Fire in the hole!'

Eddie heard the warning shout. 'Oh, *fuck!*' he gasped, scrambling forward as a flat shotgun-like blast echoed from below—

The 40mm grenade hit the crystal bridge – and detonated.

Maslov was almost directly above the point of impact. The blast disintegrated the slab beneath him, sending his shredded body cartwheeling across the bottom of the shaft to slam into a dagger-sharp crystal growing from the wall, the black point bursting out of his chest in a spray of blood. The man hung grotesquely for a moment, limbs swaying, before his weight tore the spike loose. He fell into the cavern, landing with a crack of bones on a bed of broken shards.

Eddie was flung into the air as the broken bridge kicked upwards beneath him. He made a hard landing on the stump of the destroyed crossing, his momentum sending him skidding over the edge.

He fell—

And landed on one of the inflatable light globes.

It ruptured with a flat bang, but still cushioned him just enough to survive the drop without breaking any bones. The touchdown was far from painless, though, the battery pack and light clusters inside the globe leaving heavy bruises. The destroyed bridge plunged past him to crash down on top of the rubble piled up below.

Hoyt quickly reloaded the launcher. 'Oh, I got you now . . .' he said with a cruel grin, lining up his sights on the dazed Englishman—

'Don't!' Lock shouted. Hoyt looked at him in surprise. 'We still have to get out of here, you idiot! If you take out any more of the big crystals, we won't be able to climb back up!'

Annoyed, the mercenary leader brought his hand back to the SIG's trigger – only to see Eddie jump down and drop out of sight behind the debris. 'God damn it!' he snarled.

Kagan had flinched back from the explosion's shrapnel. Now he recovered and brought his gun back towards the targets below—

Hoyt spotted the movement and fired, forcing the Russian to retreat as crystalline splinters stabbed at him.

'Orbach!' Lock shouted to the man at the lake's edge. 'Secure the sample! We've got to get it out of here.' The mercenary nodded, closing the lid over the black poison inside the steel jar and pushing a button. A latch snapped into place, and a red LED turned green to confirm that the container was sealed.

Nina looked fearfully down at the cavern below, then back up at Berkeley as he managed to brace his other foot against the rock. He strained to lift her, raising her by several inches, but still couldn't manoeuvre her within reach of a firm handhold. 'Nina, I – I can't get you any higher!' Their eyes met. 'I'm sorry,' he whispered, the apology completely genuine.

She saw helpless surrender in his gaze – but refused to accept it. 'Swing me,' she gasped.

'What?'

'Swing me!' Instead of holding on to the broken nub, she pushed against it, rocking herself sideways. 'I can reach that ledge!'

'You'll never make it!' The crystal spar she had spotted was about ten feet below her – and almost as far off to the side.

'I will if you throw me hard enough.' She gave him a pained grin. 'Come on, I'm sure you spent your time in jail thinking about tossing me off a high cliff.'

'Don't remind me,' he replied, but with a very faint hint of amusement. His grip tightened as he prepared himself. 'Okay, you ready?'

Nina took a breath. 'Yeah.' She tensed her arm. 'All right, and . . . *swing!*'

She shoved against the rock as Berkeley hauled her sideways. Her legs swung across the gap. Not far enough; she pulled herself back, then pushed again. Another sweep of the human pendulum, wider this time – then again, going even further. 'One more!'

He complied, grunting with effort. Nina swept back, then pushed herself off the protruding rock for the last time. '*Let go!*'

Berkeley released her – and she sailed across the gap, gravity reclaiming her at the top of her arc. The crystal rushed past—

She threw out both arms to catch it, hitting hard. The impact felt like a baseball bat across her chest, the pain so intense she couldn't breathe. Her nails rasped at the scabrous surface, but she couldn't get a proper grip, her own weight dragging her inexorably over the edge . . .

A gasp of sheer terror – and she dug her clawed hands into a crack in the crystal. Fingernails snapped, but adrenalin blotted out the pain. Drawing on some deep reserve of strength, she dragged herself on to the span, exhausted.

Below, Lock looked around at Orbach as the masked mercenary, carrying the container of eitr, hurried up from the lake towards his employer. 'Have you got it?' Lock demanded. The other man showed him the green light on the canister. 'Okay, good. We need to get moving.' He raised his voice. 'Cover us! We're leaving!'

'I'm gonna take care of Chase,' Hoyt insisted, his tone making it clear that he would not accept any orders to the contrary. Lock frowned, but nodded. 'Franks, with me – the rest of you give the boss cover!'

One of the mercenaries joined Hoyt, the pair hopping from spar to spar as they advanced on the Englishman. The other two resumed their assault on Kagan as Lock and Orbach ducked between the crystalline columns to reach an ascending span.

Kagan saw them go, but was forced to pull back as more bullets smacked against his cover. 'Chase!' he shouted in warning. 'They're coming for you!'

★

Behind the slabs of broken black crystal, Eddie had caught his breath, but he now faced other threats apart from the approaching gunmen. The heat at the bottom of the cavern was nauseating, and every inhalation stung as the rising fumes scoured at his nasal passages. He was only just above the surface of the eitr lake – and puddles of the deadly ooze swelled up through gaps in the raft of debris as his weight pressed down on them. He hurriedly sidestepped away from the nearest, horribly aware that a mere splash could kill him in minutes.

If he lasted that long. 'Go around that end,' he heard Hoyt order. Footsteps crunched over broken shards on the other side of his cover, the two mercenaries separating to circle him. He raised the Wildey, but knew he would only have time for one shot – he would never be able to turn and aim fast enough to take out the second man behind him.

Unless he drove one of them back, even for a couple of seconds . . .

A section of smashed stalactite about two feet long poked up nearby, one end submerged in the eitr. As far as he could tell in the unnatural light from the globes, its upper end was free of splattered black oil.

If he was wrong, he would die. But that was about to happen anyway—

Eddie grabbed the stalactite. Momentary relief that it was dry, then he tugged it. Eitr glooped up from below as it came free. He swung it around, using centrifugal force to keep the deadly substance dripping off the crystal away from him – then lobbed it at one end of the makeshift barricade.

'*Fuck!*' Hoyt gasped. The American jumped back from the poisonous missile, arms swinging as he stumbled on the uneven surface.

Eddie took full advantage of his enemy's moment of

distraction, spinning as Franks rounded the opposite end of the broken bridge, SIG at the ready—

The Wildey boomed, the bullet blowing the man off his feet. He crashed down on his back – and part of the unstable floor shattered, the steaming ooze beneath welling up and swallowing him. Limbs flailing, the mercenary was sucked down into the lake.

The Englishman was already rushing in the other direction. He had to take out Hoyt before he recovered—

He rounded the smashed span – to find that he was too late.

Hoyt had regained his footing. Both men's eyes met as they swung their guns towards each other—

The American fired first – but his shot was not a bullet. His forefinger was on the grenade launcher's trigger.

Another shotgun blast – and Eddie reeled in pain as the projectile struck his shoulder.

But it didn't explode. The grenade needed to travel a minimum distance before arming, a safety feature to protect the shooter. Instead, it was deflected away across the cavern.

Hoyt saw Eddie stagger and drop the Wildey, grinning in triumph as he brought his hand back to the rifle's grip to finish him off—

The grenade hit a cluster of crystals – and detonated.

Eddie was sent sprawling by the blast, broken fragments hitting his back. Though Hoyt was further away, he was facing the explosion, and he screwed up his face in pain as shrapnel stabbed at his eyes. He lurched backwards, this time falling. The rifle landed stock first and was jolted from his hand.

Above, Nina heard the explosion and fought through her fatigue to look down into the cavern. A swelling cloud of smoke marked where the grenade had hit – and worryingly close to it she saw her husband lying face down. Hoyt was a few yards away, one hand to his face – then he shook off the pain to search for his gun. 'Eddie, look out!'

Eddie heard his wife's voice through the ringing in his ears. He raised his head and saw Hoyt crawling for the fallen SIG. 'No you fucking *don't*,' he snarled, forcing himself up with a surge of pure hate-driven energy.

Face cut and bloodied, Hoyt reached the gun – just as Eddie dived at him. Both men rolled across the unstable ground, rivulets of eitr stabbing towards them as the crystals shifted and sank. 'Twat!' the Yorkshireman spat as he drove a punch into Hoyt's stomach. The American let out a strangled gasp. Eddie got on top of him, clamping one hand around his throat as he drew back his arm to deliver another brutal blow at Hoyt's face—

Hoyt's groping hand found a coconut-sized hunk of debris – which he smacked against the side of Eddie's head. 'Yeah, you son of a bitch!' he rasped as his opponent cried out. Another strike, and Eddie fell sideways, releasing his hold. 'Come on, you bastard!' He jumped up, kicking the Englishman in the ribs and sending him tumbling towards the edge of the eitr pool.

Nina helplessly watched the brawl – then spotted something below her. Dull highlights along dark metal were picked out by one of the glowing globes.

Her AK-12. It had landed atop a crooked spar that crossed about nine feet below her position. 'Logan!' she called. Berkeley peered over the ledge. 'I'm going for the gun. You try to reach Thor's Hammer – we've got to get it to the pool, no matter what!'

'But it's all the way down there!' he objected, pointing at the canister. It was still wedged between two intercrossing arms of black crystal.

'You've got more chance of getting to it – the gap's too wide for me to jump over. But you can reach it by going down that.' She indicated one of the snake-like columns, which in its growth had spiralled around part of the shaft's circumference before a slow-motion collision with another rising crystal pillar had forced it back upwards.

'It's too steep! I'm not a monkey.'

'If you don't, then in about ten minutes you'll be a radioactive cinder!'

Berkeley rapidly reconsidered. 'Okay, I'll try.' He gingerly lowered himself over the side of the outcrop.

'Good!' She crawled along the slanting span until she was above the gun, then gripped the crystal and slid over the edge – becoming acutely aware that her landing zone was barely a foot wide, and directly above the eitr . . .

No time to hesitate. The missile was still on its way. She looked down again, lining up with her worryingly narrow target, then dropped.

Hanging down, the actual fall was only a few feet, but that was still enough to jar her as she landed, making her tip backwards over the void. She gasped, flailing—

The movement counterbalanced her, just for a moment. She seized it, bending at the knees to drop to all fours, gasping for breath.

The Kalashnikov was a few feet away. She scrambled to it.

'Nina!' Kagan shouted, seeing what she was doing. 'Lock is getting away! I need cover!'

Nina retrieved the rifle. Her first thought was to help her husband, but as she looked down, she realised that the Russian's demand had to take priority. Lock and the man carrying the eitr sample were scaling the angled crystal pillars, zigzagging upwards. She didn't have a clear line of fire on them, the two men flitting in and out of her view between other black columns – but she *could* see the mercenaries still in the cavern, both of whom had their weapons locked on Kagan's position.

She took aim at one of the men below, and fired.

The bullet missed by mere inches, cracking off a crystal. But it achieved its purpose. Both men swung their guns around to find the new threat. Nina jerked back as shots ripped into the span beneath her—

Kagan popped out from his own cover and fired. One man went down in a spray of blood as several rounds struck him in the head and chest. The other immediately realised where the greater danger lay and spun back to retarget the Russian.

He wasn't fast enough. Another burst from the AK-12 hit home. He screamed, losing his footing and plunging into the eitr. Sizzling steam gushed up around him as he sank into the turgid depths.

'Get Thor's Hammer down to the lake!' Kagan called to Berkeley, who was unsteadily picking his way down the wall. 'I'll get Lock!' He made a running jump to another spar to intercept the American and his follower.

Nina turned her attention back to Eddie, whose battle with Hoyt had taken them out of sight behind more crystal columns. 'God damn it!' she hissed. She slung the rifle, then searched for a line of sight.

Below, Eddie was still on the defensive as Hoyt forced him ever closer to the edge of the eitr. The mercenary's height advantage over the former SAS soldier also gave him greater reach, and he was making full use of it, able to strike repeatedly while preventing Eddie from retaliating. 'Looks like you screwed it all up again, Chase!' said the American, feigning an attack with his right hand only to dart in with a painful punch from his left. 'I guess failing's what you're best at, huh?' Another blow, the Englishman barely deflecting it.

'You don't fucking know me,' Eddie growled.

'And nor does your wife up there! You didn't tell her you *murdered* the girl you were supposed to rescue? I'd call that a major-league fuck-up!'

Another punch rushed at Eddie's head—

This time, he wasn't quite fast enough to block it, taking a sense-jangling blow that left him staggering. One foot came down heavily on a crystal shard – which sank, forcing up a boil of dark slime. Only the Yorkshireman's reflexes kept his boot from slipping into the eitr, but he still stumbled backwards against one of the large vertical pillars.

Hoyt saw his chance and aimed a vicious kick at his adversary's groin. Eddie snapped down his right arm to shield himself from a blow that would have ended the fight on the spot – but still screamed at a searing bolt of pain as the American's steel-toed boot fractured one of the bones in his hand.

The mercenary struck again, this time slamming a knee up into his stomach. Choking and sickened, Eddie slumped against the base of the column.

Hoyt drew back to deliver a kick to the winded man's face – then spotted something at his feet and picked it up instead. It was a shard of black crystal, over a foot long, with a razor-edged tip as sharp as a spearpoint. He grinned as he raised it, ready to plunge it into Eddie's throat. 'Been waiting eight years for this—'

Blood and shredded flesh burst from his shoulder.

Hoyt reeled, staring in shocked agony at the bullet's exit wound – as Eddie fought through the pain of his own injuries and grabbed the black dagger, twisting it to point vertically. 'Me too.'

He sprang from the floor, all his strength driving the shard upwards into Hoyt's jaw.

The tip stabbed through the tissue under the mercenary's chin, tearing through his tongue and the soft palate above before striking and snapping bone. A wet crackle came from inside the American's skull.

Hoyt stared in bug-eyed horror at Eddie, too shocked to move – and unable to scream with his airways choked by gushing blood. The Englishman twisted the spike, corkscrewing it deeper into his enemy's brain. 'I didn't fail,' he said in a growling whisper. 'I *won*. I beat you eight years ago, you just didn't know it . . .' He yanked out the shard, more blood sluicing from the gaping hole under the mercenary's jaw. 'And I won again now.'

Hoyt clawed desperately at his torn throat, then slumped to his knees, a strangled rattling sound escaping his gaping mouth. The Yorkshireman stared coldly at him for a moment – before launching into sudden movement. 'Now *fuck off*!' he roared, kicking Hoyt hard in the side of his head and bowling him into the lake.

The mercenary was still alive as the steaming black ooze swallowed him. His skin sizzled on contact with the lethal poison, a gurgling howl finally escaping from Hoyt's mouth as the eitr bubbled up over his neck, his face . . . and then he was gone, nothing but sludgy ripples left to mark his passing.

Eddie dropped the gore-soaked dagger and wearily turned to find his saviour. It took him a moment to spot Nina in the shaft high above, having found a clear firing angle between the crystalline pillars. 'Are you okay?' she asked anxiously.

'Just about,' he called back. 'But it would've been a lot easier if you'd aimed at his head.'

She raised the AK-12 with a helpless shrug. 'I *did*!'

He managed a pained smile, then heard another shout from above. 'Nina!' cried Berkeley. He had reached Thor's Hammer. 'I've got it, I've got the—'

Another burst of gunfire echoed through the chamber. Not from Nina's AK-12, but a SIG.

'Logan!' she cried, seeing her former colleague flinch, then collapse. Lines of dark red trickled down Berkeley's coat from the three scorched bullet holes across his chest.

35

Orbach lowered his rifle. 'Good shot,' Lock told him. 'Now keep moving.' He pointed to a nearby crystal span that angled upwards. 'That way.'

Nina was still above the pair. She brought her Kalashnikov around, but from her current position couldn't see them through the serpentine columns. 'Oh my God, Logan!' She looked back at the other archaeologist. 'Logan, can you hear me?'

He was still for a moment, then slowly raised his head. 'Nina, I . . .' he gasped, blood oozing from the side of his mouth. 'I'm sorry, I . . . I messed up. But at least . . . I can do this.'

With his dying breath, he stretched out a trembling arm – and pushed the steel canister over the edge.

The heavy container plunged down the shaft—

It hit a damaged crystal lancing across the cavern about ten feet above Eddie. Glassy splinters showered over him, but the metal vessel didn't fall any further, wedged into the broken surface.

'Eddie!' Nina shouted from high above. 'It's Thor's Hammer – get it to the eitr!'

He searched for a way to reach it. A pillar rose at an angle close to the canister. Weaving around the pools of eitr bubbling up through the rubble, he headed towards it.

*

Lock had also seen Thor's Hammer fall. 'Dammit!' he snarled, pausing midway through his climb to another ascending spar. 'Orbach, don't let him reach that cylinder! Take him out!'

Orbach stopped and looked down the shaft, finding that Eddie was partially obscured behind a damaged spire. He put down the eitr, propping the sealed container against a stubby spike jutting from the span beneath his feet and backing up to find a clear line of fire.

He only had to move a couple of metres to get an unobstructed view. The SIG locked on to its target . . .

The crunch and scrabble of running footsteps came from one side, above him.

Orbach looked up – as Kagan leapt from a higher crossing to slam down beside the eitr canister, AK-12 in one hand.

The mercenary whirled—

Kagan was quicker.

The Kalashnikov's thudding bark echoed through the shaft, a burst of bullets stitching bloody rents across Orbach's torso. The spasming American fell over the edge back into the cavern below. The point of a stalagmite was waiting for him, the man's agonised scream cut short as he was impaled on the ragged spike.

The Russian turned, drawing back one foot to kick the eitr into the pit below—

A single gunshot came from behind him.

Kagan let out a startled gasp, shock blotting out the pain of the bullet that had just ripped into his back. The AK fell from his hands and dropped down the shaft. He tried to complete his movement, to send the eitr over the edge . . . but his body would not cooperate. His knees buckled, and he slumped across the top of the spar, legs hanging over one side. The canister was just out of reach, and the mere act of reaching for it shifted his balance, the weight of his lower body slowly dragging him over the edge.

Lock jumped back down and advanced on him, faint wisps of smoke still streaming from the barrel of his handgun. 'You made the same mistake Chase did in 'Nam, my friend,' he said smugly. 'The guy giving the orders – you thought he never gets his hands dirty, huh? Afraid not.' He reached the fallen Russian. 'And you want to know something else, Kagan? Back in Vietnam, you went to all that trouble to find out what you could about the eitr from that girl – but there was nothing *to* learn!'

Kagan forced out words, tasting blood. 'What . . . do you mean?'

'The BSA had already secretly taken samples from her before she even left Germany, but the results were worthless. We didn't find out anything about the nature of the eitr from her . . . but we used Slavin to make you think that you *could*. She was just a decoy, a way for us to learn about your lines of research.' Lock leaned closer, gloating. 'You exposed Unit 201 for *nothing*! I just wanted you to know before you died – payback for all the trouble you caused me in Washington, you bastard.'

And with that, he raised his boot to Kagan's head, about to shove him over the edge—

'No!' Nina cried. She had moved across the shaft to get line of sight on Lock below, emerging from cover by one of the light globes. The surprised American raised his gun, but Nina had already lined up her AK-12 . . .

She fired – just as Lock jinked sideways. The single bullet shredded his left sleeve, a small puff of blood amongst the torn material. Lock barked in pain, but the wound was only superficial.

And the charging handle of Nina's gun had locked back with a sharp *clack*. She had used most of the AK's ammunition fighting the wolves, and now the rifle was empty.

Lock recovered from the shock of his injury. He took aim at her, a tight smile of triumph twisting his face—

Nina kicked the light globe like an oversized football, sending it sailing across the gap at Lock.

He fired. The bullet punctured the inflated latex sphere, but cracked against the cluster of LEDs and batteries at its heart rather than continuing through. Before he could react, the deflating globe hit him and knocked him back.

He gasped in sudden fear as he lost his footing – and fell.

The drop was only eight feet, on to a narrower span below. He clawed desperately for grip to save himself from another, deadly plunge, but was forced to let go of his gun. The weapon spun down the shaft and vanished into the glutinous void.

Kagan's slide continued inexorably, the Russian's grip faltering. 'Grigory!' Nina called, scurrying to a position where she could jump to reach him. 'Hang on, I'm coming!'

'No . . .' Kagan growled. His waist was now over the side, only his hold on the edge of the crystal keeping him from falling. 'I am . . . gone. But so is . . . the eitr!'

'Don't!' shouted Nina, but too late.

Kagan dug the nails of his left hand into the scabrous surface and lashed with his right at the container of eitr. His fingers just caught it, jarring it loose from where it had been wedged – but the movement cost him his life. He slipped and plummeted without a sound, hitting the eitr lake with a flat splash and vanishing for ever beneath the oily liquid.

The canister wobbled . . . then tipped over the edge—

Its strap caught on the crystal spike.

Nina and Lock were both frozen for a moment, staring at the steel cylinder as it swung above the cavern – then they burst into motion, Lock dragging himself up to reach it from below as Nina dropped the empty AK-12 and leapt across to the span from which Kagan had fallen.

Eddie reached the canister containing Thor's Hammer. He had heard the gunshots from above and was filled with fear for his wife, but he could do nothing to help her. Instead, he picked up the heavy steel container and jumped back down to the unstable island of rubble, debris crunching and shifting beneath his feet.

There was a handgrip set into a recess in the lid. Holding the cylinder as steady as he could, he clenched his fist around it and twisted. A moment of worry as it refused to move, then he felt the seal give as he applied more force. Still unscrewing the lid, he made his way to the broken shoreline.

At first he thought that the level of the eitr had risen, but then he realised that the smashed crystal remnants on which he was standing were sinking into the ooze. Black boils swelled all around him, threatening to burst. 'Let's fucking get this over with,' he muttered, coughing as the acrid vapour rising from the lake stung his nose and throat.

Another turn – and the lid came free.

He tossed it aside, seeing what was inside the canister for the first time. Article 3472 – Thor's Hammer – was, like the substance it was intended to counter, a thick black slime, a new and even more foul odour coming from it. Eddie recoiled; while the fumes from the eitr might not be lethal, he had no idea if the same was true of its counter-agent.

The rubble shifted beneath him, the liquid lapping closer to his boots. He took a step back, supporting the container with both hands. No time for speeches, or even smart-arse comments: he knew what he had to do.

With a grunt, he lobbed Thor's Hammer into the eitr.

The container flipped over as it arced down towards the heart of the lake. The black fluid sluiced out. The effect was immediate as it splashed into the eitr, a sizzling reaction sending up bursts of steaming vapour. A moment later, the canister hit the surface with a wet smack and sank out of sight . . .

The eitr immediately began to change.

A swirling, churning whirlpool of froth erupted where the cylinder had landed, and around it the glistening black oil turned a dull, sickly grey, the metamorphosis sweeping outwards.

As it reached the base of the great crystals, they too changed. Black scales turned grey, then flaked and crumbled, stress fractures stabbing upwards through the dark spires. One spar, angling almost horizontally from the surface until it hit the cavern's far wall, collapsed into the lake of ooze with a thunderous boom. Whatever else Thor's Hammer was doing to the eitr, it was clearly also affecting the crystals that had grown from it, removing the slight flexibility in their structure that had allowed them to curl and zigzag up the shaft like serpents – and without it, the huge natural formations were unable to support their own weight.

More crystals splintered with gunfire cracks as the discoloration seeped upwards. Eddie saw that his position was more dangerous than ever, any doubts disappearing when one of the light globes floating on the eitr ruptured as the sizzling froth ate through it. 'Oh, *fuckeration*!' he yelped, jumping back from the lake's edge as it crumbled and sank into the slime.

He ran for the crystal that Lock had used to make his ascent, hoping it would survive long enough for him to follow the American's route upwards – but swerved as he spotted his Wildey. The rubble beneath it was being eaten away by the chemical reaction spreading through the eitr, and the toxic substance was surging up from below, about to swallow the weapon—

Eddie snatched up the gun just before the liquid claimed it. 'No you fucking *don't*!' he gasped, changing course back to his escape route and pounding up it as fast as he dared. The span shifted under his weight, pieces shearing away where it scraped against other crystals below it.

Nina made an awkward landing, having to drop to all fours to keep her balance on the crystal bridge. She gripped it for a few seconds until she had stabilised, then looked down to locate Lock and the eitr canister.

The latter was still swaying from the jutting black spike, the green LED glowing. Lock was below it, standing on another span and reaching up for his prize—

Still on her knees, she lunged just as he clamped his hands around the sides of the cylinder and jerked it upwards to flick it free. She grabbed the strap as it fell away – but was now caught in a tug of war against a much stronger and heavier opponent. And Lock had secure footing, while she was unbalanced, arms outstretched as she struggled to keep her knees on the crossing's upper facet. She pulled as hard as she could, trying to snatch the canister from Lock's grip . . .

It wasn't enough.

A sharp yank from below tipped her forward – and for the second time in mere minutes an awful shock of fear slammed her heart as she fell.

She screamed – only for it to be cut off as she slammed to a joint-straining halt.

The strap had caught again, this time over the top of a cluster of larger spikes stabbing out from the flank of the crystalline span. They creaked alarmingly, black turning almost to white as fracture lines formed, but held firm. She was dangling just a couple of feet from Lock, but while he was standing firm on the narrow crossing, there was nothing below her except the now-seething surface of the eitr lake. *Eddie must have used Thor's Hammer*, she told herself as she glanced down, but that gave her neither help nor comfort.

She looked back at Lock. He was still gripping the inverted canister with both raised hands, but with Nina's entire weight now pulling against it was straining to keep his hold on the slick metal. If he let go, Nina would drop to her death – but he would also lose the eitr sample.

If he leaned across to *kick* Nina loose, however, the container would drop neatly back into his arms as she fell . . .

Lock had realised this too. His knuckles whitened as he tightened his grip on the stainless-steel cylinder, then he hesitantly lifted one leg to check that he could maintain his balance – before lashing out.

The toe of his boot hit Nina's calf. She imprisoned a cry behind clenched teeth, squeezing her hands more tightly around the strap. Another blow, this one less painful, but Lock was already lining up for a third strike. She looked up. The strap was bunched up in her grasp. She jerked one hand, clamping it back around the tough woven nylon and pulling herself upwards by a few inches.

Lock redirected his attack as Nina dragged herself up by another palm's-width. His boot cracked viciously against her ankle, her own sturdy Arctic footwear saving her from an agonising injury. Even so, she still squealed in pain as she dragged herself higher once more.

'God damn it, woman, you don't know when you're beaten,' he growled. 'Just give it up!' He struck again, this time landing a solid hit on her shin. Nina shrieked, the muscles in her hands burning as she clutched her lifeline. 'The eitr's mine!'

He pulled back his leg for the last time—

Nina strained to pull herself another few inches up the strap – and to Lock's surprise let go with one hand. 'You want it?' she gasped, stretching out her arm towards the eitr canister. '*Take it!*'

She jabbed her forefinger at the latch button. There was a click, the green LED turning red . . .

The lid released.

'*No!*' Lock cried – then his voice became a gargling scream as the container's deadly contents gushed over his face, his skin blistering and his nostrils and mouth filling with the black poison. He thrashed in mindless agony, globules of eitr flying from his dissolving flesh—

One of them hit Nina's left cheek.

It was only the tiniest drop, but it still felt as if she had been stabbed by a red-hot needle. A new terror filled her as she realised what had happened – but she had no time to react as Lock let go of the now empty container.

She plunged—

Strong hands seized her wrist.

'Gotcha!' Eddie yelled.

Lock let out a final choking wail. Most of the eitr had now run off his face, exposing the ruination it had wrought. Both his eyes were gone, black-tainted blood oozing from their sockets where the caustic toxin had dissolved the soft tissue. The flesh on his cheeks had almost liquefied to expose teeth and bone beneath. Bubbles gurgled from his throat . . . then he keeled over, tumbling back down the shaft to hit the seething froth filling the bottom of the cavern with a sizzling splash.

Eddie hauled Nina up, her feet gratefully finding purchase. 'You okay?'

'Yeah, but—'

'Great, now fucking *run*!' He hurried up the slope, pulling her behind him. 'Kagan's goop worked, but all the fucking crystals are *melting*! They're going to collapse!'

She looked down – and wished she hadn't as she saw a wave of diseased grey seeping up the crystalline pillars after them like ink through tissue paper. The smaller spars within the cavern were already breaking apart and falling back into the lake; the thicker structures snaking towards the surface could not be far behind.

A nightmare ascent followed. Every step was a strain as the pair clambered up the steep spans, switchbacking from one side of the shaft to the other as they hunted for navigable routes through the vertical maze. Nina spotted Berkeley's body as they passed, but there was no time to acknowledge his redemption and sacrifice.

Instead, she followed Eddie upwards, climbing and jumping between the crystal bridges. The cracks and booms from below grew ever louder as more of the eitr formations were destroyed by Thor's Hammer. Fractures scythed through the crystals around them—

Eddie abruptly stopped and shoved Nina against the rock wall, shielding her with his own body as one of the thinner of the great serpents disintegrated and plummeted past them, cascading debris smashing crossings as it fell. He looked up to see that the collapse had torn away almost a quarter of the winding pathways above. 'Shit! If another one goes like that, we'll never reach the top!'

'I can see the ropes,' Nina said, narrowing her eyes against the glare of the sky. They were about fifty feet from the lip of the shaft, the lines placed by Lock's team dangling over its edge.

Eddie scanned their surroundings. 'That way,' he said, pointing at one of the surviving crystals. They made their way around a ledge, then scrambled up. The span trembled underfoot, echoing snaps reaching them from below as more spires crumbled. 'Nearly there!'

They leapt across a gap to the final span, the ropes hanging tantalisingly above its top. Escape was in sight, but now Nina remembered that there was another danger waiting for them. 'How long before the missile gets here?'

Eddie glanced at his watch. 'Fuck! Two minutes, if that!'

'You're faster than me – get to the radio and tell the Russians. Don't worry about me.'

'Sorry, love, but that's my job!' He reached the ropes, then stopped and waited for her to catch up. 'Come on, come on!' he said, holding one out to her. 'Grab it, quick! The crystal's about to—'

A colossal boom came from far below.

Nina dived, grabbing the rope—

The remaining crystals lurched, then plunged down the shaft in unison as their corroded bases finally gave way, breaking apart as they smashed against each other. Even the sections that had spiralled up the walls and bonded with the blackened stone were scoured away by the falling debris, leaving only a vertical drop into the bowels of the earth.

Long seconds passed before the pounding clamour finally began to fade. Dust swirled around the shaft . . . and then, coughing, two figures painfully dragged themselves up the ropes on to the steep incline above. 'Oh my God,' gasped Nina. She wanted nothing more than to sit down and rest, but knew she had to keep going. 'Are you all right?'

'I'll live – but only for about a minute if we don't call Moscow,' Eddie replied, grimly hauling himself onwards. The slope became shallower. They let go of the ropes and ran for the surface, feet like lead. 'You know,' he gasped as they scrambled up the final few yards, 'if Tova's got any sense, she'll have buggered off in the chopper already.'

'Yeah, but I hope she left us the radio,' said Nina. The lip of the pit came into view as they both emerged into the light, the snow-topped runestone beyond. A gap had opened in the clouds, weak sunlight finding its way through, but her eyes were locked on the nearby helicopter. 'Thank God! Tova!'

Eddie ran ahead of her. 'Radio!' he yelled as Tova peered out of a cabin window. He waved furiously for her to open the hatch. 'Radio, radio! Radioradio*radio*!'

She opened the door and jumped out, the gun still in one hand – and Kagan's satellite transmitter in the other. 'Eddie, Nina! What happened!'

'Just turn on the radio!' the Englishman shouted as he pounded through the snow. By the time he reached her, she had done so. He snatched the unit from her. 'Hello, hello!' he said into it. 'Can you hear me? It's Eddie Chase – we used Thor's Hammer, we've neutralised the eitr! Abort the missile!'

Nothing for a few seconds, then a voice replied – in Russian. 'What the hell's he saying?' panted Nina as she arrived.

'I dunno!' Eddie turned to Tova. 'Do you?' She shook her head. 'For fuck's sake! English, *nyet Russkie*!' he told the radio. 'Abort! Abortski!'

His wife clutched his sleeve. 'Uh, Eddie . . .'

'What— Oh, fuck.' He looked around to see a small black dot against the grey clouds to the north-east.

Small . . . but growing.

'It's the missile,' Nina said in disbelief. 'Oh God, it's here!'

Eddie tried the radio again. 'English, English! Er . . . *Anglijski*!' he said, dredging up something from his limited knowledge of the Russian language. 'Speak bloody English, and *abort the missile!*'

Nina held him tighter. 'It's too late.' The dot was still growing. A faint jet-engine shrill became audible over the wind. She exchanged a last look with her husband. 'Eddie, I love—'

The missile suddenly angled steeply upwards, disappearing into the overhanging cloud layer. 'What happened? Where's it going?' she asked.

'They aborted it!' Tova cried with an astonished smile.

Eddie's expression told Nina that was not the case. 'It's going up – so it can drop straight back down into the hole.' As if in response, the missile reappeared through the gash in the clouds as it kept climbing . . . then reached the top of its arc and rolled over to make a final plunge to earth.

He shouted into the radio once more, gripping it so tightly that its casing creaked. 'The eitr's been neutralised, Thor's Hammer worked – I repeat, Thor's Hammer worked! Abort the missile!' The cruise began its vertical descent. 'Abort the missile! Jesus Christ, *abort the fucking missile!* Come on, you stupid beetroot-eating bastards, *abort—*'

The pale grey pencil of the Kh-102 rocketed towards them—

And exploded.

Nina shrieked, thinking that the nuclear warhead had detonated – then realised that if it had, she would not still be there to have the thought. 'Whoa, *cover!*' Eddie yelped, grabbing both women and pulling them against the helicopter's fuselage as smoking debris showered over the plateau.

The missile's burning engine and warhead, the heaviest parts of the weapon, continued on their final course and plunged into the opening. Further crashes and explosions echoed up from below as they hit the collapsing remains of the serpentine crystal pillars.

Smaller chunks of debris smacked into the chopper, denting aluminium and cracking Perspex. Then the metal hail stopped, the explosion's echoes fading to leave only the ever-present moan of the wind.

The Englishman peered cautiously at the pit. Dark smoke had replaced the pale steam rising from the gash in the earth. 'Buggeration and, well, you know,' he said, moving into the open. 'That was *too* bloody close.'

Tova gazed wide-eyed at the scene. 'Is it safe? The nuclear bomb – if it exploded, won't it . . .'

'We're okay,' Eddie assured her. 'The missile blew up, not the warhead. It's down in the pit somewhere – hopefully at the bottom of a big pool of slime where nobody can dig it up.'

'And what about the eitr? Did Thor's Hammer work?'

'Yeah.' He gave the Swede a smile. 'Ragnarök's cancelled. We killed your Midgard Serpent, and didn't even get poisoned by it. So we came out of it better than Thor. Didn't we, love?'

He addressed that last to his wife, but got no answer. 'Nina?' he said, looking back at her.

Her face was turned slightly away from him. There was no relief or triumph in her expression, just a stricken horror. 'Eddie, we . . . we didn't get all of the eitr.'

He moved closer, feeling a rising sense of dread even without knowing why. He had never seen such a look on her face before – but he *had* seen it on others, in combat. It was the realisation of the trapped, of the wounded . . . of someone who knew they were going to die. 'Nina,' he said, now fearful. 'What is it?'

Nina looked straight at him. On the pale skin of her left cheek was revealed a small red mark, as if she had been burned by a flying ember.

But there had been no fires in the pit.

Her voice quavered as she spoke. 'When I poured out Lock's eitr—'

'No, don't,' Eddie begged her. If she didn't say the words, it might not have happened . . .

But she continued, tears swelling in her eyes. 'I got . . . I got splashed. It was only a drop, but . . . oh, God.' What remained of her resolve crumbled. 'Oh my God,' she gasped, her voice breaking.

Eddie moved closer, but Nina backed off, turning her reddened cheek away from him. 'Don't touch me,' she whispered. 'There could be more of it on me, I might be . . . contaminated.'

He reached out, desperate to comfort her, to feel her skin – but stopped short, letting his shaking hand slowly fall. 'Nina . . .'

'We need to get out of here,' she forced herself to say through her tears. She opened the helicopter's hatch and climbed inside.

Eddie stared after her, for a long moment unable to move. Tova spoke, but he didn't register her words. 'I'm fine. Let's go,' he said in gruff automatic reply, taking the gun from her and stepping away to let her board the aircraft.

Hoyt's mocking words returned to him. *Just can't protect your women, can you, Chase?*

He looked back at the pit – then emptied the weapon at the sneering ghosts above it with a roar of fury and despair.

Epilogue

New York City

Oswald Seretse regarded the letter on his desk with solemn dismay. 'Are you *absolutely* sure this is what you want to do, Nina?'

She had to compose herself before replying, emotions churning beneath her outward calm. 'Yes, I'm afraid so. That's my resignation from the IHA, effective immediately.'

'Mine too,' Eddie added curtly from a chair in the corner of the official's office.

'But why?' Seretse asked. 'You haven't given me a reason.'

'Do I need to?' said Nina.

'No, but—'

'Then can you please respect my decision?' He was taken aback by her hard tone; she softened it in apology. 'Believe me, if the circumstances were different I wouldn't be leaving. But . . . I have to. There are other things I want to do – *need* to do.'

'Such as writing your book?'

533

She was a little surprised. 'You heard about that?'

'Having my own office at the UN does not isolate me from the latest gossip. And I would be a poor diplomat if I did not keep my ear to the ground.'

'I guess so. But yes, I've already accepted the offer to write it. Don't worry, I'll vet everything through the UN before publication. The IHA's secrets are safe with me.'

'I never doubted it,' Seretse assured her. 'But on the subject of secrets, you clearly have some of your own. I am being pressured, particularly by the US State Department, to find out exactly what happened on your most recent operation. We know there was a gun battle at the lake in Norway that resulted in several deaths, and that according to Mr Trulli and the other survivors you left the scene with a Russian; but after that you vanished from the radar until reappearing in Moscow, then travelled back to Sweden . . . and finally turned up in northern Canada! All without a word of explanation beyond your decidedly sparse report. And Dr Skilfinger has been equally uncommunicative, except to say that you and Eddie saved her life.' He leaned forward. 'What *is* going on, Nina?'

'I can't tell you, Oswald,' she replied. 'I'm sorry. But part of the IHA's remit from its founding six years ago was to make sure that potentially dangerous archaeological discoveries stayed out of the wrong hands. As director of the IHA, I made a decision to restrict all information about what we found, for reasons of global security.'

'Even from the nations funding the IHA?'

'*Especially* from them,' Eddie rumbled.

Seretse eyed him. 'I see.' He leaned back. 'Would I be correct in assuming that if the information were to be released, it could result in, shall we say, *disagreements* between certain members of the UN Security Council? Certain nuclear-armed members?'

'To put it mildly, yes,' Nina told him.

The diplomat nodded. 'Then I had better accept your resignation immediately.' He slid the letter across the desk to an out-tray. 'After all, I can't use my position as United Nations liaison to demand answers from somebody who no longer works for the organisation, can I?'

Nina managed a faint smile. 'Thank you, Oswald.'

'Oh, I don't doubt *I* have not heard the last of this. But now that you both no longer work for the IHA, such matters are no longer your concern.' He stood, straightening his immaculate suit before extending his hand. 'I may have only worked with you briefly, but you both lived up to your reputations.'

Eddie rose and crossed the room to stand beside Nina. 'Good or bad?'

Now it was Seretse's turn to smile slightly. 'It's perhaps best that I do not say.' He shook their hands. 'Good luck, to the pair of you.'

'Thanks,' said Nina. 'I'm sorry to have dropped this bomb on you' – Eddie suppressed a sarcastic comment on her choice of words – 'but we need to do this. We want to . . .' She was more careful with her phraseology this time. 'We want to spend as much time with each other as we can.'

'Ah, yes, I can quite understand that. A job like this can keep us away from our families for too long.' But there was something in Seretse's eyes that suggested he had picked up a little more meaning from Nina's remark. 'I hope you do everything you want to achieve.'

'So do I,' she said, heartfelt.

He rounded his desk to show them out. 'If I may ask, what *are* you going to do?'

'Travel, for one thing. And not with my archaeologist's hat on. I want to see new places, meet new people.'

Seretse nodded. 'It sounds most agreeable. Where are you going?'

'Vietnam first,' Eddie said. 'There's a place I want to visit there. And then, well . . . kind of a world tour.'

'We're going to see some friends in Hollywood too, at some point,' said Nina. 'Do you know Grant Thorn? The movie star?'

Seretse shook his head. 'I must admit to preferring French cinema to Hollywood blockbusters.'

'Me too, actually. Although I don't think I'll ever talk Eddie round to my point of view.'

'You know those Jason Statham *Transporter* movies technically count as French cinema, right?' he said with a grin.

Nina sighed. 'Yes, this is the man I'm going to be spending the rest of my . . . time with.' She shook Seretse's hand again. 'Goodbye, Oswald.'

'Bye, Ozzy,' Eddie added. Seretse gave them both a tired look, but smiled in farewell.

Nina held her upbeat expression as she and Eddie walked to the elevators, but her facade crumbled as they descended towards the lobby of the Secretariat Building. He put his arm around her. 'It's okay,' he said, trying to reassure her. 'It's okay.'

'It's *not* okay,' she replied, struggling to keep her composure. 'Eddie, I'm going to *die*! You saw the doctor's report. Even if they didn't know what was wrong with me, they still knew it was bad. The eitr infected me, and . . . I don't know how long I've got.'

'It might be years.'

'And it might be weeks! The Russians told us how quickly the stuff can kill, even in small doses.' She unconsciously touched her cheek; the red mark had faded, but was still visible, a hardened blemish against her otherwise smooth skin. 'I only got hit by a drop, but we both know that's all it takes. I've lasted longer than the nine steps Thor took, but . . . it's only a matter of time.'

The elevator doors opened. She blinked away tears before stepping out. 'All right then,' said Eddie softly as he walked beside her. 'We don't know how long you've got. But there might be a cure out there somewhere. We can't give up on finding it, ever – I'm sure as fuck not going to, and I'm not going to let you either! And until we find it, we can make what you've got – what *we've* got – as good as it possibly can be. Okay?'

'Okay,' she managed to say.

They crossed the lobby, heading for the exits to the plaza outside. Eddie looked around at their modernist surroundings. 'You know, I'm actually going to miss this place.'

'So am I,' Nina replied. 'But there's something I'm going to miss more.'

'What?'

'Being—' Her voice caught, choked off by a sudden rush of emotion. She breathed hard, forcing out the words. 'Being the mother of your children.'

Eddie couldn't reply, as overcome as his wife. Tears streaming, they went through the doors and out into the winter cold of New York.

Two days later, the weather was considerably warmer.

'Are we there yet?' said Nina in joking complaint as she wiped sweat from her forehead. Even though the rented 4x4 had air conditioning, the temperature at midday was still stifling.

'Not much further,' said Eddie as he guided their vehicle down the bumpy jungle track. Under normal circumstances, to hire a car in Vietnam he would first have had to apply for a Vietnamese driver's licence, which would have taken at least a week. However, on this occasion the time to process the paperwork had been reduced to a couple of hours; they were both grateful to Seretse that their United Nations documentation would remain valid for a few months.

'So this is where you came eight years ago?' She watched the brilliant greenery roll by. 'It's beautiful.'

'Yeah, it is.' He sounded almost surprised, prompting a questioning look from his wife. 'I didn't really get the chance to play tourist last time I was here. Besides, it was pissing it down.'

'At least it's not raining today. I wouldn't fancy trekking through the jungle in a monsoon to find Natalia's grave.'

He gave her a slightly confused glance. 'Sorry, what?'

'Natalia's grave? That's why we came here, remember. How far from the village is it?'

'Oh, yeah.' He seemed distracted, but there was something else to his attitude as well. Nina couldn't quite tell what, though. Almost . . . *expectant*? 'Not far.'

He guided the Nissan Patrol around a bend in the narrow track, bushes whipping at the vehicle's flank. Ahead, a cluster of buildings came into view: the village of Ly Quang. 'Is that it?' Nina asked.

'That's it. Hasn't changed much.' He brought the 4x4 down the hill and pulled up outside the largest building.

The sweltering heat hit them the moment they opened the Patrol's doors. Nina screwed up her eyes as pinpricks of sweat beaded around them, then surveyed their surroundings. It was clear that the village did not get many visitors; the few people in sight had already taken an interest in the new arrivals.

One of them, a woman Nina guessed to be in her mid thirties, regarded Eddie first with uncertainty, then dawning recognition. 'Ay up,' he said. 'Looks like somebody remembers me.'

The woman hurried to the car to meet him, speaking

excitedly. 'Sorry, I still don't speak Vietnamese,' he replied with an apologetic shrug. 'But this does.'

He took his phone from inside his leather jacket and brought up an app: an English–Vietnamese translator. A set of phrases had already been saved, a tap of Eddie's finger prompting the phone to say the first in a mechanical voice. The woman did not seem wowed by the technology – the country's cellular phone network had been massively expanded over the course of eight years – but her reaction to what it was saying was more excited.

'What did you ask her?' said Nina.

Eddie didn't answer, instead tapping a second phrase. The woman listened, nodding enthusiastically, then waved for him to wait as she ran into the large building. 'Eddie?' Nina asked again. 'What did it say?'

'Just checking something,' he replied, though he was having trouble holding back a smile.

'What . . .' Nina began, stopping as the Vietnamese woman reappeared – followed by someone else.

A blonde Caucasian woman in her late twenties, whose eyes widened in delighted shock at the sight of the Englishman. 'Eddie!' she cried. 'My God! But that means . . .'

'Yeah, that means.' Eddie's grin could no longer be contained. He turned to his wife. 'Nina? I'd like you to meet Natalia Pöltl.'

Eight Years Earlier . . .

'But you know I am right, Eddie,' Natalia continued, desperation entering her voice. 'And it is what I want to do. Please!' She wrapped her hands around his. 'I will not let anyone else die because of me. You have to do it. You have to!' She squeezed his hands, then let go and turned away, getting down on her knees.

'You . . . you know how to make it not hurt, don't you?' she said quietly.

'Yeah, I do,' he replied. 'But—'

'Then do it. It is the only way to end this.' She raised her head, and closed her eyes.

He stared down at the young woman. 'Are you sure this is what you want?'

'Yes,' came the reply.

He was silent for a long moment. Then he slowly raised the gun.

'Please,' whispered Natalia. 'Do it.'

Chase hesitated – then pulled the trigger.

Natalia shrieked, flinching . . . before slowly opening one eye, not daring to speak for several seconds. 'You . . . did not shoot me.'

Chase's gun was pointed towards the sky, smoke curling from its barrel. 'Course I didn't bloody shoot you. I'm not a psychopath!'

'But – you have to! If the Americans or the Russians take me alive, they will use me to—'

'They won't,' he said firmly. 'And you know why? 'Cause they're going to think you *are* dead.'

Natalia stood, regarding him in confusion. 'I do not understand.'

'You will. You won't *like* it, but you'll understand.' He set off, heading south-west. 'Come on.'

'Where are we going?'

'To find your dead body.'

Bewildered, she followed him. 'Eddie, what are you talking about?'

'I'm going to keep my promises – both of them,' he told her. 'I promised to protect you, and you made me promise not to let anyone carry on your grandfather's work. And I just had an idea how to do both of those things.'

They continued through the jungle. The valley floor was muddy, still sodden from the storm, but the relatively flat ground let them move at a decent pace. Before long, the trees thinned out as they neared the steep earthen wall of the valley's west side.

Chase looked up at it. 'Okay, somewhere at the top of that's the camp where they were keeping you and your friends. So a bit south of it there'll be a big mudslide.' His gaze moved along the stepped cliff, spotting an area largely stripped of vegetation about a quarter of a mile away. 'That's where we fell down.'

They picked their way along the valley until they reached the swathe of destruction. Chase turned his attention to the ground, trying to match what he remembered from the darkness of the previous night with what he saw now. 'There!' he finally said, pointing out a shape half buried in the mud.

Natalia recoiled when she realised what it was: the body of a woman. 'Who is she?'

'One of the Russians – she came after me when I was carrying you out of the camp, but we all got washed away by the mud-slide.' Feet squelching in the sludge, Chase went to the broken-necked corpse. Insects had already started to feast on it; revolted, he swatted the flies away before picking up the body. Its head lolled horribly.

The young German was appalled. 'What are you *doing*?' she shrilled as he carried the dead woman towards her.

'Saving your life. Take your clothes off.'

'*What?*'

'You need to swap clothes with her.' He laid the body on the ground and, with a degree of disgust at himself even though he knew it had to be done, started to undress it. 'I'm going to do

541

what you asked me to: put a bullet in your head and burn your body. Except *she's* going to be you – that's hopefully what Lock and his people'll think, anyway.'

Realisation dawned. 'You are going to trick them into thinking you have killed me?'

'Yeah. I'll make damn sure that they find me and see what's left of the body. If it's so badly burned that they think they won't be able to get anything useful from it, then they'll leave – and they'll stop looking for you.'

'But if they find you with the body, they will kill you!'

'They can *try*,' Chase said, with a confidence he didn't feel. 'The main thing is that you'll be safe.' He looked away as Natalia started to remove her clothing, concentrating on the unpleasant task of stripping the dead Russian. 'Once you've got dressed, I want you to go back to the village and stay with your friends. I know roughly where we are, so if you head east,' he gestured over his shoulder with a thumb, 'you'll get to the river, and then you can follow it back to that crossing we used. If you even *think* there's anyone nearby, hide until you're sure they've gone – and for Christ's sake don't step on any more landmines!'

Even without looking at her, he could tell she was dismayed. 'You . . . you are going to leave me?'

'No,' he replied. '*You're* going to leave *me*. And here's another promise. I'll never tell anyone – *anyone* – that you're still alive until I'm absolutely sure that nobody'll be able to use you to restart your grandfather's experiments. You won't ever see me again unless I'm one hundred per cent sure of that. Otherwise there's a risk I might lead somebody to you.' He removed the last piece of the Russian's clothing. 'Here. Put these on,' he said, still not looking around at Natalia as he held up the bundle.

She took the damp and dirty garments from him, then passed him her own. 'Let me help.'

Chase shook his head. 'No. Soon as you're dressed, get to the village. I'll take it from here.'

'But—'

'Don't argue. It's the only way to keep you safe, and you wouldn't want me to break a promise by not protecting you, would you?' He began to dress the body in Natalia's clothes. The Russian was slightly bigger than the young woman, but the clothes she had borrowed from her friends in the village were loose-fitting enough that it did not matter.

He was halfway done when he felt a hand on his shoulder. 'Eddie? I . . . I am ready to go.'

Chase turned to see that Natalia was now dressed – and that despite her words, she did not want to leave. He stood and faced her. 'Are you all right?'

'No,' she admitted. 'I am frightened. And not just for me. These people, when they find you, they will—'

'Hey, hey. It's okay.' He put his hands on the young woman's shoulders and kissed her on the forehead. 'I'll be fine. It's the only way to keep you safe. Although,' he added as an idea came to him, 'sorry about this.'

'Sorry about what— Ah!' She gasped as he twiddled a skein of her blond hair around his forefinger and tugged hard, strands snapping. 'That hurt! Why did you do that?'

He tucked the hairs into a pocket. 'Her hair's darker than yours. If I make sure they find these, it'll be more convincing. Now go on, get moving.'

Chase straightened, gently but firmly pushing her away. Natalia got the message and, with an expression of deep regret, set off into the jungle to the east. Then she paused, looking back. 'Eddie. Thank you.'

He nodded. 'Can you make *me* a promise?'

'Of course. What is it?'

'That you'll make the most of the life you've got.'

Tears shone in her eyes. 'I will. If you do the same.'

'Always do.' He gestured for her to go. Reluctantly she turned away and headed into the trees. Before long she was lost to sight amidst the undergrowth.

Chase watched until he was sure she had gone, then looked back at the dead woman. 'Okay,' he said with a sigh, 'sorry about this, but I'm going to have to kill you again.' He finished dressing the corpse, then raised it over one shoulder in a fireman's lift. 'Now, where's the best place to start a fire?' He got his bearings, and headed back into the jungle . . .

'So that's what happened,' finished Eddie. He and Nina were seated with Natalia on the same makeshift bench on which the young woman had told the Yorkshireman her story eight years earlier. 'Lock and Hoyt bought it, and so did Kagan and the Russians. They actually believed I'd executed Natalia. As if!'

'Yeah, and I believed you too,' said Nina, still reeling from the revelation. 'You jerk! You lied to me!' She punched him, only semi-playfully, on the arm. Natalia looked on with a mixture of amusement and concern, unsure exactly how angry she was.

'No I didn't!' he protested. 'And by the way: ow.'

'You did, you said you killed her!'

'No, I said I *did what she asked me to do*. Which was to make sure nobody used her DNA to recreate the eitr. Lock and the Russians both thought she was dead, so they stopped looking for her. Problem solved!'

'I did not agree with him at the time,' said Natalia. 'But now I am very glad that he did what he did. It has not been easy, but the friends I have made here, the help I have been able to give to the children – I would not give that up for anything.'

Eddie's expression became more serious. 'So how are you?' he asked her. 'Have there been any more . . . symptoms?'

She gave him a sad look, then discreetly rolled up the hem of her thin cotton shirt. Several lumps, ranging in size from the width of her little finger's tip to slightly smaller than a golf ball, ran in a ragged line up from her waist. 'The first one appeared last year,' she said, indicating the largest. 'The others came soon after. They are only growing slowly . . . but they are growing all the same.'

The sight of the tumours filled Nina with a sickening chill. Was this a glimpse of her own future? She had to clear her throat before speaking, mouth suddenly dry. 'Have you seen a doctor?'

Natalia shook her head. 'I did not want to risk anyone learning that I was still alive. I was afraid that the Russians or Americans would come after me again.' She lowered her shirt.

'They won't,' said Eddie. 'I promised you eight years ago, the only way you'd ever see me again was if I was one hundred per cent sure that wasn't going to happen.' He spread his hands wide. 'And here I am!'

'You are completely sure?' she asked, hesitant.

'The second eitr pit has been destroyed,' Nina told her. 'The Russians developed a substance to neutralise the eitr, and as far as we know, it worked. And I heard Lock say there's nothing anyone could learn about the eitr from your DNA. So if you want to see a doctor . . .'

'I do not think they will be able to help me,' the German said with a sigh. 'You did not say that the Americans or Russians had developed a cure.'

'Afraid nobody's found anything. Yet,' Eddie added for Nina's benefit. 'But if you want or need anything, we can arrange it.' He nudged his wife. 'See if Seretse cancelled your IHA credit card yet, eh?'

Natalia shook her head again, but this time in gratitude. 'There is nothing I need.'

'Really?' Nina said.

'I have everything I want here already. I have lived my life the way I promised Eddie.' Seeing that he was unsure what she meant, she continued: 'That I would make the most of everything I had.' She smiled. 'It was very good advice.'

'Maybe I should write a book about it. I might get a six-figure advance too,' he said, grinning at Nina.

'But if you could get medicines and toys for the children, that would be wonderful,' Natalia went on. 'Anything you can give them will help.'

'I'll see to it,' Nina assured her.

The three of them continued to talk for some time, curious villagers occasionally joining them with questions for the visitors. Even the boy with the missing leg, now in his teens and keen to show off his agility on his prosthetic limb, made an appearance. Eventually, however, the conversation came around to what Eddie had been doing since his last visit, which in turn led to the events in the eitr pit. 'You . . . were infected?' Natalia asked Nina in a quiet voice.

Nina touched the little mark on her cheek. 'Yes,' she said, sighing. 'Just a drop, but that was all it took. I don't know how long I've got left.'

'I am so sorry.' She looked down at the ground. 'This is all my grandfather's fault. He was an evil man. I wish he had never been—'

'It's not *your* fault, though,' Eddie cut in firmly. 'And Nina, I didn't just bring us here to tell Natalia that she was safe. I wanted to see if she was still okay – and to show you that it's not all over. You can't just give up and accept it. You might have years, bloody *decades* even, before any symptoms show. That's plenty of time for someone to find a cure. You just don't know. Christ, look at everything we've survived up till now. We should be dead fifty times over, but we're still here! So I'm not going to give up on you, ever, and I won't let you give up either. Like Mac always told me: fight to the end.'

Nina tried to take solace from his words, but struggled to overcome the gloom in her heart. 'I wish I had your confidence.'

'No, Eddie is right,' Natalia insisted. 'Because of him, I have had eight more years of life. Sometimes they have been hard, but they have always been worth it.' She smiled at the American. 'And you are very lucky. You have a wonderful man to share your life with. He will look after you and protect you – I know this, because he did the same for me.'

Eddie put his arm around Nina. 'She's right. I'll always be here for you, love. You know that.'

Nina's gloom evaporated as she turned to look at her husband's smiling face. He was not handsome in any conventional sense, yet she couldn't imagine anyone else she would rather see each morning for the rest of her life. 'Yeah, I know. I love you.'

'I love you too.' They kissed, making Natalia smile and blush.

They stayed in the village for a few more hours, talking. 'Afraid we've got to go,' Eddie eventually told Natalia after checking his watch. 'We've got a plane to catch from Da Nang tomorrow, and I don't want to drive back there at night.'

'That is a shame, but I understand,' she replied, with a small grin. 'I love the people here, but they are very bad drivers!'

'I'll make sure that the medicines and other things are couriered to you,' said Nina.

The German nodded in thanks. 'Oh, and I've got something else for you,' Eddie told her. He produced a slip of paper and offered it to her.

'What is it?' Natalia asked.

'Your dad's phone number. He's still in Hamburg.'

She regarded the paper almost fearfully before taking it. 'I . . . do not know what I should say to him. It has been eight years – he will have thought I am dead . . .'

'Yeah, I know,' said Eddie with sympathy. 'But whatever you say to him, I'm pretty sure he'll be happy to hear it.'

Tears glistened in her eyes. 'Thank you, Eddie. For everything.'

They went to the 4x4, and made their farewells. 'I will say to you what Eddie said to me,' Natalia told Nina. She paused for a moment to remember his words. 'Make the most of the life you have got.'

'I will,' said Nina, smiling. 'Thank you.'

Natalia kissed her cheek, then did the same to Eddie. 'And you too.'

'I never do anything else!' he said, kissing her in return.

The couple got into the Patrol. Eddie started the engine, giving Natalia a final wave before turning the vehicle back towards the jungle track. The sun had wheeled around the sky during their stay, illuminating the jungle with a gorgeous honey-like glow as it began to descend towards the tree-shrouded horizon. Nina took in the view. 'Look at that,' she said. 'It really is an amazing world, isn't it? And I want to make the most of it with you while I can.'

Eddie hugged her, then they kissed again. 'I'll be with you all the way,' he told her.

'Fight to the end,' she replied, smiling.

Another kiss, then they set out into the waiting world.

TURN THE PAGE FOR AN EXCLUSIVE EXTRACT FROM THE NEXT
WILDE & CHASE BOOK

KINGDOM OF
DARKNESS

BY

ANDY
McDERMOTT

OUT IN HARDBACK AND EBOOK ON
28TH AUGUST 2014

Prologue

Greece, 1943

The military convoy ground through the darkness shrouding the muddy country road towards its next destination.

In the lead car, a four-seater Kübelwagen utility vehicle, SS-Sturmbannführer Erich Kroll used a torch to check a map of the farmlands around the town of Pella. His Waffen-SS unit, soldiers of Hitler's feared *Schutzstaffel* elite force, were on a mission direct from the Führer: to locate and round up any Jews remaining in the Nazi-occupied zone for deportation to the concentration camps of Treblinka and Auschwitz. The operation had, by now, been mostly completed to German satisfaction, but, Kroll mused, the *Juden* were as hard to eradicate as rats – and the task had been made harder by Jewish sympathisers amongst the local population.

The Nazis had their own sympathisers, though. Fascist collaborators had provided their new masters with lists of those suspected of harbouring fugitives, and now the SS was checking each one. On this night, they already had five prisoners in the truck behind them, two Jewish women and a boy found in a farm's outbuilding, as well as the farmer and his wife who had been sheltering them. A good catch, but Kroll hoped there would be more.

He swapped the map for his list. The next target was the property belonging to the Patras family. According to his information, they liked their privacy, keeping to themselves. That alone made them worthy of a visit from the SS; even if they were not harbouring any enemies of the Reich, they still needed reminding who was now in charge of their land.

The Kübelwagen's headlights picked out a crossroads ahead. 'Go right,' Kroll ordered the driver, Jaekel. The young storm-trooper had already impressed the unit commander, shrugging off a vicious slash across his face from a knife-wielding Jew in order to bayonet him and the family he was protecting. At the moment, the scar was still a raw red line, the stitches visible; in time, it would be a stirring reminder of his bravery and a magnet for women.

The car made the turn, the truck and half-track behind it following. The road led up a hillside to the house near its summit. Jaekel pulled up outside the front door. The truck jolted to a halt behind it, the half-track heading around the building to watch for anyone trying to run from its rear.

Kroll marched to the door and pounded on the wood with a gloved fist. 'Open up!' he barked in Greek. He had studied the ancient form of the language in his youth; learning its modern derivation to a reasonable standard had not been difficult. 'This is the Waffen-SS – we are here to search your property for Jewish fugitives. You are ordered to let us in, immediately!'

He stepped back and waited impatiently. Behind him, his men held their weapons at the ready as sounds of activity came from inside. 'How long do we give them?' asked Rasche, Kroll's senior lieutenant.

'Thirty seconds, no more,' Kroll told the SS-Obersturmführer. 'Then we kick the door down.'

Rasche smiled, manic eyes widening. 'I hope they don't rush. I always like to make an entrance.'

'Open the door at once!' Kroll shouted. He heard voices behind it; that the occupiers had not immediately complied suggested they were trying to conceal something. 'You have ten seconds! Nine! Eight! Seven!' Sub-machine guns came up.

A clunk as a heavy bolt was shifted, then the door opened a crack. An elderly man nervously peered out. 'What do you want?'

'You heard me,' Kroll snapped. He shoved the door open, sending the old man reeling back. 'You are Alejo Patras?' he demanded.

'Yes, I am,' Patras replied.

'Who else is in the house?'

'My wife, Kaira, my two sons, and my oldest son's wife and their daughter. But we have nothing to hide here, we are just farmers.'

'Five others,' Kroll told his men before turning back to Patras. 'Bring them all here, now. Anyone who is not here in one minute will be shot when they are found.' He made a show of raising his left arm to check his watch.

Patras called out urgently. Before long, others filed into the stone-floored hallway: an old woman and a couple in their thirties, the wife fearfully holding a six-year-old child. The German regarded his watch again. 'Where is your other son? He is running out of time!'

'Dinos!' cried Patras, following it with an exhortation for him to hurry. Seconds ticked by, Rasche's malevolent smirk widening as he fingered his gun – then a door banged somewhere deeper inside the house. Running footsteps, and a man in his twenties hurried into the hall.

Kroll's cold gaze turned upon him. 'What were you doing?' he demanded in Greek. 'Why were you hiding from us?'

'I – I wasn't hiding,' the young man insisted. 'I was in the cellar, I didn't hear you.'

'Give the cellar a full search,' Kroll ordered, not taken in by the protestation of innocence. 'Look for hatches, hidden doors, false compartments – anywhere people might hide.'

Rasche nodded, then addressed one of the men watching the family. 'Rottenführer! With me.' The trooper, a squat, round-faced man named Schneider, followed him out.

Keeping an eye on the prisoners, Kroll waited as his unit searched the house. One by one they returned, reporting that they had found no sign of fugitives. The elder Patras appeared relieved to be vindicated, but the Nazi commander detected a rising tension in the faces of his sons – particularly the younger.

Only Rasche and Schneider had not yet come back. Kroll went to the doorway through which they had gone. 'Obersturmführer!' he called. 'Have you found anything?'

A pause, then: 'I'm not sure. Is Zoller there? We need him to move something.'

Kroll glanced at the huge stormtrooper, whose head reached to just centimetres beneath the ceiling beams. 'Sturmmann, go and help him.'

Zoller's arm snapped into a rigid Hitler salute, his finger-tips actually brushing the plaster overhead. 'At once, Herr Sturmbannführer!' Hunching down to fit through the doorway, he headed for the cellar.

There was now definite concern in the brothers' expressions

– no, Kroll realised, the whole family's. Even the young granddaughter had the look of a child whose lie was about to be exposed. 'If you are hiding Jews down there, you will be treated just like them,' he warned the group. 'Give them up now, and I may be lenient.'

The elder Patras shook his head. 'This is a very old house, it has many cubbyholes. But we are not hiding anyone, I promise.'

'I would prefer to see for myself,' Kroll replied with a sneer. He listened as thumping sounds echoed up from below. Then—

'Sturmbannführer!' Rasche shouted. 'Come quickly!'

'Bring them,' Kroll snapped to his men. The prisoners were hustled along in his wake, guns pressed against their bodies. The cellar entrance was a crooked door at the back of a cramped pantry, stairs leading down a steep passage lined in white-washed stone. A flickering lantern provided weak illumination at the bottom. The SS leader led the way underground, noticing the polished curve to each stone step; the passage was either regularly travelled, or had been here for a very long time.

He reached the foot of the stairs. The lantern revealed a grotto-like space, sacks and boxes lining the irregular walls. Grunts of exertion came from around a corner. Beyond it, Kroll found his three men standing at what appeared to be a dead end – except that Zoller had managed to get his thick fingers into a gap that had been concealed behind some barrels and was pulling at it. Wood creaked with each tug.

'There's a mark on the floor from a hidden door,' explained Rasche, pointing at a faint line arcing across the flagstones. 'But we can't get it open.'

Kroll drew his Luger and faced Patras as the family was pushed into the subterranean space. 'How does it open? Tell me now, or I will shoot your wife!' He pointed the gun at the old woman's head. She gasped in fear.

There was a tense silence – then the younger son shoved his mother aside, lunging at Kroll—

The gunshot was deafening in the confined space.

A jet of blood sprayed across the cellar from a bullet wound in Dinos' throat, almost black in the low light. Kroll stepped back as the young man collapsed at his feet, twitching like a dying fish. His mother screamed.

'Open the door!' Kroll yelled. The young girl shrieked in terror as the other SS troopers slammed her parents against the walls. 'Open it, or I'll kill you all!'

'Wait, wait!' cried the horrified Patras. 'I'll open it!'

His older son shouted in protest even as gun muzzles were jammed against him, but Patras scurried to the dead end and pulled aside a stack of boxes. Behind them, at floor level, was a small nook. He slipped his hand inside, curling his fingers around a concealed catch.

A loud *clack* came from behind the fake wall. 'It will open now,' he told Kroll. 'Please, let my family go!'

'How many people are hidden back there?' the German demanded.

'None, there is nobody there. It is just a room. Take what you find and go, I beg you!'

Again, his son protested. 'Father, no! You can't let them into the shrine!'

The last word caught Kroll's attention. 'What shrine?' he said, rounding on the elderly man. 'What's back there?'

The conflict on Patras' face told him that the Greek did not want to give up his secret. 'It . . . it is our family's heritage,' he finally said, each word practically forced from his lips. 'We have protected it for many generations, many centuries.'

Kroll regarded him for a moment, then addressed Zoller. 'Open it.'

The big man slotted his fingers back into the gap. This time, there was little resistance when he pulled. The hidden door swung outwards, one corner rasping faintly against the floor.

'Step back; let me see.' Kroll shone his torch into the newly revealed darkness to find another set of steps heading downwards. He directed his light to the bottom. There was a chamber below.

'Sir,' warned one of the stormtroopers, a thin-faced man named Gausmann, as Kroll began to descend. 'If there is someone down there, they could be armed.'

Kroll stopped, shining his torch back at his prisoners. 'If it turns out anyone is down there, kill the family,' he said. Their lack of reaction told him that they did not speak German. 'But . . . I don't think he's lying. Rasche, follow me.'

The assault unit commander led the way down the second set of stairs. These seemed even older than the first, the irregular stones in the whitewashed walls held in place by the weight of the ground above them rather than mortar. But, as it came into view, he saw that the room at the bottom had been built with more care. Elegant columns supported the ceiling of the roughly circular space. *Ancient Grecian architecture,* Kroll thought, directing his torch beam over the nearest. *But later than the Classical period . . .*

He turned his light into the centre of the room – and froze.

'My God!' he gasped, astonishment reducing his voice to a whisper.

The shrine was filled with treasure.

Gold and silver glinted everywhere his torch beam darted. Coins, jewellery, statuettes, even armour and weapons: the spoils of several lifetimes, all arranged as if on display to the figure at the chamber's far side. A marble statue of a man, flakes of coloured paint still visible on the pale white stone, watched over the room of wonders.

Kroll heard Rasche let out an exclamation, but he ignored the

SS section leader, advancing on the statue. The light picked out a name on the plinth. Ανδρέας: *Andreas*. A common enough Greek name, but what had this man done to arouse such adulation?

Rasche's own torch flitted excitedly over the gleaming riches. 'It's a fortune!' he said. 'It must be worth millions of marks. And those farmers have been hiding it from us!'

'Not just from us,' Kroll said quietly as he examined some of the items in more detail. The inscriptions upon them were in Greek – *ancient* Greek. 'These are thousands of years old.' He illuminated a line of carved text beneath the name on the plinth. 'It says, "Friend and follower of the king Alexander" . . . Does it mean Alexander the Great? It must do!'

'I'll take your word for it, sir,' said Rasche. 'I never studied Greek.'

'You should always study the past, Obersturmführer,' Kroll replied, reading on with growing intrigue. 'It can teach you a lot. Especially when it concerns Alexander the Great. He was born near here, near Pella – it was the capital of Macedonia.' He stepped back, almost reflective. 'Alexander was my childhood hero, actually; he was the greatest military leader in history, never defeated in battle. He'd conquered most of the known world before he was thirty years old. If he'd lived longer, who knows what else he could have accomplished.'

'Sir,' Rasche replied, with clear disinterest. He moved to prod at one of the piles of coins.

'Philistine,' Kroll muttered as he read more of the text. It *was* referring to Alexander the Great, he was sure. 'These dates, they're long after Alexander died. But this Andreas, the inscriptions say he knew Alexander personally . . .'

He regarded the statue. The man it portrayed was old, bald-headed with a long beard, yet still had the upright posture of youth. The remaining scuffs of paint on its face were enough to give the impression that it was looking back at him, expression almost challenging. 'Andreas, Andreas . . .' he whispered, searching his memory. The name was connected to Alexander's, somehow, but the link was elusive—

Suddenly it came to him. The rational part of his mind instantly dismissed it as ridiculous. It couldn't possibly be true! But . . .

His gaze fell upon something behind the statue. It was a pithos, a large earthenware jar as tall as a man and almost a metre across at its broadest. More Greek text had been inscribed upon it. He went to the vessel, having to stand on tiptoes to examine the spout. It had been sealed, black pitch around a silver stopper. The rim was silvered too, as if the jar's interior was lined with the precious metal.

'Silver,' he said out loud. However ludicrous it sounded, the connection between Andreas and the Macedonian conqueror had now solidified in his thoughts.

'And gold,' said Rasche, coins clinking from his fingers.

'Forget the gold – we may have found something even more valuable.' He turned, ignoring his subordinate's look of confusion. 'The old man, and his family. Bring them down here!'

Rasche shouted an order up the stairs. The surviving members of the Patras clan were quickly hustled into the hidden chamber, their dismay at their secret having been revealed mirrored by the amazement and raw greed on the faces of the Nazis. 'Andreas,' Kroll said to the patriarch in Greek, indicating the statue. 'He is who I think, isn't he? Andreas the cook, from the *Alexander Romance*?'

The defeat and resignation in the old man's voice told Kroll that he wouldn't need to resort to threats to get the truth. 'Yes, it is he.'

The commander's pointing finger shifted to the pithos. 'Then the jar – it really contains what Andreas found in the Land of the Blessed?'

Patras' son gave his father a look of alarm. 'How could he know?' he hissed. Zoller pushed down hard upon the man's shoulder to warn him to be silent.

Kroll's sneer turned upon the prisoner. 'You think we Germans are all uneducated thugs? You need to remember that Greece is no longer the centre of civilisation. Yes, I know about Andreas, and what he discovered. But until now, I thought it was only a legend, another of the *Romance*'s chapters of fantasy.'

'Andreas *wrote* the *Alexander Romance*,' Patras replied, a certain pride entering his tone despite his fear. 'He hid the truth inside the fantasy.' A flick of one hand towards an unimpressive wood and metal chest, considerably newer than the treasures around it. 'A copy of his original is in there.'

The urge to open the chest and read the ancient text rose in the Nazi leader, but he restrained it. There were more important answers he needed first. 'Why did he hide the truth?'

'So that only someone who believed they were a worthy successor to Alexander could find it.'

Rasche's impatience at being shut out of the Greek exchange reached bursting point. 'Sir, what are you both talking about? We've found their treasure – what else do we need from them?'

'Information,' Kroll told him. 'That's how wars are won, not with swords or bullets. I told you, you should learn from history.' He returned to the pithos, signalling for Jaekel to join him. 'Open the jar.'

'Sir!' Jaekel snapped in reply. He raised his gun, flipping it around to smash the stock against the pithos's spout—

Kroll's yell of 'No!' and the horrified cry of '*Óchi!*' from

Patras were simultaneous. 'Idiot!' the Nazi growled. 'Use your knife, not your gun! Take out the stopper.'

The chastened stormtrooper slung his weapon and unsheathed his combat knife. Kroll watched as he began to work the plug loose, then turned his attention back to the Greeks. The adults all seemed appalled at the prospect of the great jar's opening – or was it apprehension? He looked back at the text upon the pithos. More mentions of Alexander, but from the perspective of history. Andreas may have known the great king, but these words had been written long after his death.

Which meant that if Andreas himself had been the author, then the pithos really might contain the stuff of legends . . .

A crackle as Jaekel worked loose a chunk of pitch. He tossed it aside, then jimmied away at the stopper itself. More of the black resin crumbled. Then there came a sharp rasp of metal – and the stopper moved.

'Careful, now,' Kroll warned, but Jaekel had learned his lesson. He used the knife to lever the cap upwards. It was indeed solid silver, as the Nazi leader had suspected, but he was now less interested in the value of the metal than what it contained. Waving Jaekel aside, he hopped up on to the statue's plinth so he could look down into the container.

Water shimmered gently in the torchlight. The jar was almost full to brimming, holding hundreds of litres, maybe more. He leaned closer, briefly moving the torch away as he adjusted his balance . . .

The shimmering remained, even without light.

For a moment he thought it was just an after-image. But the same thing happened when he lowered the torch again to check. 'Jaekel, point your light at the floor,' he ordered. 'Rasche, Gausmann, you too.'

The SS troopers obeyed. The chamber went almost fully dark

as Kroll flicked off his own light. He closed his eyes for a few seconds to let them adjust, then opened them again.

The water in the pithos was *aglow*.

It was faint, like moonlight reflected from a pond on a misty night, but there was definitely light coming from inside the jar. 'What is it, Sturmbannführer?' asked Rasche.

'Wait,' said Kroll. He flicked his torch back on and cautiously reached out, dipping the tip of his little finger into the water.

The resulting sensation made him twitch. 'Sturmbannführer!' Rasche said again, with more concern. 'Are you all right?'

'Yes, yes,' Kroll replied, slipping his finger back into the pithos. This time, he was prepared, and did not flinch. His skin tingled, very slightly. The effect was not unlike a mild electric charge.

The Nazi withdrew his hand, thinking for a moment. Then he scooped up a small amount of water in his palm. He raised it towards his mouth—

'That is not for you,' said Patras. Kroll looked sharply towards him. Even surrounded by SS troopers, guns aimed at him and his family, the old man's attitude was suddenly defiant, warning clear in his words.

'Who are you to decide?' Kroll demanded in Greek.

'We are the descendants of Andreas – once a humble cook, and later the guardian of the Spring of Life. We have protected his shrine for over two hundred centuries, and kept his secret from those who think themselves better than the great king. Is that what you believe, German? That you are a worthy successor to Alexander?'

Kroll bristled at the challenge. 'I believe that the Third Reich will become the greatest empire the world has ever seen, yes.'

'But you are not its leader.'

'I act in the name of its leader, Adolf Hitler. Therefore I *am* worthy, since Hitler is the greatest leader in all of history.' Kroll allowed himself a smug smile, pleased with his own irrefutable logic.

Patras was unimpressed, however. 'You may believe what you wish to believe. But the water is not for you. Andreas thought to keep it for himself rather than share it with Alexander, and though he soon regretted that decision and tried to change it, by then it was too late.'

'Then the water *is* the same as in the *Alexander Romance*, yes?'

The old man nodded. 'It is.'

Kroll felt almost breathless with excitement. He had been right; the gold and silver treasures were nothing compared to the value of the water. 'And . . . you know how to find its source?'

A firm shake of the head. 'No. This is a shrine to the memory and works of Andreas, marking his birthplace – but it is not his tomb. He is buried at the spring.' Another shift in Patras' attitude; now he seemed almost condescending, like a schoolmaster looking down upon his pupils. 'The path to the spring is hidden, but it begins here. If you truly think you are superior to Alexander, then perhaps you *deserve* to find it.'

'Of course I deserve it,' Kroll snapped. With that, he brought his hand to his mouth and sipped the water. The faint tingling was stronger upon his tongue. He gulped down the rest and swallowed. For a moment he felt nothing. Then . . .

'Are you all right, sir?' Rasche again, shining his torch into his commanding officer's face.

Kroll blinked in annoyance. 'Get that damn light off me. Yes, I'm fine. I'm . . .' He paused as an odd feeling rose through him – almost *elation*, the tingle swirling through his veins to every part of his body.

'The water – it could be stagnant, or polluted. Or even poisoned.'

'I'm fine,' Kroll repeated. The sensation passed, but somehow, he knew that something good had just happened to him. And his knowledge of the *Alexander Romance*, a Greek recension of which he had read as a student, suggested what it might be.

He made a decision. 'Close the jar,' he ordered Jaekel. 'Put the stopper back in and find something to seal it with. I don't want to lose a single drop of what's inside.'

'What *is* inside it, sir?' asked Schneider, who was holding Patras' daughter-in-law and granddaughter. Even in the low light, Kroll noticed that he had wound his fingers into the woman's long dark hair and was slowly stroking the strands.

'Something that will make us very rich. All of us. Now listen. Gausmann, bring down the other men outside – I want the whole unit to hear this.'

'What about the prisoners in the truck, sir?' Gausmann asked.

'Shoot them. I know you have wanted to since we arrested them, so now is your chance.'

Gausmann was surprised, but pleased, a cold grin crossing his face as he saluted.

'Yes, sir.' He hurried up the stairs.

'If I may ask, sir,' said Rasche, barely hiding his impatience, 'what is this about?'

'It's about a long and rewarding life, Rasche,' Kroll told him. He stepped down from the plinth and waited. Muffled gunshots soon came from above.

The prisoners flinched at the sound, the little girl beginning to cry. Schneider slid his fingers into her hair. 'Hush, now, little one,' he said, giving her a snake-like smile. She buried her face into her mother's neck, trembling.

Footsteps echoed down the tunnel as the other troopers clattered into the shrine, gazing at the treasures with awe. 'Oster, come on,' said Kroll, waiting impatiently for the last straggler to enter. He stepped forward to address his men, letting them see the sternness in his expression. 'Attention!' All those not holding the Patras family snapped upright. 'I want everyone to listen very closely. You've all seen what this room contains. It's full of treasure . . . and we are going to take it.' Eyes widened in avaricious delight. 'But the gold and silver and jewels are *not* the most valuable things here. The water in that jar,' he gestured towards it, 'is worth the most of all. I will explain why this is later, but for now, I need to make it clear that no one must know about this outside our unit. *No one.* You are either with me, or you leave now.'

He regarded them silently. He did not expect any departures, and there were none. 'Good. Here is what we are going to do. We will close up the cellar and secure this house until we can arrange for the treasure to be transported safely out of the country.'

Rasche gave Patras and his family a sidelong glance. 'And what about them?'

Kroll stared hard at the old man – who looked back with equal intensity. 'You know already. And so do they, I think.' He switched to Greek. 'We are going to take everything we have found here.'

Patras nodded in resignation. 'I had guessed. And what about my family? Please, they have done nothing. My granddaughter – she is only a child. She at least deserves to live.'

The SS commander gave the girl a look, then frowned at Schneider, who reluctantly withdrew his hand from her hair. 'Very well. You have my word,' he told Patras, before speaking again in German: 'Take them outside and dispose of them. All of them – including the child.'

The troops encircled the prisoners, pushing them back to the stairs. Patras spoke quietly to his family, trying to reassure them, but with a leaden fatefulness they quickly understood. All three hugged and kissed the little girl as they were led away.

Rasche watched them go, then went to Kroll. 'Sturmbannführer, I agree that we should take the treasure, but I *have* to know: what is so important about the water? How can it possibly be more valuable than gold?'

Kroll smiled thinly. 'Obersturmführer Rasche, which is more valuable to a person – gold, or their life?'

Rasche was puzzled by the question. 'Unless they are a fool, their life, of course.'

'Of course. Now, answer this: how much gold would you give to live for ever?'

'I don't know – a lot, I suppose . . .' He trailed off, staring at the pithos before snapping his gaze back to his commander. 'Wait, you think—'

'I *know*,' Kroll interrupted. 'The moment I drank it, I knew. A long time ago, someone found the secret of immortality.' His smile broadened. 'And now . . . it belongs to *us*.'

IF YOU LOVED THIS BOOK, WHY NOT TRY THE
REST OF THE BRILLIANT **WILDE & CHASE** SERIES BY

ANDY McDERMOTT

GO TO

WWW.HEADLINE.CO.UK

TO FIND OUT MORE ABOUT THESE INTERNATIONAL BESTSELLERS